The jet climbed, thrusting its way through the murk, folding its flaps in stages, transforming the wings for highspeed flight. Everything was fine.

Then I saw the monoplane.

It materialized, suddenly, shockingly. The tiny blur in the darkness became a terrifying form. High wing, fixed undercarriage, spinning propellor, a blurred disc. The sight triggered a kaleidoscope of visions: a mid-air collision, the front of the jet dissolving; awful, cataclysmic impact; flesh ripped and torn, bones shattered, blood spraying, atomizing, limbs spinning like bits of broken toys, a screaming, blinding torrent of freezing air, the aircraft, a miracle of precision and balance, reduced in an instant to pathetic bits of scrap tumbling, spinning, trailing passengers and their belongings.

There was no time.

And then it was gone.

Had it ever been there at all?

SPENCER DUNMORE

A TOM DOHERTY ASSOCIATES BOOK

To William G. Booth
in affectionate memory

Courage is the price that life exacts for granting peace.
The soul that knows it not, knows no release
From little things;
Knows not the livid loneliness of fear,
Nor mountain heights where bitter joy can hear
The sound of wings.

AMELIA EARHART PUTNAM

This is a work of fiction. All the characters and events protrayed in this book are fictional, and any resemblance to real people or incidents is purely coincidental.

THE SOUND OF WINGS

First Tor printing: January 1988

A TOR Book

Published by Tom Doherty Associates, Inc.
49 West 24th Street
New York, NY 10010

ISBN: 0-812-51714-8
Can. No.: 0-812-51715-6

Library of Congress Catalog Card Number: 84-21355

PRINTED IN THE UNITED STATES OF AMERICA

0 9 8 7 6 5 4 3 2 1

1

Tomlinson died approximately twenty seconds before we were due to touch down on Kennedy's runway 13 Left. We had been descending through the mist and muck for the better part of twenty minutes. A Category Two landing, this one, instruments all the way. In such conditions you rely totally on your needles and numbers; only they can tell you whether you are the right way up or whether the airport is in front or behind you. The visual references upon which you have depended since birth are denied you; they are buried somewhere in the bosom of that inscrutable enemy, the endless grey. You monitor the panel with the devotion of the zealot at his altar, observing the steady unwinding of the altimeters and the airspeed indicator, checking and rechecking the glide slope and localizer needles, confirming and reconfirming that you are still on the correct path at the correct height at the correct angle of descent.

The In-Range and Before-Landing checks had been completed: ignition, lights, seat-belt signs, radios, airspeed indicator and altimeter bugs set, fuel switches, gear down, no-smoking switch on; several score switches flipped and gauges gazed at. Hydraulics? Checked. Flaps? Twenty-two degrees.

Tomlinson ordered full flap.

As I depressed the two levers I glanced ahead through the windscreen. It was my first look outside since we had begun our approach. I could have saved myself the trouble. There was still nothing to see but murk. The radio altimeter said 262.

I called, 'One hundred above,' conveying to Tomlinson that we were now a hundred feet above the decision height and that in a matter of seconds he had to make up his mind whether to land or to go around. Still nothing to see outside. An uneasy little voice somewhere in the region of my solar plexus mentioned the faint but very real possibility that a minute but significant component in the radar-guided blind landing system might have gone catastrophically wrong . . .

'Decision,' I called when the altimeter read 162.

Which was when we first glimpsed the runway —and I silently apologized to the gauges and needles.

'Landing,' Tomlinson responded. Thus did he signify that he had control and was in sight of the runway and that everything was in order for a gentle return to Mother Earth.

Which was when he died.

He emitted an odd gasping gurgle. And turned. For an instant his eyes met mine and his mouth opened as if he wanted to say something. Then something strange happened to his eyes; they misted; the life went out of them; his head rolled to one side, comically, as if his neck had suddenly turned to rubber.

It was by any reckoning a devastatingly inappropriate time to depart this life.

At such moments the priorities sort themselves out with astonishing rapidity. Forget poor Tomlinson. Concentrate on the aircraft and its passengers. Grasp the control yoke with your right hand. Simultaneously wrap your left hand around the three thrust levers. Push them firmly up to the EPR bugs. Then pull them a fraction back with a neat little twist of the wrist. No need to over-boost the engines. Plenty of power available. Left hand up to the flap lever. Thirty-three to twenty-two degrees for the go-around. Beautifully instant response from the three Rolls-Royce RB211-

524B4s. Thrust, power, urge, to wrest the 1011 away from its disquieting proximity to the runway. When there's an emergency you instinctively seek height as does any winged creature. Height means safety, height provides time to review a situation, time to consider the alternatives, time to take the appropriate action.

I gestured to Jorgensen, the Second Officer, who sat directly behind me.

'Get his seat back,' I told him. I wanted Tomlinson's legs clear of the control column and his hands well away from the levers on the console. But I was calm now. The instant of acute danger was past. Gear up, the 1011 was climbing at a positive rate, beautiful, obedient creature that she was.

While Jorgensen tended to Tomlinson's inert form I called the tower and explained the situation, requesting their cooperation. Captain taken ill. Seriously ill. Arrange for an ambulance at the ramp. Then I called the company frequency and told them what had happened. I remember the tingling mixture of conflicting emotions as I flew the eager bird clear of the runway. There was relief, of course, that we had avoided flying into the ground and spreading ourselves and 221 passengers along runway 13 Left. There was pity for old Tomlinson too. The poor bastard looked so pathetic and shrivelled. And it was all tangled up with an odd feeling of pleasure—yes, pleasure—that I had this opportunity to demonstrate what a thoroughly competent, marvellously professional airman I was. Not a very admirable emotion, you say? I don't deny it. Nevertheless that's what I felt. I informed the passengers via the interphone that everything was under control and that a technicality had caused us to abandon our landing approach but that we soon would be safely on the ground and that Anglo-World regretted this minor inconvenience and it would mean a delay of only a few minutes and that there was absolutely no problem, etcetera, etcetera. Mine was the voice of the father-figure providing everyone with a confidence-fix. I reached up and pressed the button to summon the cabin attendant. She appeared a moment later, a rigid, anticipating-the-worst look in her hazel eyes. No doubt it had been there since the moment she heard the engines spooling up and she felt the aircraft being wrenched away from the runway. Sensible girl, she quickly closed the flight deck door behind her. Few sights are more demoralizing for passengers than that of the Captain slumped helpless at his controls.

'Christ,' she said, biting her lips as she approached Tomlinson.

I asked her to do what she could for him.

'I think it's too late,' said Jorgensen.

* * *

'Bloody shame,' said Wheeler, the New York Operations Manager. He was a burly man who wore a perpetual frown and looked as though he got insufficient sleep. 'Poor fellow, only had a year to go before retirement. Heart. Not fair, is it? But why should it be? Funny how we expect things to be fair, when there's nothing in nature that's the least bit fair. Seemed all right when you left London, did he?'

'Perfectly.' Just before take-off the late Captain Tomlinson had told me an endless story about Margaret Thatcher and The Rolling Stones. 'Does his family know?' I asked.

'We sent London a signal. They'll ring his home or send someone to see the wife. Nasty job, what? Captain Porson is coming over on 823 in the morning.' He accorded me a weary smile. 'Must have been a bit of a shock for you.'

'It got the adrenalin flowing.'

'Good show. By the way, I don't think the media know anything. Better that way. Usually the buggers smell a story even before it happens. But it looks as if they've missed this one so far. I want everyone to keep their mouths shut. Bloody bad publicity, captain dying in flight.' He shook his head as if to convey to the late Captain Tomlinson that the manner of his departing left much to be desired. 'So if anyone contacts you —not that I'm saying they will, mind, but simply that they might—I'd be obliged if you'd deny any knowledge of the incident. Can we count on you for that? Very good of you, old man.'

I had flown with Tomlinson three or four times over the years but I hadn't known him well; at least six months had elapsed since we had last sat side by side in a 1011. It was the luck of Crew Scheduling; you might find yourself with the same individuals half a dozen times in a row then not set eyes on them for a couple of years. Airline crew members are as interchangeable as engines or wheels or any other component.

I remember the rest of that day with remarkable clarity. I enjoyed it intensely. There was an exhilarating sense of being alive, a heightened awareness of everything around me. Reaction, of course. But I suppose the truth was that I was feeling brighter and better because of someone else's bad luck. I kept hoping it didn't show. After dinner I went to Jimmy Ryan's on West 54th Street and caught most of a set of strident Dixieland that suited my mood perfectly. I had been tested. And I had not been found wanting. Ten out of ten for Master Beale. Not that the fact would make much difference to the speed with which I became promoted to the left-hand seat on the 1011; the seniority system made sure of that. But if the management had harboured any doubts about my fitness for that august post they must surely have been dispelled the instant I touched down at Kennedy with all passengers safe and sound and in total ignorance of what had happened. The left-hand seat of the 1011 was the pinnacle of my ambition in this life. A delectable aircraft, the 1011, capable of carrying eighteen first class and two hundred and twenty-six economy passengers five thousand and fifty miles at a top speed of 548 mph. It had taken fifteen years to get this close to my goal: five years as a second officer—variously known as a 'stoker' or 'oiler'—on VC10s, then to the right-hand seat on Tridents. Six years later I made the big move to the left-hand seat. *Captain* Adam Beale. Four golden stripes. It was my European Period: London to Paris to Brussels to Cologne, Manchester to Prestwick to London to Dublin and Belfast with occasional trips to Malaga and Rome and Turin. Then I had bid for the 1011; it meant reverting to the co-pilot's seat on the right-hand side of the flight deck; but it was the only way to gain the pinnacle. How long now? Assuming the company remained solvent—by no means the certainty it once had seemed—I should make the final move within three years. Just about coincident with my fortieth birthday. A depressing milestone. Like untold millions of men in their late thirties I told myself that I didn't look my age. My trousers still fitted well; I was the same weight as I had been for the last ten years or more. Five ten; a spot over eleven stone. The slightest gathering of flesh above my belt? Well, didn't it more or less disappear the instant I stood up? Indeed it had probably been there all my life but simply hadn't been noticed before. No scrawn around the neck. No fullness under the chin. A touch of grey here and there in the dark brown hair, which Joyce said added a touch of distinction, but which I sometimes considered ripping out—hair by painful hair.

On my way to Operations that evening I bumped into a Pan Am flight attendant. I had an instant impression of masses of black hair and the brightest of blue eyes combined with a smile that was positively dazzling. No problem, she assured me when I apologized for the collision. Her fault. Perhaps neither party was looking where he or she was going, I offered. Well, that just could be, she admitted. She had dropped her paperback. I retrieved it. Faulkner. Good, was it? Real good, she assured me. I said I hadn't read any of Faulkner's works. She said I should. I said I most certainly would. Was she absolutely sure she was all right? Nothing damaged or wonky? At which she grinned as if I had said something witty. No, she assured me, there wasn't anything wonky. And I agreed that I couldn't see anything the least bit wonky. Did she hail from the South? She nodded. Mississippi, a li'l place called Waveland. Come to think of it, didn't I have a kind of an accent too? No, I told her, the language was called English and that was what I was speaking. Another high-intensity beacon of a smile. Where was I headed? London? She sure wished she was headed there too, but it was L.A. for her. We told each other to have a good trip.

A delicious little encounter. No significance to it, of course. A mere brushing together of passing souls. But there had been a reaction, I burbled to myself, we had responded, one to the other, and we had gone on our separate ways changed for ever in some infinitely subtle way. It pleased some romantic nerve in me to muse that because of that chance meeting neither of us would ever be quite the same again. I watched her as she walked away. No doubt she was supporting some idle good-for-nothing of a husband who lazed through the days in Mississippi quaffing mint juleps while she plodded up and down Pan Am aisles. Would she glance back as she turned that corner? Unquestionably—but those two cretins of sailors got in the way at the critical moment. By the time they had dragged their horrible selves out of the way she had vanished. I wondered what her name was. Then I informed myself that I shouldn't be wondering anything of the sort. You're well and truly wed, mate. Her name's Joyce. Remember her? Hadn't forgotten her for a moment, I informed myself with a touch of asperity for my cheek in even suggesting such a thing.

2

Jorgensen came in from his external inspection of the aircraft. He dripped rain.

'Pouring down,' he complained in that end-of-the-world tone of his. 'Turning bloody cold too.' He took off his cap and shook it, sending a fine spray about him. 'Turn to snow soon, I shouldn't wonder.'

Some of the cabin crew were making their way to the door, a pretty cluster of royal blue uniforms and neat, just-done hair-dos. Pert caps at precisely the right angle. Fresh make-up. Energetic dragging on the last cigarettes before take-off. Molly Stevens, the chief stew, puffed out smoke from the side of her wide mouth, picking tiny fragments of tobacco from her lower lip, while she eyed her crew. One by one, from nape of neck ('Hair must not touch collar') to tips of toes ('Shoes must at all times be properly shone'). Rumour had it that Molly was a grandmother. She had been flying since the days of the DC-3s and Tudors. The Steam Age. I recognized about half the girls; the rest were strangers. A couple of them looked no more than sixteen, even with the diligent application of eye shadow and First Blush. Someone had once said that when the stews start looking too young to fly you were beginning the grim slide into middle age. Balderdash, of course. Did incredibly attractive Pam Am stews get dewy-eyed over pilots on the brink of middle age?

'This damned coat isn't waterproof,' Jorgensen complained. 'My tunic's soaking, absolutely soaking. It really is a bit much. You pay for waterproofing. It's *extra*.' He held the garment at arm's length before him and examined it critically as he moved it from left to right.

'Olé,' I said.
'Pardon?'
'Nothing.'
'It's a bit thick, if you ask me.'
'A tragedy,' I said.
'I'm not calling it that,' Jorgensen assured me seriously. 'I'm merely pointing out that it's not what it's advertised to be.'

The great man came striding out of the men's room, body inclined as if he was making way against an enormously powerful wind. A solid little fellow, was Captain Edward Porson. A shade too short, rather too ample in the waist and a trifle too squat in the neck. He had a beefy face with a prominent nose and a jutting, almost prognathous jaw. Captain Porson had been with Anglo-World even longer than Molly. He was one of the *senior* senior captains, a man at the very top of his profession. But not for long. In a few months he would be retired—protesting vigorously, no doubt—to his farm in Sussex to raise chickens and remember his days of glory. (Why, I wondered, did so many airline pilots raise chickens after retirement?) One of the old school, Porson, something of a martinet, a mite short-tempered at times, but a solid professional.

He nodded at Jorgensen and me.

'All set, are we? Everything under control? No problems? Let's be on our way then.'

Off he went, marching as if to do battle. I fell into step beside him. He said nothing. I didn't mind; in some ways taciturn captains were easier to live with than the garrulous types who wanted to discuss everything from sex to advanced aeronautics. Discussion had been known to lead to disagreements. And disagreement could be dangerous on a flight deck. Through the passenger terminal. Past the rows of bored faces in the rows of identical seats. Funny, the similarity of people waiting in airports, no matter where; they might be a permanent display set up in airports all over the world. A nod here to a British

Airways acquaintance; another nod to an engineer from Air Canada. Ignore the curious, sometimes admiring glances from passengers. Sweep past them, earnest and intent. An odd little pleasure, a secret thrill to be a member of the élite corps.

Our 1011 wore the maroon and silver livery of Anglo-World. You breathed in her fragrance the instant you boarded her, a subtle mingling of metal and plastic, oil and fuel. She was breathtakingly beautiful and magnificently disposed; she possessed no bad habits; she reacted in a thoroughly lady-like manner in any given situation; treat her considerately and she would invariably do your bidding; indeed she would perform minor miracles if you wished. I adored her. I settled in my seat, automatically reaching for the lap straps and adjusting the rudder pedals to my liking. I surveyed the instruments before me, above me and beside me on the central console: everything at hand, logically, rationally arranged. Basic gauges directly in front: airspeed indicator, altitude and direction indicator, radio altimeter, barometric altitude meter, marker indicators; below them the Distance Measuring Equipment, the horizontal situation indicator, the rate of climb and descent indicator; in the centre of the panel between the two pilots, the flap and landing gear levers; below them, the landing gear lights; in the centre, a bank of dials recording the pulse and energy of our three jet engines.

Rain spattered angrily against the windows. It was coming down with a vengeance now, striking the aircraft like little bullets. Another dirty night. How long was it since I had taken off into a sunny sky? Visibility had deteriorated to less than half a mile; the clouds were hanging overhead at no more than three or four hundred feet. We would be clambering up through the stuff the moment we were airborne; it would be as bumpy as hell until we reached a calmer altitude. Colossal oceans of cold air were nudging equally colossal masses of warmer air. Turbulence and precipitation were the result.

There was the crew's oxygen system to check. And the intercom. And the rows of lights. And navigation aids to be programmed.

You could see heads moving along the jetway, the telescopic umbilical cord made of steel and aluminium connecting aircraft to terminal. The passengers put you in mind of an endless belt of targets at a funfair rifle range.

Behind me, Jorgensen was setting up shop, peering at the dials and switches that controlled the 1011's systems: hydraulics, engine bleed control, cabin pressure, brake temperature, cooling air, fire detection, fire extinguishers, electrics, engine controls, humidity control, waste water, fuel. A boring job, the oiler's; he was the lowest form of aircrew life.

The passengers continued to shuffle aboard; in the main cabin there would be the usual confusion with seat numbers, the inevitable frayed tempers. The ground crew reported that all the aircraft's doors were closed. Porson advised that the brakes were firmly set.

Porson scratched his right knee, blew his nose with vigour and said 'Let's have the Before-Start check, if you please.'

Galley power off. Hydraulics: pumps set. Harnesses fastened and secure. Navigation equipment, cabin signs, switches, knobs and levers by the score: thus we droned our way through our litany.

The outside temperature was hovering around the freezing mark, creating the unpleasant possibility of freezing rain. Nasty stuff, it turned to ice the instant it landed on the aircraft, building up rapidly and enthusiastically on fuselage, wings and tail. Deadly, because of the weight it created and because it literally changed the shape of the flying surfaces, diminishing their ability to create lift. But with a bit of luck we would be off before the temperature slipped any more; we would be speeding on our way to comparatively balmy London.

Porson and I had studied the flight plan in Operations, reviewing the latest pilots' reports and weather information, checking a few random examples of computer's calculations with those provided by the manual, making sure that the clever gadget that had spawned the cornucopia of information was still in good working order. Funny, how you got the feeling the computer resented such checks of its competence. Funny, too, how you longed to be able to demonstrate, just once, that it was generating pure bilge. But you had to admit that the ingenious, industrious little devil was infinitely better at the job than the pilots and navigators who used to labour over mountains of data, wearily calculating loads, routes, altitudes, alternates and economical cruising speeds. The computer did it all with consummate, almost insulting, ease, absorbing the intelligence that our aircraft was to fly from Kennedy to Heathrow, then mixing in all the data concerning winds and temperatures and every conceivable aspect of the aircraft's capabilities. It took only a second or two to sort the facts out, then, in meticulous chapter and verse, we were told the story of the flight before the aircraft had moved an inch from its ramp. It was all here, on a few inches of yellow paper: the weight of the aircraft upon take-off, consumption of fuel during the journey, length of time that would elapse between take-off and touchdown at Heathrow, weight of fuel that would be remaining in the tanks upon touchdown, length of time of the journey, average temperatures that could be expected on the route, wind velocities, the length of each leg of the trip in nautical miles together with cumulative totals, the magnetic course of each leg, altitudes, groundspeeds . . . information by the shovelful: the computer had all the answers before the questions were asked. No need for navigators now with their sextants and charts; accelerometers and gyros had made them as obsolete as riggers. How long before the indefatigable little monsters made pilots obsolete too?

I tuned in 135.5 on the VHF radio. 'Kennedy Clearance Delivery, this is Anglo 824. We're at Gate Bravo Twelve. Request clearance to London Heathrow.'

A Brooklyn accent responded. 'Anglo 824, you're cleared London Heathrow via Belle Three. Flight planned route. Depart 22 Right. Squawk 31007. Call Ground for taxi.'

'Easing off a bit,' observed Jorgensen, squinting through the windows, his eyes half closed as if dazzled by intense sunlight. 'I think.'

'I think not,' Porson declared.

'Perhaps you're right,' Jorgensen murmured. 'On second thoughts.'

The flight deck door opened. Molly Stevens appeared, an odd little smile on her carefully shaped lips.

'Do you know who's aboard?'

She sounded breathless with excitement.

'The Ayatollah?'

'*Who*? No. Vince *Baker*.'

Porson glanced across at me.

'Who's this Vince person?'

'A singer, I think.'

'Not just any singer,' said Molly, her tone betraying utter disbelief that there could be anyone in the world who had not heard of Vince Baker. 'He's *the* singer,' she added. 'There just isn't anyone else.'

'He's fruity,' Jorgensen declared airily. 'He wears a falsie in those tight pants of his.'

'He certainly doesn't,' Molly responded with fire in her voice.

'Wears a *what*?' snorted Porson.

'An aid to nature,' I told him.

'Jesus Christ,' he muttered as a ground crewman's voice intruded on the interphone.

'All set down here, Cap'n. Ready to start when you are.'

Molly took the orders for coffee and soft drinks, then hurried aft, her pretty nose aflare.

'Stand by for starting engines. Starting number two.'

He pushed the ground start switch. I reported the valve open light. A gentle rumble was audible as the huge Rolls-Royce unit stirred itself, sucking in copious quantities of the damp and chilly air of New York, compressing it, igniting it with the aid of kerosene atomized to droplets about one millionth of an inch in diameter, then ejecting it as white-hot gas in a lethal stream from the tail pipe.

Now number one engine; finally number three. Stabilizer trim to be set to take-off band, flaps to be set, hydraulic systems and air-conditioning systems and electrical power to be checked and activated. Galley power switches on. Fuel system, tank pump, crossfeed valve.

Then came the After-Start check: continuous switches for ignition, for windscreen heat, for engine anti-ice. Checks of stabilizer trim, flaps and slats, hydraulic systems, air-conditioning, door lights, elevator jam warning system, electrical power, fuel pumps, APU . . .

'Kennedy Ground, this is Anglo 824, ready to taxi. Over.'

'Anglo 824, you're cleared to taxi to the holding position runway 22 Right. Wind is three seven degrees at fifteen knots. Current altimeter is two nine nine five.'

'Anglo 824.'

From the flight deck it always looked as if the big aircraft was barely moving along the taxiway; in fact it was travelling at over 30 mph. During the trip out to the runway there were yet more checks of the aircraft's systems: pressures, data, controls, lights . . .

Our path was marked by twin rows of blue lights between which ran the taxiway, shiny with rain. Two DC-10s and a 747 were ahead, waiting like impatient monsters at the threshold of the runway.

'This is your captain speaking, there are a couple of aircraft in the queue ahead of us. The delay will be brief. We'll be on our way in a matter of minutes.'

Porson looked around the cabin, spending two or three minutes on the task, peering at everything and everyone, satisfying himself that we were all in working order. When I had met him at the hotel earlier that evening, he had said, 'Pity about Tomlinson. Shame.' And that was it. He would probably argue that I had merely done what I was expected to do, no more. He was right, of course; nevertheless it wouldn't have given the old bugger a coronary to have said it was a good show or something of the sort.

An instinctive glance at the instruments, little glowing beacons of information in the darkness. Every pilot thrills to the prospect of a take-off, no matter how many he has performed. Every flight is another brash leap into the unknown; there is always the possibility that you will encounter some condition totally new to your experience. A particularly violent windshear, for instance, or the simultaneous failure of all engines due to ingestion of volcanic dust. Such things happen—and the fact that they so seldom happen is little comfort. At all times you must expect the unexpected. Like your captain expiring.

A British Airways 747 settled itself with ponderous dignity upon the runway, its eighteen-wheel main undercarriage unit sending up a frenzy of spray.

The first DC-10 waddled out on to the runway and departed. A DC-8 landed. We inched forward until it was our turn.

'We'll be away in just a moment now, ladies and gentlemen. Will the cabin staff please take their positions for take-off.'

My first alone-and-unaided take-off had taken place nearly twenty years earlier. My aircraft was a little high-wing Auster with a Gipsy Major engine that sounded as if it belonged in a motor cycle. Mr. Evans was my instructor, a lugubrious looking man who wore funeral grey suits that were baggy and ancient. I always thought he was pining for a lost love. After a couple of circuits that morning he had instructed me to taxi back to the ramp. Then he had asked me if I thought I could do it all by myself. A disbelieving nod. The moment every student pilot dreams of! I experienced a sudden tightening of the throat muscles; a hitherto undiscovered nerve in the left hand began throbbing violently, threatening to paralyse my left side. Should I beg off for medical reasons? Unthinkable. The strip was already unrolling before me like some endless black carpet. A bump-squeak from the undercarriage. Uneven ground. What if a tyre blew? What would happen? Why didn't I think to ask Evans about it? I hadn't the *faintest* idea. Too late; she was half flying, tail up, bouncing, ready to take off. Then she rose, surprising me with her eagerness. I shouldn't have been surprised. In his doleful, tedious way Mr. Evans had explained that without his weight aboard the aircraft could be expected to become airborne with considerably more than the accustomed alacrity.

Now the centre line of Kennedy's runway lay glistening before us. Porson followed the book, performing a rolling take-off procedure, advancing the thrust levers while the aircraft was in motion. He set them right up to take-off setting, then I leant over and held the levers firmly in position. The runway stripes accelerated. There was a soft rattling of something loose beneath the floor.

'Minus five,' I reported.

'Minus five,' Porson repeated as per the book.

The airflow past the rudder was strong enough now to provide control. The runway hurtled beneath the nose, the stripes a single, wobbling, wavering line. A touch of rudder to keep the line slicing the aircraft down the middle. On either side the great, swept-back wings flexed and trembled with the feeling of flight as the air swept over their surface; finding strength, creating lift.

'V-One,' I said, my eyes on the ASI.

'V-One.'

The point of no return. V-One was the now or never speed; it was too late to abandon the take-off; there was insufficient runway left to brake and stop.

'V-R.'

Rotation speed. Porson eased back on the column, adding a touch of aileron to keep the wings level. Nose high, the jet was poised, her main wheels still pounding the runway. A moment later the rumbling ceased.

Now she was flying, free of the bonds of earth, each engine gulping down fuel at a rate of one hundred and fifty gallons a minute, to provide the power to thrust the four hundred and fifty thousand pounds of aircraft and occupants skyward.

'V-Two,' I reported.

'V-Two,' Porson acknowledged. V-Two was the minimum safe flying speed. At this weight, in these weather conditions, at this runway altitude, the speed was precisely 172 mph. The computer had worked it all out.

We climbed at an angle of fifteen degrees to the horizontal, as verified by the flight director's symbol on the instrument panel.

'Undercarriage up.'

Nothing to see but putty-coloured mist and muck that smeared the windows like ethereal hands hopelessly attempting to grasp at the speeding jet.

We climbed, thrusting our way through the murk, folding our flaps up in stages, transforming our wing for high speed flight.

'You're the cream in my coffee,' Porson half-sang, half-hummed.

Then I saw the monoplane.

3

It materialized, suddenly, shockingly. The tiny blur in the darkness became a terrifying form. High wing, fixed undercarriage, spinning propeller, a blurred disc. The sight triggered a kaleidoscope of visions: a mid-air collision, the front of the 1011; dissolving; awful, cataclysmic impact; flesh ripped and torn, bones shattered, blood spraying, atomizing, limbs spinning like bits of broken toys, a screaming, blinding torrent of freezing air, the aircraft, a miracle of precision and balance, reduced in an instant to pathetic bits of scrap tumbling, spinning, trailing passengers and their belongings.

A crazily prolonged scintilla of an instant. Something had happened to time; there was enough for thoughts, for fear, for the air to choke in my throat as I tried to cry out, to warn the others . . .

But I had to act.

Only one thing to do: grab the controls from Porson. Swerve, try to avoid the monoplane.

And hope.

A glimpse into the cockpit of the monoplane. A fleeting image of hands clutching an old-fashioned joystick. An angled wing, fabric-covered, the ribs defined beneath the delicate membrane.

No sound of impact. Incredible!

Missed! Christ, actually missed!

'What the bloody hell!'

Porson's white face, mouth open, eyes wide and indignant.

Straighten up. Did the flimsy little monoplane touch the 1011 as it hurtled past?

'My God,' I told Porson in a voice that was not quite

my own. 'That was a hell of a near thing.'

'What was?' Porson snapped, his hands on the controls.

'That aircraft,' I said, pointing forward as if the monoplane was still there to be seen.

'*Aircraft*?' He hissed the word. 'What bloody aircraft?' He picked up the interphone with his right hand. 'This is the Captain speaking, ladies and gentlemen, our apologies for that . . . er, manoeuvre. A spot of very rough air. That's why we asked you to keep your seat belts on until we reached cruising altitude. We don't expect anything else that violent, I promise you, but please keep your seat belts on until the sign is switched off. Thank you. I'm sure the rest of the trip will be much smoother.' He glanced at me. 'I didn't see any bloody aircraft.'

Half-numbed by the suddenness of it all, I still kept seeing the damned monoplane, angled, a fragment of a second before it should have hit us. Why couldn't anyone else see it? I turned to Jorgensen. He shrugged, apologetically. No doubt he had been busy with his dials and gauges.

I called the controller. A light plane, I told him, fixed undercarriage, high wing, single engine.

'No other traffic in your vicinity,' the voice reported, disinterestedly.

Could a light plane—probably of wooden construction with fabric covering—be invisible to radar because of the presence of rain and squalls?

'It was a near-miss,' I told him. 'I'm concerned that the other aircraft might have been damaged and might have come down.'

'Are you reporting damage?'

'Negative, at least we're not aware of any.'

Porson refused to turn back to Kennedy. There was no bloody reason he said. Anger caught me about the throat; the pompous old fool didn't believe something because he had failed to see it.

'If they had your other aircraft on radar then I'd turn

back,' he declared. 'But there's nothing to suggest that we're damaged. Except your manoeuvre might have taken the bloody wings off.'

'But we would have hit it . . .'

He shook his head.

I did see the thing. Clearly. Horribly clearly. Dead centre of the window panel. If I hadn't banked we'd have collided. Why didn't that cretin of a controller spot the other aircraft? I could answer that one. The light aircraft had already broken up, torn to bits by the violence of our passing. Yes, that had to be it. The remnants were still fluttering down. It would take them a week to find them all.

A slight warming of the visceral chill.

Except that they wouldn't find the bits for the simple reason that they would all have fallen in the ocean.

'Everything all right?'

Molly's voice was tinged with alarm.

'Perfectly all right,' Porson snapped.

'I thought we were looping the loop,' she said with a somewhat sad attempt at a smile.

'I can assure you we weren't,' said Porson tightly. I had the feeling that I no longer existed as far as Porson was concerned. 'Passengers all right, are they?'

'A bit shaken up, that's all. A couple of overhead racks came undone. Some coats and hats fell out. Nothing serious.'

'Good.'

'What was it?'

'Rough air. I told you.'

'Oh.' Molly recognized the tone of Porson's voice. He didn't wish to say anything more on the matter. She cleared her throat.

Why, I asked myself, don't you ask Molly if she saw that monoplane? Why the hell just sit and wait and hope she is going to announce that she saw it missing us by a couple of feet?

'I'm turning off the seat-belt sign now,' Porson told

the passengers in his best avuncular voice. 'We're clear of the rough air. It should be a most pleasant trip all the way to London. We're advised that the temperature there for our arrival will be fifty-one degrees Fahrenheit or, if you prefer, eleven degrees Celsius.' He managed to make it sound as if the temperature was being especially arranged for the arrival of the Anglo-World flights from exotic places. 'At the moment we're travelling at an airspeed of a little over five hundred and sixty miles per hour, about eighty-five per cent of the speed of sound—that's a little faster than a bullet emerging from the barrel of a revolver. The temperature outside is just under sixty degrees Fahrenheit. That's below zero, by the way. We're flying at our cruising altitude of thirty-three thousand feet, but your cabin has been pressurized to about five thousand feet above sea level. On behalf of the entire crew I wish you a most pleasant trip and I do thank you for travelling Anglo-World.'

4

The post box contained nothing more interesting than a card from the Irvines, whoever they were. Spending a week in Nassau. Having marvellous time. Weather glorious. Getting lovely tan, ha, ha. Must be friends of Joyce's. I stuffed the card in my pocket and relocked the box. My head throbbed; my eyes were heavy, the lids stiff and inflexible. My insides churned; it felt as if someone was conducting an experiment in advanced chemistry down there.

I thought of that bloody monoplane. And every fibre of me seemed to contract anew, shrivelling with sheer, unalloyed terror. The fear came fresh and keen; it sliced vertically through me, numbing yet stinging. I lived through that moment again and again. An appallingly, incredibly near thing. An instant that was seared indelibly into my mind. Would it haunt me for the rest of my days? There was no doubt that if I hadn't acted as I did, they would be looking for bits of us in the ocean. Porson, the silly sod, should have been on his fat bloody knees thanking me for what I did, not criticizing me, for God's sake . . .

But what was the use of telling myself? I should have told Porson the instant we shut down at Heathrow. Should have insisted that he listen. Should have *made* him understand. But I had done nothing of the sort. And he had gone stalking off on his own, no doubt heading straight for the Chief Pilot's office to make a damning report about that nitwit of a First Officer by the name of Adam Beale . . .

'Ah, Mr Beale.'

Christ.

'Hullo, Mrs Halliwell.'

An imperious but slightly dotty old girl of about eighty-five, Mrs. Halliwell lived in the next-door flat. She spent her days stalking about the building, nose held high as if noting nasty smells. She wore a fur about her shoulders, winter and summer.

'I called upon your wife this morning,' she declared, the grand lady of the manor addressing a minor tenant. 'But there was no reply when I rang the bell. I rang it several times,' she added, a hint of vexation in her brittle tones.

I told her that in all probability Joyce had gone to work; it was something she did almost every day.

'Work? Ah yes, of course.' Although we had known Mrs Halliwell a couple of years she still seemed to have difficulty accepting the notion of Joyce being employed. In Mrs Halliwell's day it was presumably considered infra dig for a young lady of quality to be part of the labour force.

She glanced at me in her haughty way, frowning at my uniform as if seeing it for the first time. No doubt she thought I was a bus conductor; I vaguely half-expected her to refer to me as 'my good man.' Nodding, she pointed a bony, oddly autocratic finger at me. 'And aren't you working today, Mr Beale?'

'I was. I've just got back from New York.'

'From York?'

'*New* York, Mrs Halliwell.'

'Ah, yes of course. Your wife informed me. You're something to do with the airlines, aren't you?'

So she didn't think I was a bus conductor.

'Yes, I work for Anglo-World,' I told her. But not for long, I thought, wondering if they were already considering my case, Porson and Forbes, the Chief Pilot.

'I suppose it's changed.'

'Changed?'

'New York.'

'Yes, I rather think it has changed, Mrs Halliwell.'

'It possessed a certain quality of crude vigour that wasn't totally unattractive,' she said, wrinkling up her ancient nose in a rather touchingly girlish way. 'We stayed at the Savoy-Plaza the first time we were there. Quite a reasonable establishment, if I recall. Where did you stay, Mr Beale?'

'At the Sheraton.'

'I don't know that name. Is the Savoy-Plaza still there?'

'I really couldn't say.'

'Beside the park.'

'Central Park?'

'That's correct. I remember, Whispering Jack Smith was appearing at the Mirador on 51st Street; I met him. He was quite charming, for an entertainer.'

'How interesting,' I said. I had never heard of Whispering Jack Smith or the Mirador or, for that matter, the Savoy-Plaza.

Mrs Halliwell reminisced about the dining-room at the Savoy-Plaza; 'Really not too terribly bad, for an American hotel.' She added, 'Of course, in those days no one thought of going out to dine without dressing properly. Nowadays no one bothers. It's a sure sign, Mr Beale, of the disintegration of our civilization. Lack of respect for occasion inevitably leads to lack of respect for individuals and institutions. Sad, and now I fear it's too late to put a halt to the rot.'

'Oh dear.' My head felt as if it was shrinking.

'It was barbarically hot in New York. I remember it quite clearly. There was insufficient air. I suspected at the time that it was something to do with all those absurdly tall buildings. They took up too much space, that was the simple fact of it. And all those people! Are you all right, Mr Beale?' she asked abruptly.

'Pardon?' I pulled myself together. 'I'm perfectly all right, thank you.'

She frowned. 'Are you sure?' She peered at me as if I was in a test tube.

'Quite sure,' I muttered even as a chill travelled the length of my spinal cord.

'I must have been mistaken,' she said. She peered at me again. 'But I'm rarely mistaken,' she added, conversationally, as if saying that she seldom drank champagne. Then she said it was pleasant to talk to me but she couldn't spend the day in idle chit-chat; she had a great deal to do, so she wished me a very good morning.

I gaped at her as she made her grand exit, head at regal angle, little frail sticks of legs carrying her through the front door with the dignity of a duchess departing from Buckingham Palace. Why did she ask if I was all right? Did it *show*? I shivered as I saw the monoplane again, coming through the glass entrance doors. When would I stop thinking about it? I picked up my bag and made my way across the lobby, past the potted rubber tree plant, the statue of a nymph holding a lyre and the small fountain into which visitors were wont to toss pennies. As a rule I bounded up the stairs two at a time. Not today. I trudged, step by step, to the second floor. The landing was quiet and cool; the traffic noises were muted, a soft hum. Somebody had been making coffee; it reminded me that it was nearly noon, London time. I had nibbled a morsel of toast for breakfast; but the prospect of lunch wasn't the least bit appealing; my viscera still lurched uneasily. I found my key and let myself in. Ours was an attractive flat, all mod cons, finished in voguish greys and purples. The interior decorating was Joyce's work; she had a flair for it. Actually, I wasn't particularly keen on the results but since I was unable to suggest any reasonable alternative, I didn't. The wretched place cost a hundred and seventy quid a week. All very nice, of course, to have a Kensington address but wouldn't it have been more sensible to put the money into some property of our own? Joyce agreed in principle; yes, she could see what I meant but on the other hand she was the one who had to travel into town every day and frankly she wasn't all that keen on wasting large chunks of her day squashed in buses and tube trains, arriving home halfway through the evening and then having to start worrying about getting something to eat. It was all very well for me, she had declared on a number of occasions; I had only to nip out to Heathrow three or four times a month, whereas she was at the *mercy* of London Transport. She had a point of course. She usually did. Bleakly I wondered if I, too, would soon join the army of commuters travelling up to some rotten desk job . . . No! Mustn't think like that. Things would sort themselves out. They had to.

Cup and saucer and plate in the sink; tube of toothpaste and brush on the side of the basin in the bathroom; a couple of pairs of shoes lying like wounded creatures on the bedroom floor. Every morning Joyce agonized over her choice of shoes. She had dozens of the things. Too many, that was the truth of it.

I tossed my bag on the bed, hung up my tunic, slipped the stripes from my shirt epaulettes and loosened my tie. Back to the living room, straight for the cabinet. Three-quarters of a bottle of Johnnie Walker there, thank the Lord. I poured myself a generous portion, splashed in some soda, put on an Oscar Peterson cassette and settled down in the long sofa to gaze unseeingly at the Azoulay that Joyce had bought for five hundred pounds a year ago and which, she claimed, would shortly be worth ten times that amount.

Disquietude was a soft, nagging ache that seemed to stretch like some weird membrane somewhere deep inside. You couldn't pinpoint its position; it was capable of subtle movement to elude you. The Scotch drowned the feeling momentarily, then it reappeared somewhere, a few centimetres to the right or left, up or down.

A large blot on the career of Adam Beale. On the perfect record. Comments would now be added to my file, comments that would haunt me the rest of my career, if indeed I was to have a career after this. Pilots had been discharged for a lot less. There had to be a simple, totally satisfactory explanation, I told myself as I poured another Scotch. There was always an explanation. It was simply a question of searching diligently enough to find it. The fact that Porson and Jorgensen hadn't seen the other aircraft meant nothing. If the truth be known, Porson's ageing eyes were probably incapable of responding to a situation that occurred with such breathtaking speed. The important thing, the *really* important thing, was that I *had* seen it and *had* taken the appropriate action.

Again my mind grappled with the enormity of the tragedy that had very nearly taken place. I saw bits of aircraft and bits of occupants scattered like chaff in a windstorm. I told myself that the monoplane had disintegrated. The poor little thing had probably fallen to bits the moment the 1011 screamed past it, missing it by a matter of inches. (At Heathrow I had examined the leading edges of the wings and the tail unit to see if there were any marks that might have been made by fragments of another aircraft. In vain.) But eventually the mystery would be cleared up. I would be exonerated. Indeed, if there was any justice left in this disagreeable world I would be hailed for my superb reaction. 'Had it not been for the brilliant evasive action taken by the First Officer . . .' The blot would disappear. The record would be virgin-pure once more.

But the truth was, the bloody light plane might have survived the near-miss and might have flown on its stupid way, its cretin of a pilot wondering what the hell all the noise and wind had been about. Thc fact that the little plane had not been seen on radar may have been due to the heavy rain showers in the area at the time; a flimsy craft didn't register like a big metal jet . . . Sod the both of them. Another Scotch without delay.

Awful, that moment when Porson had looked at me as if I was mad. I think there was a glimmer of fear in his eyes. Thought I was going beserk, did he? Sod him too.

Damn it, I *did* see the bloody aircraft! I saw it; it was a high-wing monoplane, single-engined, fixed gear. What else? Type? I couldn't identify it; some sort of light plane, that's all I could say. It was dark, damn it, and the thing was gone in a split second. I could hardly be expected to provide any more information, could I?

I was arguing with myself.

I finished the glass and poured another. A modest one. The Oscar Peterson cassette had stopped. I played the other side but thought about the monoplane and heard nothing. Apologies to Oscar. An hour later I telephoned Joyce's office number.

The girl from Trinidad answered.

'Justin and Crang, good afternoon.'

'Hullo, Sally. It's Adam Beale. May I speak to Joyce, please?'

'Sure thing, Mr Beale. Hold on a jiff, will you?' She made the request sound like instructions for some intricate Caribbean dance step.

Joyce came on the line. Brisk and businesslike as usual. 'Hullo, Adam. You're at home?'

'Just got in.' Not quite true but what the hell.

'Good trip?'

'Good enough.'

'Nice time in America?'

'It was all right.'

'You don't sound very enthusiastic. Tired, are you?'

Her voice had that irritatingly detached quality. I would have bet a fiver she was reading some damned memorandum or dashing off a perfectly marvellous headline for somebody's sanitary napkins while she was talking to me. It was something to be mentioned to her. One day. But not today.

I said, 'What do you say to having a bite at that funny little Italian place in Rupert Street or Dean Street or wherever it is. Then we could go to a film. I feel like a film. Something light.'

'A *film?*'

She sounded appalled at the suggestion.

'Yes. Remember them? Flicks? Movies? The cinema?'

'You're in a lovely mood,' she said—still sounding as if she was only half involved in the conversation. 'You've forgotten all about it, haven't you?'

'It?'

What the hell was *it?* Birthday? Anniversary?

'You've forgotten.'

'That's what you think.' A nasty little fragment of a memory began to dig somewhere deep down.

'I reminded you before you left for New York.'

'Ah.'

'The Art Directors' Ball.'

'Yes.' Christ.

'We have to be there between six and half past.'

'Only if we go,' I said with a dismal attempt at jocularity.

'We are going,' she declared. 'We didn't go last year. You were in Bombay or somewhere. We're going to this one. I told you when we got the invitation.'

'Did you? Yes, I suppose you did.'

'I want to go,' she said. 'You said you'd be back from New York in time.'

'But I'm very tired.'

'Then have a couple of hours' sleep. You always say a couple of hours are enough to freshen you up.'

Yes, I believed I had been known to say that.

'I'll be home about five.'

'Good.'

'Have a doze.'

'Yes. Rather.' Defeated.

'Sleep tight.'

I tried. But the moment I closed my eyes I saw the damned monoplane again, hurtling at me at lunatic speed. And I heard Mrs Halliwell. I got up and had another Scotch.

5

'You must be frightfully proud of her,' said Jeremy Forsythe.

'Frightfully,' I agreed, wondering what time it was and how long this ordeal was going to last. I felt slightly sick. Dinner had consisted of leathery roast beef and sticky pink pudding. I was conscious of the food bobbing about uneasily in alcohol. The mixture felt slightly volatile.

'She has quite an exceptional ability,' said Forsythe. 'She *grasps* a concept and, you might say, extracts the *essence* of it.'

He was a tall, very thin man of indeterminate age; his long face and slightly cavernous cheeks put one in mind of a prophet of Biblical days. But his suit spoilt the image: green corduroy with leather piping. His lightish brown hair was combed forward, Caesar-style, no doubt, I thought nastily, to camouflage incipient baldness.

Forsythe was Joyce's superior, something called a Creative Director. An awfully sound type, according to Joyce, absolutely tireless when assisting members of his team, developing their potential. But there was something about his hands that irritated me; the fingers were too long and they moved incessantly. They seemed to possess a life of their own, independent of the rest of him.

The band consisted of seven men of mature years who kept demonstrating how loudly and enthusiastically they could bat out the latest rock rubbish. I tried to ignore it but the music was like an intrusive pet pawing, begging for attention or food or a bullet through the brain. God, why did this foul ball have to be *tonight*? The maddening thing was how much Joyce was enjoying it. Prancing about with some dimwit in a fringed leather jacket, wagging her shoulders and bottom as if she was doing toning-up exercises. Indeed, everyone seemed to be having a simply marvellous time. Chatting. Laughing. Flirting. Peeping down the ladies' dresses. Whispering witticisms in ears. Exchanging knowing winks. At our table sat representatives of the creative department of Justin and Crang, a motley bunch, the men all beards and floral waistcoats, the middle-aged woman sporting long straight hair like eighteen-year old folk singers. Chaz Somebody and Liz Somebody-Else, Freddy and Ferdy, Pen and Clarice. Fat ones and skinny ones. Ugly ones and uglier ones. The ballroom was full of clones of them.

According to my watch we had been at this table little more than two hours. Absurd. Something was obviously wrong. I held my watch to an ear. Blast the thing. It was still working. I compared times with Chaz Somebody. Blast again! Not only was my watch working, it was mercilessly accurate. How many more hours of this mob? I watched them, pointing delightedly at one another, back-slapping, hand-shaking, hugging everyone, apparently ecstatic to be seeing everyone again after all these years. Two was it? No, just one. At the last ball, don't you recall? Ha, ha, bloody ha.

I dragged myself to the gents and washed my face in cold water. It was going on in there too. Two bearded gents embraced one another like grizzly bears. Each told the other that he didn't look a day older. 'Haven't changed one iota, I swear to God. How on earth do you do it, you old reprobate? Still sleeping with seventeen-year-olds twice a week? No? Three times? Jolly good!' I returned to the main ballroom and spent a few minutes studying the exhibits from competing agencies: advertisements, pamphlets, posters, record jackets, book covers and half a dozen other categories of commercial art. Works of genius, according to a couple beside me. They oo'd and ah'd as if they were in the Tate. God knows how Joyce could work with such twits.

A blonde woman with large breasts enquired if I was Sammy. I assured her I wasn't. She said she couldn't find Sammy. A shame, I commented. She asked me if I'd like to go back to her hotel.

'Unfortunately I'm here with my wife,' I said.

'Shit,' she said and made off.

I went back to the table. Joyce was engaged in an intense and obviously uproarious conversation with three or four of her colleagues. No doubt about it, she revelled in all this. I sat down and sipped my lukewarm coffee. A slim man with ginger mutton-chop whiskers told me that he would adore to learn to fly. Was it difficult?

'Planes are female,' said a weary-looking woman with a cigarette in her mouth. 'You wouldn't like them at all, Ferdy.'

'You're being beastly, Mary Lou.' Mutton Chop looked at me, one eyebrow slightly raised in an almost provocative manner. 'I could learn to fly an aeroplane, couldn't I?'

'If you can ride a bicycle,' I said.

'Well, actually I can't,' he admitted with a giggle. 'Never quite got the hang of it. Tried over and over again.'

Another woman recounted at length her experience aboard a Trident of British Airways. The thing simply dropped, she said. People's meals went flying, plastering the ceiling with sole and tartare sauce.

'An air pocket.'

'Probably,' I said, lacking the strength to explain that there were no such things as air pockets.

'Well,' said Mutton Chop, 'I know I would feel *perfectly* secure if I knew Captain *Beale* was in command.'

'He's not interested,' said the woman called Mary Lou. 'He's married to Joyce, for God's sake. You remember her, Ferdy. I know it'll come as a hell of a shock but you've got to face it. He's *normal.*' She pointed a finger at me. 'At least I assume you are.'

'I certainly was when I came in here,' I replied.

Joyce returned to the table. Was I having a good time? Fun, wasn't it? I said that I couldn't remember a night like it. The smile remained on her lips but it hardened perceptibly, the corners of her mouth becoming frigid and fixed. Her eyes told me not to dare to cause any trouble. Or I would regret it.

'To be honest,' said Forsythe, the Creative Director, 'I'm always a bit nervous about taking off. All those people. All those cases and whatnots in the cargo compartment. How the blazes is all that weight going to drag itself up into the air? I know it isn't really dangerous . . .'

'But it is,' I said.

'It is?' He paled.

'Certainly,' I said. 'So many things can go wrong. A large bird might be sucked into an engine on lift-off and cause a flame-out. You could run straight into wing-tip vortices from the 747 that took off before you; the eddies are powerful enough to flip you upside down. You might collide with some other aircraft wandering around, trying to find its way home. Things happen. Flying is not a particularly safe way to travel. But it is fast. So people accept the risks. But if I were you I'd avoid flying when there's any thunderstorm activity in the area, or when there's high humidity and when the temperature is close to freezing. And it's always as well to make sure your seat is securely fastened to the floor before you sit down because they might have used your aircraft for carrying cargo during the night; they would have taken all the seats out, you see; but sometimes the chaps are a little casual about putting them back again.'

'God,' said Forsythe. 'I was thinking of flying to Spain in August.'

'Have a good trip,' I said.

Joyce said, 'Adam sometimes derives a certain pleasure scaring people about flying. I suspect there's a rather nasty sadistic streak somewhere deep inside him.'

I opened my mouth to make a suitable reply, but the conversation had shifted rapidly from the dangers of aviation to the horrors of the advertising business. The one called Chaz said that he was fed up with the rat race.

'*Rat race?*' challenged a flabby man in a silk sports jacket. 'My dear boy, you don't know what a bloody rat race is till you've worked on Madison Avenue. They *consume* writers and artists, simply *consume* them on Mad. Then throw away the remains like yesterday's fish and chips.'

They babbled on about copy and layouts and story boards and billings and budgets, topics that meant little to me and in which I had absolutely no interest. The people in advertising seemed as insubstantial as the ideas they worked on all day. It still amazed me that Joyce could enjoy it—and take it all so seriously. She loved it, with its nervous strain, its frustrations, its disappointments, its grotesque cast of characters. One of her colleagues, a skeletal woman with dark-rimmed eyes told me an interminable story about an advertisement that was brim-full of *double ententes*, subtly disguised insults directed at the client.

I had consumed far more Scotch than was good for me. It hadn't made me drunk but I had a nasty feeling that the next swallow, or the one after that, might fell me for a week. I was suffering from the fearsome combination of jet lag, fatigue and alcohol. But I found that I could now think about the monoplane with a degree of equanimity: the memory of it was as unreal as everything else in view.

A stocky man in a frilly parody of evening dress clambered on to the stage and stood in front of the band, who were lighting cigarettes and drinking surreptitious drinks behind their music stands.

'Ladies and gentlemen,' he began in a surprisingly shrill voice. 'Now for the moment we've all been waiting for! The moment when your peers select the finest work in the industry—the top of the crop!' Even to be nominated, he declared, was a signal honour; then he went on and on about categories: black and white newspaper, full-colour newspapers, campaigns of radio and television . . . As he spoke colour slides flashed on the screen behind him. But there was something wrong with the focus. I kept blinking; it didn't help. I winced as then they played television commercials that hurt my eyes as much as the radio spots had stung my ears. For some incredible reason everyone seemed to be enjoying the whole business. Winners kept running up to the stage to receive plaques and handshakes and kisses from the long-legged girls who led them off stage. The applause was thunderous.

I blame it on my distinctly fuzzy condition; I had reached that stage when you are only partially aware of the world around you; I knew where I was, of course, but it seemed to have no real connection with *now*. I didn't hear the announcement. Not a word. I was looking into space, thinking, wondering, wandering. Then, suddenly, I became conscious of the people at our table getting to their feet with a scraping of chairs. It took a moment to sink in. The next thing I saw was Joyce. Standing. Grinning. Glancing at me then turning away and hurrying across the room and up on to the stage.

At that point it finally dawned on me. Ye Gods, Joyce had won . . . something or other. I tottered to my feet and started to chatter about it being a jolly good effort but no one was listening. All attention was focused on the stage. Joyce was up there; around me the place was erupting in applause. Forsythe and Chaz Somebody-or-Other were on the stage too, beaming, grinning, shaking hands with the fat bloke with the high-pitched voice.

'They deserved it,' declared Mutton Chop.

'Absolutely,' I said. I wanted to ask what they deserved but I had the sense not to. I seemed to recall something about a nomination; Joyce did mention the word at some misty point in the past. At the time it hadn't seemed very significant; I thought it was the agency that won. It never crossed my mind that it was *her* award. Why the hell didn't she tell me?

'Jolly good show,' I said to her when she returned with Forsythe and Chaz, all of them clutching their awards, fingers encircling the plaques as if fearing that they might fly away. 'You deserve it,' I added for good measure. To which she responded with one of her on-again-off-again smiles.

'Marvellous, darling,' someone bellowed in my ear. 'About time the silly buggers recognized real ability.'

I wished I could think of something suitable to say. But it was too late; she was angling her head, receiving kisses of congratulation from one and all.

Her name was engraved on the brass: JOYCE BEALE, COPYWRITER, Beneath JEREMY FORSYTHE, CREATIVE DIRECTOR and above CHARLES P. COE, ART DIRECTOR.

'Jolly good show,' I burbled and still no one was listening to me.

'Extraordinary, getting a Felix for the Adler Account,' said Mutton Chop. 'Adler of all accounts.'

'Extraordinary,' I said. Was the plaque a Felix? And who was Adler?

'No question that the Peerless campaign deserved it even more.'

'No question at all,' I said.

'But *Adler*.'

'Incredible,' I said.

* * *

I should have explained the whole thing while we were driving home, wending our way through rain-soaked streets. God knows why I didn't. Pride, I suppose. No doubt pride taken to extreme is a form of insanity. Practically everything seems to be. Why did I have such a lunatic reluctance to admit any sort of failing to my wife? Everything had to be all right. A year earlier, I had suffered a toothache. It hit me on Sunday afternoon while I was watching a football match on the box. I put up with it until Monday. Went off to the dentist after Joyce had departed for work. The tooth was seen to and as far as I know she was never aware of it. Would a psychiatrist jump on that one and point to it as some sort of mental failing? Perhaps I can justify my behaviour, at least partially, on the grounds that I don't like people fussing about me when I'm feeling under the weather. But I have to admit that I had no excuse for not telling Joyce about the monoplane. I should have said, 'Look, I know I wasn't the perfect guest tonight but the fact of the matter is, I've been under a lot of strain. A very distressing thing happened on the trip home. I saw a plane that no one else saw. I took the controls and banked violently because I thought we were going to hit the damned thing. The trouble was, no one else saw the other aircraft. The captain thought I'd popped a rivet. God only knows what sort of a report he's put in to the office. It could mean dismissal. It's possible. It's a very real possibility.'

What would have been so hard about saying that to her? Nothing, absolutely nothing. She would have melted at once. That tight-lipped expression would have changed; she would have become the soft, warm and exceptionally lovely female she is under all that pasted-on corporate bullshit.

As I negotiated Hyde Park Corner I said, 'It was a very good show indeed, your winning that award.'

'Thank you,' she said, her voice icy and controlled.

She didn't say anything else.

'Obviously,' I said, choosing my words with care, 'your colleagues thought it was a fine effort too.'

Then it came out.

'Was it necessary to be quite so hostile to Jerry?'

'Who?'

'Jeremy Forsythe.'

'I wasn't, at least I didn't think I was . . .'

'I would remind you that he is my superior. I would have thought you might at least have had some consideration for my position there.'

'But I hardly said a word to the man . . . I was

talking to that pouf with the whiskers most of the time . . .'

'Ferdy's a very sweet person.'

'Ferdy?'

'He may be a little bit different. But that's not a crime, not in this day and age. Perhaps it was in Victorian times, but we've progressed a little. Or hadn't you heard?'

'Heard what?' My head felt as if it had a giant pendulum inside, swinging freely, walloping first one side of my skull then the other. 'Look, I really don't know that I want to talk about friend Ferdy. There simply isn't anything I want to say about him.'

'Everything's so black and white with you, isn't it? Something is right or it's wrong. No grey areas. No subtleties.'

God, she could be the most infuriating bitch at times. 'What the hell are you talking about? Am I supposed to be enthusiastic about homosexuals simply because they happen to be in advertising? You weren't so keen on that faggot who got in the Tube that day and started to put on his make-up when you were with your parents.'

'He was an exhibitionist—'

'Don't you call those bloody whiskers a trifle exhibitionistic?'

'—and it's a condition, a fact of life, something he can't do anything about.'

'So is leprosy, but I'm not particularly keen on chatting at meals with lepers either.'

She didn't respond, but I could sense her drawing away from me, squeezing herself into the corner of the seat as if afraid that I might reach out for her. The muscles on my hands grew tight on the steering wheel; I had to blink away the slightly blurred images; at any moment I expected to see that bloody monoplane flying into us . . .

I could at least have said, 'I'm sorry. I haven't been

feeling well. Jet lag, I suppose. Couldn't sleep. Feel rotten. But I'm as proud as Punch of you. They all say you're brilliant. And I agree. You are. Have I ever denied it? I think it's absolutely marvellous that you've won the award. It's not every fellow who has a wife who can write brilliant advertising and win awards.' But I didn't say that, or anything else, for that matter. We both stared fixedly ahead as if we had been charged with the job of memorizing every detail of every foot of Beaufort Street. We drove home without exchanging another word.

I was too weary and fuzzy-minded to make any more attempts at reconciliation. She was in one of her Iron Maiden moods. Sod her. She would snap out of it the moment she found out that Anglo-World had sacked me. I blinked heavy eyes. Weird the way the mind sometimes works: here I was, deriving some sort of upside-down satisfaction from the thought that I might be able to shake Joyce by announcing that I was unemployed. Devastating strategy. I played the Oscar Peterson tape again while Joyce readied herself for bed. Was life simpler for jazz pianists than for airline pilots? Did Oscar Peterson really possess only ten fingers? If I, Adam Beale, ever became rich, fantastically, incredibly rich, I would hire the Oscar Peterson trio on a permanent basis, having them ready to play at any time of the day or night, at my bidding. But would Oscar be prepared to work under such conditions? For a few idiotic moments I actually wondered about it. Ridiculous. I had consumed far too much alcohol, that was the truth of it. I saw myself slumped in the chair, a slightly pickled lump of disconsolate humanity, bleary of eye, despondent of soul. Did I regret what I had said to Joyce's playmates? Christ, I didn't know. Neither did I bloody well care. What a tiresome bunch they were. How could they be compared with Beresford and Bill Gates and Harry Green? Jolly types, damned good company, with plenty of interesting, stimulating things to talk about. On the other hand, it was undeniable that Joyce deserved kudos. Loads of kudos. And an evening of fun to celebrate her win. Which she didn't have. Because of me. Therefore it could be assumed quite safely that at this moment she was filing a Major Complaint. I had Spoiled Things For Her. I had done it before, according to her. A streak in me, she claimed; I derived some pleasure by Spoiling Things. Quite untrue, of course. Nothing intentional about it; if it happened it was nothing more significant than a collection of circumstances all combining to create the bloody problem. After all, if that nonsense with the monoplane hadn't happened I would have had no more than my customary single Scotch on my return home; I would have enjoyed a refreshing sleep before Joyce got home and I would have been the soul of affability and charm during the evening. Damn the bloody monoplane once again. And damn the bloody Art Directors' Ball for being on that one night. If Joyce had stayed in that insurance company, life would have been simpler. But Joyce had ambition; editing an insurance company employees' magazine wasn't enough for her. She could *write*. So off she went to an advertising agency. And succeeded. I had encouraged her. Good show, old girl, show them how to do it. She had. Her progress had been rapid; now, after five or six years with the agency she was in charge of several junior writers; she worked on the leading accounts, attended board meetings, visited important clients. And tonight had become a national award winner, 'a *name* in the game', as someone at the table had remarked. Good for her. She had worked bloody hard; she deserved it all: her private office, the secretary and assistants, the fat salary (which was almost totally gobbled up maintaining this hideously expensive, *prestige* address and keeping the Jaguar in silky running order), the expense accounts, the stock options. No question she had done extraordinarily well. And she seemed to love the business in spite of

The Pressure, getting the better of it, whisking the perfect headings out just in time, dazzling the clients with her charm and good looks. And she had a plentiful supply of both commodities—though she was fond of deprecating them, declaring that looks should never exert influence on a person's career. She was like the millionaire who says that money isn't important. Astonishing how self-assured she had become. The quality must have been there all the time, lying dormant, waiting to be extricated by circumstance. When I first knew her she tended to be 'artistic', rather charmingly sloppy in her appearance, apt to go into delights about poems or pictures. Now there was nothing the least bit sloppy about her. Even her speech had changed; she had trained herself to choose her words meticulously; she enunciated with clarity. Admirable, of course. She was a person to be admired for so many things. And if I was honest about it, perhaps I did tend to take her a little for granted; perhaps I hadn't always thought of her job as being that important; perhaps subconsciously I considered it a sort of convenient occupation to while away the time until she settled down and attended to the business of being wife and mother and homemaker and all the things women were said to want to be. Perhaps it was time I made some official pronouncement on the subject. A Declaration of Recognition. One of those wry apologies that in the old, dear days used to lead to such marvellously erotic makings-up. The days when we couldn't wait to get our hands on one another. When unbuttonings and unzippings were still breathlessly exciting. Why couldn't the freshness, the sense of discovery last forever? And where was that adoration of the early days? Once she had looked up to me as if I was Churchill and Bader and Richard Burton all rolled into one. She had listened to my every word, bright-eyed, expectant. Now it had all been said and neither of us had any surprises left for the other. Christ, on this day more than any other I had wanted to be with her, a quiet, intimate meal at that funny Italian place, the precise location of which we could never quite remember; we always had to go looking for it, in one seedy Soho street after another. I had wanted a little warmth and comfort from my wife because I had had a harrowing experience and I was a little frightened about what was going to happen. That wasn't too much to ask for, was it?

The first side of the cassette came to an end. I turned it over.

The next morning the office telephoned. I was to call at the Chief Pilot's office at three in the afternoon.

6

'Captain Forbes has someone in his office at the moment,' said the auburn-haired girl; she spoke apologetically, as if it was a matter of personal concern that Captain Forbes could not see me immediately. She asked me to sit down on one of the three chairs. Would I mind waiting a few moments?

It was like a dentist's waiting room, with magazines to while away the waiting minutes. *Aviation Week*, *The Economist*, *Flight*, Anglo-World's own magazine, *A-Way*. I leafed through pages without absorbing a word. From Captain Forbes' closed office door there emerged fragments of conversation. Was Porson with Forbes? Discussing *me*? Was my fate now being decided? No doubt they regretfully were agreeing that any pilot exhibiting such glaring signs of peculiarity should be dealt with immediately; obviously unworthy of promotion to the 1011's left-hand seat; instant dismissal was probably the best solution, considering the vast numbers of perfectly truthworthy pilots now eagerly seeking employment in the country's airlines . . .

'Rotten weather, isn't it?'

'Pardon? Yes, quite rotten,' I responded to Forbes' secretary. Did she know something? Had Forbes already told her what he intended to do with me? Was she smiling sweetly and being conversational for that reason? Pity? My hands tingled; I could feel the dampness in the palms; I had an uneasy feeling that I was exuding a sour, frightened smell. In a little while I might be leaving the head office of Anglo-World Airlines for the very last time. Jobless. Just another unemployed pilot. The world was full of them. What then? Would I lose my license permanently? Would even the salt-mine possibility of instructing be denied me? Take up some other line of work? At thirty-six, almost thirty-seven? Selling insurance? Driving a taxi? The truth of the matter, I told myself, is that you're not capable of doing anything but flying aeroplanes. Except possibly doing washing-up in a café in the Mile End Road.

I felt a ridiculous twinge of self pity.

Twerp!

Every commercial pilot knows that ill-health can rob him of his licence at any time in his career. The twice-yearly examinations by CAA-approved doctors are meticulous, ordeals to be dreaded for weeks ahead. The older the pilot, the greater the medical odds against him. Cardiovascular problems are the most likely to ground him, according to the statistics. And what about the second? I knew the answer. Mental disorders. Not eyesight, not cancer, not digestive disorders, not the business of breathing in and out. Mental disorders. I shivered. Could seeing an aeroplane that no one else sees be classified as a mental disorder?

My heart thudded as Forbes' door opened. But it wasn't Porson who emerged; it was a pilot named Hartman, a genial, moustached man who wore a suntan all year round. He nodded to Forbes' secretary then to me. He greeted us in a maddeningly cheerful manner; everything always seemed to be totally right with Hartman's world.

'Cheerio, Rosemary,' smiled Hartman. 'Don't do anything I wouldn't—which should give you lots and lots of scope.'

Christ, the wit of the man.

'Captain Forbes will see you now.'

I sucked in air and nodded to the secretary as I made my way into Forbes' office, to God only knows what fate.

A tall, rather weatherbeaten-looking man in his late fifties, Forbes was Senior Pilot, responsible for the efficiency and safety of the pilots who flew Anglo-World's 1011s.

He asked me to close the door and sit down.

He hardly glanced at me as he spoke. Was that significant? Should I plead for mercy? Initiate a counter-complaint against Porson? I kicked his desk as I sat down. It emitted a hollow, drum-like boom. I apologized; Forbes shrugged. It was said that Forbes was one of the very few men still alive who had flown Hampden torpedo bombers during the war; according to the experts, a Hampden TB flyer had a rather poorer life expectancy than your average Kamikaze pilot.

'First of all,' he said in that slow, measured way of his, 'I want to say that you did well when poor old Jim Tomlinson died. Must have come as a bit of a shock, his . . . er, fading out of the picture like that.'

I nodded in what I hoped was a casual way. The cool professional. I admitted that it was certainly unexpected. Tomlinson had apparently been in good health. Hadn't complained of chest pains or a heavy left arm. Seemed quite chipper until the fatal moment.

'Extraordinary.'

I nodded again. Keep agreeing.

He cleared his throat and studied the file before him. 'I'm puzzled about this business, this *incident*, just after you took off from Kennedy the other night. Apparently you frightened some of the passengers out of their wits.'

'I was pretty frightened myself.'

'Quite so. I've spoken to Ted Porson. He says he didn't see anything.'

Yet another nod. 'He made that clear at the time.'

Forbes caressed his bony chin. 'You think he was mistaken?'

I considered that for a moment, mind spinning like a runaway compass. 'I'd like to say yes. But I'm sure he's absolutely sincere in what he says. On the other hand, so am I. I saw that aircraft.'

'And you seem to be the only one who did. Odd, isn't it?'

'Very,' I said.

'You contacted Control?'

'Yes. They had nothing on radar.'

'And no one else in the aircraft saw it either.'

'Apparently not.'

'Captain Porson seems to be of the opinion that it was probably one of those illusions created by reflection of the navigation lights and the cloud; a not unreasonable thought, what?'

'Not unreasonable at all.'

'But not correct?'

'I don't think so. That aircraft nearly hit us. We came within a hair's-breadth of a mid-air; I'm certain of it.'

Forbes tugged his right ear lobe and half closed his eyes, as if trying to picture the scene. Had I any idea of the type of aircraft? Nationality? Colour? Markings?

'It was a high wing monoplane, with a fixed undercarriage. That's really all I can tell you. I think it had a radial engine but I wouldn't want to swear to that. It was gone in a flash.'

'Of course.'

'It came right across our path.'

'What was your altitude at the time?'

Forbes knew; it was all there before him in the report. But presumably it was a little test: see if the accused remembers the story the same way as the report.

'We were still climbing to cruise altitude. We would have been close to twenty thousand feet at the time.'

'A fair altitude for the type of aircraft you describe.'

I nodded. 'That occurred to me too.'

'A puzzle,' Forbes observed. 'I remember once when I was in the right-hand seat of the DC-4. The captain jolly nearly wrote us off taking off from Athens. Very dirty night. Low, patchy clouds; you were in and out of the stuff the instant you got off the ground. You know the sort of thing.'

'Yes.'

'More confusing than solid cloud sometimes. At any rate this fellow was flying visually—a real old-timer, you know; had more confidence in himself than in the instruments. The silly bastard was utterly convinced he was still climbing when he was in fact diving. Quite steeply. Something to do with the forward acceleration causing him to feel the nose was tilting upward when it wasn't. Had no visual references, you see. Scared some of the passengers that time, too.' He gazed at me for a moment. 'I suppose you're thinking the passengers would have been a bloody sight more scared if they'd had that aircraft coming through the flight deck door.' Forbes sniffed with vigour. 'Is that what you're thinking?'

'Something like that, yes.'

Forbes slipped metal-rimmed spectacles on and perused the file, turning over a couple of pages; then he sat back and clasped his hands behind his head.

'You've got a good record with us, Adam.'

'Thank you.'

'To be perfectly frank, if I didn't know you as well as I do, I'd probably be quite convinced that you imagined the whole thing. But I know you. I've known you for nearly fifteen years, all the time you've been with us. You get to know people and you get to rely on them. I put a lot of weight in anything you tell me.'

'I appreciate that.'

'Mind you, that isn't to say that I put any less weight on anything Ted Porson says. Quite the contrary. I've known him even longer than I've known you. I've got a lot of respect for both of you. Which puts me in a difficult position.' He took off his glasses and rubbed the bridge of his nose. 'I'm going to recommend to the Director of Flight Operations that the incident be closed. We'll keep our eyes and ears open, of course, and perhaps we'll sort out the explanation eventually. How's your wife? I forget her name, forgive me.'

Relief was as good as the first swallow of Scotch. To hell with the Director. If Forbes supported me I was safe. 'Joyce, sir. That's my wife's name.'

'Yes, I remember now. Pretty. Children?'

'No, sir. My wife's a career woman. Advertising. Copy Chief, actually.'

'Splendid,' said Forbes, who clearly hadn't the foggiest idea what a Copy Chief was.

'Actually,' I said, 'I think she's starting to get tired of it. She'll be staying at home and raising a family before too long. That old maternal instinct. They all want to eventually.'

Bull-feathers, of course, but it seemed to suggest the sort of symmetrical home scene that fitted in well with the corporate image.

Forbes tugged his right ear lobe again as if to satisfy himself that it was still attached and in good form. 'It's funny,' he said, 'how we tend to think of women as being far more uniform in hopes and ambitions than men. It's been my experience that the reverse is often true. The female seems to be even more infinite in her variety than the male. Fascinating species, aren't they?' He smiled and extended a hand. 'Nice to chat with you, Adam.'

'Yes . . . and thank you.' I kicked his desk again as I got up; my exit sounded like the opening of 'Sing, Sing, Sing'.

'By the way,' said Forbes when I was at the door, 'it wasn't Ted Porson who told me about the passengers being frightened. It was one of the passengers—who happened to be a director of the corporation. When I mentioned the incident to Ted he said the matter had slipped his mind. Cheerio, old chap.'

'Cheerio,' I said. I thanked Forbes again and closed the office door. I had to compose my mouth; it was involuntarily twitching into an absurdly large grin. If I wasn't quite firm with it it was liable to emit unbecoming carols of joy and relief. Reprieve! Acquittal! All those idiotic fears about being sacked and having to drive taxis! Ridiculous over-reaction on my part!

I noticed that Forbes' secretary was regarding me, a half-smile on her lips. I also noticed that her lips were perhaps a trifle too prominent; on another face they might have been almost ugly, but on her they were as sexy as hell. It was something to do with the line of the underlip and the way the flesh swelled and curved, all aided and abetted by the auburn hair and the eyes of pellucid green, plus a fragment here and there of brown and perhaps even of blue. Quite a dish, Captain Forbes' secretary. Odd that I hadn't observed the fact earlier; no, on second thoughts, perhaps not odd at all.

'And how long have you been working for Captain Forbes?' I asked her in that ultra-sincere, intensely-interested-in-you voice that I used to consider a weapon of no mean potence in my dealings with the opposite sex.

'Three months,' she said. 'I was in Accounting before then.'

Now I remembered. Someone had mentioned

Forbes' new secretary. Recently divorced. Hot stuff, according to the someone.

'Your name's Rosemary, isn't it?'

A charming touch of colour in those bounteous cheeks. 'How did you know?'

'Actually it was a bulletin from the pilots' association. They keep us informed about really important happenings in the aeronautical world. When you took over from Edna Witherspoon the news was flashed far and wide.'

'Oh, *you.*' More pretty pinkening of the cheeks. A couple of undone blouse buttons revealed glimpses of intriguing hills and valleys. There was a veritable treasure down there—in fact, I told myself, barely able to stop myself chuckling at my own devastating wit, one might even call it a *treasure chest*! Worthy of Noël Coward, that one, I thought. Which perhaps reveals something of my insanely euphoric mood.

'I'm glad everything was all right,' she said.

I thanked her. Then departed, light of step. It was over. All that ridiculous worrying and wondering; a total waste of time and energy. And all those uncomplimentary things I had said and thought about Porson—all undeserved! The old boy probably wouldn't have said anything at all if it hadn't been for some cretin of a director who happened to be on that particular flight at that particular time.

I thought of Joyce. I had given her the very devil of a time. Poor girl. You could hardly blame her for being miffed, could you? Again I asked myself why I didn't explain the problem to her at the very first opportunity. The whole business could have been *shared* and it would have been that much easier to bear. You're a damned fool at times, I informed myself as I pushed open the front door and went out into the car park. That was when I decided: a celebration was called for. No question about it. I turned on my heels and went back into the Anglo-World building, heading straight for the public telephone in the foyer. I dialled Joyce's number.

'Justin and Crang, good afternoon.'

I said, 'Sally, my angel, why don't we run away to Trinidad together?'

'Fine, Mr Beale. I'm finished work at five. But what about Mrs Beale?'

'She can come too.'

'I bet she can, mon,' she chuckled. 'I'm putting you through now.'

'Mrs Beale's office. Good afternoon.' A young man's voice. Very correct but a trifle high-pitched. It was Trevor, Joyce's assistant.

'Is Joyce there? It's her husband calling.'

'I'm afraid she's in conference.'

In conference. In plain language, having a good old jaw.

'When will she be finished?'

'I'm afraid I couldn't say. She's with a client.'

Oh well, we couldn't possibly interfere with that magic moment. God knows, the world might fall apart at the seams.

'All right,' I said. 'Tell her I'll ring her back in an hour.'

'Yes, of course. Thank you. Goodbye.'

Officious little twerp. A slap-up feast at the Café Royal, that's what the occasion demanded. Wine and food to blissful excess. Bury the petty irritations under an avalanche of calories, pickle them in alcohol. Let joy be unrestrained. Totter off to the theatre. Something light. Frothy. Lots of chuckles. Then to glorious, eventful bed.

I decided to telephone my parents in Golders Green. My father answered.

'Hullo, old man, everything all right?'

He always asked the question at the outset of every conversation. Get the bad news, if any, over and done with at once.

I assured him that Joyce and I were in good health.

'And you and Mother?'

'Still breathing in spite of all the efforts of man and anno Domini.'

'You'll both live to be a hundred.'

'Heaven forbid! My father had recently retired from a life assurance company where he had been an actuary for some forty years. 'Where are you calling from? In Town? Well, that's a change, I must say.' He seemed to think I lived in a state of constant motion, hurtling around the world, rarely stopping anywhere long enough to catch my breath. 'Ah, here's your mother,' he said. 'Cheerio, old man.'

My mother said she had been getting worried because she hadn't heard from me for more than a week.

'I had to take a couple of unexpected flights,' I lied. 'How are you, dear?'

'A bit achy,' she said. 'But we mustn't complain. When are you and Joycie coming to see us. Sunday?'

'Yes, I expect so, Mother. But there's a possibility I may have to work. Can I let you know a little later on? Tell you what, don't cook anything. We'll pick you up and take you out for a drive. We can eat somewhere.'

'That would be lovely,' she said.

I rang off with that vaguely uneasy feeling that I always had after speaking to my parents. There were so many things that I should have said and hadn't. When would I say them? I drove into town, found an inordinately expensive place to park and rang Joyce's number again. More chuckles from Sally. Then Trevor, the Twerp. No, he was afraid she was still in conference.

'It's important,' I said.

'Well . . . ' You could almost see the sweat bursting out of the spotty little forehead. Gulp. 'All right, I'll see if I can interrupt her. One moment.'

I smiled a self-satisfied smile and adjusted the knot of my tie in the dusty glass of the telephone box.

Joyce came on the line, her voice edgy and tense.
'Adam, whatever's the matter?'
'I didn't say anything was the matter.'
'But Trevor said it was important.'
'It is.'
'What is it, for God's sake?'
'I've decided that we're going to the Café Royal tonight. Gorge ourselves. Then go and see something funny. After that, go home and have an orgy and gorge ourselves on each other. You see, darling, I simply want to apologize for being something of a pain in the neck the last few days. I know it was all my fault and I'll explain it all over dinner and I'll meet you at six or so at the corner beside Boot's . . .'
'I'm sorry, Adam.'
'What?'
'I can't. It's impossible. We've got a client from Liverpool. It's a bit of a crisis actually. We're going to continue the meeting all afternoon then take him out for a bit and perhaps come back here afterwards. I really am sorry, but there's nothing I can do about it.'
I frowned at my reflection in the glass. I said, 'There most definitely is something you can do about it. You can tell the client that you can't talk about his bloody advertisements this evening because you're going out to dinner with your husband.'
'I said I was sorry, Adam. It's out of the question. Tomorrow perhaps.'
'Surely to God you can get out of it.'
'No, I can't, I really can't.'
'It's a bit bloody hard . . .'
'It was a bit hard when you had to fly to Toronto and miss the Overells' cocktail party.'
'Yes, but I didn't have any choice.'
'I don't have any choice now. It's business. Let's do it another time. I do appreciate your asking me, honestly, but . . .'
'I might not want to do it another time.'

I heard that little, impatient sigh. She said, 'I suppose that's a risk that has to be taken, isn't it? Look, I really must be getting back.'

I hung up and glared at the receiver as if blaming it for what had transpired. There was an urgent rap on the door. An elderly lady. Had I finished with the telephone? Other people were waiting.

I shook my head. No, I most definitely had not finished, not by a long chalk. I put another 5p coin in the slot and dialled the Anglo-World number.

'Captain Forbes please . . . er, perhaps you'd better put me through to his secretary.'

'One moment.'

She answered. 'Captain Forbes' office.'

'Rosemary?'

'Yes, who's this?'

'Adam Beale. What do you say to a slap-up feast at the Café Royal tonight?'

'Me? Tonight?'

'Why not?'

'Well.'

'Well what?'

'I was going to see my aunt. She's having an operation on her foot. Something to do with a bone that's growing the wrong way.'

'Sounds painful.'

'Yes, it is, I think.'

'But I'm sure your aunt is a very understanding type.'

'How do you know how understanding she is?'

'From the way you talk about her. One senses these things.'

Another giggle. A tiny pause. Then: 'All right.'

'Good show,' I said. But was it? What had I done? I knew damn well what I had done. I had made a date to meet another woman for dinner. It was the first time since marrying Joyce. There had been temptations, of course, and opportunities galore, in Melbourne and Manchester, in New York, in Toronto, even in

Golders Green, but until now I had managed to resist . . .

* * *

'My aunt was very understanding,' Rosemary said that evening, spooning her lobster bisque with enthusiasm. 'You said she would be, didn't you? I didn't know she would be so understanding. But you did, you knew. I think that's marvellous, being able to sense things about people. How do you do it? I can sometimes but not always. I can't rely on it, if you know what I mean. Very important, being able to rely on it, I think. Don't you think so too?' Her eyes roved the ornate interior of the Café Royal. 'This is lovely. I've never been here before. Have you been here before? I expect you eat in these sort of places all the time, don't you? It must be nice to eat in lovely places like this all the time.'

'I'm glad you like it,' I said. 'Oscar Wilde and his friends used to dine here.'

She nodded. 'I know him,' she said. 'There was something funny about him, wasn't there? A scandal, wasn't it? I know I read something about him once. I know that was the name. I don't forget names. Faces sometimes, but names I never do. Oh I suppose I shouldn't say I *never* forget them, but I *hardly* ever do; that's a fact. Oscar Wilde. I'm sure there was something funny about him, I'm sure of it, I am, really.'

'Oscar Wilde was a poet and novelist and a great wit,' I said, when at last there was a brief moment of silence. 'I think he may have spent some time in advertising before he was convicted of buggery. A funny chap in all sorts of ways.'

A little smile. 'You're funny too.'

'But not that way.'

'You're married, aren't you?'

'Whatever gave you that idea?'

'Your records,' she said.

'Ah yes.' One of the snags of illicit dining with the Chief Pilot's secretary was that one could have few secrets.

'I used to be married,' she said. 'But it didn't take,' she added as if talking about an inoculation. 'Sid and I led separate lives for six months, no, it was nearer nine months. Well, eight anyway. We lived in the same house, well, flat, really. It wasn't a marriage, not in the real meaning of the word, if you understand.' She sipped her wine. A tiny morsel of bread stuck to one corner of her mouth resting on that marvellously sensuous lower lip. Odd, how unsavoury it might have been on some people, but on her it looked delicate and childlike. She was a remarkably sexy creature; I wanted to reach across the crisply starched tablecloth and grasp those superbly rounded breasts—miracles of proportion, they were. Plump yet not over-ripe; prominent yet not obscene. Pity to waste the whole evening at the theatre. I nodded as she said, 'Sid changed. He just wasn't the same chap I married. Something happened to him. Something mental, if you ask me. It affected his whole being. He got very irritable all the time. You couldn't say anything to him; he'd snap at you and tell you to get off his back and stop making his life a misery. Me? I didn't make his life a misery. If you ask me, he made his own life a misery. I mean, after all, what can you do when someone starts to change like that? People do get these funny mental upsets, don't they? I'm not saying it's their fault. I'm not saying this was Sid's fault. I mean, I don't *blame* him for it. D'you see what I mean? You can't blame someone for something that they don't have control over, can you? It's really something you should be sorry for them not angry with them because they can't help it. But the trouble is, you can only be understanding for so long. I mean, an *angel* could do better, I'm sure, but I've never ever claimed to be an angel. I have my faults. I accept that. I'm sure I've never thought of myself as perfect and I really don't think I'd mind if someone honestly pointed out some of my faults. But you couldn't talk to Sid about his faults. He'd explode. He'd really get pink in the face. A couple of times I feared for my life. I did. I thought he was going to go off the handle. Something about his eyes. They sort of bulged when he got really angry. I expected to feel his hands around my throat. Very powerful hands, Sid had. If he wasn't careful he could break someone's fingers, shaking hands with them. He didn't know his own strength, really, that was the truth of it . . .'

* * *

I arrived home a few minutes before midnight. Paused at the front door. Listened. Swallowed. Felt slightly sick for some reason. It wasn't any question of my being scared of Joyce and what she might say. Nothing of the sort. But I had to admit to a certain trepidation; it was, after all a totally new experience for me. Never before had I come creeping home in the middle of the night like one of those red-nosed drunken husbands on funny seaside post cards. There was simply no way to know how Joyce would react. Might she hurl saucepans and other kitchen utensils? Scream like a harridan? Rip my face with her finger nails? All highly unlikely of course. Joyce wasn't the sort. Besides there was a good chance that she would already be fast asleep. I might be able to slip into bed without waking her. Or perhaps she would roll into my arms as she used to in the old days, forgiving every transgression in a high tide of fleshy adoration. Once again I asked myself what had happened to that marvellous spontaneity with which we used to conduct our lives? It was hardly the moment to ponder such questions. I slipped the key in the lock and turned it. Gently. The door emitted a nervous squeak as I eased it open. Startled, I stepped back. Then looked in again. Darkness. And total silence, broken only by the ticking of the grandmother clock on the far wall. I entered, crossed to the bedroom. Door wide open. No sign of habitation. Quite obviously, quite definitely she hadn't come home yet. What a bloody cheek. I pushed the front door shut with my heel and loosened my tie. The grandmother clock announced midnight. At the same instant I heard Joyce's step in the hall. Her key clicked into the lock. Hastily, I dropped into a chair and crossed my legs, picking up a magazine from the coffee table. Damn, it was *Vogue*. Too late to exchange it for *Punch*.

'You're still up,' Joyce said. 'Sorry I'm late.'

'Quite all right,' I said. 'Perfectly normal time for a wife to come home from work.'

'I rang,' she said. 'But there was no reply.'

'I went out for a walk.'

'*You*?'

'I felt like a walk.'

'What time was that?'

'I forget exactly. Ten or so.' Clearing of throat. 'Possibly later. Or earlier.'

She didn't seem interested in pursuing the matter. She took off her coat and dropped it on the back of a chair; she left her briefcase on the floor. She was frowning as she sorted the post, tossing the envelopes on the table without interest.

'Did you have something to eat?' I asked.

'Mm?' She nodded. 'Yes. Late supper. Some overcrowded place in Chelsea. Awful service and the food wasn't much better. I think we've lost the account.'

'Pardon?'

'The account. The business. I've got that feeling.'

'Shame.'

'It's a damned sight more than a shame,' she said with a terse sigh.

'Life goes on.'

'It matters, Adam.'

'I'm sure it does.'

'People's jobs depend on it.'

'Of course.' I asked her if she wanted a drink.

She shook her head. 'No thanks, Adam. I'm going straight to bed. Do you mind? I'm exhausted.'

I sat there with *Vogue*, feeling oddly deflated.

7

I could be totally, completely assured, said the lady in the Hazelton Lanes shop, that the jacket was quite up to the stylistic standards of the Louis Feraud and Frank Usher garments that filled Joyce's cupboard at home. 'Lots of flair but with a charming element of the sporting spirit added,' she told me solemnly. I nodded as if I knew what she was talking about. I bought the jacket at a dizzying price and had it gift-wrapped in pinks and golds. I purchased a 'Thinking of You' card and trudged through wet and slippery snow to the Park Plaza Hotel where I wrote a short but rather fetching note, admitting that I had been something of a bear recently and apologizing profusely. I explained that there had been a couple of tricky problems at work but it was all sorted out now. In any event I realized that I shouldn't have taken it out on her; I asked humbly and contritely for forgiveness. It was all rather overdone, of course, and somewhat tongue-in-cheek. But it would work wonders. She would laugh and kiss me and look at the jacket and laugh and kiss me again. I was looking forward to it all. End of crisis. I slipped the note into an envelope and applied it to the gift-wrapped box with an artful inch of Scotch tape.

In the lobby an hour and forty minutes later I met Captain Swettenham and our oiler, a wiry young man with blond, almost white hair, name of Miles.

'Snowing,' Swettenham observed with a nod at the street.

So it was. Heavily. Bloor Street was already slick and dangerous. The passing traffic sent tidal waves of slush washing over the pavement.

'They forecast flurries,' said Miles reprovingly, 'not this.'

We clambered aboard a taxi and set off for the airport, making slow progress along the snowy thoroughfares.

Swettenham became increasingly edgy. 'I'd very much appreciate anything you can do to get us there quickly,' he told the driver. 'We've got a plane to catch, you see.'

The driver glanced at us in our airline uniforms and shrugged. 'Is the plane going to go without you?'

'Do what you can, there's a good chap.'

'Okay.'

Swettenham wondered aloud why the City of Toronto permitted itself to become totally gummed up by a bit of snow. It wasn't as if snow was unknown in the region; indeed it might be said that a certain amount of the stuff could be guaranteed to fall on the bloody place between the first of December and the middle of April. Was it beyond the competence of the city officials to prepare themselves for the inevitable?

'Only fifteen minutes now,' said the driver when he turned on to Highway 401 north of the city. That was when the heavy truck skidded, flipping two small cars, a Honda and a Mustang, into the guard rail, walloping a Ford LTD with its undulating rear end. The debris blocked the highway; all traffic slithered to a halt. Our driver turned and shrugged again, holding the motion as if posing for a photograph. It was, Swettenham snapped, too bloody much, far too bloody much. But there was little we could do about it. We sat and watched the snow building up on the windows. When we lowered the window a few inches to see what was going on, snow blew into the car, driven by a freshening wind. The police arrived, lights flashing, sirens wailing, followed by two trucks and ambulances. It was half an hour before the traffic began to creep on its cautious way. By the time we reached the airport Swettenham was in a fine fury, acting as if he had been compelled to commit an indecent act. It was, he said, the first time he had been late for a flight in thirty years; he should have insisted on an earlier departure from downtown; demanded it. Miles glanced at me, then his eyes rolled heavenward. Captain Swettenham did go on, didn't he? At last the taxi slopped to a halt beside Terminal One. I got out; it was pleasant to stretch one's legs after being stuck in a taxi for the better part of an hour and a half. I followed Swettenham into the terminal building, glancing appreciatively at a spectacularly chested young woman in jeans and a sweatshirt. And, at the precise instant of thinking that Joyce used to buy jeans for two pounds and now spent fifty pounds on them, I remembered the jacket from the Hazelton Lanes shop. And realized that it was no longer in my left hand. And at the same instant I recalled that I had put it on the seat beside me and hadn't given it a thought in my haste to get out of the taxi.

I turned on my heels and hurried outside. Hopeless. There was no sign of the taxi. I asked a redcap; he said the cabs dropped off the passengers at Departures then went down to the Arrivals to find a fare back into town.

I rushed downstairs but didn't see the taxi. Upstairs again. Swettenham was already demanding to know where the hell I kept scurrying away to. We had to bloody well make up for lost time. We had a bloody flight. Miles suggested that I give the taxi company a ring. Did anyone remember the driver's name? Kasanaski? Karweseki? Kawasaki? Did anyone remember the cab's company name?

'Bad luck,' said Miles.

'It's a damned sight more than that!'
'Sorry, I'm sure,' said Miles.

* * *

We were almost an hour late pulling away from the ramp. The wind was whipping the snow almost horizontally; in the snug warmth of the cabin it looked like barrages of confetti hurtling out of the darkness. We had been in motion a minute when the control tower instructed us to hold our position; a jet ahead had misjudged a turn while making its way to the runway; it had slithered off the taxiway and was stuck in the snow, blocking our path.

'Bastards!' Swettenham snorted as if the pilot of the jet had done it for the express purpose of annoying him.

Trucks swarmed past us, beacons winking, sirens blaring. Swettenham pointed to them in ire; bloody Americans, always making a big production of every damned thing.

'We're in Canada, sir,' said Miles.

'What?' Swettenham threw up his hands. 'No bloody difference; the Canadians are just as bloody bad!' He informed the passengers that there would be a slight delay, his tone leaving no doubt in anyone's mind that the delay was due solely to the abysmal incompetence of someone outside his control or that of Anglo-World Airways.

I watched the snow and cursed myself for my stupidity. By now someone would have found the jacket. A lucky day for whoever it was. But might the someone see the Park Plaza name on the stationery and return it to the hotel? Then what? How would the hotel people have the least idea whose it was? I would send the hotel a wire the moment I got to London. Good. But why, I asked myself, didn't you think to ring the hotel while you were at the airport? It would have been a simple matter to tell them that if such a parcel was returned, would they kindly please hold it until my next trip to Toronto, or, better still, send it over to the A-W office on Yonge Street . . . Marvellous, thinking of all these bright ideas *now*, imprisoned in a 1011. Should I tell Joyce? Make a joke of it? No, women were never amused by such stories. Indeed, telling her would only make a bad thing infinitely worse. Far better to swallow the loss of a couple of hundred quid courageously and pray that an honest Torontonian might find the parcel and try to find its owner. Why did I buy the ruddy jacket in the first place? Why couldn't Joyce have a sensible job, a nine to five job? Then the situation would never have arisen. But she didn't and it had. Damnable, the way things persisted in working out, becoming fiendishly complicated and confusing. In the early days life had been so gloriously simple. Being together was all that mattered. We had a flat in Earls Court that reeked of mice and old dried-out tea leaves. A seedy, depressing place, but cheap. A mad Scot lived below; he was wont to practise the bagpipes in the early hours of the morning. One day at 4:30 a.m. the police arrived. The Scot took them all on, wielding his bagpipes like a claymore; it took half a dozen bobbies to subdue him and cart him off. Afterwards his wife took up with a man from Liverpool who played the guitar. We used to buy fish and chips and eat it at the kitchen table, unbuttoning each other's clothing as we did so. I sprinkled vinegar on her breasts and filled her navel with salt; I could taste the fried fish when I kissed her and it was incredibly exciting. And we laughed like hell because the sheer joy of living was like half a bottle of champagne bubbling inside you. Wondrous times. Enough to make you cry, to think of them now. Another life.

At last Control gave us permission to move.

'Bloody good of them,' Swettenham snapped.

We took off ten minutes later, climbing through the

clag, wings rocking in the uneasy air, snow sweeping by the windows. The cloud was piled in layers; you climbed through the first and found yourself in a curiously beautiful never-never land of wispy walls and ceilings; then you ploughed through the next layer, only to find another never-never land above it. When at last we had pulled ourselves free of the muck we were close to cruising altitude. The sky above was hard and black, the moon shining brightly, cloaking the 1011 in an icy glow.

Something made me think about Rosemary. Was there any way Joyce could ever find out about the episode? It was idiotic of me; I should never have taken the woman to the Café Royal; for that matter, I should never have taken her anywhere in the western world. What, I asked myself elaborately, was I thinking of? A cretinous question. I know damn well what I was thinking of: of that sensuous underlip and those bountiful breasts. She attracted me. Sexually. I wanted to pop into bed with her. Honest answer. But nothing happened. It wasn't that she refused me. Indeed, I rather think she would have enjoyed my company in bed. But the wretched girl wouldn't, or *couldn't*, stop talking. No wonder Sid went around the bend. The poor blighter must have become randy as hell again and again, only to have his desires benumbed by her compulsive prattle. Rosemary lived in Cricklewood, near Chichele Road. I drove her home, treated all the way along the Edgware Road to an account of her problems in Accounting and a chap named Tony and a girl named Dulcie. When she invited me in for a drink I declined. Even the prospect of closer, more intimate contact with those lips and breasts couldn't compete with the balm of silence.

Christ! Something in my head seemed to snap as my vision focused on it.

The monoplane! The same monoplane. I recognized it immediately.

But this time it was flying straight and level a hundred yards to the left, its green navigation lights glittering prettily.

I reached for the controls, fingers outstretched.

But I stopped myself in time.

Swettenham turned, an eyebrow raised enquiringly.

'Back,' I said.

'What?'

'My back gave a twinge. I thought it was going out.'

Casual discussion of an inconsequential matter. Calm tone. Measured pace. A nice touch: the shifting of the shoulders to suggest an easing of taut muscles.

And all the time the monoplane flew beside us, glowing in the moonlight. It had a single word painted on its side, a short word, but I couldn't quite read it.

'All right now?'

'Fine, thanks'

'Tricky, backs. Chap I knew bent down to tie a shoelace. Didn't straighten up again as long as he lived. Something snapped.

'It was just a little muscular spasm, I think.'

I had the odd sense of being apart, of regarding the flight deck from a short distance away, seeing Swettenham and his raised eyebrow. Seeing Miles at his console. Seeing First Officer Beale going through the motions of relaxing shoulder muscles. A convincing performance. A solidly reliable looking type, Beale, I glanced past him, out through the port cabin windows.

No errant monoplane in sight. Vanished. Probably because it hadn't been there in the first place. Had Swettenham seen it? Had Second Officer Miles? No, no. Two to one. Two didn't see the thing; one did. Wasn't it therefore reasonable to assume that the one was seeing something that wasn't in fact there?

An illusion, pure and simple. How else could you describe it? Oh bloody hell, I thought, my mind's playing games. Unfunny games. Frightening games. But I had to play the part of a perfectly calm, totally competent, completely sane member of the crew.

I *had* seen the monoplane. Quite clearly. In fact, astonishingly clearly considering the fact that it was night out there. I closed my eyes for a long moment. Squeezed them tightly. High wing, fixed undercarriage, radial engine. A boxy job, like something the military might have used in the war. With something painted on the side. Not registration letters but a word. The effort of recapturing the memory was almost physically painful.

'All right?'

Eyes open. A nod. 'Yes sir, perfectly.'

'Back again?'

'A little twinge.'

'Better see the MO about it.'

'I will.'

And now the damned aircraft wasn't there. Vanished, just as it had vanished several weeks earlier. I couldn't recall the precise date. Did it matter? Was my mind really going? Seeing things. Alcoholics see snakes and insects crawling over the wall. I saw an aircraft, a funny little old-fashioned aircraft.

Old-fashioned? Yes, come to think of it, it did have a curiously ancient appearance, a heavy, rather ungainly look typical of aircraft of another era.

And a number on its tail, its rudder.

Yes, no doubt about that. A number on its rudder rather than letters along its fuselage. So presumably it was American. As far as I knew the Americans were the only ones to employ numbers to identify their civilian aircraft; the rest of the world used letters.

But the aircraft was no longer flying alongside so I couldn't check the identification. And how could I be sure that it was the same aircraft that I had seen earlier? For that matter how could I be sure of anything? Nasty stirrings of panic: a feeling of claustrophobia, of my faculties slipping away from me, one by one. I had to brace every muscle; I had to maintain tight control.

I turned again. Slowly. Casually. Nothing to see but

a pebbly floor of dirty grey cloud. No monoplane in sight.

I remembered something else: the monoplane had flown alongside our 1011 for some moments. Which meant that it had travelled at something better than five hundred miles an hour. Which was ridiculous. Or was it? Were there high-wing monoplanes that could fly that fast? Or that high? Not in my experience. That sort of aircraft would be hard put to exceed one hundred and fifty . . .

A hand touched my shoulder. My heart missed a beat. Or perhaps several.

'Sorry, did I startle you?'

It was one of the stews, carrying a tray of drinks. I said no, I wasn't the least bit startled. Bloody lie, of course. And I suspect she knew it but she didn't pursue the subject, thank God.

I begged silently, please don't let it be my mind. I imagined myself as a pathetic simpleton, slouching around the airport. The object of pity. Poor old Beale. Just popped his cork one day. Started seeing things. Odd, no history of that sort of thing in his family. Father: an actuary, sound, totally dependable type, worked for the same insurance company for forty years. Mother: former nurse, capable, reliable sort. Grandfather (paternal): railway engineer, grandfather (maternal): accountant. Solid, modestly successful people, the Beales. Good stock, as they used to say. No odd types: suicides, artists, authors. Or advertising copy writers. No mental problems. No dizziness. No sudden blackouts. No unexplained depressions or elations. Normal. Balanced. That was me.

Ridiculous; I was trying to explain the whole thing to myself, as if I alone constituted some idiotic board of review that would decide my future.

Swettenham sniffed as he drank his coffee. He said he shouldn't drink the stuff. Didn't agree with him. Too much acid. Incredible that anyone drank it, when you considered how rotten it tasted the first time you tried it. Didn't I agree? I did indeed. Nod after nod.

But the fact remained that I *felt* quite sane, perfectly capable of carrying out my duties, of taking over command of the aircraft if necessary, just as I had when poor old Tomlinson had snuffed it. Obviously a fellow had to be more or less in control of himself to handle such an emergency. But what, I wondered, if I had seen that bloody monoplane a moment after Tomlinson had breathed his last? What then? I dismissed the question. It was unanswerable. Perhaps the whole thing was simply a question of dropping off to sleep and dreaming for a moment. Like that time on the M1. Streaking along at about eighty. Actually fell asleep. Had a dream. Driving at Brooklands in the 'thirties, about to overtake Prince Bira and Malcolm Campbell by nipping neatly between the two of them . . . Woke up a scintilla of an instant later. Wandering dangerously close to a Vauxhall Cavalier. The driver had a pipe in his mouth; his eyes opened wide with alarm. The pipe fell into his lap. I nodded a greeting as I passed him.

So wasn't it possible that I might have fallen asleep and had *dreamt* about the monoplane? Wasn't it only too easy to doze off on the flight deck? Indeed it was. There were innumerable cases of flight crew members dozing off, then waking, looking guiltily at their colleagues hoping that none had noticed, only to find them *all* fast asleep. Some flights could be numbingly boring; it was a struggle to remain conscious, especially these days when accelerometers and gyroscopes did all the work of flying the aircraft, adjusting for every shift in wind, every tiny aerial hill and dale.

At first I wasn't sure about the signals. They were faint in my earphones, oddly metallic in tone.

Morse signals?

I listened, puzzled. You don't hear Morse signals in mid-Atlantic. There was a time when they were constantly beeping in the background—signals from weather ships and beacons. But not these days.

I turned to Miles.

'Hear that? Morse.'

'Morse?' he said. 'What Morse?'

Oh Christ.

In my head-set the signals were still audible, an earnest succession of dots and dashes.

'What's that?' Swettenham butted in. 'Your phones are vibrating. That's your trouble.'

'Yes, of course,' I said.

I even managed a fairly good imitation of a light-hearted, carefree chuckle while the Morse signals kept pulsing in my headset, insistent, ceaseless, then diminishing, fading, vanishing. Even when they had gone I seemed to hear them still. But no one else heard them, did they? Wasn't it therefore reasonable to assume that they were products of my own imagination? Quite reasonable. But what *wasn't* reasonable was that I hadn't *wanted* to produce the damned things in the first place . . .

Was this my punishment? Was God at last getting back at me for abandoning Him? Nonsense of course. Of course. But the old fears still had the power to sting. At one time I had embraced The Faith with an intensity that bordered on the fanatical. Indeed, for a period of a year or two in my teens, I had wanted nothing more in life than to become a priest. I remember conveying the joyous news to my mother, my fellow-Catholic. I was somewhat disappointed by her reaction. I had expected something more than guarded approval. But no doubt Mother knew how infinitesimal were the chances of my realizing the ambition. She said that it would be as well not to mention the notion (a word that seemed grossly inadequate at the time) to my father. I concurred. My father was the non-believer who talked scornfully of all things 'Popish', as he liked to describe them, often declaring his intention of forming a Titus Oates Club with himself as president. It used to mystify me how my parents could remain on such good terms with such a vast spiritual chasm yawning between them. It took me years to comprehend that their affection for one another transcended anything as trivial as dogmatic theology.

8

I examined my face in the bathroom mirror. It was unappealing: grey and peculiarly mottled as if harbouring some infection of exotic origin.

I washed and dried my face thoroughly. The mottling appeared to be more pronounced than ever. Was this the countenance, I asked myself, of someone who was in the process of going bonkers? Losing a slate? Going off his rocker? Remarkable, how many amusing little expressions there were to describe the loss of mental balance. Unfortunately the expressions lost some of their charm when the subject was oneself.

Did I imagine the Morse signals just as I had (presumably) imagined the high-wing monoplane? I asked myself the question aloud—and immediately wondered if that act in itself wasn't sufficient evidence of bats breeding in the belfry. But here, in my bathroom, clutching a towel that was one of a set given to us by Aunt Ethel and Uncle Martin of Bishop's Stortford, the question possessed a sort of academic quality; it belonged out *there*; here, the world was back in balance and felt safe and predictable. Memories of odd sights and sounds lacked substance; they were like dreams, blurred around the edges.

I examined my face again. The mottling was fading.

The door bell rang.

Mrs Halliwell. The inevitable fur at her skinny shoulders.

I managed a thin smile.

'Ah, Mr Beale, I wish to speak with your wife.'

How many times had I told the old biddy that Joyce went out to work every day? I told her once more.

'And you are at home, Mr Beale? You're not ill, I trust?'

'My hours are sometimes irregular. I'm with an airline, you see . . .'

'You told me that before, Mr Beale. I remember distinctly. It is not necessary for you to repeat things. I was calling on your wife in the hope that she might be able to let me have a quarter of a teaspoonful of saffron. I'm making Chicken la Bodega, you see.'

'Of course,' I said as if I knew all about Chicken la Bodega. But, I explained, Joyce had failed to keep me up to date on our stocks of saffron. Would Mrs Halliwell care to come in and look for herself?

'If you wish, Mr Beale,' she said. She marched into the kitchen. I followed her. It took us only a few minutes to discover that there was no saffron in the place. I apologized to her, wondering why.

'Most vexing,' she said, her bony chin jutting. 'Possibly Mrs Pitts-Michael may be able to come to my aid.'

'Quite likely, I'd say.'

She was on her way to the door when she stopped and turned and peered at me.

'Are you well, Mr Beale?'

'Perfectly.'

Her brow furrowed into neat rows of tiny corregations.

'I recall the last time I spoke to you . . .' She shook her head. 'I can't quite put my finger on it.'

'On what, Mrs Halliwell?'

Her head moved several inches closer to mine. Involuntarily I backed away. Hoping I had not hurt her feelings, I edged forward again. But she had turned around and was massaging the top of her nose as she gazed out of the window at the next block of flats.

'I sense something,' she said. 'But I really can't say what.'

'I see,' I said, not seeing at all.

'I must reflect on it.'

'Of course.'

'Good afternoon, Mr Beale.'

I wished her a good afternoon and she went on her way, leaving me amused and yet vaguely uneasy. I lay down in the bedroom and fell into a sound sleep, dreaming of Mrs Halliwell flying around in a high-wing monoplane that bore a striking resemblance to the one I had now seen on two occasions.

I woke up to the sound of classical music drifting in from the front room. I got up.

Joyce was eating a sandwich and watching an orchestra on television. She had carefully sliced the crusts from her bread and had arranged a doily on the plate: a glass of white wine stood on the coffee table at her elbow. Even when she snacked, Joyce did it with a certain panache; I admired that quality in her. I kissed her forehead and squeezed her arm and promised her a better kiss when she had stopped masticating.

She smiled. 'Did you have a good sleep?'

'Very refreshing. What time did you get in?'

'Seven or so. I thought it better to leave you. Hungry?'

I had a salmon sandwich.

'Good trip?'

'The usual. Anything earthshattering while I was away?'

She shook her head, slowly, thoughtfully. She had a striking profile and a long, extremely graceful neck that curved into shapely shoulders. Her hair was black with tiny highlights of red. A classic beauty, Joyce, in her own individual way. 'We may have a new account. A nice one. Mary Marvel.'

'Who's Mary Marvel?'

'There is no Mary Marvel. It's the name of a line of cosmetics put out by Affiliated. We made a presentation a couple of weeks ago and we hear the vibes are good.'

'The what are good?'

'Vibes. Vibrations.'

'You advertising types do love your esoteric jargon,' I remarked, casually and without spite. It was, quite simply, an observation. But it seemed to strike a nerve. Joyce counterattacked, declaring that I lived in a world that was largely incomprehensible to the average earthling. Which I quickly pointed out was simply a matter of necessity; it was essential to be able to communicate complicated facts rapidly and clearly. On the other hand, advertising people coined their private words and phrases for the specific purpose of bamboozling not-very-bright clients.

And so on and so on.

The odd thing about the argument-cum-discussion was the reluctance of either party to give way. There had been a time—and not so very long ago at that—when we had both taken pleasure in finding subjects to argue about; there had been a certain fascination in seeing how far the other opponent could be taken before everything broke up in a spluttering of laughter and a grabbing for buttons and zippers. But now, like two armies digging in, we stolidly took our positions and refused to relinquish them.

The sad thing was, I remembered afterwards that as I had clambered out of bed after my post-trip nap and made my way into the front room, I had intended to tell Joyce all about the strange sighting of the monoplane and the Morse signals. I suppose if I had, everything might have worked out differently.

* * *

I leafed through two or three books I owned on the history of aviation. I still had the feeling that the monoplane was a vintage design, from the 'forties, or perhaps even earlier.

A Fairchild FC–2W2? Similar: big wheels, slab-sided fuselage. A Bellanca Pacemaker? Yes, that one possessed much the same look. So did the Ryan Brougham, a close kin to the *Spirit of St Louis* flown by Lindbergh. The Puss Moth was too slim and its engine was an in-line. The Lockheed Vega? Too streamlined, too modern with its rounded contours. The Howard D9A too. The 1928 Travel Air A–6000 was a possibility, with its 420 hp Pratt and Whitney Wasp. And the Stinson SB–1. And the Curtiss Robin with an OX–5 motor. And the Koolhoven FK14. And the Monocoupe . . . Old relics, all of them, from half a century ago. How many of the crocks could still be in existence? The few that were belonged in museums, not in the busy airways around JFK and Toronto International. Later that morning I went to the public library and leafed through their books on the history of flight. The same aircraft kept popping up—in many cases, the same photographs. The Junkers F13, the Spartan Cruiser, the Rohrbach VIII, the PWS24, the Avia BG–52. Forgotten designs flown by pilots long dead, or at least incredibly ancient. A Widgeon taking off from Heston. A Comper Swift landing at Sandown. A Fokker F7 at Berne. Aeronautical nostalgia. But it was all a bit pointless. I closed up the last book and returned the pile to the librarian. Had I *really* seen an aeroplane? Or was it really some memory flashing across whatever memories flash across? And what about the Morse signals? Imagination too? The maddening thing was, the more I thought about it all the vaguer the elements became; it was like blowing up a photograph to examine its details, only to find that the image has become a series of big, meaningless blobs of light and shade.

It was brighter now; the pale winter sun glimmered through high cloud. I began to walk, enjoying the freshness of the cool air against my face. I buttoned up my overcoat; the wind was damp and chilly.

Then I remembered! The number on the monolane's rudder! Clear as a bell: 605Something. A frantic search through my pockets to find a bit of paper to write on, all the time repeating the number to myself: *605Something, 605Something, 605Something.* I found a receipt. But I had nothing to write with.

'Excuse me, I wonder if I might borrow a pencil . . .'

But the stout, middle-aged woman had swept on her way, perhaps thinking I was begging. In a way, I suppose I was. Mendicant Beale.

A girl, a child, a brusque-looking business man.

605Something, 605Something, 605Something.

In the end I hailed a taxi, gave the driver my home address and asked him for a pencil. He produced one and watched intently while I wrote down the number on the receipt, and nodded as I gave him back his pencil.

I gazed at the number while the taxi whisked me home.

Extraordinary, that I should remember the number so distinctly. And correctly. There was no question in my mind about it. 605Something was the number on the monoplane's tail. I remembered it. I had seen it.

In the dark? Yes, I replied to myself, in the dark.

I remember how delighted I suddenly felt. A number could be checked. The Federal Aviation people in America were the ones to contact.

I could *see* the plane. That single word on its side: it contained the letters, F, A and O. 605Something. And FAO. It was progress of a sort.

* * *

'You've lost weight," my mother said, her eyes narrowing as she peered short-sightedly across the dining-table. 'I can tell by your cheeks. You get a pinched look, there, just around the cheek bone. You see?' she said to Joyce. 'Do you see what I mean?'

'I do,' Joyce said. 'I see exactly what you mean.'

They were looking at me like a pair of shoppers at a supermarket trying to decide on a side of beef.

'Joyce isn't feeding me enough,' I said.

My mother's hand flew to her mouth in mock horror; she told me I was a terrible liar and should be ashamed of myself.

'Shouldn't he?' she asked Joyce.

'I think so,' said Joyce her eyes avoiding mine. She was still cool with me; God knows why. Idiotic, harbouring grudges and resentment the way she did. Sometimes I wondered if she wasn't the one who needed mental first aid. But one never knew with women, did one?

'Too much of that bloody awful airline food,' said Father, spiking a Brussels sprout. 'Processed muck. The extraordinary thing is that more people aren't ill from eating it. Cooked and frozen then warmed again. No nutritional value by the time the stuff finally gets down into the tummy. If they ever really investigate the whole business they'll find that half the ailments in the world are caused by the dreadful food we eat.'

My mother said she was quite sure that the authorities would never permit manufacturers to put ingredients in foodstuffs that were actually harmful.

'That,' declared my father, 'is because you have no conception of the complete and utter callousness of the average businessman. People's health isn't nearly as important as making a bob or two. If we knew the facts I'll bet we'd refuse to eat nine-tenths of the food in the shops today.'

It was raining, the drops pounding energetically on the french windows. It was Sunday evening. We spent one Sunday evening with my parents in Golders Green and next with Joyce's parents in Wimbledon, a routine broken only rarely and usually because I was working.

My mother wanted to know if I had observed any weight loss. I said I hadn't. My mother said that weight was an accurate measure of one's health. She had been saying it as long as I could remember.

'Saw a jolly good commercial on the telly the other night,' my father informed Joyce. He regarded her with a warmly approving eye. He was physically attracted to her, I was sure. He might even have been tempted to make advances if he thought he stood a chance. He was sixty-six but the juices still seemed to run vigorously. I wondered if he and Mother still had sexual relations. I was immediately ashamed of wondering such things. Father described the commercial in detail but couldn't remember the product being sold.

'Then it wasn't a good commercial,' I put in.

'It doesn't follow,' Joyce said.

'You always said it did.'

'You always take me so *literally.*' She looked past me. 'Sometimes a message has a subtle effectiveness; you find yourself thinking about it days, even weeks after seeing it.'

'Awfully interesting,' said Father, his voice tight with admiration.

'Rather,' said Mother, a trifle pettishly, I thought. Did she sense Father's feeling for Joyce? Could she actually be jealous of her daughter-in-law? It sounded like something for *The News of the World.*

'It was selling margarine or butter or lard or something of the sort,' said Father. 'She, the housewife I mean, was coming home on the bus. Very ordinary, everyday scene. Matter of fact, I thought I was watching the next act of the play. Then another woman—the one who was in that film about the Victorian family and their son who sided with the Boers. You remember.'

'No, I don't,' said Mother.

'Anyway, the woman snapped her fingers as if she'd just remembered something. Well, she had, of course . . . No, I'm getting it mixed up with another commercial.'

'I think I remember it,' said Joyce. 'It was for Smootho.'

'You're right, by Jove. Smootho, it was.'

'It won an award, last year, I think.'

'Aha!' said Father, beaming at us. 'Told you it was a good one.'

'Burgin and Ransome,' said Joyce.

'Aha,' said Father again.

'What does that mean?' Mother enquired.

'It's the name of the agency, the people who created the commercial.'

'You've done some awfully good ones,' said Father. 'I remember that jolly one with the sailor on the yacht and his wife doing the spring cleaning. I liked that one. Reminded me of my father. He was keen on sailing, y'know.' A hint of the huntin'-shootin'-and-fishin' tone sometimes crept into his voice at such times. 'Was rather fond of it myself, as a boy. Can't think why I didn't keep at it. Not too late, now, actually. I might look into it. Interesting notion.'

'Did you hear about Joyce's award?' I said.

'I rather think we did,' said Mother vaguely.

'Award?' said Father.

'It was a sort of Oscar,' I told them. 'We went to a dinner and then they read out the names of the people in the advertising business who had done all the really clever things during the year. Joyce won one of the prizes. She's highly regarded. A rising star.'

'That's lovely,' said Mother. 'I'm sure I have no idea how you can sit down and think up ideas for those commercials.'

'Thinking up the ideas isn't that hard,' said Joyce in a precise, slightly didactic way. 'The trick is to think up an idea that fits the subject at hand. One always thinks of marvellous ideas that would be perfect for stereos when one has to sell washing machines. And then, of course, when one has come up with the idea, there's the dreadful business of explaining it all to the client, getting the fellow to understand that this is really what he wants and needs. Clients don't *know* half the time, they really haven't a clue. I sometimes think companies choose the most obtuse individuals to make decisions about advertising.'

'Extraordinary,' breathed Father, suitably impressed.

'How are your dear parents?' Mother asked of Joyce.

Joyce told her that her parents were in good health and were looking forward to a holiday in Majorca. My parents talked about their trip there in 1969. Then the one in Italy. And the one in Portugal. I wanted the day to be over because I was due to fly to New York the next morning and I wanted to get there, to delve into the ownership of unidentified aircraft number 605 Something. Unfortunately my boredom must have shown. On our journey home, before we had even reached Hendon Way, Joyce opened fire. She said my behaviour had made her squirm with embarrassment. I remember being genuinely surprised. I admitted to being slightly less than fascinated by two hours of talk about resorts but I thought I had covered up well.

'I'm sorry,' I said. 'I wouldn't hurt them for the world. Or you,' I added hastily.

She said, 'I don't know what's been getting into you recently.'

Which was, of course, the whole problem.

9

An uneventful trip to Kennedy; we arrived in bright sunshine with the Big Apple laid out below us, the steel and glass edifices glittering like rows of mechanical devices in serried ranks. It all looked so immaculate and innocuous from our stacked height of fifteen thousand feet, avenues and streets mathematically arranged in neat grids, east and west, north and south, all surrounded by strips of sparkling water. A curious place, New York; it often scared me with its dirt and violence; at other times it charmed me with its excitement and its warmth. There seemed to be too much of everything jammed into those few square miles, too many people, too many cars, too many buildings, too much energy.

No inexplicable sightings during the trip, no unidentifiable signals crackling in the earphones. When we touched down on Kennedy's runway 31 Left, my relief was almost palpable. I was on top of the world, absurdly pleased with everyone and everything. (No doubt an expert would point to these extremes of mood as an indication of a basic mental instability in the Beale brain. So be it. One has to cope with the equipment one is given.)

I hoped I might be able to talk to the Federal Aviation people in Manhattan that day. Somewhere in their acres of governmental documents they probably had the answers I needed. But by the time the crew arrived at the Sheraton on 7th Avenue it was too late. I would have to wait until tomorrow. I had dinner that evening with Captain Freeman. A pleasant enough fellow, Freeman, but his conversation tended to be limited to stories about his bloody yacht and his equally bloody family. He loved them; they were flawless, yacht and family. For ten minutes his stories were quite charming; it warmed one to see how much a man could dote on his family and take intense pleasure from the business of being a father and yacht owner. But after the magic ten-minute time limit the whole business became slightly nauseating and one had an almost overwhelming desire to tell him that his wife was having a lesbian affair with the wife of a rock musician and that his children were making money acting in pornographic films. The trick was to attempt to steer the conversation away from family and lake and on to more stimulating topics such as income tax and the weather. He was due to retire in a year or so, was

Freeman. One looked with favour upon captains who were on their way out. They made room for others in the seniority scramble. A few years ago promotion for the bright and competent had been predictable; indeed, as air traffic burgeoned the need for pilots often outstripped the supply. Palmy days. Now, with the financial squeeze hurting airlines all over the world, the aircraft getting bigger and requiring fewer pilots, the opportunities were shrinking away faster than the old boys were retiring. If the present trend continued, according to some pessimists, young pilots now entering the line might spend their entire careers as Second and First Officers, never climbing that last rung to Captain rank.

We were having our last cup of coffee (the Americans will go on filling up your coffee cup forever if you let them) when Freeman said he had heard about my peculiar experience. 'Ted Porson and I are old friends. Joined the company the same day, as a matter of fact. No need to worry about the story going any further, old fellow. Ted mentioned it to me in the strictest confidence.'

Kind of him, I thought bitterly. How far had the bloody tale travelled around the A-W corridors?

'He has a great deal of regard for you,' Freeman said.

'So I gathered,' I remarked.

Freeman smiled. He had the manner of one of those old family doctors who were supposed to be so infinitely patient and understanding. 'I thought you'd be interested to know,' he said, 'that something of the sort happened to someone Ted and I knew once. Ted knows about it; that's why he told me about your Kennedy business, you see.'

'Of course,' I said without enthusiasm.

'The difference,' said Freeman with that friendly smile of his, 'was that it didn't happen in a commercial jet. Indeed, there was only one person on board, a fellow named McVail. Here's what happened: McVail was asked to ferry an old Proctor from Hull down to Gatwick. The weather started to become a trifle heavy near Cambridge, so he decided to find somewhere to put down until things cleared up. He got directions to the nearest field but things began to deteriorate rapidly. He found himself groping around in pretty thick mist. Couldn't find the field. It was a dicey do; the Proctor wasn't at all well equipped with instruments, and McVail was far from sure about the instruments he did have. Anyway, he soldiered on, groping his way through the muck, trying to find a hole. It went on for ages. His fuel was beginning to get dangerously low. Then he saw it.'

'Saw what?'

'A Flying Fortress,' said Freeman.

'A *what?*'

'A B-17. An American bomber from World War Two days. Four-engined job. McVail damned nearly ran into her. He jammed the stick forward and scooted right underneath. Couldn't have missed her by more than a few feet. Said he saw the oil stains over the engine nacelles, the guns sticking out of the belly turret. The wheels and flaps were down.'

'The B-17 was trying to land too?'

'I presume so. But the peculiar thing was, when McVail reported it, the local radar boys said they had no such animal on their screens. His was the only aircraft in the vicinity, according to them.'

'Odd,' I said, downing some more coffee.

'He thought so.'

'And what was the explanation?'

Freeman smiled sadly. 'There wasn't one. Never did find out whose it was or what it was doing there. Except for one thing. McVail did a bit of digging around and came up with a rather weird story about a B-17 coming back from a raid in 1944 and getting lost in misty conditions, in that area. I imagine it was much the same sort of weather he was coping with. Apparently, the Fort finally ran out of fuel and came down, smashing straight into a school playground. A dozen or more children were playing there and were killed or injured. Dreadful business.'

'But that was in 1944.'

'Yes. Strange, what?'

'It was the same B-17?'

'No idea, old chap.'

I swallowed. 'You mean it was a . . . *ghost*, still trying to find its field?'

'I don't mean anything, I assure you. And I have no idea whether it's even a true story, although Bert McVail wasn't the sort to make things up. I recount the whole business only to convey to you that odd things happen to other people too.'

* * *

The blue directory in the FAA office provided me with the names and addresses of citizens who operated private aircraft in the United States. All well and good, except that none of the aircraft bearing licence numbers beginning 605 appeared to be of the correct type. First on the list was Clarence M. Fogle of Ashton, Idaho. Mr Fogle owned a Piper PA 28-140, a small *low*-winged type. Might there be an error in the listing? The bespectacled young lady seemed a trifle indignant; it was, she informed me, real unlikely.

I telephoned Mr Fogle from the hotel.

A woman answered. Clarence was out, she told me, at work.

'Actually,' I said, 'I'm enquiring about his aircraft.'

'You want to buy it?' she asked her voice brightening.

'No . . .' I started truthfully, then I caught myself. 'That is, I haven't really made up my mind yet.'

'Well, I can't tell you a whole lot about it, technically speaking,' she said. 'But I know it flies real good.

What did you say your name was, by the way?'

'Edmund Thigpen,' I replied, hoping that the lady wasn't familiar with the name of Oscar Peterson's erstwhile drummer and wondering why I lied. What possible significance could the name Adam Beale have for her?

She said she used to know a Louise Thigpen in school, then she decided it wasn't Thigpen but Theakpound or something of the sort. Did I want to come over to see the plane?

'Is it a Piper 140?'

'Well, sure it is.'

'Low wing?'

'How's that?'

'Is the wing down low or on top?'

'Well, it's down low, of course. Aren't you familiar with the Cherokee, Mr Thigpen?'

I told her that I simply wanted to be quite sure I was talking about the right aircraft. Had Mr Fogle ever owned any other aircraft? No. Did he ever fly his Piper to New York? No again. Hardly surprising, since the Fogles lived some two thousand miles away. How long had Mr Fogle owned the aircraft? Three years give or take a month or two, she informed me. Was the aircraft new when he bought it? No, it was a used airplane, she said. Did she know the name of the previous owner?

'You'd better talk with Clarence,' she told me, beginning to sound a trifle testy, for which I couldn't blame her. I wished her good day.

Disappointing. I had hoped that the number might lead me to some beginning of an explanation. Of one thing I was certain, the monoplane I had seen twice was no Piper.

Then I telephoned a Mr Carmichael in Fargo, North Dakota; a Martin Slocum in Bedford, Massachusetts; Diane Kerwald in Witchita, Kansas; Stanley Niewolik Jr in Binghamton, New York; Joe Ptasinskas in

Chicago; Maurice P. Quinn 2 in Abilene, Texas; Frank Martelli in Muncie, Indiana; Charles P. Kljscek in Santa Barbara, California; and Lars Petersen in Milford, Maine. Pleasant, helpful people. They owned Cessnas and Pipers, Mooneys and Beeches. And stayed well away from JFK and Toronto International.

* * *

A series of routine trips—uneventful, except for the usual run of incidents: an elderly lady becoming locked in the toilet, two First Class passengers attempting to have sexual intercourse under the blankets but being slightly too drunk to complete the act, a heart attack, an epileptic fit, a couple of lost passports.

Then, one frigid day I stumbled upon a fragment of a clue.

I was in the local library, looking through some of their works on vintage aircraft. I had had my fill of Vegas and Leopard Moths, Farmans and Faireys and the standard assembly of shots of Lindbergh and the Mollisons, Kingsford Smith and Amelia Earhart. I actually flipped past the page in question before it registered on my brain. Then I stopped. I remembered the writing on the side of the monoplane: a single word. It began with FAO. That was what I had just seen in the book. FAO. A page at a time I retraced my literary steps.

Then I found it. A Bellanca, a high-wing monoplane. On its side in neat letters, the word FAOLAN. What, I wondered, was a Faolan? The caption said, 'Typical of the aircraft used by the long-distance flyers of the 'twenties: The Bellanca used by Mae Nolan in her unsuccessful attempt to fly the Atlantic in 1927.'

Mae Nolan?

The name meant nothing to me. According to the caption, she had failed in her attempt to fly the Atlantic. What happened to her? I looked in the index in the back of the book. Mae Nolan: page 76. A single paragraph:

One of the first women to attempt to fly the Atlantic was Mae Nolan, 24, of New York. Accompanied by Jack Thornton, she took off from Roosevelt Field, Long Island, in September, 1927, and disappeared somewhere over the ocean. No trace of her Bellanca or its two occupants was ever found.

Poor Miss Nolan.

I looked at the photograph again. The Bellanca was parked on grass, old-fashioned chocks jammed against its tyres. Had I seen the photograph before? Was that the explanation? But why should I remember *that* photograph from all the others?

10

Weird, the workings of the mind. The fact that I flew trip after trip without seeing the monoplane, seemed in some unhinged way to increase my chances of seeing it on the next trip or the one after that. Now, every flight began to have something of the tension of sitting in the dentist's chair waiting for the first jab of pain. I kept watching, wondering, studying the endless strata of clouds, layer after layer of them, murky and blurred in the semi-darkness, ghostly spumes hurtling past, tantalizing fragments, creating fleeting shapes and images that vanished the instant they were formed. Below, the ground was wreathed in wispy blackness. I strained to see through the semi-opaqueness, trying to catch a glimpse of it before it was too late . . . I even wondered whether that was all I had ever seen: no monoplane at all, but a collection of bits of water condensation in the shadowy twilight. Couldn't an infinite number of bits of cloud create a perfect representation of a high-wing monoplane just as an infinite number of monkeys at an infinite number of typewriters could, it was said, create the New Testament or *No Orchids for Miss Blandish* or something? Was it just luck that I had never seen a similar phenomenon in all the years before? But, why the same type of aircraft on both occasions? How infinitesimal were the chances of that happening? Miss Nolan's Bellanca? Yes, it had the same general lines: squarish body, radial engine, wheels on the big side. Big wheels? Yes, that was how I remembered them; big wheels that put one in mind of a toy plane. They needed big wheels back in the early days because the grass fields they used became soft and muddy and treacherous when it rained.

The captain, Trowbridge by name, fancied himself as a star of the microphone. He settled back in his seat, interphone in his right hand, elbow resting ever so comfortably on the rest, a self-satisfied smile on his over-nourished features. He informed the passengers that the aircraft had now reached cruising altitude and was travelling at eighty per cent of the speed of sound. It was to be hoped that all passengers on board were relaxing in perfect comfort, for the purpose of every member of the cabin crew was to ensure a tranquil few hours aboard this aircraft. Then on to a description of the flight path, like something out of a 'thirties travelogue with breathtaking facts on the frigidity of the temperature outside and a fervent hope that everyone had brought their brollies, for the forecast, sad to say, indicated showers, moderately heavy at times, awaiting them at Heathrow. But, Captain Trowbridge purred, one reliable thing about the Heathrow forecasts was their unreliability. It would give him enormous pleasure, he told the assembled throng, to mingle among them and answer every question about the aircraft and the flight, but such strollings were no longer permitted by the Ministry of Transport. (Trowbridge was telling the truth, though he didn't explain the reasoning for the MoT directive. In the days of the big piston-engined airliners one of the captain's prescribed duties was to visit his passengers during the flight. Then the captain of one of the early jets went for his customary stroll, leaving the co-pilot in control. Busy with some paperwork, that worthy failed to notice that the autopilot had inadvertently been turned off. The aircraft was in a shallow dive. On the flight deck everyone was blissfully unaware of the problem. But the captain observed that the aisle appeared to have assumed a slight list. He made it back to the flight deck just in time to bring the jet out of its descent before it hit the ocean.)

Irritating, the self-satisfied way that Trowbridge stroked the extremities of his moustache as he put down the interphone. He had the air of a man who has done a superlative job although it has bored him slightly. Vain sod, he was getting plump in the middle and thin on top. The girls in the cabin regarded him as a well-married old captain with absolutely no romantic possibilities. Yet he persisted in the ridiculous self-delusion that they were all eager to jump into bed with him. Was there anything in the world as pathetic as a middle-aged man who hadn't the sense to realize that he was past it?

Milky dark. Sky of velvet. No indication of life below. Not a light, not a movement. Only the quivering of needles and the logic of numerals to tell you where you were and where you were going. The INS guides the 1011 through the darkness, two hundred lives dependent upon the accuracy of three accelerometers sensitive enough to measure acceleration ranging between .0008 and 10 Gs, or, put another way, capable of measuring acceleration of something requiring an hour to get from zero to two miles per hour—and, at the other end of the scale, from standstill to 60 mph in a mere quarter of a second. Every quiver of the great aircraft was recorded on the accelerometers and the data fed immediately into the INS computer which instantly converted the information into track and distance figures, at the same time keeping a vigilant eye on where the aircraft had been, where it was and where it was going and at precisely what speed. It was humbling, the sheer bloody efficiency and tirelessness of the thing, the way it corrected the huge aircraft, adjusting for every sideways nudge of wind or hiccup in the air waves. Through it all, the little black boxes produced a casual display of numbers on the Control/Display Unit. You simply had to rotate the data selector to learn the wind speed velocity and direction. Select DIS/TIM to find out the distance and time remaining to reach any selected waypoint or the destination—with the exact time of reaching that destination thrown in for good measure. The extraordinary contraption sometimes doubted itself and would perform little tests to verify its data. When dubious about its own performance it would flash a warning light on the CDU. The three INS units aboard the 1011 could thus self-regulate each other. The unit disagreeing with the others would be summarily discarded. Clever little unit. But a bore. You could sit back and watch it perform its miracles and depress yourself by counting the years before a newer, cleverer series of black boxes replaced everyone on the flight deck.

I froze. Faint, almost inaudible, but unmistakable.

Morse signals.

I glanced quickly at the other crew members. Neither of them gave any sign of hearing unusual sounds in their headsets.

Did I glimpse the monoplane, flitting through the shadows? I squeezed my eyes shut and opened them. No, nothing. Blue-black night sky. Tranquil. Empty.

Another glance across the flight deck. The captain, Trowbridge, was sitting, arms folded, chin resting contemplatively on his chest. To the rear. Turnbull the

Second Officer was attending to his knobs and levers. A scene of almost domestic tranquillity. Perfectly ordinary. No signals now. Must have imagined it . . . What were the signals communicating? The dots and dashes were too rapid for me. I should have written them down. Had I imagined them, feeble little pulses of sound? Probably, I decided. It was the only explanation that made sense.

The sun would be up soon. Captain Trowbridge would bid his passengers a very good morning after which he would treat them to a brief news commentary taken from the short-wave BBC broadcasts. Two or three choice items, then, invariably, something about the entertainment world, usually saved from yesterday's paper. Dolly Parton or Laurence Olivier or Johnny Carson. Trowbridge took the job seriously, jotting down notes before his broadcast, editing the copy, adding a phrase here, removing another there, spicing up this one and slipping in a wry personal comment. Was he hoping to get into broadcasting when at last they grounded him?

I shrugged to myself.

'Pardon?' said Trowbridge.

'Pardon?' I said to him.

'I thought you said something.'

'No, not a thing.'

Trowbridge went back to his notes for the morning news.

* * *

I found a book in Foyle's, a fund of information about the aviators of the 'twenties and 'thirties. There was a picture of a Stinson; it looked much like the Bellanca in which the unfortunate Miss Nolan had met her end. The sides of the flat fuselage bore the name SIR JOHN CARLING. Who, I wondered, was Sir John Carling and why would his name adorn an aircraft about to attempt the long flight from Newfoundland to Europe?

Perhaps Sir John had footed the bill. 'Two Canadian pilots, Tully and Medcalf, took off from Harbour Grace, Newfoundland, at 7.25 a.m., bound for England. They were never seen again,' stated the caption. I studied their faces. Smiling. Confidently smoking a last cigarette before clambering aboard their aircraft. Were the poor bastards sick with fear or were they confident of success? What had gone wrong? Engine failure? Or had they run into some of the foul weather for which the Atlantic was justifiably famous? In England, Princess Anne Lowenstein-Wertheim—at sixty-two, no less—took off in a single-engined Fokker named the St Raphael. She was bound for Ottawa, Canada, but she vanished en route. Frances Grayson, an American, was also bent on becoming the first woman across the Atlantic by air. She purchased a Sikorsky amphibian and recruited a three-man crew. And disappeared. Undeterred by these tragedies, the Honourable Elsie Mackay, wealthy daughter of British shipping magnate Lord Inchcape, set off to fly the Atlantic from east to west. She vanished. Ruth Elder, from Florida, was luckier; forced down in the Atlantic because of engine trouble, she had the good fortune to land beside a ship, a Dutch tanker. She and her pilot, George Haldeman, were picked up unhurt.

Mae Nolan. There she was, smiling confidently for the camera at the door of her Bellanca. A pretty girl, her dark bobbed hair framing an oval face; there was a checkered scarf at her chin. The book said she was the daughter of a rich New York manufacturer and that she had taken up flying shortly after Lindbergh's history-making flight across the Atlantic. Originally she had intended to attempt the transatlantic flight alone but friends persuaded her to enroll a co-pilot possessing the necessary navigational skill and experience of long-distance flying. She hired Jack Thornton. They took off at dawn on Thursday, September 8, the story stated. 'There were reports of her Bellanca arriving safely over the Irish coast. But they proved to be false. Miss Nolan and Jack Thornton had perished, two more casualties in the quest for fame and glory offered by the ocean in those heady days following the Lone Eagle's flight.'

Poor Miss Nolan. Lots of guts but not quite enough luck. And, God knows, you needed plenty of that particular commodity to tackle the Atlantic by air in those days. One after another they tried. And failed. Often they couldn't even get beyond the boundaries of their own airfields. They ended up in giant funeral pyres—spectacular stuff for the press. The few pilots who managed to drag their overburdened aircraft aloft went wobbling uncertainly away towards the ocean; most were never seen again. I was drawn to the photographs of those fliers, fascinated by their brave smiles. How could they be so cheerful? Didn't they comprehend the appalling risks they faced? And did the potential rewards really make it all worthwhile? The fame, the money, the ticker-tape parades along Fifth Avenue, film offers, publishers waving cheque books in your face?

Another picture of Mae Nolan, in a snappy leather suit, one hand resting on the propeller of her Bellanca, the other placed casually on her hip. She was talking to a man in shirt sleeves, a handsome, well set-up fellow with regular features, his black hair shiny and brushed flat in the style of the day. Jack Thornton, her co-pilot, according to the caption. Neither of them had long to live. No doubt they both felt the colly-wobbles hard at work, but they looked positively sanguine, as if they had no plans more ambitious than to fly from Long Island to Newark, New Jersey. But did they secretly wonder whether this might be the last time they stood in the sunshine or felt springy turf beneath their feet? I searched for more references to Mae Nolan. No luck. She was just one of many who had tried and failed. No doubt her story was big news for a day or two. But the world forgets quickly.

Was there a mundane, ridiculously simple explanation for it all? Could it be that someone was making a film about Mae Nolan's tragic flight? And had the film company made a replica of her aircraft? And had they flown it in the Long Island area? Possible. But at 500 mph? And at twenty thousand feet or more? I puzzled about it as I walked along Charing Cross Road. Down here, amid the bustle of the pedestrians and the clatter of the traffic it all seemed incredibly remote and unreal. And not the least bit frightening. I could think about it all with a certain detachment. It was an enigma, an interesting riddle to be solved. But certainly nothing to concern one . . .

Was Mae Nolan still circling the lonely Atlantic?

A sort of female, aerial Flying Dutchman?

Bilge. If she was doing anything as totally unproductive as circling, the other members of our crew should have seen her. Indeed, dozens, hundreds, thousands of crews should have seen her. In fact, Amelia Earhart should have seen her when she succeeded in becoming the first woman to fly the Atlantic.

* * *

'1927?' asked the bespectacled young man in the public library. He had a slight whine to his voice.

When I nodded and said that I wished to see September or perhaps a few weeks earlier, he sighed as if it was all becoming too much for him. He peered at me through thick lenses, then he burrowed in big metal filing drawers. 'I've got August to November,' he announced, producing a small cardboard box. 'Have you ever used microfilm before?'

'I'm afraid not,' I had to admit.

Another sigh. He might have known. He beckoned; I followed him into a small room where stood three imposing devices that looked as if they belonged in a hospital. An old man in a seedy raincoat was crouched at one of the machines, studying the enlarged images of newspaper pages sliding across a lighted screen.

The young man attached the roll of microfilm and adjusted the focus.

'Turn the reel that way,' he explained in the dull way of someone who has repeated the same instructions umpteen times and no longer cares whether anyone listens. 'And when you've finished please be good enough to roll it back. By turning the handle in the opposite direction; it's quite simple. But some users just don't take the trouble. Then the reel has to be rewound before the next user can read it.'

I said I understood; he looked at me as if he doubted it. Then, with a final sigh he departed.

It was intriguing: a turn of the handle and the events of more than half a century ago came sliding into view, column after column of them. There were mechanized manoeuvres on Salisbury Plain. The Earl of Harewood celebrated his 81st birthday. The final pleas for stays of execution of Sacco and Vanzetti were refused. Severe weekend storms occurred in many parts of the UK, a typhoon struck Hong Kong and dangerous forest fires endangered Toulon. At Shoeburyness a garrison blaze resulted in the death of a gunner named Thomas. The well-known artist Richard Caton Woodville committed suicide. The liner *Adriatic* transported twenty-seven greyhounds to the United States. Charlie Chaplin obtained a divorce. King George V joined the Earl of Sefton for a little shooting in the country. The mayor of New York, Jimmy Walker, visited Ireland. Jack Hylton's band climbed aboard an Imperial Airways Argosy which flew them all the way to Blackpool then, after circling that resort, headed east for Harrogate where the orchestra performed before flying back to London; in all, the aircraft consumed 350 gallons of petrol. You could buy a year-old Humber for £250, a Bentley 4½ litre Weyman Saloon for £1495. Settlers were wanted for farms in the Victorian Irrigation Areas of Australia; a minimum capital of £400 was required. Columbia was advertising its 'Viva-Tonal' gramophone and . . . yes, a small item tucked away at the foot of page five stated that a 'Miss Mary Nolan' had declared her intention of becoming the first woman to fly the Atlantic. 'She will depart as soon as the weather conditions are propitious,' the story ran. 'Miss Nolan will be accompanied on her long journey by co-pilot Jack Thornton. She emphasizes that she will do much of the actual flying herself; she has no intention of simply being a passenger. "One of the biggest problems on a flight like this is fatigue," said the attractive young aviatrix. "It's hard to stay awake when you've got nothing to do but stare at the ocean for about thirty hours. Jack and I will spell each other throughout the flight."' According to the newspaper, Miss Nolan and Mr Thornton planned to take off from Roosevelt Field, Long Island, 'the same field from which Charles Lindbergh took off on his famous flight.'

There was nothing about Mae in the next two or three papers. Presumably she was waiting for the capricious Atlantic weather to cooperate. While she waited, Sacco and Vanzetti were at last executed, seven years after being found guilty of murdering a paymaster and guard at a shoe company in South Braintree, Massachusetts. The newspaper described Sacco and Vanzetti as 'accused anarchists who had evaded military service during the war.' The King concluded his sojourn with the Earl of Sefton and returned to Buckingham Palace. The Vauxhall Richmond saloon was being offered for £350—sliding roof £15 extra; a semi-detached house could be had for £645 in Bexleyheath. There were Wills' Flag and De Reske Ivory Tip cigarettes; BP petrol, declared an advertisement, was 'First Off the Mark'. A butler was required by a 'well-connected family' in Ipswich. The world, declared an expert, would without question run out of the means to feed itself by 1975; he advised the purchase of tinned foods to prolong life when the inevitable famine came. The pages slid across the screen: senior bank officials convicted of embezzlement; sensational divorce; sudden, violent death; disappointing football score; triumph at cricket. Major news stories. So important at the time, now forgotten by all but a handful of survivors, old people now, remembering.

Another item about Mae Nolan. This time the paper got her name right.

> Already dubbed Lady Lindy, 24-year-old Mae P. Nolan of New York is prepared to fly the Atlantic in her bright red single-engined aeroplane, 'as soon as the weather cooperates,' she says. She test flew her Bellanca monoplane for two hours this morning, accompanied by co-pilot J. Thornton, landing in a high wind which she declared to be 'no problem at all'. She plans to stay in Europe for some weeks after her flight. 'It seems dumb to travel all that way and come right back again,' she stated. She intends to replenish her wardrobe in Paris and will 'almost certainly' visit Britain and Ireland before returning to the United States. She has full confidence in her machine and in her ability to remain alert for the many hours the flight will take.

A grainy photograph depicted the Bellanca in flight over Long Island.

Then: LADY LINDY TAKES OFF FOR EUROPE.

No picture, but merely an announcement of a successful take-off followed by a rehashing of the details about her.

MAE NOLAN BELIEVED SPOTTED
NEAR IRISH COAST.

An absurd flaring of hope. Idiotic, when you know perfectly well what happened.

NO NEWS OF MAE NOLAN.

HOPE FADING FOR MAE NOLAN.

NOLAN BELIEVED LOST.

A short item about a bishop declaring that hotheaded young women like Mae Nolan should devote themselves to the home and the family. Then nothing. The last morsel of news value had been wrung out of Mae Nolan. She vanished.

* * *

The Morse signals again: but incredibly faint this time, hardly audible. I had to strain; it was almost physically painful to hear the delicate sounds. Were the damned signals coming from some fantastically distant station or were they being generated within my head? Were they in fact distress signals of a rapidly disintegrating mind?

No, bloody no, I refused to accept that. The signals had gone now, hadn't they? No, there they were, so feeble that it was impossible to distinguish dots from dashes. Sweat had stuck my shirt to my body like a second skin.

I waited, thinking that the Morse might become stronger as we approached the mainland of North America. But no, they remained the same, tiny, infinitely fragile sounds, almost imagination, but not quite.

* * *

Return trip next day. While we were still climbing to cruising altitude, I glanced out of the right-hand cabin window. There it was, gleaming, a bright red high-wing monoplane of the Bellanca type, about half a mile distant. I gazed at it, stupidly helplessly. Why didn't I have the presence of mind to bring binoculars so that I could decipher its serial number and the name on its body? I glanced at the Captain. He turned to me, casually, disinterestedly. He sniffed then looked forward again.

Now the sky to starboard was empty.

I listened, waiting for the Morse signals.

Nothing.

My throat was dry; I swallowed and smiled easily at a

joke of the second officer's. Oh very droll. Christ. How, I wondered, would I react if another pilot told me of seeing odd aircraft and hearing Morse signals where there are no such signals? Wouldn't I immediately categorize him as 'highly suspect'? Of course I would. No longer could he be counted among the clearheaded, sharp-eyed, thoroughly stable fellows who shepherded the loads of airline passengers around the hostile skies. My next medical was due in a few weeks. No doubt the examiner would take one look at me and say, 'Seeing things and hearing things, are you, old man? Ah, yes, thought so.' Then what? Would I be dismissed immediately? For 'psychological reasons'? What then? What indeed? And Joyce? No doubt she would rise to even greater heights in the advertising world. Director. President. God knows, she might form her own company and become a tycoon. How would she regard me then? Probably wouldn't regard me at all. I would be cast off like something from last year's wardrobe, a reminder of a former, less glamorous period. There would be magazine articles about her: 'Dazzling star of the advertising world, rated by some experts as the most successful practitioner of the viciously competitive craft since David Ogilvy. She has offices in London, Paris, New York, Los Angeles and Toronto. Her influence has been felt throughout the industry; her style of advertising has been imprinted upon products as diverse as new cars and floor wax. Married briefly to an airline pilot in the early 'eighties, (he was dismissed as mentally unbalanced) she went on to become the wife of the immensely wealthy . . .'

Damn it, that hurt. I could practically *see* the bloody article, photographs gleaming on thickly-coated paper; Joyce immaculately attired, stepping out of shimmering Rolls, uniformed chauffeur saluting obsequiously . . .

Why not tell her about the monoplane and the Morse signals? Damn it all, didn't she have a right to know? Didn't wives usually like to know their husbands were slithering around the bend?

All of which was undeniable. But now I couldn't bring myself to tell Joyce. A minor power struggle was still going on. I would tell her later. Later. When all this strangeness had sorted itself out. It would eventually. It had to.

* * *

'You hardly said a word all evening,' Joyce declared as we drove home from her parents' place in Wimbledon.

'Didn't I? I thought I said quite a lot.'

'Mother actually asked me what was the matter with you.'

'Did she?'

'Yes, in the kitchen when we were washing up.'

'Oh, *there*.'

Visits to either set of parents seemed inevitably to lead to arguments on the way home.

'Aren't you well?'

'I'm perfectly well.' Untrue. I was out of sorts. Hadn't slept properly since the last trip. Kept seeing that bloody plane and hearing those equally bloody dots and dashes. The last few weeks had been a mental switchback. At one time I had thought it was all fading away, one of those oddities of life that would never be fully explained and that would eventually be forgotten. Now it had all come back to nag at me, to make me doubt my sanity, to make me wonder how long it would be before something—God knows what—blew up in my face.

'I have a feeling that Father thought you might be angry at something.'

Perish the bloody thought. I shook my head. Why should the pompous ass think I was angry? Just because I didn't pay total, enraptured attention to his umpteenth telling of the story of his first days as an assistant to the chief engineer of some dismal factory in Lancashire? How many times had he recounted the tale? Did he really think we were all hearing it for the first time? Also, come to think of it, his general air of intense self-satisfaction irritated me. So did his habit of examining each forkful of food at close quarters before popping it into his mouth. As did his execrable taste in neckwear.

'I don't know what's happened to you lately,' said Joyce.

Neither did I.

11

Two trips to Mirabel, one to Kennedy. Category: Uneventful; no inexplicable sightings or hearings.

I had a thirty-six-hour layover in New York. I spent half a dozen of those hours at the New York Public Library, studying microfilm films of 1927 newspapers. The stories were essentially the same as those I had read in the British papers, although there was considerably more detail about Mae Nolan herself ('born in Abbottsport, N.Y.') and the Nolan family ('Miss Nolan's father is James M. Nolan, President of the well-known pharmaceutical company that bears his name'). I found Abbottsport on the map; it was in the north-west part of the State, thirty miles or so from Rochester: 'Upstate', a bearded librarian informed me. According to the newspaper stories, Mae had spent much time immediately before her flight in a place called Mineola, near Roosevelt Field on Long Island. I asked how long it would take to drive out to Long Island. No time at all, my bearded friend told me.

* * *

There is nothing inherently difficult in driving on the right-hand side of the road. I had done it before. Twice, I think. But I don't recommend trying it in

New York City until you have practised diligently in more tranquil territories. The moment I eased the Cheverolet out of the rent-a-car driveway I was tempted to abandon it. But a sort of tidal wave of traffic swept me along, block after frightful block. The man at the office had told me to 'hang a left' at 44th Street. But I was already at 53rd Street and unsure whether I was travelling east or west, north or south. It was a nerve-jangling journey, along pot-holed streets, some littered with the rusting hulks of abandoned cars that looked as if they had sickened and died in their journeys and had been cannibalized by their fellows; then past gracious buildings and splendid shops; a block further on there were abandoned apartment blocks, crumbling, fire-ravaged. A city of contrasts, New York. And one that seems to do very little to help the total stranger find his way around. I found signs aplenty, but they informed me only how to get to the Bruckner Expressway or the Bronx River Parkway or half a hundred other thoroughfares. It had apparently not occurred to the sign-installers that there might one day be a driver out there who had not the slightest idea what points of the globe were connected by the Bruckner Expressway or the Bronx River Parkway. After half an hour of wandering I found the Throgs Neck Bridge which, I had been told, would take me to Long Island. Joy! Definitely the right road now! But as I approached the bridge I discovered that it would cost the sum of $1.25 to cross the thing. Bloody outrageous, the tolls on some of the American bridges; they must have paid for the wretched structures ten times over, yet they continue to extract cash from every hapless traveller. Ahead, another sign pointed the way for those motorists having the exact change. Fair enough: a speedy lane for those who didn't require change. I fumbled in my pocket and found a dollar bill and a twenty-five cent coin. I steered into the Exact Change lane. At the toll booth the truth hit home: 'exact change' meant coins only. Too late to change lanes now. As I jumped out to obtain change of my already-sweaty dollar bill, I could feel the waves of hatred emanating from the cars lined up behind, a vast huddle of trembling machinery. How long would it take for such concentrated loathing to prove fatal?

Long Island is a great finger of land some one hundred miles long extending east-north-east from the mouth of the Hudson, separated from Manhattan by the East River. Once it was the home of Indians. Now some six million New Yorkers live there.

After the confusion of Manhattan, it was pleasant to drive along a wide highway, through wooded country. The traffic was lighter now. A sign told me I was in Nassau county. Another pointed the way to Mineola. It was a prosperous-looking area with substantial homes on impressive properties; lawns neatly tended, woodwork crisply painted. Cadillacs, Mercedes and BMWs decorated the driveways. Smart shopping areas dotted the place like miniature clones of Beverly Hills. I found Roosevelt Field. But the airfield had disappeared under the concrete of yet another shopping centre, a monster this time, complete with Macy's, Alexander's and Burger King, plus a car wash for good measure. A handsome book shop carried volumes on every conceivable subject except the historical field upon which the premises stood. A bespectacled assistant was only vaguely aware that Lindbergh himself had set off on his famous flight from this very spot. Yeah, it seemed to her she did hear something of the sort but, no, she didn't have any books about it. Why, she seemed to ask, would anyone still care? Perhaps she had a point. I went out into the chill. The sun had gone down; the bright lights of the stores cast a frigid glow. It was a curiously emotional moment, standing there, realizing that Lindbergh and umpteen others had walked near here, pacing, worrying, wondering if their brutally overloaded machines would succeed in dragging themselves off the cinder strip. Fonck's Sikorsky almost made it in 1926, then its landing gear collapsed; the big biplane was burnt to a crisp, along with two crew members. This was hallowed ground for those who cared about such things; the field had been named after a son of Theodore Roosevelt, Quentin, who was killed flying in France during the First World War; my research had also armed me with the information that nearby Mitchel Field had been named after a former mayor of New York who enlisted in the air service during the same war and met his end when he fell out of a training aircraft. I was becoming the custodian of a wealth of aeronautical trivia.

I made my way back to the Chevrolet. I had left it in a roofed parking area adjacent to Macy's.

That was when I saw her. She was standing in the shadows, beside my car. Bobbed hair; leather breeches and a short jacket with a checkered scarf at her throat. Just like the photograph.

I remember muttering something, God knows what, as I started towards her. I was oddly conscious of the sound of my feet on the asphalt as I walked. My pace quickened.

A family—father, mother and four or five children—crossed in front of me. Chattering, laughing. Damn it, I was only fifty feet or so from the car. Almost there . . .

Gone.

I stared, horrified, as if I had been witness to a murder.

There. That spot. Beside the right front wheel. That was where she had been standing. I had *seen* her.

'I didn't imagine it,' I said.

'Uh?' queried a man unlocking a Mercury.

'Sorry,' I said. 'Talking to myself.'

'Yeah, I find myself doing that,'.said the man with a lopsided grin.

I examined the asphalt around the car's front wheel, although heaven knows what I expected to find. I *had* seen her. No dream, that. No drunken vision. I could almost have reached out and touched her.

Mae Nolan?
No, I couldn't accept that.
Could I?

* * *

That Sunday evening at my parent's home I enquired about foreign connections in the family.

'Whatever made you think about that?' asked my mother, her eyebrows arched, looking for all the world as if I had enquired about homosexual communists in the family.

'Just interested,' I said.

My father said, 'Your Uncle Rupert nosed around the family tree fifty or sixty years ago. In fact, it might have been even longer than that, some time before the war, wasn't it?'

'I'm sure I haven't the faintest idea,' said my mother. 'At that time I didn't know the Beale family existed.'

'A mere schoolgirl, were you?'

'I most certainly was.'

'Uncle Rupert said there was a Dutchwoman,' said my father. 'She married your great-grandfather, or possibly your great-great-grandfather. At any rate, it was a long time ago. He was of the opinion that there was a French male or female somewhere but I don't think he was very sure about it.'

'Any Irish connections?' I asked.

'I should hope not!' declared my mother indignantly; she was convinced that all Irish citizens, male or female, were members of the IRA.

'American?'

'I don't think so,' my father replied.

'A distant cousin of mine married an Egyptian,' said Joyce.

'Ah, now, I shouldn't like *that*,' said my mother.

'He was really quite nice,' said Joyce.

Which led to a chat about the neighbour's daughter who married a Free French officer during the war and how he had left her in Lyons with two children; and about the Canadian who married Aunt Gladys and how they lived in Calgary and how I had never yet managed to pay her a visit despite my many trips to Canada.

'It's approximately the same distance,' I told her for the umpteenth time, 'from Toronto International Airport to Calgary as it is from London to Moscow.

'Yes, yes, I know all that,' said my mother, 'but it's not the same thing at all; if you really wanted to visit Aunt Gladys you'd find a way.'

Which was undeniable.

I enjoyed the evening. I felt calm, able to think almost dispassionately about the peculiar case of Mae Nolan. Curious, how adaptable we are. Somehow, for some reason, I had become involved in a series of events that took place a lifetime ago. It made no sense and I was as far as ever from sorting it all out. But I could face the fact without cringing. That odd visit to Roosevelt Field had, in some odd way, reassured me. Lord knows why, but I seemed to sense that I had no reason to fear her any more. I decided that on my next layover in America I would travel up to Abbottsport, Mae's home town.

12

The bus was less than half full. I sat immediately behind the shirt-sleeved driver who hummed tuneless melodies as he steered his big vehicle along the damp, slippery highway. He had pulled his peaked cap forward as if to shield his eyes from the glare of the sun. But there was little sun that day; it would glimmer weakly for a moment, then the sky would become leaden and snow—large, wet flakes—would whirl past the bus windows on a brisk wind. On either side of the road the trees were laden with snow; it lay precariously on the branches like over-generous helpings of icing sugar. We passed through several small communities; a few shops, some houses, cars angle-parked along Main Street, every little town had at least one elderly citizen who seemed to spend his or her time gazing suspiciously at the bus as if it was some dangerous intruder. I enjoyed the pageant of small-town America from the overheated comfort of the bus. This, according to some, was the real America; New York and Chicago were cultural aberations and one should depart from them as rapidly as possible.

I was not at all sure just what I was going to look for in Abbottsport. What appealed to me was simply the prospect of nosing around the place where Mae was born and spent much of her short life. I had used my airline identity card to obtain a cut-rate seat on US Air to Rochester, then I had found this bus to take me on to Abbottsport. I had to return that evening to catch a flight back to New York; we were leaving for London at eleven the next morning.

The bus came to a splashing stop in a place called Flitchburg. A stout lady clambered aboard, puffing and shaking her head. The driver asked how she was keeping and she told him she doubted she'd see the winter out. The driver winked at me as the lady made her groaning way aft. Across the street a man was clearing his driveway with a snow blower, sending up a fountain of the stuff that sparkled in the feeble glimmer of sunlight like showers of tiny gems.

The bus began to roll then stopped as a man in a navy blue pea jacket came running, carrying a large brown parcel.

'Much obliged,' he said to the driver as he boarded.

'No sweat,' was the driver's response.

We drove on and passed a road sign informing us that Abbottsport was only five miles away.

It was strangely exciting to realize that Mae Nolan herself must have travelled along this very road and must have seen many of these same sights. That old frame house looked as if it had occupied that half acre since the Civil War. The stone bridge looked even older: perhaps Mae had stood on it as a child, looking down at the narrow river below. What river? Damn! There was a sign but we were past it before I could read the name. There was a date carved in the stone above the main door of that schoolhouse: 1922. It would have been brand new when Mae saw it, paint gleaming, bricks fresh from the kiln. The slogan CHEW MAIL POUCH TOBACCO was faded and almost illegible on the side of a sagging old barn; when Mae lived here it was no doubt bright and vigorous, up to date advertising of a popular product. Model Ts, Hupmobiles, La Salles and Nashes must have cruised this road in those days. Did the barnstormers come here, with their Jennies, their wing-walkers selling five dollar rides? Did the 'twenties roar here in upstate New York? Did the young blades call themselves sheiks and did they smoke Melachrino cigarettes (thirty cents for twenty)? The Jazz Age: F. Scott Fitzgerald. Swallowing live goldfish. Sitting on flagpoles for days at a time. Bix Beiderbecke and Paul Whiteman. George Gershwin and Louis Armstrong. I discovered that you can feel the tug of nostalgia for an age you have never known.

One more stop, at a hamlet apparently consisting only of two petrol pumps and something called a feed store.

'Abbottsport next,' the driver announced.

* * *

The snow began in earnest the moment I set foot on the pavement of Abbottsport. I shivered in the light raincoat I had brought with me from relatively mild London and watched the bus pull away. Abbottsport had a population of some twenty thousand, according to the Welcome sign on the outskirts of town. But I could see only two at the moment: a lady with blue hair getting out of a Mazda and a portly old gentleman shovelling the snow from the pavement in front of Hiller's Hardware. A sleepy and rather rundown little place, Abbottsport. Perhaps it was the sheer boredom of it that prompted Mae to try her luck over the Atlantic.

At one end of the row of shops an attempt had apparently been made to give everything a Colonial look, complete with white shutters and suitably quaint 'period' signs. But interest seemed to have waned halfway along the block. Mason's Drugs had a special on Kotex Slims. The Family Shoe Store had snow boots on sale. Meade for Liquors. An A & P. The Sixty-Minute Dry Cleaner. Dr B. W. Irwin, Dentist. Joe's Barber Shop, Frederick Electric, Zenith Chromacolor TV, New York Telephone Company, Kentucky Fried Chicken. The Abbot Hotel offered live entertainment ('Your C & W Favorites'). At the American Legion Post, the Stars and Stripes fluttered over a weary-looking artillery piece of 1918 vintage.

Then I saw the library. It was a sturdy grey stone building beside a tiny grassed area opposite the fire station. I crossed the street and went up the steps to the library's imposing oak door. The lintel stone bore the pronouncement BOOKS ARE LIKE AN OPEN DOOR TO SET THE SPIRIT FREE.

Beside the front door another sign informed me sternly that the Book Drop was not to be used for records, cassettes or films.

A quiet, rather cosy place, the library; it was almost empty but for an elderly man nodding at a study carrel, an open newspaper before him, and a sharp-featured woman of middle age peering suspiciously at the titles on the fiction shelves, perhaps bent on finding works that should be banned.

There was no one at the librarian's desk.

Then suddenly there was. A dark-haired girl wearing horn-rimmed glasses, popped up into view. She seemed surprised to see me.

'I was looking for that darned pencil-sharpener,' she explained, touching at her hair. 'How do you suppose a pencil sharpener always gets itself lost under a desk?'

I said it was a subject deserving of a lot of thought. She smiled and rather charming dimples appeared on her cheeks, the one slightly higher than the other. Was there something she could do for me?

I told her I was looking for information about a former resident of Abbottsport.

'Be glad to help you if I can,' she said. 'What's the name?'

'Mae Nolan.'

A thoughtful nod. 'I've heard of her. She was a flyer, wasn't she?'

'That's right. And she died trying to fly the Atlantic back in 1927. I'm trying to find out more about her and her flight.'

Another thoughtful nod.

'Seems to me we do have some files on her. I guess it was a pretty big story at the time. When did you say it happened?'

'September of 1927. And to be perfectly honest I'm not at all sure what I'm looking for. I found out she came from Abbottsport, so I caught a bus and . . . well, here I am.'

'You're English, aren't you?'

'How could you possibly tell?'

Another smile, even broader and warmer. 'Beats me.' She fingered her chin. 'Mrs Cochrane had all the archival data at her fingertips. Lots of stuff, books and newspaper clippings about the area. Historical, mainly. They moved it all, stowed it in the back. No one's asked about Mae Nolan since I've been here.'

'And how long is that?' I asked for no very good reason.

'Four years. Just before Mrs Cochrane retired.'

'Pleasant little town you've got,' I said, not entirely truthfully. It seemed the right thing to say.

'So you like it? That's nice. What part of England are you from?'

'London.'

'Lucky you. Went there once. Vacation . . . sort of.'

'I hope you enjoyed it.'

'Loved it. London and Rome are my favourite places in all the world. Not that I've seen a whole lot of the world,' she added with a grin. 'Wouldn't want to come off as a world traveller. Anyway, I'm rambling. You're here to find out about Mae Nolan, not my vacation. Look, do you want to wait a couple of minutes? I'll take a peek in the back room and see what we've got. Okay?'

'Certainly. Shall I stamp out the books for you while you're away?'

'You want to get me fired?' She glanced about the library. 'It's kind of quiet. If anyone comes tell them I'll be right back, okay?'

'Okay,' I said.

She strode to the rear of the library with the enthusiastic step of someone interested in what she is doing. A most agreeable young lady, the librarian, apparently pleased to assist a total stranger. A samaritan in slacks—and charmingly filled slacks at that. Her name was Beverly Sutton, according to the plastic sign on her desk.

'She gone again?' An elderly man asked the question, his thin-lipped mouth puckered in annoyance.

'She's in the back room looking for something,' I told him.

'Is that so?'

'Yes, it is.'

'Back soon?'

'I rather think so.'

'Jeez,' complained the old man. 'Old Maggie Cochrane never went into the back room. Always there. At her desk. Where she was supposed to be.'

'I'm sure Miss Sutton won't be more than a minute or two.'

'Missus,' said the old man.

'I beg your pardon.'

'It's *Mrs* Sutton, not Miss Sutton.'

'Yes of course,' I said. A knot of disappointment lodged somewhere mid-chest. Silly, damned silly. Of course.

Beverly Sutton—*Mrs* Sutton—emerged from the back room. She carried a couple of weatherbeaten cardboard boxes.

'Found something,' she announced, a light of triumph in her brown eyes. 'Not too sure just what it is. Mostly newspaper clippings, I think, but maybe you'll be able to find what you're looking for.' She put the boxes on the counter. 'They're kind of dusty; mind your clothes.'

'I will. And thanks very much indeed for your trouble.'

'You're quite welcome.'

'You through?' the old man wanted to know.

'I'll be right with you, Mr Mehlenbacher,' said Beverly. She smiled briefly at me. 'Let me know how you make out. You can sit right over there at a carrel.'

I thanked her again. A bit of luck finding such a helpful soul. The old man stirred as I took off my coat and draped it over the back of the chair. He glared, then frowned down at his newspaper. I seated myself as quietly as possible, placing the two boxes on the desk before me.

A tingle of anticipation: it was exciting, contemplating what might be in there.

Don't expect too much, chum, I told myself as I removed the lid from the first box. It was as the librarian had said: a collection of newspaper clippings, browning and brittle with age; a few letters, some 8 x 10 prints, curling at the edges. I took these first. Was this Mae Nolan, this young woman standing in front of a desk? A white haired, distinctly corpulent man sat opposite her. There was writing on the back of the print, the ink now rusty and faded: 'Mae Nolan, left and Mayor Lennex.' No date, damn whoever it was. I studied the girl in the photograph; her features were already familiar to me from the grainy images in the newspapers and the aviation history books. Another glossy showed her sitting in the rear of a large white car; a uniformed chauffeur sat at the wheel, gazing dutifully ahead; someone had scribbled something completely illegible on the back of the print. Next, a shot of Mae in leather helmet and riding breeches clambering into the cockpit of a frail looking biplane: 'Mae Nolan in training airplane, Corey Field.' Again, no date. Next came a picture of Mae Nolan in another office, signing something at a desk; around her were four men in their forties and fifties. According to the scribbles on the back of the print they were Zedekiah Folger, Willard Jenkins, Edwin W. Emerson and Thaddeus P. Osborne. Prosperous pillars of the community, apparently, they all looked remarkably pleased with themselves. Another photograph, this time of Mae talking to schoolchildren, 'telling them of her plans to fly the Atlantic. Copyright the *Abbottsport Star*.' The local paper had contributed several photographs: Mae on a bike, Mae studying a map of the North Atlantic, Mae stepping out of a Packard tourer. Stiff, obviously posed shots, all of them. She seemed barely able to conceal her impatience. No doubt she regarded the whole thing as a waste of time. But publicity was inevitable; in a modest little place like Abottsport the story of her flight must have been a sensation. More photographs: Mae outside a jewellery shop admiring a large banner in the window: GOOD LUCK, MAE! In the doorway, an immense cigar clamped between his jaws, stood the ubiquitous Zedekiah Folger. Mae shaking hands with a middle-aged man outside a factory building. 'Left, Aviatrix Mae Nolan; right, J. M. Nolan. June '27.' J. M. Nolan? Her father?

So much for the photographs. I turned to the newspaper clippings. Most were from the *Abbottsport*

Star, but there was also a selection of clippings from New York papers and a couple of magazines. More than half a century old, they had to be handled with care; I had visions of them crumbling to dust between my fingers.

ABBOTTSPORT GIRL FLYER ANNOUNCES ATLANTIC BID announced one headline. The sub-head ran: MAE P. NOLAN TO FOLLOW LINDY'S AERIAL FOOTSTEPS, PLANS TO BE FIRST WOMAN IN WORLD TO CONQUER ATLANTIC BY AIR. I glanced through the story. No new facts; the same basic information I had seen before —except that the final paragraph provided more gen on the Nolan family.

> Mae Nolan is the daughter of Mr and Mrs James M. Nolan of Beach Boulevard. Neither Mr Nolan, President of Nolan Pharmaceutical Company, nor his wife have been available for comment on their daughter's planned flight. A friend of the family, however, has informed this correspondent that Miss Nolan's parents are deeply concerned about the dangers of the venture, pointing to the number of experienced aviators who have already lost their lives in attempts to cross the Atlantic by air. Miss Nolan took flying instruction at Corey Field, obtaining her aviator's license in July of this year. She is a noted local sportswoman, skilled in riding, golf and tennis.

The article was illustrated by a photograph of Mae driving an enormous open sports car; later in the same story I found a portrait that had apparently been taken when she was about eighteen. She had a perfectly oval face and a firm, well-shaped mouth; there was a hint of shrewdness and determination in her eyes that even the coarse newspaper screen couldn't blur. An individual with a will of her own, no doubt about it. I gazed at the image of her and wondered about the manner of her death. A hell of a way for a brave girl to end up, feeding the fishes somewhere in the middle of the ocean. Was the flight really that important to her? Was it worth risking everything for? Foolish question; obviously this girl with the level gaze must have thought so. I studied the photographs again, looking deep into her eyes. I was beginning to know her; already some of her expressions and gestures were familiar to me. She had a slight twist to her smile that suggested a wry sense of humour. Was this really the same person I saw on that parking lot on Long Island? A few weeks ago I had never to my knowledge even heard of Mae Nolan; now she seemed like an old friend.

More stories: MAE TAKES OFF FOR EUROPE! MAE NOLAN: DEPARTURE. MAE REPORTED SIGHTED NEAR IRISH COAST. I scanned the columns, works of fiction, some of them, full of 'reports' and 'reliable sources'. Then, MAE NOLAN OVERDUE. NOLAN AND THORNTON FEARED LOST. At last a mention of Jack Thornton. No doubt he had handled the take-off from Roosevelt Field. He was a far more experienced pilot that Mae. But Mae was the more newsworthy. Besides, she was paying for it all.

MEMORIAL SERVICE FOR MAE NOLAN. A picture of black-clad relatives arriving at the church; the men with tall hats, the women in veils, a Monsignor talking of her courage and skill and how she would be sorely missed by all who had the privilege of knowing her in this life. End of story. End of file.

I took the boxes back to the librarian. She greeted me with a friendly smile.

'Find what you were looking for?'

'It was very helpful,' I told her. 'Mae must have been quite a girl.'

'I guess so. Imagine trying to get to Europe in one of those funny old airplanes.'

'I'd rather not.'

'It scares me, flying in a big jet,' the librarian confessed. 'I know it's safe. I've read all the statistics.

But I just don't *feel* safe.'

'It's your sort,' I told her, assuming a suitably severe expression, 'who will be the ruin of the airline business.' For an instant I think she took me seriously, then she grinned, revealing even, perfectly white teeth. I asked her if she knew much about the Nolan family.

She shook her head. 'They were before my time,' she said. 'But I guess they were just about the biggest family around here in the old days. There's a Nolan Street down near where the railroad station used to be. And the high school has a James M. Nolan Auditorium.'

'Do any of the family still live here?'

'There's a widowed lady, a Mrs Villate. She lives up on the hill in back of town. A real pretty property, she's got. I think she's an aunt or a cousin of Mr Nolan's. Someone said she's sick. Heart trouble, I think. What do you say we look in the phone book for more Nolans?'

'The phone book: a brilliant suggestion!'

'I didn't take those years of library training for nothing,' she commented easily. A most pleasant person, this Beverly Sutton. I congratulated myself on encountering her.

'Is Abbottsport your home town?' I asked her as she turned the pages of the slim telephone book.

She shook her head again; a small curl of dark hair tumbled across her forehead. 'I grew up in Illinois,' she said. 'Near Chicago. I moved to New York when I got married. Albany. Do you know it? It's the State capital. I worked in the library there. Then they needed a librarian here so I moved. With Russell. That's my son,' she added, her cheeks colouring. I asked her how many children she had. Just Russell, she said.

'Do you like Abbottsport?'

'It's okay. It's not exactly Las Vegas—or even Albany, come to that. But it's quiet and kind of pretty and everybody knows everybody. Do you mind if I ask you why you're interested in Mae Nolan? Are you a writer?'

'No,' I said. 'But I supppose I might write something if I find anything particularly interesting. I'm not sure. But actually what I do for a living is fly jets. I work for Anglo-World.'

Her hand flew to her mouth. 'Oops! Sorry what I said about being nervous in a jet. I was only a little bit nervous.'

'Were you flying Anglo-World?'

She shook her head.

'Try us next time.'

'I will. I promise.' She turned her attention to the telephone book. 'B. Nolan, 23 Delaware, G. S. Nolan, 451 West Rush, M. D. Nolan, 129 Fourteenth Street. That's all. And here's Mrs. Villate.'

I copied the names and numbers. 'I'll give them a ring. There might be some connection. I understand the Nolans used to have a house on Beach Boulevard. Do you know where that is?'

'Beach? It's at the north end of town. Near the lake. Nice area. Lots of fine homes there, private beaches, everything.'

'I thought I'd go up and have a look at the house.'

She nodded. 'Good idea.'

'Excuse *me*,' The speaker was the thin, middle-aged lady. She handed two books to the librarian.

'Awfully sorry,' I said.

'Mm,' she muttered, moving to the counter in a meaningful way.

'I'm getting you into trouble,' I said when the lady had gone on her way.

'That's Mrs Pottruff,' said the librarian as if mention of the name alone was enough.

'Not *the* Mrs Pottruff.'

'Yes, that's right . . .' She stopped, grinned. 'You're putting me on.'

'Only a little bit,' I assured her. 'We have lots of Mrs

Pottruffs in England too. Well, I suppose I'd better be on my way.'

'Do you like flying?'

'It's better than working for a living. Much better. I've been potty about aeroplanes since I was a little boy. I still think I'm one of the truly lucky people to be able to fly and make a pretty good living doing it.'

'But the travelling must be tough . . . on your family, I mean.'

'There's just my wife,' I told her. 'No children. Joyce is in advertising. Smart girl. She's busy with her job so I don't think it matters much when I'm away for a few days.'

'I'll bet it matters more than she lets on.'

I smiled, unsure how to respond. Was there a smattering of intensity in the way Beverly Sutton had spoken? Or was I mistaken? Probably. I usually was.

'You've been awfully helpful,' I told her. 'I'm very grateful.'

'My pleasure,' she said.

'Is Beach Boulevard within walking distance?'

'A couple of miles, I'd say. Too far to walk on a cold day. Why don't you try over by the bus station. There's usually a cab there.'

'I'll do that. Thank you.'

'Let me know how you make out,' she said. 'If you get a chance, that is.' Her cheeks flushed pink again.

'I will. Thank you again.'

'I enjoyed it,' she said. And apparently meant it. A warm and delightfully approachable person. A shame to leave her and plod out into the chilly wind. The pity of it was, I could think of no reason to linger in the library any longer. Perhaps I would come back later and talk to Beverly Sutton again. I found myself looking forward to it—and told myself to stop being a twerp.

I made my telephone calls from the A & P. No answer from the residences of B. Nolan or M.D. Nolan. G. S. Nolan was at work, a woman told me, and she sure as hell wished he was related to the Nolan Pharmaceutical Company but the truth of the matter was, her old man was an alcoholic son-of-a-bitch who couldn't even spell 'pharmaceuticals' let alone make them. I inserted my last dime and dialled Mrs Villate.

'The Villate residence.' Frosty female voice.

I asked to speak to Mrs Villate.

'What is the nature of your business?'

'I believe Mrs Villate is related to Mae Nolan who was born in Abbottsport and who was killed trying to fly the Atlantic in 1927 .'

'What of it?'

I said, 'My name's Adam Beale. I'm doing some research on Mae Nolan here in Abbottsport and was on my way down to the old family house on Beach Boulevard and I thought I'd give all the Nolans in the phone book a ring and . . .'

'Is that all?' Still frosty.

'I'd very much like to talk to Mrs Villate about Mae Nolan.'

'That will not be possible.'

'But why? I wouldn't take up much time. I . . .'

'I'm very sorry. Mrs Villate is confined to bed and never grants interviews. Good day to you.'

She had hung up before I could respond. Blast her. I had been looking forward to a cozy chat about the old days. But if Mrs Villate wouldn't talk to me there wasn't much I could do about it. I went across the snow-slick street to the bus station. A taxi was parked in front, just as the librarian had said.

The driver was a fleshy young man wearing a soft flat cap.

'Are you free?'

'No, but I ain't too expensive.' Throaty chuckle. 'Where you wanna go, Mister?'

'Beach Boulevard. Number seventy-six.'

'Hop in.'

He reached back with his left hand and opened the rear door. Before I had settled myself in the back, the driver had enquired how long I was staying in town and was I here on business or maybe visiting relatives? Did I know the Beach Boulevard area? Real nice area. Lotta great real estate up that way.

I smiled to myself. People in small towns liked to know everyone else's business. I told the driver that I was visiting Abbottsport on a confidential mission.

'No shit?' said the driver, interested. When I told him that I couldn't say more, he nodded understandingly, like a colleague sharing a state secret.

Beach Boulevard was an attractive area beside the lake—which appeared to be about the size of the English Channel. Here, the houses were large and imposing, obviously belonging to the well-to-do. Most of the properties fronted the lake and possessed boat houses and jetties.

Number seventy-six was a splendid and quite immense house with an ornate, rather fussy character that dated it to the 1920s or earlier. It had a gabled roof with dormers poking up like eager little eyes; the columned portico was carpeted; large brass coach lamps adorned either side of the carved oak front door. But on closer inspection it was apparent that the white clapboard was peeling in places; the cement had spalled here and there. It looked as if the house might be just a little too much for its present occupants' purse.

'Have a card,' said the cabby when I had paid him. 'You'll maybe need a cab again while you're in town. You want I should wait?'

'No thanks.'

I put the card in my pocket and watched the old Checker slither away. Perhaps I should have asked him to wait. Well, too late now . . .

The house had an imposing semi-circular driveway; it would have made an ideal location for a Jaguar advertisement.

I felt peculiarly tiny as I made my way up the path to the front door. Suddenly I questioned the whole business. What the hell was I doing here, in a funny little town in upstate New York in the dead of winter, about to knock on some stranger's front door for no better reason than the fact that a particular young lady once lived here? Well, that *was* the reason of course. She grew up on this spot. Must have stood here a hundred thousand times. Must have run across that lawn. Must have splashed in the lake.

I raised the heavy brass knocker, a fearsome looking lion's head.

The sound of the knocker seemed to reverberate through the house. Did Mae look at that lion as a child and wonder when she would be tall enough to reach it?

A footstep. I felt a twinge of excitement. I tried to avoid gazing directly into the security eye in the door but I was conscious of being inspected by someone within. There was a clatter of metal and the turning of a lock. The door opened; a substantial chain was taut across the jamb.

A young man of about twenty stood there. He wore jeans and a crumpled jacket that might once have belonged to a Viet Cong trooper.

'Yeah?' Not exactly the soul of friendship.

'Hullo. My name's Beale,' I announced. 'I'm here on rather an odd mission. I'm doing some research on a young lady who used to live here in this very house.'

'Yeah?' Still not friendly, or even interested.

'Her name was Mae Nolan.'

'So?'

'Her family used to own this house.'

'So?'

'Well.' I seemed to have lost my train of thought. The youth was so obstructive, so downright unpleasant, it was hard to think. 'This girl, Mae Nolan—er, she was lost in an attempt to fly the Atlantic, back in the 'twenties, shortly after Lindbergh—you've heard of Lindbergh, haven't you? I'm doing some research on her and I thought I'd like to see the house where she grew up, you see.'

'Uh, huh,' said the loathsome one, shaking his head.

He seemed to be saying no. 'You don't get in, fella, without written permission from my father and he's outta town right now, so get lost, uh.'

'Just a minute,' I said as the door began to close.

'Beat it.'

'Bastard,' I breathed as the door slammed in my face.

I shivered in the wind and backed up a few steps to look at the house again. Conscious of the youth peering at me through the heavy curtains at a side window, I went back on the driveway. A three-car garage adjoined the house.

Then I saw her. Leaning against the side of the house. Leather helmet, breeches, big grin, checkered scarf at her throat.

13

A woman's voice was addressing me. It possessed an insistent, abrasive tone. I blinked. I was seeing things again. No one at the side of the house now. No female figure in jodhpurs. No female of any description there.

But there was unquestionably a female figure at the front door.

'What are you *doing*?'

She was short and plump; she wore purple slacks and a pink blouse.

'Doing? Well, just looking, actually.'

'Looking at *what*?'

As I walked toward her, she seemed to shrink into the doorway, grasping the glass-covered storm door as if it were a shield.

I said. 'I'm here on rather an odd mission. I hope I haven't disturbed you. I was telling that young man all about it,' I added, spying the unpleasant youth in the rear. 'It's about Mae Nolan.'

'Thorbert *said*.'

Thorbert. He looked like a Thorbert.

'Her family used to live in this house,' I said.

'Whose family?'

'Mae Nolan's.'

'They don't live here *now*.'

'I realize that.'

'So what d'you *want*?' She had an odd way of emphasizing certain words.

She had to be Thorbert's mother; they both had the same irritating mannerisms.

Standing in the middle of the front garden, I explained that Mae Nolan had died under rather tragic circumstances and that I was doing research on her.

'What *for*?'

'I'm thinking of writing a book, or article perhaps. I'm not quite sure. I was at the library in town and I found out that the Nolans lived in this house back in 1927 when Mae got an idea that she wanted to become the first woman in the world to fly the Atlantic.'

'What?'

I repeated my story. The woman scowled suspiciously.

'So what's all that got to do with looking at our *house*?'

'Merely a way of finding out what she saw when she was growing up.'

'She isn't *here* now.'

'I know that.'

'So there's nothing to *see*, mister.'

'I know that too.'

'So go away. Now. You're tres*pass*ing.'

'I'm sorry to have disturbed you.'

'You get *along* now,' she snapped, flicking a finger at me as if I was a particularly revolting insect.

'Good day,' I said. With as much dignity as I could muster I made my way back to the road. A last glance back; I paused in spite of the pink face at the door. Did I glimpse someone moving by the back door? Was there the hint of a laugh in the wind? I shook my head.

Association of ideas, that's all it was. The mind working away on a lot of forced-fed input. Stuff yourself with enough old newspaper stories and photographs and you could find yourself back in the Jazz Age wearing twenty-eight inch wide bottoms on your trousers, listening to bully chaps twanging away on ukeleles. And seeing young girls in flying togs. Snow was peppering the air again; the flakes stung my face. I hunched my shoulders and headed back towards the town. I should have asked the taxi driver to wait; I should have never bothered to come to the house in the first place. Damned silly. What the hell did I think I was going to accomplish anyway?

I heard the car but paid it no attention.

It drew alongside me. I glanced to my left.

ABBOTTSPORT POLICE DEPARTMENT read the legend on the white door.

'Just hold it there, fella.'

God.

The cop was large, tall as well as portly. He swung out of his car, hand on the butt of his revolver.

'Just where d'you think you're going?'

'I'm walking that way, to the town,' I said, pointing. 'What's wrong with that?'

'I'll ask the questions, fella.'

I cleared my throat. 'Very well, officer,' I said as pleasantly as possible. 'Ask away.'

'Have you been at the Wendelmeyer residence?'

'The what? Oh, if it's number seventy-six, yes. I didn't know that was her name.'

'So if you didn't know the name how come you were calling at the house? What kind of a scam are you working, fella?'

'Scam? Look, officer, I can assure you I was on a perfectly innocent mission. Here's my card. I work for Anglo-World Airlines. I'm a pilot and . . .'

'Says here you're a cab driver.'

'What? Dreadfully sorry. Wrong card.' A strained chuckle-unreturned by the stony-faced sentinel of law and order. 'Got that one from a local chap, you see. Drove me out here. Should have asked him to wait. He offered but . . . Here's my card. Adam Beale. Anglo-World, see? Says so there. The truth is, a rather noteworthy resident of Abbottsport used to live in that house: a girl by the name of Mae Nolan. She died in 1927 trying to become the first woman in the world to fly the Atlantic.' Bloody hell, I seemed to have told that story a hundred times. 'I'm doing some research on her. I was in New York and I flew up to Rochester this morning. I took the bus from there. Went to the library where I saw some newspapers and odds and ends. Then I thought I'd have a look at the house where Mae Nolan used to live. I'm afraid the lady didn't take too kindly to my presence. I hope I didn't frighten her. I tried to explain but . . .'

'Maybe you'd better come down to the station,' said the cop. A chubby forefinger indicated the back door of the police car.

'Whatever for?'

'A little checking.'

* * *

It was almost dark when I left the Abbottsport Police Station. I had been obliged to sit on a hard wooden chair while a porcine, gum-chewing police sergeant telephoned Anglo-World in New York and disinterestedly took my career apart. Was a party by the name of Adam Beale known to them? Was there someone there who could verify his ID number? Was it true that said Adam Beale had left New York City by air for Rochester and had then taken a bus to Abbottsport? And was said Adam Beale due to fly as a member of the flight crew on Anglo-World Flight 824 from Kennedy to Heathrow tomorrow morning? Was there someone there who could describe said Adam Beale and could in fact vouch for him? It took an age. There was no one on duty who knew me by sight; the crew with whom I had flown from England weren't in their hotel rooms; yes, the name checked out all right; an A. Beale was scheduled as First Officer but there wasn't anyone around who knew him . . . I squirmed; within hours everyone in the corporation would know of my incarceration by upstate New York police. There would be more head-shaking over the odd bod named Beale.

No apologies from the police when at last I was released. I could take off, the sergeant announced. He seemed to have lost interest in me. I said I thought it was all a bit thick. He nodded and said it sure as hell was but life was like that, wasn't it?

I thanked him for his hospitality; he barely glanced at me, impervious to my feeble sarcasm.

Bastards. I went out into the snowy street, shivering after the overheated police station. I was hungry; I suddenly realized that I had missed lunch; now it was almost six o'clock in the evening, Abbottsport time. My stomach gurgled emptily. I looked up the street, as if seeking the one friendly face I had encountered in this insular community. A couple of minutes' walk brought me to the library. But it was closed, its windows in darkness. I turned away, disappointed. Sod Abbottsport. I would get out of it immediately. Back to Rochester, then on to New York on the first available plane. God knows why I came here in the first place. I had succeeded only in making a bloody fool of myself. Now my name was in the files of the local constabulary. Adam Beale: highly suspicious, odd-sounding stranger whose MO was to call on the houses of residents mumbling about people long since dead. Again I experienced that odd sense of being apart, of standing back and watching the man in the light raincoat in the snow before a closed library clutching a small flight bag—the contents of which were now rumpled after repeated searchings by heavy-handed Abbottsport police. A forlorn-looking figure, clearly a dubious character, someone to be avoided by the good citizens of Abbottsport, the sort who spent a good deal of time in police stations. There was a lethargic, defeated look about him as he trudged along, trying to find somewhere to eat.

The Paradise Restaurant.

It was ill-named. A narrow, rather shabby little establishment, it seemed to have been decorated by someone with a passion for cheap chromium plating. Perhaps it had looked ultra-modern in its day; now, its chrome dented and scratched, it put one in mind of a second-hand car that has been driven too hard and has been involved in a series of minor accidents. One sign said no credit, another said that one did not have to be crazy to work here but it sure helped, exclamation mark.

I was the only customer. I sat down on a stool at the counter.

'Wanna menu, mister?'

An elderly gnome asked the question.

I nodded and he handed me a soup-stained card that looked as if it had been handled by a couple of hundred people that day. It listed 'plump eggs' and 'sizzling steaks' plus 'mouthwatering sea food.'

'A ham sandwich, please.'

'Toasted? Plain? White? Brown? Got rye if you wannit. Give you an open face with fries and peas, if you like.'

'Just an ordinary sandwich, please. On rye bread.'

I really didn't like rye bread. Why then, I asked myself elaborately, did you order the bloody stuff? I didn't know. The list of things I didn't know seemed to be growing by leaps and bounds.

My stomach growled again.

'Mustard?'

'I beg your pardon? Yes, mustard. Thanks.'

The man behind the counter had an oddly squashed shape; he was too broad for his inconsiderable height; his trunk and even his head seemed to have developed horizontally; he possessed no neck. He wore a grubby white T-shirt, an apron and a small white cap. His face was weatherbeaten; he looked like a good-natured pugilist who has lost every fight.

'Still snowing?' the gnome asked as he prepared my sandwich.

'Yes. Cold wind too.'

He wagged a wise finger at me. 'Shouldn't be surprised if we don't have two, maybe three feet by mornin'. Wind outa the east. Sure sign of shit on the way.'

'Really?'

'You can bet on it. From outta town, are you?'

'Just visiting,' I said, as if to establish my harmlessness.

'It's not a bad place in the summer,' said the squashed man now wagging his finger at the street, 'but it's hell this time a'year. I tell you, if I could sell up I'd be on my way to Florida. Want to buy the joint?' he asked with a toothy chuckle. 'What line of work you in?'

'I'm a pilot,' I said. 'I work for Anglo-World.'

'No kiddin',' he said, interested. 'What the hell you doin' in this neck of the woods?'

Americans in general seemed remarkably interested in knowing my business. I told my story yet again.

'The girl's name,' I said, 'was Mae Nolan.'

'Sure,' said the squashed man. 'Used to see her in here all the time.'

I felt my mouth drop open. 'You mean you *met* her?'

'Well, not exactly formal, you understand. But I knew her to say hullo to. My dad ran the joint then. It was a soda fountain; nice place in them days. Fact is, it was *the* place in town for the kids to meet. I worked here, making sodas and sundaes, all that stuff. I've spent my whole life in this joint. Depressin', ain't it? You look around and you start to add things up and what the hell have you got? I once tried to figure out how many miles I've walked in here. Figured I must've walked far enough to go clear around the goddam world and I've never even been outa State, 'cept for a wedding in Indianapolis. My uncle Fred's daughter, Josie; she married a guy who got busted for tax evasion. Can't recall his name. Real nice guy.'

'Very interesting,' I said. 'But about Mae Nolan; can you tell me anything about her? By the way, my name's Adam Beale.'

'Charlie Vogel,' was the response. 'Nice to know you. You wanna know about Mae? What can I tell you? It was a hell of a long time ago. We all thought she'd make it to Europe and put Abbottsport on the map like Lindbergh did for St Louis, although I got to admit that St Louis had one hell of a head start on this burg. Never figured Mae would fail. She'd always done whatever the hell she wanted to do. Ahead of her time, I guess you'd have to say. Sort of woman's libber; anything a man could do she could do just as well. Maybe better. Real strong personality, Mae. Always the centre of attention. A bunch of them kids would come in. Pretty ritzy group. Well dressed, you know. None of this jeans crap like today. They'd park outside there in their snappy roadsters: guys in blazers and boaters and girls in those cute little short dresses they used to wear. They'd come in and order orange phosphates and malted milk and lime rickeys, stuff like that. Real big, they were, back then. Kids didn't count calories, I guess. They used to zap down two or three of them apiece, then go out in their cars and put away a few belts of bootleg hooch. Rot-gut stuff it was, too, let me tell you. Sent some of 'em outa their minds. Not Mae, though. Never saw Mae sauced. Took too much care of herself.'

'Was she pretty?' I asked. An idiotic question, but for the moment I could think of no other.

'Pretty? Sure, cute as a button. I was nuts about her,' said Charlie Vogel with another toothy chuckle. 'She did everything I wanted to do: drove fast cars, flew her own plane, spent dough like there was no tomorrow. And there wasn't, was there, for her? She was maybe eight or ten years older than me. Had everything. Nolan was a big name in Abbottsport back then. They had a big summer house down on Beach. Summer house? Jeez, it was bigger than the public school I went to. I was real broken up when Mae died. Felt as I'd lost a real friend. I hadn't of course. I bet she didn't know me from a hole in the wall but I liked to think she did. So what you doin' coming all the way up here to find out about Mae Nolan?'

'I'm doing research on the women fliers of the time,' I said. 'Mae Nolan was one of several who tried to fly the Atlantic.'

'No kiddin'.' The man was pleasant in a rough-diamond way, apparently genuinely interested in my mission.

'Can you tell me anything about her family?'

'Family? Jeez, they were way outa my class, lemme tell you. All kinds of dough. Nolan Pharmaceuticals. Seems to me they had a plant in Buffalo, no Syracuse, I think. One of them big conglomer-what-you-call-'ems took over in the 'forties. Big family, the Nolans. I dunno, mebbe seven, eight kids. That's why the old man built that big son-of-a-bitch of a house down there by the lake; it had to be that size to get 'em all in! They used to spend the summers up here. Abbottsport was a real popular summer place then; lotta people still come here, of course, but nothing like in the old days. I'd say the Nolans were just about the richest family in these parts. Biggest house. Bunch of cars. Big power boats. You name it. They had it.'

A customer entered, a tall man in work clothes who addressed Charlie Vogel by name, ordering a hamburger with the works and a black coffee.

I munched my sandwich. Here, within touching distance, was someone who had actually known Mae. Here was Opportunity. But how to take advantage of it? What questions to ask? Odd how quickly my despondence had vanished; now, with most of a ham sandwich inside me, I felt rather better disposed towards the community of Abbottsport. I glanced about the restaurant. Mae had walked in here, had undoubtedly touched this counter and planted her shapely bottom on that stool. Listen carefully and you could almost hear her, laughing with her well-dressed friends, dazzling the callow, spotty-faced youth behind the counter.

'Somethin' else I can get you?' Charlie Vogel enquired.

'No, thank you, that was very tasty.'

'Yeah?' Charlie had a hint of surprise in his voice.

'Do you know what happened to the other sisters and brothers?'

'Hell, no. There was a whole bunch of them. I guess they got married and went all over the place. Seems to me ol' man Nolan sold the house on Beach right after Mae got herself killed.'

I finished my small meal and thanked him for his time and trouble.

'No sweat,' he assured me. 'Nice talkin' about Mae. I often think about her. Funny, how some people stick in your mind and the others just sort of fade away, know what I mean?'

'I think so.'

'I tell you, there are times I'd swear I can see Mae comin' in through that door like she used to back then. I'm mebbe at the cash register or talkin' to a customer and I think I hear her voice again. I look up and there's no one there. Dumb, uh?'

'Perhaps not,' I said.

14

There were snow showers when we took off from JFK. Rotten visibility and lots of traffic. Aircraft were coming and going like a swarm of bees around a hive.

Except that bees have more sense than to fly on such a dirty night. I handled the take-off. And I did everything absolutely by the book, for the captain on this trip —sitting beside me, silent and apparently bored beyond endurance—was none other than Edward Porson. It was, in fact, the first time he and I had flown together since the unfortunate encounter with Mae's Bellanca. I prayed I wouldn't see the damned thing on this trip. I wanted to show Porson how smooth and totally uneventful a journey could be with me in the right-hand seat.

* * *

The members of both the Megford-Schollenberg Medieval Ensemble and the Kent Consort of Viols were late additions to the passenger complement of AW 842. Fate, aided and abetted by the vagaries of the musical profession, brought them together to journey to Heathrow on that wintry day. For the Megford-Schollenberg musicians—skilled performers on such esoteric instruments as douçaine, alto shawm, sackbut, gittern and rebec—their presence on 842 was testimony to their redoubtable reputation among the musical intelligentsia of a number of leading North American universities. The Ensemble had originally been booked to return to London three days earlier, but impassioned pleas for additional concerts led to the change of plans. That very afternoon they had performed for four hours after which they had been rushed to JFK by a small convoy of limousines. Unhappily, the Kent Consort of Viols had enjoyed considerably less success in America. Gallantly attempting to take their art to the concert halls, they had encountered critical acclaim and immense acreages of empty seats. After two rather nerve-racking weeks the promoter had declared, 'I want you should know my decision is in no way a reflection of the Consort's skills and dedication, but circumstances compel me to cancel the last half-dozen concerts, which I am, at my discretion, permitted to do, according to Clause 19, sub-section (e) of our contract.'

Thus it was that Ernest Shipperbottom, sackbut player with the Medieval Ensemble, came to be seated in the economy section of A W 842 beside Druella Hart-Lintlock, a member of the Kent Consort of Viols and a virtuoso on the viola da gamba.

Ernest Shipperbottom was sorry to be leaving America. He had enjoyed the adulation and the enthusiasm. But it would be good to see dear old London again and his little house in Streatham and his two near-Persians, Staccato and Spiccato. It would be pleasant too, to spend a few days unwinding, pottering about, sorting through the post—though he didn't expect much of that—and generally getting back into the familiar routine. In recent years, the familiar routine had become increasingly appealing. Had Mrs Flanagan looked after Staccato and Spiccato properly? How many times had he wondered? How many times had he imagined the most awful happenings: Mrs Flanagan dropping dead, the cats starving, the house burning down, the supply of cod and haddock suddenly drying up? Ah well, soon he would be home. And in a day or so it would seem as if he had never gone away in the first place.

The moment the seat belt sign went off, Bernard Hinkley-Forbes came ambling up the aisle. Constitutionally incapable of sitting still, was Bernard, a performer on both alto and soprano shawm. Shawm players were an odd lot, in Ernest's experience.

'Where's Carter-Weybourne sitting, old man?'

'Haven't the foggiest.'

Bernard beamed. 'Trust you to get yourself sitting next to one of the ladies of the Consort. The Kent Consort of Viols,' he added, noting a blank look on Ernest's face. Then he went breezing off, leaving Ernest to apologize to the sturdy female with the iron-grey hair cut incongruously in page-boy style. He said he was most awfully sorry but he really had no idea the Kent Consort was travelling on the plane.

'Druella Hart-Lintlock,' she introduced herself, extending a sizable hand and shaking Ernest's in a brisk no-nonsense manner.

'My name's Ernest Shipperbottom. I'm awfully pleased to meet you. I know of your ensemble's work, of course. Most impressive.'

'Good of you to say so, Mr Slipperbottom.'

'It's Shipperbottom, actually.'

'Rather. I seem to recall that our two ensembles worked together a few years ago. Tanglewood, wasn't it?'

'I say, you're right. I remember it well. A moving experience. Are you just returning from a tour?'

A curt nod. 'A bit of a bore. You?'

'Yes. And I suppose our tour was really a bit of a bore too.'

'There's something terribly *lacking* there.'

'There?'

'In America,' said Druella Hart-Lintlock, dismissing the entire continent with a wave of her beefy hand.

'Quite.'

'Culturally speaking.'

'Of course.'

Like professionals of most fields, they talked less of the artistic side of their endeavours than of the practical: of draughty dressing rooms and cretinous stagehands, of noisy air-conditioning that drowned the delicate sounds of their instruments, of hideous hotels and bone-shaking buses, of cough-racked audiences and avaricious impresarios, of baroque bows, of gut strings.

'But we have to keep on,' said Druella Hart-Lintlock sounding like a weary Crusader after five years of battle.

'I do most definitely agree.'

'It's up to us.'

'Indubitably.

It was turning out to be a thoroughly enjoyable

journey, chatting like old friends with this quite spectacularly forceful female about a subject so dear to his heart. Cocktails arrived. Then dinner, with several glasses of wine. The conversation might well have continued along the same lines. But it didn't. Somehow it wandered, indecisively, to the profession as a whole.

Druella Hart-Lintlock pointed out that virtually every one of the countless members of anonymous instrumentalists had entered the profession with secret ambitions of being star soloists with their names on the posters outside the Albert Hall.

'You're absolutely correct,' said Ernest.

'I myself entertained such notions at one time,' said Druella Hart-Lintlock.

'Looking at me now,' said Ernest, sipping his third glass of wine, 'You'll probably find this hard to believe; but I was once considered an infant prodigy.'

'On the sackbut?'

'No. In those days I played the trumpet. And, even if I say so myself, I was quite good. At the age of sixteen or so I used to appear with dance bands as a solo act. You'll laugh.'

'Certainly not.'

'They called me "The Teenage Harry James".'

'My goodness.'

Did he sense a certain excitement? A tension? A sexy instrument, the trumpet, he'd heard. It affected some women in quite extraordinary ways. Which was more than you could say for the sackbut.

'You have heard of James, haven't you?'

'I do believe so. You must have been very good.'

'Well, I don't mind telling you that I played with a lot of top names of the day. Loss, Rabin, Roy, Payne. I used to come on stage and toot "Flight of the Bumble Bee". That was my specialty. Lots of high notes and triple-tonguing. Funny to think of it now, all these years later.'

Her gaze was rapt, intense.

'Did you use your own name?'

'Dear me, no. Ernest Shipperbottom wouldn't do for that sort of thing. So the promoter cooked up a brand new name for me. Billy Brass!'

Which was when the wine hit Ernest in the left eye.

* * *

Captain Porson was enjoying his grilled sole. His jaw worked with an enthusiastic rhythm that I found irritating. I would have liked the sole. But since regulations forbade Captain and First Officer to select the same main dish and since Porson as Supremo was entitled to first choice, I found myself grappling with plastic chicken. Tasteless stuff, it jammed itself between my teeth in obstinate, sinewy little threads tough enough to make parachute cords.

A call from the cabin crew.

Porson picked up the interphone.

'What?' He scowled, then turned to me. 'Better go back and have a look. Some sort of bloody disturbance in Economy.'

* * *

'You *bastard*,' Druella Hart-Lintlock had said, crisply, loudly.

Ernest gaped at her.

'What?'

'You . . . *sod*!'

'Sod?'

'My sister *Marjorie*!'

'Madam, I assure you . . .' *Marjorie*. Christ. Like a creaky scene from an ancient film it came back. 1944. The Palais. A marvellously successful engagement. Enthusiastic servicemen and girls in pretty frocks. One, a slim and winsome redhead. She positively bubbled with adoration for the brilliant young fellow with the trumpet. Marvellous snogging session in the band bus. Spectacular co-operation from the winsome one.

Then, triumph!

A heavenly interlude of tenderness.

Then, a hasty scrambling back into assorted garments as voices and steps neared . . .

'But that was . . . *ages* ago.'

'He's nearly forty,' snapped Druella Hart-Lintlock.

'Who is?'

'Your bloody *son*. And he's a dead loss. Been in and out of prison . . .'

'But I didn't *force* . . . I mean, she was more than willing.'

Which may have been true but it was not the moment to say it.

A large and powerful hand connected with Ernest's cheek, setting off a deafening series of bells in his skull. His knee jerked, quite involuntarily, striking his fold-up table, tossing his tray and most of his dinner into Druella Hart-Lintlock's lap. At that moment Bernard Hinkley-Forbes came ambling up the aisle. His mouth dropped open in astonishment. The Kent Consort of Viols were attacking! Were they furious that their tour had been such an abysmal failure? Were they jealous of the Megford-Schollenbergers? He rushed to Ernest's aid, imploring Druella Hart-Lintlock not to strike Ernest on the lip. Then Freda Posthwaite of the Kent Consort of Viols hurled herself upon Bernard Hinkley-Forbes, to be followed a moment later by Halbert Hewitt who played gittern and lute with the Medieval Ensemble.

Such was the situation when I arrived on the scene. It was a brief battle. But eventful. One of Freda Posthwaite's flailing feet caught me in the groin. Then a hand clutched my shirt front and ripped it, scattering buttons like pellets. Something sharp and exquisitely painful walloped me in the rib cage. In a few moments we had the situation under control. Three of the stews escorted Druella Hart-Lintlock to the rear of the cabin and made her promise to sit quietly. We cleaned Ernest Shipperbottom up as best we could and found him a seat up front.

Then I went back to the flight deck and reported to Captain Porson.

I didn't like the way he looked at me. Simultaneously puzzled and peeved.

'Tell me something, Beale,' he said. 'Why do odd things happen when you're about?'

15

'Justin and Crang, good afternoon.'

'Hullo, Sally, it's Adam Beale. Put me through to Joyce, will you?'

'I'll put you through to her office, Mr Beale, but I don't think she's there. Just a mo', please.'

Trevor Whatever-his-name-was came on the line. Self-important little twit, he sounded as if he was discussing grand strategy for the recapture of the Falklands.

'Yes, Mrs Beale did mention that you would probably be telephoning. She asked me to inform you that she had to go up north for a couple of days.'

'North?'

'Yorkshire, actually. The Peabody Group.'

'The what?'

'A new account,' said Trevor, clearly surprised that I didn't know. 'Quite an important new account. They're in furniture manufacture and retailing and several other related activities. In all, the account should be up in the three million region.'

'How fascinating,' I said.

'Yes, isn't it,' he replied enthusiastically.

'When did my wife have to go to Yorkshire?'

'This morning, first thing. She caught a train about eleven for Leeds.'

'Where is she staying?'

'Actually we don't know. Yet. The Peabody people said they would make all the arrangements and put us in the accommodation picture later on in the day.'

Just like Trevor to talk about 'the accommodation picture'.

'When will she be back in London?'

'Can't say precisely. Tomorrow, I would think. Or possibly the day after if things don't proceed according to plan.'

'All right. I'm at Heathrow,' I told him. 'I'll be at home later. Will you give me a ring when you know where she's staying?'

Trevor said I could count on him. A bit over-effusive, young Trevor.

* * *

I poured myself a Scotch and downed it before doffing my overcoat.

I refilled my glass. Sod those potty medieval musicians. And sod the Peabody Group.

I was looking forward to seeing Joyce, damn it. I had been away for four days, four distinctly harrowing days. Was it too much to expect her to be in London when I returned? I thought back over the events of the early morning. And had another drink. Johnnie Walker was doing his job admirably. I was feeling good now, almost buoyant. Then I thought of the utterly poisonous Abbottsport Police Department. And I felt a little less buoyant. Reports might already be circulating in A–W's executive suites: '. . . demand by the local police for identification of this individual . . . behaviour that hardly seems to conform to what is expected of a senior pilot of the line . . .'

I could look forward to a second interview with the long-suffering Captain Forbes. Another blot on my record. Blots eventually begin to form a pattern in employers' eyes . . . 'Something odd about Beale . . . this man is continually getting himself into controversial situations . . . he could be a potential problem . . .'

'It wasn't my fault,' I informed the drawing by Michael Barnes. I re-armed my Scotch. The thought of A–W connecting this episode with the business of the mysterious monoplane near Kennedy was disquieting to put it mildly. The thing was, here, in the sanctuary of the flat, it all seemed so remote, so downright *unlikely*. How could I possibly explain it to Forbes or to anyone else for that matter? There was this funny old monoplane at twenty thousand feet, batting along at Mach .8 . . .

I spilt Scotch on the cabinet. And swore. No doubt the Scotch would do something to the finish and no doubt Joyce would have a number of things to say about it. But she had to be here to say them, didn't she?

I nodded vigorously, as if I had made a telling point.

I reread the note Joyce had left on the hall table: *Darling, sorry, had to go north on short notice. Another client crisis! Office will advise my hotel. Cold meat and salad in fridge. Will ring you. Love, J.*

The thing to do, I told myself, is to snap out of it. Get something to eat. Have a sleep. Then pop out to the flicks or something.

Lethargy lay like some immensely weighty blanket.

The telephone rang.

'Mr Beale? Trevor Murdoch here, Justin and Crang. We just heard from Herbert Milne at the Peabody Group. They've arranged accommodation for Mrs Beale at the Queen's Hotel in Leeds.'

'Right,' I said. Why did Trevor Murdoch's voice jar me so much? I pictured a pallid-faced individual with small, weasel's eyes and damp hands.

'I have the telephone number. Do you have a pencil?'

'Yes. Go ahead.'

I didn't have a pencil but I told myself I could remember the number. I was wrong. I cursed Trevor

Whatever. Then I felt sorry for him. Poor little turd, he was doing his best. Did Joyce keep him hopping? Did he secretly worship her? Both for her ability and her beauty?

'She's a smasher,' I said to no one in particular.

That was when I saw Mae Nolan's reflection in the mirror. But a blink later she was gone—for the perfectly simple reason that she wasn't there in the first place. I realized that my mouth was open, my lower jaw hanging loosely as if the muscles no longer had power to hold it in position.

The fact seemed to call for another Scotch. I knew I shouldn't have it. I possess a low tolerance for alcohol, particularly when my body is suffering from jet lag—or 'diurnal disturbance' as it is officially known. I was tired, yet I was far too tense to sleep. Another Scotch—just one more—might do the trick and I would lay myself down and sleep it all off and when I awoke Joyce would be home and Mae Nolan would have gone off to wherever she was supposed to go and leave me in peace.

I don't know how long I sat there, musing and drinking and feeling sorrier and sorrier for myself. I do, however, know and acknowledge that I downed far more Scotch than was good for me.

The telephone rang.

I dropped the receiver on my first try; my hands seemed to lack their usual deftness. I said hullo.

Joyce sounded disappointed, as if I had failed her yet again. 'Adam, you've been drinking.'

'Under the circumstances,' I began, 'it's not too surprising . . .'

But she seemed not to hear the comment. 'I'm at the Queen's in Leeds.'

'Do say hullo to Prince Philip.'

No chuckle from Central Yorkshire. 'I expect to be back tomorrow,' she said, her voice tight, as it invariably was when she knew I had had a drink.

I hung up the receiver and regarded it, smirking to

myself at how humbled Joyce would be when she found out why I had downed a gill or two. Whereupon the telephone rang again, startling me. I stepped back and almost lost my balance.

Was there something Joyce had forgotten to chide me about?

'What now?' I enquired.

It was Joyce's mother. '*Adam*?'

'Good evening . . .' I began, oozing charm.

'Is Joyce there?'

'No, she's with the Queen in Leeds.'

'Pardon?'

'My little joke,' I explained. 'The Queen's Hotel, you see. Joyce is there on business . . .'

'In *Leeds*? Oh God.'

'Well,' I began, 'I suppose it isn't everyone's idea of heaven but the place has its points . . .'

'Martin's had a heart attack.'

For a moment I couldn't think who Martin was. I usually addressed Joyce's father as 'Dad'.

'Oh dear,' was my hopelessly inadequate response. 'Where . . . how?'

'He's in hospital. I'm just leaving for there myself. Will you please tell Joyce?'

'Yes, of course.'

'He's at St James's.'

'Yes, I'll tell her,' I promised.

But when I rang the Queen's they told me that there was no answer from Mrs Beale's room. I instructed them to tell her to call home. It was important, I added, really important.

Then, for some inexplicable reason, I felt my presence was required at the hospital.

* * *

It was a nightmare, squatting on those unyielding seats in that torture chamber of a hospital waiting room, exchanging banalities with Joyce's mother, trying desperately to be sober, to be rational, to be a rock of Gibraltar when I was feeling like the Hackney Marshes. I kept wanting to giggle—at a fat nurse, at a skinny patient, at a cartoon in the tattered copy of *Punch*. Thank God Joyce's mother appeared not to notice. She kept telling me that Martin had been perfectly well just that morning. I told her that it makes you think.

When might I decently escape? Why, I wondered, didn't others come and take over the vigil? Joyce had a brother, Gerald, a surveyor. Where was he, the sod? A neighbour arrived, a Mrs Hesketh, who said that she came rushing here the instant she heard the news and was there anything she could do, anything at all, just say the world. A hefty, ruddy-faced woman, she spoke to me as if I was a child. I was not to worry; she was absolutely convinced that my father was going to be all right; the thing was to have faith. Everything would be all right as long as everyone *believed.* Then, before I was able to explain that I was the son-in-law, not the son, and perhaps because she smelt my breath, her attitude hardened. Her eyebrows angled in disapproval. The doctor materialized, a pious-looking individual with a lugubrious expression and a fringe of white hair bordering a naked pate: perfect casting for one of the monks in *Becket*. The next twenty-four hours would be critical, he informed us; they would, in fact, tell the story, whatever that meant. The patient was resting as comfortably as could be expected. His condition appeared to have stabilized. Somewhat, he added. It could, he said, be considered a fairly good sign. Although, he hastened to declare, there was no guarantee that further attacks wouldn't take place. It was a volatile period, he said. Twice. He looked at me and seemed to expect me to ask a telling question or two. But I had none. I said, 'I see.' The effects of the alcohol were wearing off, leaving in their stead a ghastly sourness. My head ached; my stomach groaned periodically. I sat in gloomy introspection while the women talked. And talked. What were we accomplishing by being here? I wondered. Joyce's mother seemed to regard the vigil as a duty. Perhaps it was an act of expiation for something she had done to poor old Martin. Perhaps, I ruminated, she was the cause of his heart attack. I was considering the various ways in which she might have accomplished this when a nephew turned up, a pasty-faced individual; I remembered him from some wedding or funeral. Everything that had been said for the last three hours was relayed to the nephew who nodded woefully and kept saying 'I see' precisely as I had done.

* * *

The next day things looked brighter. Joyce got back to London at noon; I met her at King's Cross and we went to the hospital together. Her father had had a night that was officially classified as 'comfortable'; even the melancholy physician seemed mildly optimistic.

As we walked out into the car park, Joyce took my hand.

On the way home she asked me to stop at a wine merchant's. She trotted inside and emerged a couple of minutes later with a bottle of Mumm's. A little celebration, she said. We went home and drank the champagne and went to bed and made love and slept and woke and made love again. Joyce was a complex and sometimes infuriating female, but quite marvellous in so many really important ways. I was her slightly sodden but utterly devoted slave.

It was a beautiful afternoon. A perfect afternoon.

Why, then, did I keep wondering about it afterwards? What was it that troubled me? I didn't know. I eventually came to the conclusion that if there was anything that had cast a bit of a pall on the proceedings it was Joyce's perfectly understandable concern about her father. You couldn't blame her for that, could you?

16

I explained that the whole thing was a complete misunderstanding; my enquiries were quite innocent and the suspicion of trespassing was totally without foundation. I was merely looking at the bloody house and, while it would have been interesting to have seen inside, I had not at any time attempted to gain entry.

'But what were you *doing*?' Captain Forbes asked, puzzled.

'Research,' I said. 'Mae Nolan once lived there.'

'Who?'

'Mae Nolan. A girl who tried to fly the Atlantic . . .'

His eyes narrowed. He nodded. 'Nolan. Disappeared, didn't she? A few months after Lindbergh. Yes, I remember the name. You're doing research on her?'

'Yes.'

'What for?'

'A book perhaps, or an article.'

Forbes stroked his bony chin as he regarded me. 'This research into Mae Nolan, is it anything to do with that odd business of the monoplane you saw at JFK?'

I thought rapidly. 'I suppose it did sort of set my mind thinking along those lines.'

'The company doesn't like having policemen telephoning, demanding identification of our pilots.'

I realized that, I assured him, and I was sorry that I had caused the problem but it really hadn't been of my making. My conduct, I declared, was exemplary at all times and in the best traditions of the company.

More stroking of the chin. Old Forbes seemed to drift off in thought for such long periods that it was a shock when he suddenly spoke again. 'Did you get much material?'

'Material?'

'About Mae Nolan?'

'Not as much as I'd hoped. But I talked to a chap in a restaurant who said he remembered her; and I got quite a lot of odds and ends from the local library. I found out that one of Mae Nolan's relatives still lives in Abbottsport. But she wouldn't talk to me.'

He smiled in his distant way. 'Possibly it was your accent.'

'My accent?'

'It's remarkable how bitter many Irish-Americans still are towards the British,' he said. 'The sins of our forefathers.'

* * *

Since first light the temperature and the dew point had remained in disquieting proximity. Then the warm front moved in bringing more moisture. Temperature and dew point converged. The water vapour that had been invisible and therefore relatively harmless now emerged for all to see, becoming tiny droplets that chose to perch upon the billions of infinitesimal particles of smoke and air pollution that floated in the air.

Fog.

Freeman announced, 'Ladies and gentlemen, this is the captain speaking. I'm sorry to have to tell you that weather conditions have deteriorated even since we started taxiing. The tower advises us that the fog has become too thick for us to attempt a take-off. So we're going to turn around and head back to the ramp. We ask you all to stay in the terminal building so that we can advise you by public announcement the moment we can resume our journey. Again our most sincere apologies. Anglo-World usually manages to arrange more propitious weather conditions for our passengers. My regrets that we didn't manage it this time.'

He settled back with a self-satisfied sigh, his public relations duties done for the day. As he taxied the big aircraft between the narrow rows of lights, using only two engines to save fuel, Freeman regaled the flight deck with his memories of the peasoup fogs of London back in the bad old days when everyone was burning coal in their grates. 'Couldn't find your way around Heathrow; a chap in a light plane was lost on the airfield for two days during that killer fog in the 'fifties. Another chap taxied right into a hangar, and didn't even know he was doing it. Didn't hit anything. Incredible luck.' A veritable cornucopia of stories, was Freeman. An amiable soul, he usually wore a somewhat cherubic grin on his round, jocular face. I had flown with him half a dozen times in the last couple of months: the luck of the Crew Scheduling.

We parked at the terminal and closed down the aircraft system by system, switch by switch: throttles, parking brake and lights, ATMs, fuel and ignition switches, engine valve switches, seat-belt signs, air data sensor heat switches, wind-screen heat and defog fan, side window switches, wing anti-ice switches, engine anti-ice switches, wing flood and wheel well lights.

'Ah, hullo, m'dear,' Freeman exclaimed as a pretty stewardess looked in through the flight deck door. 'Everything under control back there? Passengers unloaded, are they? No mutiny?'

The stew reported everything under control.

'Clap 'em in irons if they give you any trouble!' Freeman added with a chortle. 'Lovely,' he said when the girl had gone. 'I'm sure females didn't have such lovely tits when I was a bachelor. Or such nice bums either, come to think of it. What do you chaps think, is their shape improving as the years go by, or is it just my appreciation of them?'

'My wife's shape isn't improving,' said Enright, the Second Officer. 'She's seven months pregnant.'

'Jolly good,' chuckled Freeman. He sniffed at the fog

curling about the 1011's nose. 'Grand weather for ghosts, what?' he remarked with a grin in my direction. My heard did a hop-skip-and-jump. Perfectly harmless comment; of course. Freeman meant nothing by it; it was merely friendly chit-chat; people had often said such things to me before, hadn't they? I tried to remember. And failed. As we made our way into the terminal building Freeman dipped again into his apparently inexhaustible fund of flight lore.

'Used to know a captain named Reeves. He's retired now. Lives in Cornwall. Or is it Devon? Has a charming little place with a view of the sea. Still hale and hearty at seventy or so. He was a captain when Anglo-World were flying Tudors, and you know how long ago that was. Reeves had been on Halifaxes during the war. Collected a DFC too, I believe. The chaps used to wear their wings and ribbons on airline uniforms in those days. Then, all of a sudden the practice was out of date. Strange, the way things come and go, eh? I digress. Back to Reeves. He and his crew did twenty or so trips together—not a scratch on any of them. Then, over Hamburg or Berlin or somewhere they got walloped by flak. Blew half the nose of the aircraft off, the navigator and bomb aimer with it. Hell of a mess. God knows how the thing stayed in the air, but it did; and friend Reeves managed to steer it home at tree-top level. And plopped it down on the first friendly airfield. A few days later they gave him a new aeroplane complete with replacement navigator and bomb aimer and off they went on another trip. Well, dashed if they didn't run into a hell of a lot of trouble again. Clobbered by flak. Engine on fire. Bits falling off. Reeves said he had his work cut out just staying in the air. He called for his crew to report in. Everyone was alive. So far. The navigator worked out a course for home and away they staggered, bits continuing to fall off, but the aircraft still staying aloft. Then, according to Reeves, a Jerry night fighter attacked them. Hit one of the gunners. Set one engine on fire. Reeves headed into some cloud and managed to evade the fighter. The crew set to work to put out the fire. By this time they were down to about five thousand feet. Dangerous height, so down they went to tree-top level, just as before. They only had three engines—or, rather, two and a half, because one of the remaining engines was coughing and wheezing a bit by this time. They continued to head for home, nipping over church steeples and transmission masts and generally hoping not to be seen by any of the locals. The gunner was quite badly wounded; the others tried to do what they could for the poor fellow but of course he needed medical help. The winds seemed to have strengthened, Reeves told me. The navigator kept giving him course corrections. Eventually they reached the Channel; by this time the crew were tossing out bits of equipment and various odds and ends to save weight. They were down to about fifty feet; they could all see the water quite clearly, splashing and swirling down there. The faulty engine was still emitting disquieting noises and there was some doubt as to whether they would get across to England. But they did. Reeves said he'd never been so glad to see a coastline in his life. He landed on the emergency strip at Manston. It was about two miles long; they had put it there for just such emergencies as this.'

'They got down safely?' Enright asked.

'Absolutely,' said Freeman. 'No brakes or hydraulics, electrical system shot to hell. They just went wobbling down the runway until they came to a stop. Then they all got out, presumably thanking their lucky stars. But they observed that the navigator wasn't with them. Reeves went back inside the aircraft and found the navigator still sitting at his desk, dead as a doornail. When the MO looked at him he said the poor chap had been killed instantly. A chunk of flak had hit him at the base of the skull. Reeves said he was going to suggest that the navigator be recommended for the VC; he said the brave fellow had been working like hell all the way home in spite of his wounds.

'"Impossible," said the MO. "That man was killed outright. He's been dead for hours." 'Which puzzled friend Reeves and the rest of his crew.'

'Very odd,' I said.

'Actually,' said Freeman with the pleased look of the storyteller whose tale has been received well, 'that wasn't the oddest thing. A little while later something struck Reeves. The voice he'd heard over the intercom, giving him course corrections and positions, wasn't the voice of the new, replacement navigator, but that of the original navigator, the one who'd been killed on the last trip but one.'

'He could have been mistaken,' said Enright. 'Voices tend to sound alike on the intercom.'

'True,' said Freeman. 'But the original navigator came from Lancashire, a place called Droylsden. Quite definite twang to his voice; in fact the other fellows used to kid him a bit about it, called him George Formby and that sort of thing. His replacement was a Londoner with what you might call an Oxford accent, rather lah-di-dah, in fact. D'you get the point? Reeves recognized the voice of the Lancashire fellow on the intercom but he was so used to hearing it that he hadn't given it a second thought.'

'The original navigator came back from the dead to guide the aircraft home, is that it?' I said, trying to sound as cynical as possible.

'I know it's hard to swallow,' said Freeman. 'I'm not even vouching for its authenticity. Could be quite apocryphal, I admit it. But old Reeves wasn't the sort to make up ghost stories for the fun of it. If you'd known him, you'd have agreed with me.'

'I'm sure we would have,' said Enfield diplomatically. 'But I think there has to be an explanation. Something. I don't know what. What do you think?' he asked me. 'Have you ever run into anything like that?'

I shook my head. Automatically. Deny such things. Keep denying them. Never let it be thought that there might be anything the least bit questionable about Adam Beale. A sound, thoroughly reliable type. Rock of Gibraltar.

17

Joyce's father was making satisfactory progress. We all had a great deal to be thankful for, was Joyce's mother's comment; she repeated it several times. We all declared how well the patient looked; he said he had a feeling his number wasn't up, not yet. We dutifully stood around his bed and looked at each other until it was time to say that we really should be getting along.

I drove Joyce back to her office. On the way I remarked that it was really the very devil to know what to say to people in hospital. For some reason which still escapes me she seemed to take exception to the comment. I assured her that I wasn't referring to today's hospital visit in particular but to hospital visits in general. Her mouth had that tight-set look to it all the way to Justin and Crang. She permitted me to peck her on the cheek but she was out of the car with celerity. A cheery 'See you later!' was acknowledged with an almost imperceptible nod as she disappeared into the agency's doorway.

I drove home in glumly reflective mood. Despite her many admirable qualities there was no getting away from the fact that Joyce was appallingly touchy. What had happened to the girl I met at the folk music concert at the Festival Hall? The one who looked up to me as if I was standing atop Nelson's Column. Who hung on every word. Who listened, wide-eyed, to my endless dissertations on the marvellous world of aviation and, in particular, my place in it. Was it all a sham? Was she in fact bored to death by my ramblings? If so, she did a remarkably good job of concealing the fact. When I thought about it objectively I came to the rather disquieting conclusion that one of the things I had enjoyed most about Joyce in those days was how much she seemed to admire me and my profession. Heady stuff, admiration, a frighteningly close kin to flattery, against which our species possesses no known defence. I suppose I might have been considered a reasonably good catch then: not bad looking, exuding a modest charm, with good teeth and healthy gums, a clear complexion and a fairly appealing future. Joyce presumably absorbed these data into her personal computer—the one that is built into every female—and my pros and cons were instantly listed in declining order of significance, factor weighed against factor, shortcomings, prospects, habits, presentability. Then, in micro-seconds, came The Rating. I was classified. Christ. I shook my head. Cynicism depressed me. Particularly my own. I thought back to that concert at the Festival Hall. Were we really the same people? Even our tastes in music had diverged dramatically since then: mine to jazz, hers to the classics.

I drank instant coffee and read the paper. The usual chaos: hell and hopelessness on all fronts. I had been reading such stuff throughout my adult life. Every disaster word, every end-of-the-world prognostication had been used and re-used so frequently that they no longer had any impact. What phrases would the fourth estate dig up on doomsday?

The telephone rang. It was my mother, enquiring about Joyce's father.

I told her that he was coming along as well as could be expected. We had a great deal to be thankful for, I added.

'I rang their number,' said Mother, 'but there was no reply.'

She must have been disappointed. My mother, like most women, seemed to revel in grim news, endlessly repeating the ghastly details to anyone who would listen, squeezing out every last drop of agony.

'I'll tell Joyce that you rang.'

'Please do. We didn't know it was happening.'

How could she and Father possibly have known? They were in Ludlow at the time, visiting a cousin.

'Poor Joyce, is she taking it well?'

'Joyce takes everything well.'

'That's true,' she said. Then added. 'That's very true.' I knew she would and I didn't like myself very much for knowing.

Then a salesman with an oily voice rang and wanted to talk about something absolutely, brilliantly new in vacuum cleaners; I told him that I was the butler and that decisions concerning household appliances did not come within my realm of responsibility and that the Chief Housekeeper was on holiday in the Bahamas. Half an hour later a woman telephoned to burble about the joys of owning a freezer and how she could help us cut our food bills by a third or even more, followed almost immediately by a shrunken, shifty-eyed man who called at the door with a bagful of religious publications and a lot to say about how the Bible had predicted all our current problems with devastating accuracy and how there was still time for me to join the group which had all the answers. It was one of those days.

I went out to buy some Scotch, shoe polish and a pound of butter.

I encountered Mrs Halliwell not ten paces from the front door.

'Ah, Mr Beale. Not at work today?'

Was she asking or accusing? With her, it was hard to tell.

I admitted that I was indeed idle today.

'And does your wife also have the day off?'

'I'm afraid not.'

'A somewhat unsatisfactory arrangement.'

'I think so too,' I began. Then stopped. Her old head had moved closer to me. Her eyes narrowed.

'There is something,' she said.

'Something?'

She looked me up and down. 'I have a sensitivity to these phenomena.'

'What phenomena?'

She continued to peer at me, her nostrils flared. Her face was etched by a web of wrinkles; her skin like an ancient parchment within which her eyes sparkled, mobile and alert. 'Am I wrong, Mr Beale, or have you indeed had some form of supernatural experience in the recent past?'

'Supernatural experience? Me?' My voice thickened as I spoke. I felt as if she possessed X-ray vision and was examining me component by component. I had to clear my throat. 'Not me, Mrs Halliwell,' I rasped.

One eyebrow rose in stately disbelief.

'Curious,' she said. 'I am rarely wrong about such things.'

I thought rapidly.

'But as a matter of fact,' I said, 'a rather odd thing happened to a . . . friend of mine. He told me all about it.'

'Ah,' she said. 'That could be the explanation.'

'Could it really?'

She nodded slowly, thoughtfully.

I said, 'It's quite remarkable . . . to be able to sense such things.'

She shrugged. 'Not really, Mr Beale. Some people are born with a gift for art, for poetry, others are born with different gifts. Would you like to recount your friend's story?'

'Do you think I should?'

'Why not?'

I didn't know.

'My interest is purely professional, Mr Beale.'

'Quite so, Mrs Halliwell.'

I told her the story, carefully relating the facts as if they had happened to someone else . . . 'a close friend, a fellow pilot with Anglo-World, very solid type, not at all given to visions or that sort of thing.'

'What sort of thing?' Mrs Halliwell enquired sharply.

'I mean, I don't think he ever had any similar experiences before . . . a very uncomplicated person, you might say.'

'None of us is uncomplicated, Mr Beale.'

'No, of course. Anyway, the odd thing was that he noticed some markings on the monoplane. Later on he was able to discover an aircraft of similar type with much the same sort of markings. It had belonged to a young lady who died trying to fly the Atlantic. Her name was Mae Nolan; she was an American; she disappeared in September of 1927.'

'Mae Nolan,' murmured Mrs Halliwell, seeming to run the name over her tongue as if she was tasting a wine. 'The name does seem faintly familiar. Of course there were so many then; every day, it seemed, another madcap was flying off somewhere. So many of them were killed.'

'Nothing was ever found of Mae Nolan,' I said, 'or of her aircraft or the man who was flying with her.'

'And you think that your acquaintance saw this Mae Nolan in her aeroplane in the vicinity of New York aerodrome?'

'I'm simply repeating what he told me.'

'You think there is some other explanation?'

'I don't know. I wish I did. But I . . . he also told me that he's heard Morse signals over the radio, in the middle of the Atlantic, signals which no one else on the flight deck seems to have heard.'

Mrs Halliwell pondered this. 'I know of several

highly qualified people. I would suggest that you put your friend in touch with one of them.'

'He won't talk to anyone else.'

'Why ever not?'

'Airlines are very touchy about the fitness of their pilots. So pilots don't like it to be known for anything that might be considered, odd, if you see what I mean.'

She pursed her lips; the brittle flesh seemed in imminent danger of breaking into fragments at the corners of her mouth. 'Do you know of any reason why this young lady, this Miss Nolan, should go to so much trouble to contact your friend?'

'Not the slightest.'

'No family connections that you know of?'

'None at all.'

'Possibly she wished to tell him something or wished him to *do* something. As Schopenhauer pointed out, the difference between those who now live and those who have passed over is most definitely not absolute. The will to *exist* is present in both, you see.'

'Yes, of course,' I said.

'The will has an existence of its own,' she said, her small, frail hands outstretched. 'And that existence cannot be destroyed by anything as trivial as death.'

'I see.'

'You sound dubious, Mr Beale.'

'Do I? I'm awfully sorry. I don't mean to. It's simply that it sounds so unlikely, a 1927 monoplane getting in the way of a jetliner and signals coming through the radio where they couldn't possibly be heard. I suppose I'm looking for a different sort of explanation.'

'Consider, if you will, how incredible electricity, wireless and television would have seemed to people of two hundred years ago. Isn't it possible that we are just as ignorant and confused about the supernatural, Mr Beale, as they were about electricity?'

'I suppose so.'

'Wasn't it Camille Flammarion who said that "the

unknown world is vaster and infinitely more important than the known world"?'

'I'm not sure,' I said truthfully.

'And consider Julian Huxley's words: "It becomes increasingly clear that probably all living matter which is connected in the brain with mental processes has two sets of wholly distinct properties—those which we usually call material which can be dealt with by physics and chemistry, and those which we call mental which are dealt with by psychology."' She wagged a bony finger at me. 'Everything that I have learnt leads me to support that view without reservation.' Another wag. 'We see but one world, Mr Beale, but we have business in both.'

'Ah,' I said.

'What you tell me suggests that the young lady in question wishes to convey something to your friend. Of course, I have not the slightest idea as to the nature of that communication. My advice, Mr Beale, is that your friend should seek expert counsel . . .'

I said, 'Do you mean that you think I . . . that a ghost . . . a *spirit* . . . is trying to get in touch with . . . my friend?'

She cocked her head at an angle. 'My dear young man, I really don't think there's the least doubt of it,' she said as if recommending the best shop to buy my pound of butter.

* * *

The remarkable thing about patently absurd notions is how they become progressively less absurd the longer you live with them. Familiarity gets to work on them, shaping them, moulding them until they start to assume a specious rationality. If you don't remain on guard at all times you might find yourself beginning to accept them. Mrs Halliwell's explanation was a perfect case in point. What did she know about aircraft and radio signals? Why did I even *listen* to her senile ramblings? Balmy old bird, she talked about ghosts as if they were as natural and matter-of-fact as mothers-in-law.

* * *

After signing in for the flight I wandered downstairs to look in my post box. There was the usual collection: a newsletter from the company, statistics from the safety department, association bumph, a memo from Operations about scheduling, a note about an impending flight number change . . . then I saw the blue airmail envelope.

CAPTAIN ADAM BEALE, ANGLO-WORLD AIRWAYS, LONDON, ENGLAND, it said in bold characters. An American stamp adorned the upper right-hand corner; the postmark said Abbottsport, N.Y. In the upper left-hand corner was the return address: B. SUTTON, 120 W. UTICA, APT 4, ABBOTTSPORT, N.Y.

Beverly Sutton, the librarian who was so helpful; Beverly of the horn-rimmed glasses and the big smile.

'Dear Adam,' she wrote, *'I hope you don't mind me sending a letter to you at your company—and I hope I spelled your name correctly and got the name of your company right! If not, well, this letter will undoubtedly come right on back to me post-haste. (Sorry about that one! Quite unintentional!) After you left I did a little more digging here in Abbottsport and that's the reason I'm writing: to tell you something you'll be interested in, at least, I think you will. By the way, before I forget, I've got to apologize for those dumb cops of ours. I heard they picked you up and questioned you for* hours. *I'm really sorry. I hope it didn't make you too sore at us all. I guess the officers thought they were doing the right thing but it beats me how they could have thought you were a suspicious character. So, please accept my apologies on behalf of Abbottsport and New York State and President*

Reagan and Congress too! OK, it's time I got around to telling you what I dug up. This is it: I think I've located the man who taught Mae Nolan to fly an airplane, way back in 1927! I was thrilled when I found him and I figured you would be too—that's if you're still interested in finding out about Mae. (Maybe you've abandoned the whole project by now, but I hope not.) The man's name is Earl Diebner. He's nearly ninety and he lives in an old folks' home in Merton, which is a small town about twenty miles from here. I called him on the phone. It took a couple of minutes to get him to understand what I wanted but in the end he said OK, he would talk to you if you wanted to find out about Mae when she was learning to fly.'

She provided the address of the nursing home, plus the telephone number, complete with area code. After which she signed off: *'Yours sincerely, Beverly Sutton.'* Three cheers for Beverly, the indefatigable searcher. How on earth did she run this old chap Diebner to earth? And was I really glad she had done so? I didn't relish the prospect of going back to Abbottsport. I imagined the police ambushing me, Bonny-and-Clyde-style, as I approached that town sign festooned with insignia announcing the presence of Kiwanis, Optimists, Rotarians, Lions, the Abbottsport Garden Club, the Volunteer Fire Company, the Veterans of Foreign Wars and the U.S. Jaycees, whatever they were, immediately above the stern admonition to motorists to Protect our Children. A curiously hostile town, Abbottsport. A community of xenophobes, was it? No, that didn't make sense. America was full of foreigners from every corner of the globe. The Nolans themselves had once been foreigners.

I was flying to New York that day. The flight was thirty minutes late due to minor trouble with cargo compartment fire warning lights. We landed at JFK at about four-thirty local time; I telephoned Mr Diebner from the Sheraton on Seventh Avenue.

'Langley Home,' a woman's voice answered.

I asked to speak to Mr Earl Diebner; she said that he was eating his supper and I should call back. I explained that I was calling from New York City. She seemed taken aback; her voice became subdued; it was as if long distance calls invariably meant bad news at the Langley Home.

I could hear sounds in the background: a rumble of rather lethargic conversation, the clatter of knives and forks. I held on to that telephone for an inordinate length of costly time until, with a banging and sighing, it was at last answered.

'Yeah?' A cracked, throaty old voice. 'This is Earl Diebner.'

'My name is Adam Beale, Mr Diebner.'

'Never heard of you. And whatever you're selling, sonny, I don't want none and even if I did want some I ain't got any dough.'

'I'm not selling anything, Mr Diebner. I'm calling about someone I believe you knew a long time ago. I understand you were a flying instructor at one time.'

'Wassat? Instructor? Yeah, that's right. Say, come to think of it, some woman called me a couple weeks ago about the very same thing.'

'Did you teach Mae Nolan to fly, Mr Diebner?'

A sort of chuckle emerged from the receiver. 'Sure I did. Taught her everything she knew. Which didn't do her a hell of a lotta good. She got herself killed.'

'Yes, I know that, Mr Diebner.'

'What the hell year was that? Twenty-nine? Thirty? Not so good on dates any more. Remember a lot of things real good but I screw up when I try to figure the dates. Brain gets sluggish, like a motor that's got oiled up plugs, know what I mean?'

'I think so, sir.'

'No, you don't, but mebbe you will one day.'

'I was wondering if it might be possible for me to come and talk to you about Mae Nolan.'

'About who? Mae? What for?'

'I'm doing research on her. For a magazine article,' I added.

'Yeah? All right, I guess we can talk. When you comin'?'

'I'll have to arrange my schedule. Perhaps I could call you back and discuss a time and day.'

'Sure. Call.' Cackle. 'But you'd better not leave it long, sonny.'

'Pardon?'

'At my age it just ain't wise! Listen, I'll try to hang on but I can't promise nuthin'!' He chuckled again.

I called Beverly at the library.

'Adam!' She sounded pleased to hear from me. I told her that I had spoken to Mr Diebner and thanked her for finding him.

'I was glad to do it, really. Are you going to see him?'

'I'd like to. I'm going to be flying to Toronto next week. It's actually a good deal closer to the area than New York City is, so I thought I'd pop over to Rochester . . .'

'That's great,' she said enthusiastically.

'Are there buses to Merton from Rochester?'

'I guess so. But I'll tell you a better way.'

'What's that?'

'I'll drive you. I can meet you in Rochester.'

I said I couldn't possibly put her to the trouble.

'No trouble,' she said. 'I'd like to follow this up. There's only one thing.'

'Yes?'

'Can you put up with a little Honda? I mean, a *little* Honda!'

I told her that I adored little Hondas. She laughed. I asked her if she was quite sure she could find time to drive me to Merton. Yes, she told me; as long as I gave her a couple of days' notice so she could arrange for a sitter for Russell and, if necessary, find someone to fill in for her at the library. I promised to telephone her as soon as I knew what time I would be arriving in Rochester.

* * *

A dream, a shatteringly vivid dream, that's what it was. I'm quite certain of it.

I awoke with a start. A hell of a start. The way one always wakes in New York when there appears to be a total stranger in one's hotel room.

She was standing at the foot of my bed, her slim form just discernible in the shadows. She wore a leather jacket with a checkered scarf at her throat. She seemed to be laughing silently. Her teeth glinted softly in the gloom.

My mouth dropped open. I tried to assemble a word or two, but she beat me to it.

'Did I startle you?'

'A little.'

'Sorry.'

'Don't mention it.'

'So you're going to see Earl.' Bright, businesslike voice.

'Who?' Something had lodged in my throat. The word emerged as a kind of croak.

'Earl Diebner,' she said. 'You're going to see him.'

'Yes, that's right. Do you mind?'

A shrug. 'No. Why should I mind? How is he?'

'I'm not sure. Old, of course. He's in a nursing home. In Merton.'

'So he didn't ever make it to Bali.'

'I beg your pardon.'

'He always said if he made any money he'd retire to Bali.'

'I see.'

'He didn't get very far east.'

'What?'

'Merton is east of Abbottsport,' she explained.

'Of course. Do you mind if I ask you something?'

'Shoot,' she said.

'What are you . . . well, what I mean is, why are you *communicating* with me?'

'Isn't that kind of obvious?'

'Not to me,' I said.

I heard her emit an impatient little sigh. 'I want you to let everyone know what really happened.'

'But how am I supposed to do that?'

'Don't you *know*?'

'No, I really don't . . .' I began.

And stopped. Because I was talking to myself. For some reason I looked at my watch. That was when I realized that I couldn't see the hands. So how, I asked myself, could I possibly have seen *her*? I looked across the room at where she had been standing. Blackness. I couldn't see the picture of Concord, New Hampshire, on the opposite wall. So I didn't see any slim girl in any leather jacket. I had dreamt the whole thing. Obviously. It had all been spawned by my conversation with the old Diebner fellow . . . All quite logical and understandable when you stopped to think about it. Why, then, was my heart pounding as if I had just run ten miles? The damned *presence* of her. I could almost have reached out and touched her. Why didn't I, then? Why lie in bed, motionless as a cadaver? There had been a curl of hair bobbing across her forehead and her eyes had been huge and bright when she smiled. She had held something in her left hand. What? I frowned with the effort of trying to remember. Something soft; a pair of gloves perhaps. She had a marvellously self-confident way about her, standing there, talking. No shyness about conversing with a perfect stranger . . . Christ, I told myself, you're thinking about her as if she was really *there*. You're on your way, chum. Around the bloody bend. She wasn't there, for God's sake. You dreamt about her. Remember that, keep remembering it. Several deep, calming breaths. Heart still pounding away. Thud-thud-thud-thud. Was this the sort of weirdness chaps went through immediately before suffering heart attacks? Or brain haemorrhages? You feel peculiarly off balance when you're not sure about your mind, what it's going to tell you, what it's going to do next. It's not quite under your control any more. Bits seem to be constantly threatening to break off and go spinning away on their own. What, I wondered, if it suddenly *went*, just as I was bringing an aircraft into land at JFK? No, mustn't even consider the possibility. I sat upright in that bed in that pitch-black room, shaking my head. A ghost? A spirit? Just as Mrs Halliwell said? Nonsense. Bilge. Poppycock, piffle and hogwash. I turned on the light. Not quite four o'clock. Wide awake: the inevitable result of flying from London to New York: body still on British Standard Time; but brain back in 1927.

18

It was supposed to be something of a celebration: the first time Joyce's father had been able to get up and have dinner with guests. Joyce and I were the guests. We dutifully made the usual cheering remarks about how marvellous it was to see him up and about again and how bonny he looked and how he would be back to his old self in no time at all.

But he was having none of it. His face was grey and his flesh possessed an oddly plastic look; if you prodded it, the dent would surely remain after you removed your finger. He refused to be cheered up. The old machinery, he declared, has been dealt a traumatic blow; it would never be the same again. Neither would he.

'You just wait and see,' said Joyce with a brave grin.

I made some idiotic remark about his soon being

back on the golf course. Idiotic, because it seemed to make him more morose than ever.

'Golf?' he muttered with a sorry shake of his head. 'What a hope. I'd last about thirty seconds. If that. No, I always say you've got to accept the realities of a situation. My golf days are over. Probably my walking days too, if the truth be known.'

I kept trying: 'I think you've made excellent progress. To be honest, I thought you'd be spending a lot more time in the, er, recuperative stage.'

'Recuperative?' he echoed. 'That's for ever, if you ask me. Ever. From now on it's permanent recuperation. That's what I've got to look forward to.'

Joyce's mother had told us about all this in the hall when we arrived. He was in a deep depression; the doctor had warned her, she said, and it had come to pass just as they had predicted.

His mood hung like a sort of miasma over the assembly. Dinner became an endurance test full of forced conversation, of pretending that things were All Right. I told the story about a New Yorker who bought a ticket for Paris and found that he was the only passenger aboard an enormous Boeing 747 with accommodation for some four hundred. The solitary passenger was whisked over to Paris with a dozen cabin attendants to cater to his every whim.

'The only problem was,' I said, 'they lost his baggage at the other end!'

'That's a very funny story,' said Joyce's mother as if she was reading a line out of a children's book.

'Most amusing,' commented Joyce's father. He pushed his plate aside and said he couldn't eat any more.

After dinner I found myself alone with him in the drawing room while Joyce and her mother washed-up. I couldn't for the life of me think of anything to say to him. He sat there in gloomy introspection occasionally emitting tiny sighs. He reminded me of an ancient monk once seen in Thailand, a skeletal, quite motionless figure who looked as if he was a victim of malnutrition. I had stared at the old monk for some moments because I thought he was dead. It was therefore something of a surprise when the ancient sprang to his feet after what was presumably a period of intense contemplation; he strode away with a surprisingly brisk step.

'Wimbledon should be fun this year,' I said.

'Fun?' said Joyce's father.

I said, yes, I thought it could be.

Another little sigh and a sad shrug.

I asked him if he would like to watch television; he said he supposed it would be all right. Mr Enthusiasm. We watched someone talking about the Labour Party and its future. Then Joyce and her mother arrived with after-dinner cups of tea. The ordeal lasted another hour and a half. When we left, it was raining hard. I stepped into a large puddle as I jumped into the car.

'Sod it,' I said to no one in particular. 'Bloody new shoes.'

We had driven a couple of miles before Joyce spoke.

'There's a horribly callous streak in you,' she said.

I glanced at her in surprise. She had that tight-lipped look, a portent of trouble to come. Why *was* it that driving home from visiting our parents seemed inevitably to lead to strife? I asked her to be good enough to explain her remark.

'It might happen to you one day,' she said.

'What might happen?'

'Heart trouble.'

'I don't recall ever claiming immunity . . .'

'Damn it,' she snapped, 'you might have tried a little harder.'

'Tried what?' I asked, genuinely puzzled.

'You virtually ignored him.'

'Your father?'

'Of *course*!'

'Ignored him? For God's sake I was stuck with him after dinner while you and your mother went trotting off into the bloody kitchen . . .'

As soon as the words were uttered I knew I had chosen unwisely.

'*Stuck* with him?'

'What I mean is . . .'

'He nearly *died*!'

'I'm aware of that. I was at the hospital, if you recall . . .'

'You're quite unbelievable,' she said, as if she was comprehending the fact for the first time.

'I don't think you quite understand . . .'

'When I think what he's been through.'

'I know what he's been through . . .'

'And he's always been so good to you.'

'I know that too,' I said. 'I also happen to know that it's up to him to snap out of this. He's up to his ears in self-pity . . .'

'You bastard,' she said.

I started to say that I was merely pointing out the truth. But somehow I didn't get the opportunity.

Thank God I had to fly to Toronto the next morning.

* * *

Beverly met me at Rochester Airport. The same big smile, but no glasses. Then I saw them in her left hand. Presumably she had used them to pick me out of the arriving passengers, and then had removed them. I found it rather touching that she had bothered.

I told her it was awfully good of her to meet me.

'No problem,' she said. 'I'm just real glad you could find the time to get up this way. How is London?'

'Unusually warm at the moment,' I said.

'Lucky,' she grinned. 'It's still winter up here.'

So it was, I observed, as we went outside; snow had

fallen recently, the air was crisp and icy. We made our way to the parking lot and to her diminutive blue Honda.

'Do you want to go right over and see Mr Diebner? Or do you want to eat or have a coffee? Or maybe tea?' she added.

I told her that I had to return to Toronto first thing in the morning for the trip back to Heathrow. 'So it's tonight or never,' I added. Which made her blush a little. That in turn made me blush. I had made the remark in all innocence but it had taken on an extra meaning somewhere along the way.

She put her glasses on. 'Okay,' she said. 'Merton it is. Stand by for take-off!'

The little car bounded forward with a sort of puppy-like enthusiasm. Beverly shifted gears in a deliberate, grind-if-you-dare manner; she nodded, satisfied, when she was safely in top. We scurried southward out of the city, along roads that still bore traces of snow and ice in streaky patches. The traffic was sparse. We talked of trivialities. Yes, I had had a good trip over. (Not a single odd sighting or hearing, although I didn't mention this fact to Beverly.) No, they appeared not to have had as much snow up in Toronto as in the Rochester area. She said that very little had been happening in Abbottsport since my last visit; the biggest excitement of the season was the arrest of the local United Way chairman; he was accused of interfering with young male workers.

'I guess,' said Beverly, 'they didn't know what they were volunteering for!'

We chuckled companionably. I was enjoying the drive. And the company. It sounds less than complimentary to call someone relaxing, yet this was the case with Beverly. The little Honda was our world and it was snug and warm and safe. For the moment.

As we headed further out of the city we found areas where the snowfall had been heavier. Ploughs had cleared the roadways, leaving miniature mountain ranges on either side; they glistened and sparkled in the car's headlights. Here and there abandoned cars had been buried in the ploughed snow; they looked as if they would remain there until the spring.

I began to feel drowsy. Hardly surprising. It was midnight London time. I should have been tucked up in bed, fast asleep. Perhaps I was; perhaps I was dreaming this just as I dreamt that Mae Nolan came to visit me at the Sheraton on Seventh Avenue. Indeed the sheer improbability of this journey made the dream idea seem quite reasonable. What could Mr Diebner possibly tell us that would make all this worthwhile? It was undeniably of interest that he was the man who had taught Mae Nolan to fly an aeroplane. But so what? When one stopped to think about it, this was an awful waste of time and money. Was it the sort of slightly irrational thing done by someone in my condition, whatever that condition was?

I stirred my sluggish self into wakefulness. Beverly was announcing our arrival at Merton.

'If you were dazzled by the sights and sounds of Abbottsport,' she said, 'you're going to be knocked right over by this place!'

The Honda bounced across railway lines and clattered over a narrow steel bridge that looked as if it had been there since Abraham Lincoln's time. 'Pop 5890' said the Welcome sign; another sign admonished us to drive carefully while in Merton.

A cluster of shops and houses. A post office in solitary splendour. A flag pole but no flag. A gas station. A billboard advertising vacations in Hawaii.

Beverly turned off the main street and pulled up in front of a large and slightly decrepit looking house.

* * *

Mr Diebner eyed us without enthusiasm.

'I'm missing "Barney Miller",' he said.

'Who?' I asked.

'Never hear of "Barney Miller"?'

He sounded incredulous, as if I had admitted not having heard of Ronald Reagan.

'It's a TV show,' said Beverly.

The old fellow nodded approvingly at Beverly. 'She knows,' he said. 'It's my favourite.' He was ancient and bent, the skin on his face like old, dried-up putty. He had a large and rather imposing nose that seemed to have retained some of its youth while the rest of his face had withered into old age. He gazed at Beverly a few moments, then he seemed to remember my presence. 'You're the fella who called me?'

'Yes, Mr Diebner. My name's Adam Beale and this is Beverly Sutton.'

'Did you bring somethin'?' Earl Diebner looked expectantly, first at me then at Beverly.

'Bring something?'

'To eat,' snapped the old man, suddenly irritable. 'Goddam food's lousy here. No bulk. Lost eight pounds since they stuck me in this dump. Goddam meat loaf's made of cardboard, I swear.'

'I'm very sorry,' I said. 'I had no idea. I never thought of it.'

'Tell you what,' said Beverly. 'What do you say I drive down to that Colonel Sanders I saw a couple of miles back on the highway. I'll pick up some fried chicken. Be back in fifteen minutes.'

'Now you're talkin'.' At last we were treated to a Diebner smile. 'Smart girl,' he told me as Beverly departed. 'Not your wife, I guess, her havin' a different name. Livin' with her, are you? Don't blame you. Pretty girl, too, under them glasses.'

'No, she's merely an acquaintance.'

'Yeah?' said the old man sceptically.

'I assure you . . .'

'Anyway,' said Earl Diebner, 'you were talkin' about Mae Nolan over the phone. I'm missin' "Barney Miller",' he added.

'Yes, you mentioned that.'

'Did I? Don't recall. My favourite show, "Barney Miller".'

'I see.'

'After "MASH". I guess I've seen every one of the shows they ever made. Some ten, twenty times, maybe fifty times. Know what they're gonna say before they say it. You watcha hell of a lot of reruns when you're in a home, lemme tell you, sonny. What did you say your name was?'

'Adam Beale.'

'You talk like a Limey.'

'Yes, I am.'

'And you're tryin' to find out stuff about Mae Nolan?'

'Correct.'

'What for?'

'I'm not sure. It all depends on what I find out. I made some enquiries in Abbottsport—that was where Mae Nolan was born.'

'No need to tell me that, sonny.'

'Of course not. Anyway, Beverly managed to find out that you were here in Merton and so we thought we'd come over and talk to you. It's kind of you to see us.'

'Yeah, it is,' he agreed, nodding in the grave way of a senior executive whose time is fully occupied with pressing matters. 'So what you want to know? I told Mae it was dumb for her to try and fly the Atlantic. She wouldn't listen. She was like that. Thought she could do anything in the world if she set her mind on it. One time, she even tried to get me to fly with her to Europe. I told her she was outa her skull. Dumb bastards were fallin' in the water every other day. Not me, buddy. 'Course the thing was, I knew what she was up against. She didn't. I'd been flyin' a long time even then. 'Twenty-two it was when I started. JN4—Jenny. OX5 motor. Goddam thing was always oiling up. The Hisso

Jenny was one hell of a lot better airplane but they were tough to find. No brakes on them ships. You had a tail skid to slow you down. Not that you needed much slowin' down. You touched down at about thirty-five, seems to me. You could get yourself blown backwards sometimes. It happened. A lot of wing; too much—cross-wind'd flip you upside down before you knew what was happenin'. Funny thing, it was right after the war, you know, and everyone was talkin' about Rickenbacker and all the other fighter pilots; whole world was crazy about flyin'—as long as someone else did the flyin'! It was tough as hell to get any sort of work with airplanes. A guy I knew flew right across the country, clear to California, just taking folks up for rides. Somebody asked him what was the most dangerous part of flying. Know what he said? "Starvation"! Good, eh? That guy had a point. Real tough to make a living then, not like today with all the big jets.' He shook his head sadly.

'Was Mae a good pupil? Quick to learn?'

The old man looked up, frowning as if trying to remember who I was talking about. 'Mae? Yeah, seems to me she was pretty good. But she wanted to do it all in a day, know what I mean? Impatient. Over-controlled a whole lot in the beginning but she soon got the hang of it. She was better than most of the women I tried to teach. Something in women, they work too hard driving a car or flying a plane. Can't let the plane fly itself. They're like that with a lot of men, uh?' he added with an unexpected chuckle, a hoarse cackle, that terminated as abruptly as it had begun. 'You ever do any flyin'?'

I told him of my association with Anglo-World. He sniffed. Then he asked me if I had ever been an instructor. I said no.

'You should. Good for you. Makes you remember all the basics all over again.'

'I'll remember that, Mr Diebner. But about Mae . . .'

He wagged a sadly deformed finger at me. 'You teach others you teach yourself. Trouble was, there was no dough in it. After 'twenty-nine it was nuts. For mebbe six months I had one pupil. *One*. A dentist. The only guy in town who had any dough. Fat little bastard. If he decided to take a flying lesson, I ate. Bad as that, it was. A bitch. I quit. Worked at a coupla different things. Then went to Chicago. Worked in the yards a while. Meat-packin'. The pits. You know what my job was? Hosing down the casings—the intestines. God-awful job. You got about 45 cents an hour for standing about ten hours up to your knees in water and God knows what other shit. That's where I got the rheumatism,' he declared tapping his leg and indicating his bent back with his right thumb. 'I shoulda sued 'em, I guess.'

I asked him how well he had known Mae personally.

Again he seemed to have to make an effort to return to the subject at hand. 'She was a real nice lookin' girl. Smart too. College education. Had a degree in pharmacy, far as I recall. Would've taken over the family business, mebbe. Nice clothes, car, dough, everythin'. She used to tell me about her boy friends. Real intimate stuff sometimes; she had no respect for any guy who wasn't a pilot. She liked me a whole lot. Mebbe I could've made some time with her if I'd really tried. But the truth of it,' he revealed with a twinkle in his rheumy old eyes, 'is I had a wife at the time. Judy, her name was. Bitch took off in 'thirty-two with a printing company salesman. That was just before I went to Chicago. I was workin' in a movie theatre at the time. Real tough to keep an eye on your wife when you're workin' nights.'

We talked on, about how Mae had been planning the Atlantic flight from the first time she clambered aboard Earl Diebner's training biplane, about her endless questions concerning radio equipment and life rafts and where she should go to obtain the best navigational training. Earl Diebner had apparently taken her only half seriously. It was the post-Lindbergh era of Atlantic madness; almost anyone who could pilot an aircraft had considered the possibilities of a long-distance flight, preferably over an ocean. It was the way to achieve instant fame, fortune and, presumably, happiness.

Beverly returned with a cardboard bucket of fried chicken, coleslaw, three coffees—and, slipped in her handbag, a small, flat bottle of bourbon.

'Rare woman, this one,' Earl told Adam as he unscrewed the bottle. 'Wish I were forty or fifty years younger, I'd marry you,' he told her. He poured a generous helping of bourbon into his coffee, but ignored ours. 'Gives it a little body,' he said. 'Helps digest the food.'

As he munched the chicken and drank the fortified coffee, Earl recounted how Mae had originally talked of making the flight solo; eventually, however, she had agreed that she lacked the flying experience and the navigational knowledge and had contacted several pilots, eventually selecting Jack Thornton. 'Heard tell she signed him up for twenty-five grand. A lotta dough back then.'

'Do you know much about her family life?'

'Not really. Seems to me her ma and pa came up to the field once. They didn't like the idea of her flying a plane. But she was free, white and twenty-one so what were they going to do about it? She had a real nice car, I remember. A Nash Special Six with a rumble seat. Roadster, we used to call 'em. Never hear that name any more, do you? Roadster.' He finished his coffee and sighed in satisfaction. 'Real good,' he muttered in Beverly's direction. His eyes had become heavy; I sensed that the old man might soon doze off.

'Do you remember how many hours of solo time she had when she went to Roosevelt Field for her transatlantic flight?'

He shook his head. 'Could be in her log book, though. We could look.'

'You have her log book?'

'Sure. She left it at the field—Corey Field, it was. Field's gone now. They put up apartments or a power station or something. Anyway, when she went off to New York she left her log book. Meant to pick it up later, I guess. Never got the chance. So I kept it. For old times' sake. You wanna see it?'

'I'd love to.'

'Okay. Be right back.' He staggered to his feet. Winked at Beverly and made his plodding way out of the room.

'Cute,' said Beverly.

'Master-stroke of yours, the whiskey.'

She smiled modestly.

'I'll settle with you later,' I told her.

Earl Diebner returned, his carpet slippers flopping noisily. He handed me a faded book. The words AERO OIL were barely legible on the cover; the name M. Nolan had been written on a dotted line; it was almost invisible; age had etiolated the ink, leaving only a shadow on the paper.

'Aero Oil used to give you log books if you'd buy their oil,' the old man said. 'But seems to me we used to charge the students two bucks for 'em. They could afford it, most of 'em.'

The log book's pages were filled with neat lines of faded writing. *'May 31, Pilot in command Earl Diebner; students M. Nolan. Familiarization. Take-off 8.45, landed 9.40. Aircraft: Standard.'* Two sessions that day. She flew again after lunch, this time taking the controls for approximately thirty minutes, practising straight and level flight.

'Had a lotta trouble getting it fixed in her mind that you got to co-ordinate the rudder with the ailerons. Got real frustrated about it, I recall. I thought she was going to quit after that first lesson. But she stuck to it, got to hand it to her for that. She stuck to it until she was pretty good and then she never forgot it. She'd have been flying all day if I'd let her. Impatient as hell, she was. Never had a student as impatient as her. She'd be bouncing up and down on her toes waiting to get in the plane. I tell you, I often think she had a premonition she didn't have much time left so she had to pack it all in right away.'

I glanced through the pages, noting an entry here and there; you could almost sense the enthusiasm of the girl, the wonder with which she described her experiments in turns and stalls, landings and take-offs. Two and three hours in a single day were common.

'She'd get mad as all-git-out if the weather grounded her,' said Earl Diebner with a tooty grin. 'One day it was blowin' about forty knots. She said, "What's the matter, Earl, it's just a bit of wind." I said, "You go and kill yourself if you like, honey, but you'll have to find somebody else's plane to do it in. You're not takin' mine." I tell you, she got madder'n hell. She said she'd go and buy her own plane and I said that was just fine with me; she could do what she damn well pleased but while she was flying my plane she had to do what I told her. I used to talk kind of rough to her once in a while. She needed it. She'd always had her own way in everythin' else, know what I mean? She used to ask me what sort of ship she should get for her Atlantic trip—and this was when she still couldn't land without shaking us both like we were on a roller-coaster. But, hell, that was a detail far as she was concerned. She was going to fly the Atlantic; she was going to be the first dame to do it! She'd make the whole damn world sit up and take notice! She'd be famous. That was her. A lot of drive. Ran in the family, I guess.'

'What type of aircraft did you recommend that she use for the Atlantic flight?'

He scratched his ear. 'Seems to me I said the Ryan guys would most likely be real happy to make another

Spirit of St Louis for her. Or there was the Bellanca. Italian feller, Bellanca. Made a pretty good airplane. So did Eddie Stinson. And Curtiss. Any one of them would have been okay, with extra fuel tanks and some other changes. Beefed-up gear, for one. They had the Whirlwind J-5. Real good engine, for its day . . .'

It was time to leave the old boy to Barney Miller.

I stood up and told him it had been a great pleasure meeting him.

Earl Diebner looked up, surprised. 'You goin'?'

'It was kind of you to spend so much time with us.'

'Yeah, well, funny thinkin' back all them years. Long time ago. Different world then. Better in some ways, worse in others, I guess. You wanna keep her log book, you go ahead. No good to me, not now.'

We said our goodbyes at the door with its grimy stained-glass windows. Earl Diebner nodded and raised a weary hand in farewell as we turned to leave.

Then something occurred to me.

'Mr Diebner, I wonder if I might ask you one more thing.'

'What?'

'Did you ever have an ambition to retire to Bali?'

'Bali?' The face cracked into a smile. 'Yeah, I did. How did you know about that?'

'I forget,' I said. 'I suppose someone told me.'

19

I spent most of the journey to Abbottsport trying to convince myself that lots of people have had dreams of retiring to places like Bali. Indeed, if one took the trouble to stop passers-by in New York or London or perhaps even Djakarta, asking them what they considered the place to retire to, wouldn't it be almost certain that some would say Bali?

Not very convincing, I had to admit. Think of something better than that. Coincidence? When you have dreams you have to cook up some sort of conversation and by sheer chance you might get something right . . .

'You're quiet,' said Beverly.

'Sorry,' I said. 'I was thinking.'

'About Earl Diebner?'

'Yes. He was an interesting old boy. How on earth did you manage to find him?'

'I asked a lot of questions and got a lot of answers and pretty soon I found someone who just came right out and said, "Why in tarnation don't you go and see Earl Diebner? He taught the girl to fly an airplane!" Why, I'd never heard of him! But it wasn't too tough to find him once I knew his name.'

'Talking to him was like talking to a history book.'

She nodded with that contagious enthusiasm of hers. 'I know what you mean. I used to ask my grandfather about an old man he said he knew when he was a little boy. Seems the old man had fought in the 4th Minnesota regiment in the Civil War. And he claims to have *seen* Abraham Lincoln. Imagine! My grandfather actually spoke to someone who *saw* Abraham Lincoln! That's *exciting*! The old guy died seven or eight years ago. He was about as old as Mr Diebner. Nice old man; you'd have liked him.'

'Is your father still alive?'

'Uh huh.' She nodded. 'He's retired now. Used to work on the railroad. Doesn't like airplanes very much. Says they're unsafe.'

'He's quite right. I'm terrified every time I go near one.'

She laughed. 'Dad was in the Corps of Engineers in the war. He spent a whole lot of time in England. In Lancashire and Northern England. He said he loved the people but hated the weather. He had a fight with a British marine in a pub. He's got the scar on his forehead to this day. Lucky punch, he says, but I don't know. My dad is a lousy drinker.'

'It's a common failing of highly intelligent, thoroughly admirable fellows,' I informed her.

'I'll tell him,' she said, pleased.

Bali?

There was no denying it, old Diebner had reacted when I had mentioned Bali. I had stirred some memory long buried in the ancient storage battery where he kept nearly ninety years of recollections.

Yes, I told myself, but what you're saying is that Earl Diebner's desire to go to Bali was communicated to you by a girl who has been dead well over half a century. No, unacceptable. You must have read something about it in one of those newspaper stories: 'The hopeful young aviatrix declared that if she was successful in her venture she would be able to afford to send her flying instructor to Bali, since he had often expressed a desire to live in that island paradise.' An admirable explanation. Except for the inconvenient fact that I didn't read any such thing in all those clippings. Earl Diebner hadn't been mentioned in any of them. I had never heard of him until I received Beverly's letter. All right, then, file away the Bali business for a while. Eventually the solution would be found. It was down there somewhere, pleading for someone to be perceptive enough to uncover it.

'Yes,' I heard myself saying, 'a drink would be very nice, thank you, if it's no trouble. But . . .'

'But what?'

'Well . . . your, that is, might there not be objections from Mr Sutton?'

She glanced at me. 'I'm divorced,' she said. 'Didn't I tell you?'

I said I didn't think so.

'Sorry.'

I said it was quite all right.

Beverly lived in a two-bedroom apartment in a small block of flats in a residential street a block from Main Street. A cosy flat, warmly decorated in oranges and yellows, laden bookshelves occupying about half the wall area. There was a small television set and an impressive stereo system with gigantic speakers.

'When we split up I got custody of the stereo,' she grinned.

A teenage girl emerged from a bedroom putting on her overcoat. She was introduced as Sue, who 'sat' for Beverly from time to time. She said 'hi' to me then departed, saying that she would 'see' us.

'Nice girl,' said Beverly. 'I feel I can trust her with Russell. But sometimes I'm not so sure I can trust Russell with her,' she added, peeping into the second bedroom. 'He's fast asleep.'

'How old is he?'

'Six.'

'It must be difficult, bringing him up alone.'

'He's a good kid,' she told me. 'One of his real nice qualities is he isn't one bit like Chuck. My ex,' she added.

She had been divorced three years, I learnt. Beverly did not specify the grounds. A charming no-good, was her description of her ex-husband: 'He had six jobs in the five years we were married. Never satisfied. One of those men who always feels he's being unfairly treated. A clever guy in his own way. But unhappy.'

I said I was sorry it hadn't worked out.

'Water under the bridge,' Beverly shrugged. 'It hurt a whole lot at first. I kept thinking it was all my fault. I had failed. But then I came to realize that was a kind of conceit. It wasn't my fault at all. It was his, the heel. And the best thing I could do was forget about him as quickly as possible and learn to live my own life. So that's what I've been doing. Scotch? Bourbon? Gin? Rye?'

'Straight soda,' I told her. 'I'm flying tomorrow.'

'OK, I'll have soda too,' she said and poured the drinks.

'You're being very kind to a total stranger,' I said.

Her cheeks coloured prettily. 'The rest of Abbottsport seems to have treated you kind of shabbily,' she said. 'So I feel it's up to me to redress the balance.'

'Actually, it wasn't all bad. After the police let me go I had something to eat in a little restaurant near the bus station. An old chap named Charlie Vogel told me he remembered Mae. She used to buy lime rickeys from him. We had a pleasant chat. A few more snippets of gen.'

'Snippets of what?'

'Gen. Sorry. Air force slang. Information.'

Beverly asked, 'Have you decided what you're going to do with all this stuff on Mae Nolan?'

I shook my head. 'God knows whether anyone still cares about something that happened that long ago.'

'I hope you write a book,' Beverly mused, her fingers intertwined and resting demurely upon her lap. 'It'd be great to have it in the library and to think I had a little bit to do with it.'

We sat and talked about it while we finished our drinks. Oh Lord, it was all too warm and pleasant; her proximity was deliciously tempting. It would have been so perfectly natural, perfectly delightful, to lean across and kiss those softly shaped lips. I wanted to. Badly. Urgently.

So I said, 'I'd better go.'

'There's the spare room,' she said. 'I can bunk with Russell.'

Again that delicate touch of colour in her cheeks.

'I think I'd better not,' I said.

'I understand,' she said.

'I don't want to go,' I said, 'that's why I must, I suppose. Weird logic, isn't it?' I remember I thanked her in an idiotically formal way: I must have sounded like a small boy mumbling, 'Mum says to say thanks for offering to have me.'

Have me.

Christ.

* * *

The motel room was a monument to vinyl and arborite: plastic pretending to be wood, leather and bamboo. The television set bore a warning stating that it was connected to an alarm system and if any attempt was made to move the set the system would be activated —with God only knows what dire consequences. Paintings were screwed firmly to the walls—though it was hard to imagine anyone wanting to steal those monstrosities. Cigarette burns stained the edge of the dressing table. The bedside lamp looked as if it was made of ferns dipped in aluminium paint.

It was a depressing little room that possessed a slightly sour smell as if the air itself was weary and used up.

Weary and rather disconsolate, I brushed my teeth and clambered into the bed. It was moderately comfortable. I had slept in worse, far worse. One thing about being a professional flyer, you learn to sleep almost anywhere.

Why didn't I take Beverly up on her offer? She wasn't offering *herself*, was she? Merely the use of a room. Her room. But no, Little Lord Fauntleroy has to choose the noble route. Faithful unto death. Twerp. The juices within me had little patience with such twaddle. At one point I looked up her number, tempted to call her. Please, let me have another chance.

But I didn't. I turned off the light and lay in the darkness, gazing forlornly at the gap in the curtains through which a neon sign flashed at four-second intervals.

In a way, I thought, I insulted Beverly. She didn't

suggest sex, did she? Just a bed, for God's sake. Was she at this moment gnashing her teeth with vexation, hurt and humiliated by yours truly? Probably.

I called myself an assortment of names. But there was nothing for it; I had better get some sleep; it was after twelve midnight, local time. Early morning in London. Joyce would soon be awake, would soon be worrying over her shoes, would soon be setting out to Lord only knows what creative conquests . . .

'That's *it*, Ozzie! Yes! *That*!'

I opened my eyes. The female voice had drifted through the paper-thin walls from the next suite. Then it was Ozzie's turn; he said she was heaven, pure-and-simple heaven.

I squashed a pillow over my head. But the voices kept intruding, tormenting me, creating images of a veritable kaleidoscope of fleshy delights—delights being experienced only a matter of a few feet away. Sod them. But in a few minutes they would be done and they would sleep, satiated. Come on, I urged them, get it over with, be good sports. Would I ever see Beverly again. Would she ever want to talk to me? Should I telephone her first thing in the morning before I caught the bus for Rochester? Yes, I would call. And I would occupy these moments thinking of something suitable to say. Suddenly I remembered Colonel Sanders. Hell, I had completely forgotten to recompense her for the chicken and the whiskey. No matter, I would write her a note and slip a twenty dollar bill in the envelope. Say I will be in touch again very soon. Underline 'very'. No doubt the man in the motel office could supply a stamp. Pop it in the U.S. Mail box just outside the main entrance. Problem solved.

I clambered out of bed, turned the light on. Scribbled the note. Returned to bed. More breathless exchanges from next door. Ozzie seemed to be surpassing himself.

I turned on the television set. A familiar face flickered to shadowy life on the screen. Frank Sinatra, in army attire: *From Here To Eternity*. I watched it wondering why American films about the military usually depicted the non-commissioned types as the solid reliable characters and the officers as neurotic cowards. British military films, on the other hand, tended to portray the officers as the noble souls who saved the nation in time of trouble; the other ranks seemed to be included as not-very-bright light relief.

'Not yet, Ozzie, not yet.'

What, I asked myself, am I doing here? I have no business being here in this sleazy motel in the wilds of New York State in the middle of winter. It might snow all night and the roads might be closed in the morning and I would be unable to get back to New York in time for my flight. And that would mean Trouble. There were few crimes more heinous in the airline world than failure to present oneself for an assigned flight.

Bed-spring squeaks from next door.

'Fantastic, Ozzie.'

'No, you were the fantastic one, baby, believe me.'

'It was never like this with Wilmer.'

'You're not just saying that, are you?'

I watched the film, hoping to be bored to sleep. How many times had I seen it? Half a dozen? A pause for a clutch of commercials—deodorants and douches, laxatives, nasal sprays and a plea to purchase only clothing made by the United Garment Workers of America.

There was a rap at the door.

Beverly! It had to be Beverly! She was the only person in the *world* who knew I was here. I scrambled off the bed and hurried to the door. A short, balding man stood outside, bundled up in a gown and scarf.

'You wanna turn down your TV, mister?'

My what? For a moment I stared at him. Then I realized that he wasn't Beverly. A moment later I realized that he was complaining about the volume of *From Here To Eternity*. I apologized.

'Can't sleep for it,' said the man.

'I'll turn it off,' I promised.
'Okay,' said the man and turned to leave.
'By the way,' I said, 'is your name Ozzie?'
'Yeah,' said the man, suspicion darkening his brow. 'How d'you know?'
'Just a shot in the dark,' I said.

20

I was dozing when Joyce came home.
She apologized for waking me. I assured her it was of no importance; I had enjoyed a couple of hours of slumber, therefore I had almost convinced my body that it was operating in the six-thirty evening time zone in Britain and not in the middle of an Eastern Standard Time day.
'Good flight?' she asked.
'Pretty good,' I told her for the second time that day. I had called her when I arrived home and she told me that she was between client meetings, the first with the Waxoleum people, the second with an insurance company in urgent need of a new image.
'How's your father?'
'Still progressing satisfactorily.'
'Jolly good,' I said.
'Yes, isn't it,' she said.
Something in her tone puzzled me.
'And your mother?' I enquired.
'Mother's very well,' she replied. She was standing in the doorway, holding the edge of the door with one hand. She wore the turquoise silk kimono I had bought her a year earlier in Hong Kong. It suited her, draping her graceful body with a sensuous casualness that I found enormously pleasant to wake up to. I remember thinking what a remarkably attractive female she was,

with her long dark hair, her greenish eyes, dramatic cheekbones, strikingly intelligent features.

I invited her to come in. 'I rather fancy undoing that thing and having a nibble at your nipples,' I added in what I hoped emerged as a seductive voice.

'I don't think so,' she said.

'Got better things to do, have you?'

She said, 'How was Mae Nolan?'

I stared. 'Pardon?'

'I hope you're not going to tell me you've never heard of her.'

'Certainly not.'

She put her free hand on her hip. 'That's good. You seem surprised that I know her name.'

'Surprise isn't quite how I'd describe it.'

'Did you have a pleasant time at that place—what's it called?—Abbottsport?' She held the note I had scribbled several days earlier and had presumably left on the bedside table.

'It was rather cold. It had snowed the day before I arrived.'

'Shame.'

'I thought so,' I said.

'Is it serious?'

'Is what serious?'

She picked an imaginary piece of something from the tip of her tongue. I sensed that she was rather enjoying the moment.

'Please don't be evasive.'

'I'm not being evasive.'

Her brow darkened. 'Christ, Adam, you've been seeing her, haven't you, this Mae Nolan woman?'

'Not exactly,' I said with a leisurely gesture or two, 'I went to Abbottsport because Mae Nolan was born there and spent a lot of her early life there.'

'Doesn't she live there now?'

'No. She doesn't live anywhere.'

'What?'

'She is no longer of this world.'

Joyce frowned. 'What are you talking about?'

I explained. 'And she disappeared somewhere in the middle of the Atlantic. They never found a trace of her or her aircraft.'

Sharp-as-a-tack Joyce even took a moment to absorb that. 'She's *dead*?'

I nodded. 'Has been since 1927. September, to be precise.'

Joyce's eyes narrowed. You could see how rapidly she was thinking, trying to sort out things in her mind. 'I didn't know that.'

'That's what I thought.'

'What . . . well, why are you interested in her?'

'A little research project. For an article. Perhaps a book. I'm not sure at the moment.'

She stared, swallowing a couple of times.

'I thought it was something quite different,' she said.

'Did you?'

'Yes . . . and I'm sorry.'

I wondered when I had last heard Joyce utter those words. I went on:

'Even if they did manage to find her alive, she'd be about eighty. No great rival, I can assure you.'

'I had no idea you were doing . . . research.'

'Had a chat with her flying instructor. Funny old sod. Gave me her log book. Spent a lot of time talking to me.'

Nearly said 'us'.

'That must have been interesting,' said Joyce. Poor Joyce, the wind had been abruptly taken from her sails. A rare experience for her.

I said, 'If you'd like to find out more about Mae Nolan there's a book in the spare bedroom. Chapter twelve, I think.'

She didn't say anything for a moment. Then: 'You don't have to look so damned pleased with yourself.'

'I'm sorry. Unintentional, I assure you.'

Quick intake of breath. 'I apologize for thinking the wrong thing,' she said.

Something made me say, 'But has it occurred to you that you might have been thinking the right thing? Perhaps I've invented a fiendishly clever way of deceiving you.'

She shook her head without smiling. 'I don't think so. It's not your way, Adam.'

'You don't think I possess the imagination to think up anything so ingenious.'

'No,' she shrugged. 'It's simply that you're a very straight-forward person.'

Which was one of the nicest things she had said to me for a long time.

* * *

'I'm sorry to have to announce that we can't maintain altitude, ladies and gentlemen. We will have to ditch. I want to make it quite clear that the cabin crew are fully trained to handle this emergency. Please follow these instructions. First, remove your shoes and place them in the seat pockets in front of you; then be sure to take all sharp objects out of your pockets—tie clips, hair clips, pens and pencils—and put them in the seat pockets beside your shoes. Then remove ties and scarves and make sure that you loosen your collar. Put on your overcoats. Next, take the life jacket from under your seat. Remove it from its plastic pouch, then put it on in accordance with your cabin attendant's instructions. After that, fasten your seat belt as tightly as you can. Return your seat back to the upright position and make sure the folding tray in the seat-back in front of you is securely stowed. Just before touchdown, you will be instructed to clasp your hands over your head, bending forward as far as you can go with your feet flat on the floor. Look about you now to determine the location of the emergency exit and life raft nearest to you. You'll have a few minutes to review the instructions in the safety booklet in the seat pocket. After touchdown, please remain in your seats until the life rafts have been removed from the overhead compartments by members of the cabin crew . . .'

The sea ahead, grey and angry, choppy, scars of white spume whipped by the searing wind. Establish a heading parallel to the swell of the ocean, is the manual's comfortable advice. Calculate the velocity of the wind and its direction by observing the breaking action of the waves. What could be simpler? Dump fuel. Establish a rate of descent of approximately 200 feet per minute. Wheels up. Flaps fully extended. The manual advises touching down on the face of a swell, just downslope of the crest.

The theory is one thing, the practice quite another.

You can't ask anyone for their advice. You know of no one who has done this and survived. The trick is to learn the technique rapidly. Get it right the first time. No opportunity for a second try if your first approach doesn't seem right.

Aircraft trembling, shuddering, threatening to tumble like so much scrap metal. Controls spongy, as the airspeed falls away, knot by knot. Soon she will no longer be capable of flight. Only a few more moments then the cold grey sea will claim her. Hold her off as long as possible. Nose up a few precious instants longer. Sea blurring by, horribly close, the water churning, spray whipped by the vicious gale.

The moment of truth. Now. All options gone. Insufficient speed, insufficient height. Nothing left to do but to attempt to set her down as gently as possible on that angry surface.

Are the passengers prepared? Heads down, hands clasped in approved fashion? Feet flat on the floor? Meal trays stowed and secured?

Too late to enquire. Too late for anything now but the application of every ounce of instinct, every particle of skill to the business of touchdown . . .

Please, God . . .

A fearsome impact. An instant of helplessness while brains, organs, nerves and muscles fight to survive the shock. Senses reeling, trying to escape from the torture chamber the body has become. Disbelief that it would be so incredibly overpowering. Structure folding, tearing, crumbling. Shocked screams of humans and metal under hideous stress . . .

Now the onslaught of water.

It comes bursting through the shattered cabin windows. Spurting in through rips in the metal hull, bubbling up through the distorted floor.

Quickly, horrifyingly quickly.

Numbingly cold, it clasps at naked hands that still grip useless flying controls. It runs, as if in gleeful exploration, up sleeves and across legs and laps.

Splashing, surging, it creeps up the cabin wall.

Get out! For Christ's sake, escape!

Turn to the left, towards the captain's seat.

But I'm not in the flight deck of a jetliner. I am in a little cockpit.

A ridiculously cramped space of wooden struts, wing above, visible through the small, flat transparent panels . . .

A girl. A leather helmet framing her small face. Hands outstretched, fingers clutching, seeking.

'Adam, Adam, for God's sake do something . . . !'

I try to answer but frigid water fills my mouth. I see the water splashing in her face, the drops running down her cheeks like tears.

I try—God, how I try—to reach her hand. But the rushing water pushes my arm aside as if it is a trifling bit of flotsam.

The greedy water invades the cabin, bubbling eagerly into every corner and crevice. Your arms strike out in impotent combat. You try to speak. The stuff is in your mouth, choking you. Then in your eyes. Over your head. Your hands are two indistinct shapes waving ineffectively before you, like seaweed.

I see her. Still struggling, still grasping for God only knows what, trying to fight off the tons of water pouring in . . .

The words are formed but they can't emerge. I *have* to tell her. It's urgent, desperately important. But that awful, crashing weight of water keeps the message within me . . .

Five minutes past two.

Joyce looked up at me. I was sitting up in bed.

'Adam, what on earth . . . What's the matter?'

Brain tumbling, spinning. A moment's puzzling over the sight of my arms outstretched before me in the darkness. No bubbling, boiling ocean. No one drowning before my eyes.

'Sorry,' I said. My voice sounded a little odd, slightly higher pitched than was usual.

'Are you all right?'

'Perfectly,' I replied.

God, how I fancied a hearty Scotch at that moment.

'Bad dream?'

For some reason I didn't want to admit it. Did I subconsciously consider it unmanly to own up to having bad dreams? 'Must have been something I ate,' I said. 'The cream puffs probably. Or possibly the Brussels sprouts. I've never been keen on Brussels sprouts.'

'Are you sure you're all right?'

Joyce was leaning on one elbow regarding me with something midway between interest and trepidation; I fancied she wasn't at all sure what was going to happen next.

'Perfectly all right. Sorry I woke you. Go back to sleep.'

I lay back. The blood seemed to be hurtling round my body at twice its normal speed. You could hear it. Why didn't Joyce turn and ask what the din was? Damn it, the stuff was positively *thundering* through my arterial system.

I still trembled at the frightful feeling of claustrophobia, the ghastly containment, the awful, voracious water crushing the breath in my lungs, squashing the life out of my body . . .

Poor Mae, poor bloody hopeless Mae. Struggling simply because it was her body's automatic reaction. It wouldn't have done the slightest good or preserved life an instant longer. Indeed it would have had the opposite effect, helping to consume the last molecules of oxygen more rapidly . . .

But perhaps it didn't happen like that at all. Perhaps she had the great good fortune to hit the water hard enough and fast enough to smash the life out of her instantly, sparing her the agony of death by drowning. But the chances were against it. I worked it all out. Consider the dangers of such a flight at that period. The first and greatest hazard was the take-off. The aircraft would have been grossly overloaded with fuel. It was reported, however, that Mae and Jack Thornton did manage to drag their Bellanca into the air and were seen heading out over the ocean. Might the aircraft have broken up in the air? Possible but unlikely. The Bellanca was a tough, well-built aircraft. The most likely problem was engine failure. And in that eventuality, the descent would almost certainly have been gradual, a long, hopeless glide while the crew vainly searched for a ship as they worked to get the engine started again. How incredibly, horribly lonely the ocean must have looked to them as they levelled out . . . Then the frightful impact; the aircraft settling awkwardly, nose dragged down by the weight of the useless engine, water pouring in through shattered cabin windows . . .

It was sickening, contemplating what the two of them must have gone through, Mae and Jack Thornton, as the water claimed them, all hope gone for ever. How long did it take? How long before their ordeal was over?

A hell of an end for a brave soul like Mae. And Thornton, of course. Funny, how I kept forgetting about Thornton. So did most of the press, too, I gathered. Mae had been the glamorous figure; Thornton was just another male flyer in a world suddenly full of them.

* * *

'I dreamt about that girl last night, the one who was killed trying to fly the Atlantic.'

Joyce was reading *The Observer*; it was folded on the table before her.

'Mae Nolan?'

'That's the one. Had quite a nightmare. Realistic as hell. Thought I was in the plane with her and the water was pouring in. Most unpleasant.'

'Why didn't you tell me last night?'

'I thought it was the Brussels sprouts.'

'Pardon?' Eyes still on the *Observer* leader as she nibbled a slice of wholewheat toast.

'Nothing.'

It was Sunday morning. When I was at home we had a leisurely breakfast on Sunday mornings, complete with bacon and eggs, sometimes kidneys and mushrooms too; lots of coffee, lashings of marmalade.

I looked forward to our Sunday morning breakfasts. They were our private little treat for ourselves, a time for laziness and indulgence. At one time we had had interminable conversations over Sunday breakfasts, solving many of the great problems of our time, from abortion to the arms buildup. I asked Joyce if there was anything of particular interest in *The Observer*. Not really, she informed me, still reading. I was a little disappointed that she didn't find something, something to point to, to shake her head at, something to share.

Her birthday was coming up in a little over three weeks. I had no idea what to buy her. The strange thing was, back in the early days, when we hardly had a couple of bob between us, there was never any doubt in my mind about presents for her. Now, when I could afford reasonably valuable gifts, I hadn't the foggiest.

Perhaps I would see if Harrods had anything similar to the jacket I had bought in Toronto and had lost.

'Any coffee left?' I asked.

'I think so.'

'I'll do it.'

I poured the stuff.

'Thanks,' she said.

'Don't mention it,' I said.

Perfectly harmless fragments of conversation.

Why, then, did they concern me?

Was it that nothing was the same any more? And was it my fault? Or was it Mae's?

Mae's? What on earth was I thinking of, blaming *her?* Poor girl, she could hardly be blamed for my troubles at home, whatever they were—and to be perfectly honest, I wasn't at all sure. Our troubles seemed to defy categorization. As I sipped my coffee, I wondered. Was this what happened to all marriages? What *was* different? Well, I told myself, for one thing we used to indulge in a rather excellent line of insults. It used to be fun thinking up little verbal whips. Was there, indeed, some subtle streak of masochism in it? When did we stop insulting one another? Was it simply a matter of losing interest? When did we start finding it too much trouble to think up biting things to say? At one time she had been fond of pointing out how brilliantly she managed both her careers, the one at home and the one at the office.

I used to call her Saint Joyce.

She in turn called me the Intrepid Aviator.

'Do you remember, I used to call you Saint Joyce?'

She nodded, without looking up from the paper. 'Yes, I remember.'

She might have been talking about a film we had seen when we first met. Something starring Nova Pilbeam or Jack Buchanan. There was, I observed, the tiniest tightening of the mouth. On the port side. As if she was thinking, Oh God, let's hope he isn't going to become maudlin and start talking about the marvellous old days and how we should try to recapture that feeling.

Don't worry, I informed her silently, I have no intention of doing anything of the sort.

She folded the paper and put it down. Picked up the tray and started gathering the breakfast things.

'Can't sit around all day,' she said. She had said it several hundred times to my certain knowledge. At one time she used to infer that I was guilty of trying to lure her into laziness and one or two even more pleasurable sins. Not now. She simply said it as if it was a line in a play that had to be said because it was in the script and there would be complaints if she didn't say it.

'I'll give you a hand with the washing up,' I said.

She shook her head. A quick little shake. 'No need. I can manage.'

Too bloody true. I thought of the dream again. The chilling reality still lingered. It was as if I had *been* there; the events had a hard definition in my memory. Which was patently absurd. I had never experienced a ditching. I didn't know what one *felt* like. And yet I *did* know, now. I remembered tiny details about that cabin; the handwritten notes pinned to the framing, instructions on the switching on and off of the various fuel tanks in order to keep the aircraft in balance during its long flight, and wind data from the Weather Office in the last hour prior to the take-off, a single glove floating on the ebullient water surface, a sodden chart, half a dozen unsmoked cigarettes, disintegrating . . .

21

'Been feeling more or less all right, have you?'

The medical examiner had a disconcertingly bored way of talking, as if his mind was on other matters of more importance. He sounded as if he really didn't care very much about the answers to his questions. He frowned as he spoke, apparently finding the taking of my blood pressure infinitely tedious and wearying.

I told him that I had been feeling well. *Very* well. I knew the bastard of old; he had examined me dozens of times; he knew my systems better than I knew the Jag's. The old sod's apparent ditheriness was misleading; he had a reputation for uncanny skill at locating odd murmurs and rumbles that could put paid to a man's career.

'Been sleeping well?'

Tiny quiver somewhere down in the region of my solar plexus. Had he found something? Did he know something?

'I've been sleeping perfectly,' I said, not quite truthfully, but what the hell.

'Lucky. Step on the scales, will you?'

Why did he ask about sleep? Was there some tell-tale sign that told him I had been experiencing strange dreams followed by long periods of wakefulness? Were giant bags growing beneath my eyes?

'You're down four and a half pounds.'

'Good,' I said.

'Good?' Suspiciously.

'Jogging,' I said. 'Thought I should peel off a few pounds.'

'Don't overdo it.'

'I won't.'

'And do try not to get run over. I'm always hearing of joggers being run over.'

'I'm careful to look where I'm going.'

An unpleasant six-monthly ordeal, this testing of the airline's human equipment to ensure that it is in as good working order as the engines, hydraulics, electrics and airframes.

'Play any sports, do you?'

The old bastard liked to throw questions at you without warning, trying to catch you off guard.

What did I tell him the last time?

'An occasional game of tennis.'

'Occasional?'

'Once a week or so . . . in the summer.'

'What about now, in the winter?'

'I jog,' I lied.

A grunt as he peered at my records.

'Married?'

'Yes.'

'Children?'

'No.'

'Parents still alive?'

'Yes.'

'Ages?'

More grunts as he scribbled.

'How much do you drink?'

Another little flutter of guilt down there in my more vulnerable portions. 'Very little,' I told him. 'A social drink once in a while—a rare while—that's all.'

'Relax,' the old goat snapped as he applied the sticky pads to my chest in preparation for the ECG. 'Can't do this properly if you're all tense.'

'Sorry. I find it rather difficult to relax at such times.'

'Can't think why.'

He had peered into my eyes and ears and into assorted orifices. I kept expecting him to find something that would explain it all, some component that had gone wonky. But perhaps a minor operation or a bottle of medicine would put everything back in tip-top order—and I would kick myself for not having had the sense to get the problem seen to months before. A fortnight had passed since my visit to Abbottsport and Merton. I had sent Beverly the note and the twenty dollar bill. I had thanked her for her generous help. Did it sound a bit off-hand? I wondered afterwards. I had done a couple of trips to Montreal but I hadn't contacted her. I had wanted to—indeed, I had started to dial her number, then I had stopped. Why? I wasn't sure. Yes, I was. I liked her. Good reason, therefore, not to ring her.

'You seem to be in reasonably good working order,' the old quack murmured disinterestedly.

'Really?' Half of me had been certain he would find something horribly wrong. I had been subconsciously preparing myself for the worst. 'Jolly good,' I added hastily. I had a new lease on my professional life. I had been declared fit for another six months of flying an unsuspecting public all over the place. I dressed myself in the minute ante-room, then I poked my head in the office and wished the doctor a very good morning. He glanced up from his desk and looked at me rather vaguely, as if only partially sure who I was; no doubt he would have recognized my tonsils instantly.

The sun had peeped through the heavy cloud cover; there was a touch of warmth in the air, a hint that spring was just around the corner. I could feel the definite bounce in my step. A reassuring feeling, to have been given the official stamp of approval of the medic—the CAA-approved medic at that. It solved nothing, of course, I was still as mystified about everything as ever. Nevertheless, it was good to know that the basic equipment was in good working order. I breathed deeply. It was a pleasure to stride along the sun-splashed street and smell the fresh, mild air. Passers-by had an alert, alive look; the sunshine was a tonic. The well nourished businessman in the grey suit glanced about him as he walked, apparently agreeably surprised to see the fire station still in its proper position next to the sweet shop. The girl crossing the street had a pleasant smile for the bobby at the corner. A month ago she would have hurried past him without a glance. I thought of Beverly. And felt slightly guilty about doing so. Beverly had been so marvellously enthusiastic about London. How she would have enjoyed this sunny, balmy day. So many places to go, things to see. Yes, but hold on there, old fellow, wasn't I conveniently forgetting about Joyce? I remember asking myself the question quite sternly, as if admonishing myself for sins yet uncommitted.

I shrugged. A passer-by glanced at me curiously, eyebrows raised, no doubt asking himself what this odd bod was up to.

I suppose I must have tramped along for a couple of hours. Suddenly I realized that I was both hungry and thirsty. As luck would have it, a cosy-looking pub hove into view at that moment. I went in. It was a warmly furnished place, with plenty of oak panelling and large, welcoming counters. A ruddy-cheeked girl stood behind the bar. She had a merry smile, the sort of smile that said what a lot of fun life could be and that, if you played your cards right, she might even be induced to explore that thought a little with you. Charming dimples on either side of her boldly-lipped mouth. Eyes alive and bright, possessing lids that were vaguely sensuous because they had a fullness about them. Why, I wondered, did a fullness in the lids suggest frolics in the bedroom? It was, the two of us agreed, a very nice day indeed, full of promise of a summer that was taking its own sweet time in coming but which seemed perhaps to be finally on the way and about time too and no mistake about it. Easy to chat with, this one. And apparently deriving a good deal of pleasure from my company. I had a large whisky. Might she care to join me in a spot of libation? Yes, as a matter of fact she might just do that and it was to be a small Bristol Cream, thank you very much. I suggested that while she was getting it she might as well pour me another whisky to celebrate such a jolly day. Come to think of it, a spot of something to eat wouldn't be such a dusty idea. The pangs were becoming positively insistent. Yes, a ham sandwich would be perfect. Hard to beat a tasty ham sandwich washed down by Scotch, what? All sorts of nourishment there, packed with goodness, indeed you could almost feel it doing its stuff on you even before you started eating and drinking. Yes, she agreed with an appealing intensity, there was no doubt that some things just felt so remarkably *right* from the very start that they simply had to be good for you no matter what the so-called experts liked to say on the subject. And there was no question at all, we both agreed that the so-called experts had a good deal too much to say about just about every subject under the sun these days and the world would probably be a pleasanter place to live in if there weren't quite as many so-called experts doling out their advice in great helpings . . .

She went off to see about my sandwich. I sipped my second Scotch . . .

Half a dozen customers came in and ordered drinks.

The girl returned. The sandwich would be along in a jiffy, she told me with that charmingly twisted smile of hers. A fine figure of a woman. No kid, but a mature woman with heroic lines. Full of vim, a character, with a marvellous personality. Enormous asset to a place like this, no question about it. Was she married? I tried to catch a glimpse of her left hand. But she was busy with customers, gesticulating, her hand moving, never stopping. She was like a mechanical doll in ceaseless motion.

I became aware that she had changed in some subtle way. She moved *differently*. And her hair . . .

Her appearance had become downright *dowdy*.

Why didn't I notice her dowdiness before?

Something wasn't quite right. But I couldn't put my finger on it. Had I downed the two whiskies too rapidly? I felt as if I wasn't really there in that crowded, smoky, noisy bar, the babble of cockney chatter all about me, washing over me like a familiar song.

Song. Yes, there was a song; fragments of it kept emerging between the chatter. It sounded as if it was being played on a hurdy-gurdy. A jangling, discordant din, with a frightful oom-pah rhythm. Definitely not Edmund Thigpen. People chuckled, talked, gesticulated, drank. And smoked. Everyone smoked pipes or cigarettes. You could hardly see across the place for billowing, choking smoke.

Why did I keep looking at the row of bottles behind the bar?

Something was quite definitely wrong with them.

But what?

Was it my vision? Was it something the doc did to me at the medical? Why didn't the silly bastard tell me to avoid alcohol for however-many hours? That had to be it. Something not quite focusing correctly; I seemed to have a disturbingly odd viewpoint of totally familiar things.

The barmaid returned. Smiling broadly.

'Another one, sir?'

There was something peculiar about her face, her colouring.

'I'm not sure . . . yes, why not?'

'That's what I always say,' she confided with a grin.

What the hell had she done to her mouth. And what *hadn't* she done to her eyes?

'A small one this time, I think.'

'Right-oh, sir.'

She planted the drink on the counter. Again I experienced that curious sense of not being quite where I thought I was.

'That'll be elevenpence,' she said.

I stared at her. 'What did you say?'

But she was already talking to another customer. 'What was that, Harry? A pint of bitter? Half a mo'.' Now she turned to me once more. Still smiling. 'Elevenpence, if you please, sir,' she said, her smile as wide and bright as ever.

But her teeth were bad: misshapen, discoloured.

Why hadn't I noticed before?

'*Elevenpence*?'

The smile was becoming a trifle fixed.

'That's what I said. That's the price. A small whisky. That's what you asked for, wasn't it, sir?'

'Yes . . . of course.'

'Well, that's what you got,' she said, indicating the glass before me. 'A small whisky.'

The customers, all of them, they wore *hats*. Flat cloth caps or trilbies, bowlers or boaters. *Boaters*, for God's sake. Dark suits. White shirts. Lots of stiff collars. One man in glasses wore plus-fours. Another wore a bow tie beneath a winged collar.

I tried to blink it away. In vain. They were still there. And so was the barmaid, a statue, mouth slightly open, hand half outstretched, waiting for her elevenpence.

Now I saw what was wrong with the rows of bottles behind her. It was the labels. Familiar labels. But the lettering, the designs: they were different—*wrong*—in various subtle ways.

Which was when I spied the calendar.

Wednesday, the second of March.

1927.

22

I must have rushed out of the place, but I have no recollection of doing so. I found myself sprawled awkwardly on the step, halfway across the pavement.

''ad enough, 'ave you, mate?'

A chuckle from a passing youth in jeans and leather jacket; he had a long, rather grubby looking plume of hair that stuck out sideways from his head; it wobbled, flag-like in the breeze.

'I tripped,' I heard myself say.

Laughing, the youth said he believed me but thousands wouldn't.

I scrambled to my feet and brushed myself off. The heel of one hand had been grazed; blood was starting to ooze. My knee hurt. But I didn't bother to look at it. I was far more interested in the traffic.

Minis and Datsuns, Cortinas and Volkswagens. An everyday collection of mass-produced vehicles. Nothing, absolutely nothing to deserve a second look. But I kept gazing at the cars streaming by. A beautiful sight. Beautifully ordinary. An endless shuffling stream of modern traffic. Not a 1927 model among them. The people too: the youth in his jeans, the girl in slacks, the motor-cyclist in his crash-helmet. *Today* people. Above us, a 747 cruised in the direction of Heathrow.

Shouldn't have had so much Scotch on an empty stomach. Perfectly simple explanation . . .

I was startled when a man emerged through the door behind me. My insides contracted, as if I was preparing myself for a rugby tackle.

Relax. A singularly unexceptional individual. Portly. Bald. Ruddy cheeks. Pipe. Pink shirt. And no hat.

He glanced at me, moved his head in a movement so subtle, so insignificant that it might have been a nod; it might just as well have been a wobble induced by the wind.

'Mind the step,' I said.

'What? Yes, bit tricky, that. Good day.'

'Good day,' I responded.

The man went on his way. I gazed at the pub door, trepidation fluttering about within me. Ridiculous, of course, being nervous about anything as unimportant as entering that door. Just another pub; I'd been in enough pubs, hadn't I? I knew what to expect. The calendar? The people? Nonsense. Imagination plus a spot too much Scotch. That was all there was to it. What tripe to think that going through that door took you back half a century or more. Why hesitate then? I gulped; I was scared, actually *scared* of going back inside the pub. My innards seemed to shrivel within me. I had to force myself. Right foot forward; grasp handle; push.

The warm hoppy smell wafted over me as I stood in the doorway. After the sunny street, the interior of the pub was dark, the figures indistinct. But as my vision improved I saw that they were as ordinary and as *today* as the telly listings.

I turned to close the door behind me.

And froze.

A glimpse of the street. A fleeting glimpse of Baby Austins and Morrises, a boy pedalling a tricycle delivery cart, the corpulent man striding by with his pipe and his tweed suit and his tweed hat. A horse and cart. A billboard advising all and sundry that *The Vagabond King* was on at the Winter Garden Theatre. And a toothless ancient turning the handle of a hurdy-gurdy.

A woman walked by the pub, wearing a short, shapeless dress. She had a cloche hat that clung to her head like a skull cap.

The door swung to, blocking off the scene.

I think I muttered something or other. A man glanced at me oddly. Instinctively, I suppose, I turned and retreated into the pub. What was happening? What did it all mean? I was imagining it, of course. I kept telling myself that I was imagining it all . . .

'Sir?'

The girl was behind the bar, grinning as if I was an old friend.

'Your whisky. And your sandwich.'

I asked her how much I owed her.

'A pound forty,' she said.

Heavenly words.

'Thank you very much,' I said, handing her two pound notes.

The rows of bottles looked exactly as rows of bottles should look: jolly and full of promise. The labels? Perfect. Nothing the least bit peculiar about them.

The woman smiled. Her teeth were white and regular.

The whisky was gone in a moment. Another was necessary without delay. I had to sit down. Balance becoming a shade suspect. Things wobbled a trifle.

The bar kept shifting an inch or two as I settled my right elbow on it. I was, I admitted, slightly inebriated. But, considering my input in the last little while, it would, I decided elaborately, have been a miracle if I wasn't slightly inebriated. Funny, how light and frothy I felt inside.

'Thought you'd forgotten about it.'

'Forgotten?'

'Your whisky and your sandwich.'

'Good heavens, no.'

I had a bite. I was no longer hungry.

'All right, is it?'

'Superlative,' I tried to say but the word became a trifle muddled somewhere between my tongue and my lips.

I watched a nondescript fellow make his way to the door, raincoat flapping about his legs.

He pushed the door open with the air of a man who owned half a dozen places this big.

I glimpsed the street through the open doorway. Minis once more. A perfectly ordinary street scene. Everything precisely as it should be.

'Another, sir?' A man's voice this time. A small moustache. A spot of work with the comb and the barman could have done a good turn as Hitler.

'Just one. A small one.'

'Right, sir.'

I had another bite of my sandwich. Part of it seemed to stick in my throat.

The thing to do, I decided, was to follow someone out. If I did that everything should be all right. No chance for whatever-it-was to play any tricks. I downed my latest Scotch quickly. Liquid fortification for whatever might lie out there in those uncertain streets. The pub now seemed to be anchored firmly in the last quarter of the twentieth century. Gloriously contemporary. It showed no sign of wanting to slip back half a century or so.

Another patron bidding the public a farewell. Tall, lugubrious looking chap with an odd little beard.

'Cheerio,' I said to no one in particular.

I followed the man. Past the gent's toilet door. Past the pseudo-computer game. Past the picture of Queen Victoria.

The street. Nothing at all to worry about. Perfectly ordinary. Perfectly delicious.

The signboard advertised a video game. How did I manage to get it confused with *The Vagabond King*, for God's sake?

Shouldn't drink, that was the truth of it. I possessed remarkably little resistance to alcohol. Why, I asked myself, do you keep on verifying the fact? Stupid, infantile. I declared solemnly, there and then, that the stuff would never pass my lips again. A new leaf in the life of Adam Beale. Madness, glugging down Scotch on an empty stomach. That was the root of the problem, of course. Empty innards. Hadn't touched a thing all day. Quite balmy when you stop to think about it. Should have gone out and had some eggs and bacon immediately after the medical. Set oneself up for the day, a plateful of eggs and bacon. But no, I accused myself, you go trotting into the nearest boozer and *imbibe*. Shameful. Thoroughly reprehensible behaviour. Not worthy of a pilot of Anglo-World. Lucky, no one from the line saw you flopping about on your hands and knees outside the pub. Bloody disgusting exhibition. And *seeing* things! Actually seeing things from the 'twenties! Funny clothes. Old cars. I wondered about calling Joyce and telling her the glad tidings about the medical. Job secure for another six months. Hard on the wives, these medicals. Everyone said so. Hard on the victims, too. You get a trifle tense and snappy when you know they're going to be prodding and probing, testing and thumping, doing their level best to end your career . . . On second thoughts it was perhaps not the most propitious moment to ring Joyce. Voice not *quite* as precise as it might be; the ever-present danger of the odd slur and slip. Very touchy, Joyce, when I slurred and slipped, even the *teeniest* bit. Once she had the temerity to suggest that I was a potential alcoholic. Implied that given the right circumstances the habit could beat me. Lot of absolute tripe, of course. Purely social drinker. Seldom feel the *need* for a drink. Must, however, admit to a slight tendency to over-indulge to a degree at times. But hardly a major crime. What was that chap's name? Armstrong? Armitage? Captain. Drank like a fish. But never when flying—or at least, never got caught at it. Once confided to me that he spent every waking moment yearning for a drink. Couldn't wait for retirement, he said. His plan was to sit down and drink himself into insensibility. Retired now, was Armstrong or Armitage or whatever the hell his name was. Did he indeed drink himself into insensibility the day he retired?

Anyway, no danger of Adam Beale sinking to such depths. Hadn't said Adam Beale just declared himself a teetotaller?

A cinema. An oasis of darkness and rest in the sunny, noisy and rather frightening streets. I bought my ticket and wandered in, pausing to have my ticket ripped in half by a spotty-faced youth with a grubby collar.

I collapsed thankfully into the upholstered chair. I was exhausted; God knows how far I had walked. The place was almost empty; there was room to stretch out a bit. A recorded orchestra was vigorously rendering a selection from *Show Boat*. I looked up at the elaborate cornices and columns, the ceiling with its ornate paintings of angels and cherubs cavorting in simple-minded delight, clutching flowers, with a bevy of small birds fluttering about wearing slightly astonished expressions. Some long-forgotten somebody must have worked hard on that, I mused sagely. A shame that the vast majority of people using the cinema simply arrived and departed in the darkness without even looking up at the poor blighter's work. It was one of the minor tragedies of our time. The unknown artist had laboured in the belief that the place was going to be a theatre and would spend much of its time brilliantly lit, with audiences looking at one another and the intricacies of the building itself . . . Poor chap. I felt genuinely sorry for him; I shook my head thinking about it as the lights dimmed.

The darkness was a balm. Sit back. Relax. Absolutely nothing to do for the next couple of hours but look at the screen. Perhaps close the old eyes and nod off for a bit too. Didn't sleep all that well the night before; never did, the night before a medical. The old brain working away at top speed imagining all the thousands of incredibly hideous things that could be wrong with one . . .

A piano began to play, rambling phrases, snatches of tunes that wobbled rather uncertainly into snatches of other tunes, a vaguely tango-like rhythm becoming a waltz then a sort of march.

The curtains parted. The image flickered on the screen. Clare Bow in *Hula*. With Clive Brook.

Clara *Bow*?

It began. Flickering images of figures in ludicrous postures, mouths working but producing nothing; snatches of tortured dialogue *printed* on the screen; and all the time the piano clattering away . . .

'Oo, she's lovely,' hissed a woman's voice from the row behind.

'So's 'e.'

I turned. Two women, in their forties, by the look of them, plump faces framed in tight-fitting hats.

'Sorry, I'm sure,' said one.

In the lobby, I found the youth with the grubby collar.

'What film are you showing?' I asked him.

'E.T.'

'They're showing some idiotic old silent thing.'

'What?'

'Look for yourself,' I snapped.

'All right,' said the youth. He hurried into the auditorium, returning a moment later. 'Looks like *E.T.* to me,' he said. 'You'd better go home and sleep it off, mate.'

I opened my mouth to respond. But there was nothing to say. I could only glare at the youth and wonder what the hell was happening to me. I had seen the title on the screen. What was the name of it? *Hula.* Definitely. Clara Bow and Clive Brook. Without question. But the two women in the row behind me? Did I imagine them too?

'You want to go back and 'ave another go?'

Cheeky little blighter.

No, I didn't want to go back into that damned place. I didn't trust the screen and its images. Something out of kilter somewhere. I sat down on a squeaky chair.

'You all right?' the youth enquired, distaste on his undistinguished features.

People had been asking me that question all day. Starting with that sod of a medical officer. Everyone wanted to know if I was all right.

A ghastly day. All sorts of odd happenings. Undoubtedly brought about by too hasty and too enthusiastic consumption of Scotch. The truth is, I informed myself, you simply can't take it. You're going to give it up entirely, aren't you? You promised.

'You all right, sir?'

God, another one. A skinny sombre looking cove in a striped suit and a nondescript tie.

'Pardon.'

'I'm the manager, sir. I thought perhaps you weren't feeling quite up to the mark.'

'Up to what mark?'

'Just an expression, sir.'

'Did you ever show a film called *Hula*?'

'I don't recall the title, sir.'

'Clara Bow was in it.'

Frosty, prim smile. 'That would have been rather before my time, sir.'

'What? How long before your time?'

Smile fading rapidly. 'I couldn't say.'

'Don't you know when that film was shown?'

'I haven't the faintest.'

'Ten years ago? Twenty? Fifty?'

'Nearer fifty, I should say.'

'That's what I should say too,' I tottered to my feet. 'Very good of you to provide me with the information.'

'My pleasure, sir. Are you quite sure you're all right?'

'Right as bloody rain,' I said.

* * *

That evening Joyce made her big announcement.

23

I had a couple of restless hours' sleep on the sofa, awaking in a sour, dried-out state, head throbbing, limbs aching and stiff from my unaccustomed perambulations. Joyce had just come in; I could hear her in the hall stepping briskly into the front room with a brief pause to look at the post. It took a kind of mental lurch to make myself think back over the peculiar events of the day. For the umpteenth time I blamed it all on an imagination that was too active and Johnnie Walker that was too plentiful. I sat up and tried to blink away the cobwebs. My eyelids stung. An earnest-looking fellow on the television informed us of the problems of nuclear waste. I had no recollection of turning the set on.

'Hullo,' Joyce said.

'Hullo,' I said in what I hoped was a cheerful tone. 'Passed my medical with flying colours.'

'Pardon?' She stared. 'Your medical? My God, I'd completely forgotten about it. I'm glad you passed. There was no reason why you shouldn't, was there?'

A matter of opinion, I thought.

She sat down opposite me. I expected her to say something about an odour of alcohol in the place; she usually knew if I had downed a mere brown ale or two. I remember thinking that she looked as if she had just arrived at the office, not home; she had the air of someone about to start work.

'Do you have to watch that?' she asked.

'Watch what?' I had forgotten that the telly was on. 'No, I don't want to watch it,' I assured her.

She got up and crossed to the television and turned it off, then she returned to her chair and sat down again. Oddly formal movements, as if it was some sort of ceremony.

'Have you eaten?' I asked her.

She nodded. 'I had a bite in town.'

I expected her to ask me about my evening meal but she didn't.

'There's something I'd like to talk to you about,' she said.

Christ, I thought. Rarely had I felt less like talking. I was conscious of distinct stirrings of hunger, yet I could think of no form of solid food that appealed to me.

'Fire away,' I said.

'This is difficult, Adam,' she said.

'What is?' My brain still seemed fuzzy. I glanced at the digital clock beside the stereo. A quarter to seven. A quarter *of* seven, Beverly was wont to say.

'I think it's best to be honest and frank.'

'No argument there,' I said.

She took a deep breath; I saw her nostrils flare. Then the words came quickly, almost tonelessly, as if they had been rehearsed too often.

'I've decided to leave you, Adam. I've thought about it a great deal. It's not an easy decision, but I am convinced that it's for the best. I want you to know that I bear you no grudge. I just think that we've simply grown too far apart. We aren't a unit any more. We're two individuals going through the motions. And they don't mean anything.'

For a moment the truth didn't sink in. I was still hearing the bit about it not being an easy decision.

Then, laboriously, I went back to her first statement.

'*Leave* me? Is that what you said?'

'Yes, Adam.'

The way she held her head made me think she was on the point of saying, 'Yes, please,' as she did when offered a second cup of coffee.

I found myself examining my finger nails.

'Why?' I managed to ask her.

Her cheeks flushed slightly.

'I told you. We've grown apart, Adam.'

'I don't think we've grown apart.'

A tiny sigh, a tiny oh-God-he's-going-to-be-difficult sigh. 'We have, Adam. The truth of the matter, I suppose, is that we're not quite the same people we were a little while ago.'

'So bloody what?' Christ, oh, Christ, wasn't life enough of a convoluted tangle without *this*? 'Everyone changes. It's the natural order of things.'

'I'm aware of that, Adam.'

Why the hell did she keep on saying 'Adam'? There was no one else in the bloody room, was there?

She said she was sorry it had happened but it was a fact and she felt it was essential that we faced the thing sensibly.

'When did you decide this?'

For some reason I wanted to know how long she had had this in mind; it seemed important to be able to think back and say that she was thinking about it *then* and *then*.

But she said she didn't know. 'It's the truth that's been growing more and more apparent for a long time, a very long time. I'm truly sorry it's happened this way . . .'

'But it doesn't *have* to happen,' I said. It was an enormous effort to choose words that would make the point cogently. 'I mean, it's not something that's out of our hands, for God's sake. We can make up our minds about it. The decision is up to *us*, isn't it?'

She nodded. Another deep breath. 'There's someone else, Adam.'

'Oh shit,' I said. It made nonsense of everything I had just said. It seemed vaguely unfair of her to bring in an element like this. Someone *else*? 'Who is this . . . someone else?'

Yet another deep breath. Odd, the way she hadn't moved all the time we had been talking. Her legs and hands were perfectly still, precisely arranged.

'Jeremy Forsythe,' she said.

'But he's married,' I exclaimed, naïve as ever. I thought immediately: *she's* just as bloody well married as he is.

Joyce said, 'It's not easy but sometimes in life one has to face frightfully painful situations and, well, simply live with the consequences.'

'Jeremy being a consequence.'

'What?'

'Never mind.' I tried to grapple with the thought of Jeremy Forsythe—of all people—possessing the appeal to wrest my wife away from me. For a lunatic instant I thought he might be forcing her to leave me against her will. I said, 'And may one ask just how long has this been . . . going on?'

Why was I so captivated by the chronology of the thing?

'I don't think that's important, Adam, what is important is that we face up to a fact of life. You do see that, don't you? And, after all, it isn't as if we had a family. It would be awful, wouldn't it, if there were children to consider?'

'I think it's fairly awful even without children. Besides, doesn't Jeremy have a family?'

I seemed to recall the bastard babbling glowingly about his offspring.

'A little girl and a boy.'

'Isn't the boy little too?'

'He's eight.'

'Isn't that little?'

'Yes . . . but not so little as . . . as Gwen.'

For the first time Joyce exhibited a chink in her armour of confidence. 'I rather think they'll stay with their mother.'

'Penelope, isn't it?'

'That's right.'

He called her 'Pen' at the foul Art Directors' Ball. Was Pen at this very moment receiving the ultimatum from Jeremy? Awfully sorry, old girl, I realize this must come as a bit of a shock and all that but it's just one of those things, one of those bells, etcetera . . . Did Jeremy and Joyce stay late at the office this evening discussing strategy? Did they agree to break the news to their respective spouses at a certain time? Did the two conspirators synchronize their watches?

Jeremy Forsythe?

I said, 'Is it really . . . what I mean is, have you really thought about what all this *means*? I mean, *really* means . . .'

Lame as hell and I knew it. What I was really saying was, does Jeremy really possess enough of whatever thrills you to make all the trauma and the hurting worth while?

She was nodding in a jerkily, mechanical way. 'Yes, Adam. I've thought it all over a thousand times. I know what I'm doing. I'm really dreadfully sorry . . .'

'Well, that makes it all right then, doesn't it?' It was

a sort of relief to get back on the attack again.

Now she was shaking her head, in just as mechanically a way as she had nodded it. 'No, it doesn't make it all right. I know I'm hurting you and you don't really understand why, at least not yet. I hate having to do this but, well, the fact of the matter is, it's necessary.'

'Like surgery.'

'What? Yes, I suppose you might say that.'

Stupid of me not have stayed with Beverly that night in Abbottsport. After all, might that not have been the very night that she and Jeremy first clambered aboard one another? Did they do it here? On this sofa? 'Come on over, darling, leap on, he's away in America for two more days.' I kept seeing Jeremy naked: bony and white, with pimply skin. How the hell could she possibly find *that* attractive? I know that beauty was supposed to be in the eye of the beholder . . . but *Jeremy*? Was it all a terribly bad joke? Would Joyce suddenly burst out laughing and cackle with glee at how beautifully she had had me on? Nice, momentarily warming thought. But without foundation.

'Jeremy's wife will wallop him for support. Have you thought about that? Two children of tender years. My God, he'll be lucky if he has ten pounds a week left after the court gets through with him.'

Unworthy argument. Did I really expect her to click her fingers and admit that the thought hadn't occurred to her and then declare that she was forthwith abandoning the whole thing?

'We've discussed all that. We know the problems. It's going to be unpleasant. But it has to be done.'

'Why,' I asked, 'does it have to be done?'

She shrugged. Her voice was becoming tighter, losing its patient timbre. 'It has to be done because we think it will make us happy in the long run.'

'But you'll be making two other people extremely unhappy. Have you thought of that?'

'Of course, Adam, of course. But I don't feel really

sorry for you. You haven't really cared for me for years. I mean, *really*. As for Penelope, well, that's quite another thing.'

Did they rate the two victims, so many points for a child, so many for each year of marriage, and so on? Was that built-in female computer handy for such calculations?

I said, 'Aren't you being a bit presumptuous about me? How do you know I'm going to be all right? How do you know I won't go and jump off Tower Bridge?'

She shook her head. The coppery highlights in her hair suddenly became prominent. 'I'm not the least bit afraid of you doing that. You're much too stable and sensible.'

Little did she know.

'And you think you'll be happy with Jeremy?'

'I'm sure of it, Adam.'

'Why?'

'We share interests that are important to us.'

'Advertising?'

'No, art, writing, many things.' At last her hands moved. Her fingers were outstretched as if to lend credence to her next statement. 'I have a great deal of respect for you, Adam, and what you do. I mean, it's important too, in its own way.'

'Thank you very much.'

'I'm not being condescending. Honestly. What you do is difficult and demanding and not many people can do it. I know you'll go on to great things in the airline. But I'd be less than honest if I pretended that I'm deeply interested in your work.'

'Does that matter?' I asked without caring what the answer was. I had the disquieting feeling that we were uttering a large number of words because we were doing something of significance and it simply wasn't right and proper to do anything this significant without talking endlessly about it. So far, I realized, I didn't feel anything. I wondered if it was going to be like one of those serious wounds that aren't painful at first because shock anaesthetizes everything. Would the pain come later, great waves of it? I said, 'I presume you've had it off with Jeremy?'

'That's not a very nice way of putting it.'

'No, but it's apt, isn't it. Well, have you?'

'Really, Adam, I don't think it's something I want to discuss with you.'

Odd, wasn't it, that she didn't want to talk about sex, yet sex was without a doubt the catalyst that had set all this off. What had that sod Jeremy *got*?

Something had happened to the way Joyce looked at me. There was no warmth, no *involvement* in her gaze. Understandable, I suppose. All of a sudden she saw me quite differently. I had undergone a metamorphosis. I was no longer a part of her; I had become a sort of hurdle, a barrier in the way of the perfect happiness she was going to find with that ineffable *bastard*.

'I'm going to move out tonight,' she said.

'*Tonight?*' I was astonished. For some reason I had assumed that weeks of negotiation and discussion lay ahead of us.

'I think it's best,' she said.

'Hot to trot, are you?'

'Adam, please.'

'Where are you going? To his place?'

'I can't very well do that, can I?'

'Perhaps he's already tossed the wife and kids out lock, stock and barrel.'

Then I recalled that the agency had a flat in Mayfair for the convenience of visiting clients whose billings made them worthy of VIP treatment. Among agency personnel it was variously known as The Home for Semen, Erection Alley and Consummation Towers because it was so frequently used by staff members for their flings. I asked if she was moving there.

'Don't be nasty,' she said.

'Christ, no,' I said. 'Dreadfully sorry. How awful of me. How could I think nasty thoughts?'

'Adam, please,' she said again. She had that pained

look: the sensitive soul who is shocked by the rough, crude husband and his unpleasant choice of words. She got to her feet and, automatically, brushed the front of her clothes. She was wearing a tailored cloth and leather outfit that I particularly liked. I had bought it for her last birthday. Unkind of her to wear it on such an occasion, but no doubt she had slipped it on without a second thought. More important things to occupy her mind. She said she was going to throw a few things in a case. She would be back later. It was, she said, better this way.

Hadn't Barbara Stanwyck once said that? In what film?

I found myself wondering about it while I heard Joyce bustling about in the bedroom and bathroom, no doubt counting the instants until she could get out of here and into the arms of . . . *him*.

Christ and bloody hell, I thought. But it was feeble stuff, a pathetic attempt to stir myself to righteous anger. It failed. Would I feel more later, when my hangover finally moved on? Or is it, I asked myself, that you're secretly, subconsciously, rather relieved that this has happened?

I really don't know, I replied to myself.

Joyce reappeared, coat over arm, suitcase in one hand, umbrella in the other.

'Is it raining?' I asked idiotically.

'It was, a bit, when I came in.'

'Ah,' I said.

'I'll be in touch,' she said. 'Soon. And thank you for taking it so well. I really do think it's for the best, Adam. I know you'll see that in due course. You will, really. Are you sure you're all right?'

I was going to ask her if she had any idea how many people had asked me that question in the last twenty-four hours, but it seemed hardly the time or place.

'Is that it?' I enquired.

'What do you mean?'

'I mean, don't we have anything else to say? We

seem to have done all this rather hastily, don't you think?'

'What else do you want to say?' Now that her exit was only moments away some of the patient tone began to re-emerge.

'I don't know.'

'Well, then.'

'It's a sort of premature evacuation, isn't it?'

'For God's sake, Adam.' She unlatched the front door.

'By the way,' I said.

'Yes?'

'It must have been a bit of a disappointment when you found out about Mae.'

'Disappointment?'

'Well, if Mae had still been alive and if she had been a flame of mine, it would have made all this much simpler for you, wouldn't it?'

'I didn't think about that,' she said.

Which disappointed me; I expected a more honest response from Joyce. But, then, I suppose I expected too much from her altogether.

* * *

'Oh *dear*,' said my mother.

'I thought I'd better ring you and let you know,' I told her.

'Well, of course,' she responded. Then she seemed to run out of things to say. No doubt she had a couple of thousand questions she would have loved to ask me, but couldn't ask because I was her son.

'She's moved out,' I said. 'Last night, actually, at about eight.'

'She's *gone*?'

'That's the usual result of moving out, Mother.'

'There's no need to be sarcastic, Adam.'

'Sorry.'

'Are you all right?'

Christ.

'Yes, I'm perfectly all right,' I told her.

'I can hardly believe it. *Joyce.*'

'Yes, Joyce.' It had to be said so I got it over with. 'There's someone else in her life, Mother.'

'Oh *dear*,' she said again.

'Someone at the agency where she works.'

'I can hardly believe it.' The news was making poor Mother repeat herself even more frequently than usual.

'It came as a bit of a shock to me too.'

'But surely you must have had some sort of . . . well, no you say you didn't.'

'Not a bit.'

'You poor dear. Why don't you come here and spend a few days with us? Oh dear, the Websters are coming. Perhaps I can put them off. Yes, I'm sure if I telephone them immediately I can catch them before they leave; they live in Ealing, you know. I can say your father has the flu; they'll understand.'

I assured her there was no need to change her plans. I was flying very shortly, I said. I would have to be getting ready in a couple of hours.

'Do you think you should?'

'Fly? Of course. I'm glad I have to do something.'

'Yes, I can see that,' she said dubiously. 'Dear, I do feel quite dreadful about all this. Is there any chance of a, what's the word, reconciliation? Oh dear, I never thought I'd be saying that about you and Joyce. I thought you were the happiest of couples.'

'So did I.'

'Do the Scriveners know?'

'I haven't the faintest.'

'If Nanette rings . . . she does sometimes, you know.'

'If she calls, Mother, I feel sure you'll be able to tell whether she knows or not.'

'Yes, probably. I do hope this isn't too much of a shock for poor Mr Scrivener.'

Sod poor Mr Scrivener, I thought. 'How's Father?'

'Mm? Oh, the same as ever. This is going to be very bad news for him. He was very fond of Joyce.'

'Yes, I know.' The old blighter fancied her. Now that I was out of the picture, perhaps he could have a shot at winning her away from Jeremy. A piquant situation. 'Give him my best.'

'He's here, Adam. He wants to have a word with you. Just a moment.'

There were muttered fragments of words in the background, then my father's voice came over the line. 'This is dreadful news, my boy.'

'Yes, I know. Rotten, isn't it?'

Whereupon my father proceeded to repeat all the things my mother had just said. The expected things. Except that somewhere in father's voice was a slight hint of annoyance: a reproof for me; I had buggered things up and had caused much grief and embarrassment for a lot of people and most important of all, had lost the family a perfectly adorable creature like Joyce.

'Sorry about this,' I said.

'Yes, well, these things happen. Two out of three marriages go on the rocks in America, they say. Sad commentary, what?'

'Frightful.'

'All right, are you?'

Another one.

'Perfectly.'

'Good show. I understand you're flying off somewhere.' He made it sound as if I was departing on a totally frivolous holiday in some mecca of hedonism. 'Give us a ring when you get back.'

'I will.'

I hung up, with a feeling of intense relief that I had done my duty and had fed the news into the information pipeline. Presumably Joyce must have felt something of the sort when she had unburdened herself on me the previous evening. After she had left I had sat before the darkened television set, half expecting her to return or to telephone, saying that she had thought it all over and had changed her mind and would I please find it in my heart to forgive her? But I sat undisturbed. The hours passed sluggishly. At midnight I went to bed and lay for hours staring at the window, trying not to think of what Joyce was doing at that precise instant. In the morning, after a few hours' sleep, I watched the sun come up and felt sorry for myself.

I boiled an egg and ate, and drank a cup of instant coffee.

Should I have reacted differently? Become violent? Angry at least? I really didn't *do* anything, did I? I tried to remember it all, word by word. Perhaps my lack of reaction served to convince Joyce that I really didn't give a damn about her. But I did. Didn't I? I wasn't sure. Perhaps *that* was the trouble. Being unsure.

There was anger simmering inside me. I hated that bastard Jeremy more than I had ever hated anyone. But did I hate him because he had taken Joyce or because he had hurt my pride? Was it all jealousy? A bloody odd day, yesterday, undoubtedly one of the oddest of my life. And I had finished it up as a bachelor. Free! How many times had I thought how remarkably pleasant it would be to be free again? And now it had happened. And it meant nothing.

24

CAVU weather—ceiling and visibility unlimited—for the entire trip to Kennedy. Hardly a cloud in sight: sun sparkling on shimmering ocean far below, air calm and beautiful, all splendidly well with the world. The odds against encountering such weather all the way across the capricious Atlantic were staggering. I remembered reading that the *Titanic* had enjoyed similar conditions on her maiden voyage. If Mae had chanced upon such a day, she and Jack Thornton might have motored across without the slightest problem. And her name would have become as well known as that of Amelia Earhart. No doubt there would be a sign on the outskirts of Abbottsport: WELCOME TO ABBOTTSPORT, HOME OF MAE NOLAN, FIRST WOMAN TO FLY THE ATLANTIC OCEAN.

Mae had scarcely entered my thoughts for the last few days. When we left Heathrow I had wondered about her. Would she choose today to play her odd games? Mentally I shrugged the possibility off; I really didn't care. I had enough on my mind. So she ignored me. Perhaps she no longer had any interest in me now that she had succeeded in breaking up my marriage. Funny, how I kept thinking that was her purpose. Even funnier, to keep thinking that a dead girl could have a purpose.

I arrived at the Sheraton at about six—midnight London time. I was tired and depressed; I kept gnashing my teeth when I thought about Joyce and Jeremy. I found a certain comfort in thinking of the various ways in which I could end the earthly existence of Jeremy Forsythe. For the first time in my life I understood how potent the desire for revenge could be. To load your trusty Webley and Scott Mk VI with 0.455 SAA ball ammunition; to thrust it into your belt and go striding down Curzon Street looking for your quarry; to find him and see the terror in his eyes as you pull the trigger. Hash settled once and for all. The notion had an alarming appeal. Just as well, I told myself, that I don't own a Webley and Scott Mk VI—and wouldn't know how to insert the SAA ammunition if I had any. What about Joyce? Why, I wondered, didn't I fantasize about bumping her off? Why put all the blame on poor old Jeremy? You couldn't blame the pathetic blighter for responding when Joyce (for some inexplicable reason) decided to give him the glad eye. She did it so well, so subtly, with an irresistible hint of vulnerability. No wonder he was abandoning wife and children; there would have been something fundamentally wrong with him if he hadn't.

After a salad in the coffee shop I telephoned Beverly's number. No answer. I waited ten minutes then tried again. In vain. I found myself asking where she was. Shopping? At the cinema? Out on a date? No, surely if she was out with someone, there would be a baby-sitter there to look after Russell. Why was I phoning her? I knew the answer to that one. I was lonely. Boo-bloody-hoo. Just as well Beverly was out. Why complicate her life? The bar looked appealing. Two or three Scotches would have done me a power of good. But no, I had to fly home tomorrow. I sat down in the lobby and watched the guests. A man in a silk suit whined to a cigar-smoking acquaintance about the shortcomings of American hotels; he had, he declared loudy, travelled the four corners of the world; he had stayed at hotels like the Dusit Thani in Bangkok, the Grand Palace in Tokyo, Raffles in Singapore, hotels where they knew how to treat guests with 'doo' respect and courtesy, not herd them around like a lot of goddam cattle; the whole trouble with the Western world was that there wasn't any goddam service any more; every crummy waiter and bellboy thought he was just as goddam good as the guy who was paying the goddam bill.

'Excuse me, are you Mr Trotter?'

A girl with attractive, Hispanic features was asking the question: a good looking girl, well dressed and expertly made-up.

I said, no, regretfully I was not Mr Trotter.

'You fit the description,' she said. 'Sorry.'

I assured her that I didn't mind at all. She sat down in one corner of the lobby, close to the main entrance. I noticed that she kept glancing as people entered and left. She spoke to two men; they shook their heads. The elusive Mr Trotter didn't appear. Foolish Mr Trotter, I thought. Forty minutes drifted by. I straightened my tie and wandered in her direction.

Yes, she supposed she might just as well have a drink. She said she didn't know what in hell happened to Trotter. That was the trouble with agents, unreliable as hell. Something better must have come along, so to hell with everyone and everything. That was the way the sons of bitches operated. Yes, she was indeed an aspiring actress. Was I English? Boy, did she admire that Sir Laurence Olivier. There was an *actor*, man. No, she hadn't been in any shows I might have seen. Little theatre stuff. One hell of a business, the theatre. You bust your ass just trying to get a foot in the door, just trying to be *seen*, so you might get a chance to show some *creep* that you can act so maybe he might condescend to give you a crummy break. There was no one, she told me, in the entire theatrical scene in New York who was a gentleman like me.

'You want to ball?' she asked.

I smiled to myself. Did she think I was on my very first trip to the Big Apple? Did she think I knew nothing of the ways of the city?

'I suppose you're making the offer because I'm such a nice fellow and because you find me attractive.'

She nodded, briskly, matter of factly. 'Sure. You're cute. Kind of old. But cute.'

'And how much is it going to cost me?'

She frowned, surprised and hurt. 'You *shit*,' she said. 'I'm not a hooker. I'm a fucking actress,' she added loudly, her voice demonstrating admirable voice projection. Several dozen faces turned in our direction. She got up. And stalked out. It was an impressive exit. It left me feeling small and singularly stupid. I seemed to be incapable of handling any sort of relations with women these days. Perhaps I should become a monk. I finished my club soda, paid the bill and went up to my room, even more dejected than ever. I tried Beverly's number once more. Still no response. I sat down and wrote her a note on hotel stationery, telling her that I tried to reach her by telephone and that I hoped she was enjoying good health—Russell too, of course. I added the news about Joyce. Then: '*I suppose in a way I'm telling you this item of news so that there is no misunderstanding about my marital status. We have something in common, besides Mae Nolan. I want you to know that I have enjoyed your company enormously and of course your help has been invaluable, and I would very much like to see you again in the not too distant future. This trip is a very brief one but I should be having a two-day layover later in the month. I will be in touch. Yours very sincerely, Adam Beale.*'

I reread it. Not exactly effusive, but warm enough. And did I want it to be anything more than it was? I decided not, so I sealed the envelope and mailed the letter downstairs before I changed my mind. Then I had a cup of tea. You have to specify 'hot tea' in the United States to ensure that you aren't given the iced variety. I asked the black waitress please to see that the water in the little chrome-plated tea pot was actively boiling when she brought it to me. No sweat. Glad to oblige, was the pleasant comment. But it made not the slightest difference to the temperature of the water; luke-warm as ever.

* * *

The Morse signals again, faint but insistent in my headset. The same pattern of dots and dashes, repeated endlessly. I jotted them down. Dot, dot, dot, dot, dot. Dot, dash, dash, dash dash. Dot, dot, dot, dot, dash. Dash, dash, dash, dot, dot. Dash, dash, dash, dot, dot. Dot, dot, dash dash dash. Then a moment's pause after which the whole sequence began again. And again. I checked the signals against my notes. No change. I listened to it half a dozen times. Exactly the same series of signals.

I scanned the darkened sky about us. No sign of the Bellanca.

I consulted my Flight Manual. My knowledge of Morse was adequate for identifying navigation signals from beacons and airfields but I couldn't identify these dots and dashes.

I compared my scribblings to the neat columns of type. Without success. The dots and dashes were just a lot of meaningless sounds.

Ah, but were they? I had been looking for *letters*. What about numbers?

Success!

Dot, dot, dot, dot, dot, was *five*.

Dot, dash, dash, dash, dash was *one*.

Dot, dot, dot, dot, dash was *four*.

Dash, dash, dash, dot, dot, was *eight*.

Dash, dash, dash, dot, dot, was another *eight*.

Dot, dot, dash, dash, dash was *two*.

Five, one, four, eight, eight, two.

514882.

I stared at the numerals. They meant nothing.

I listened. No signals now.

514882.

I folded the paper and slipped it into my wallet.

* * *

The emptiness of the flat was overwhelming. I wanted to turn around and go back to the airport. There were people there who knew me, who would engage in conversation over a pint or a cup of coffee, talking of sports or airlines, taxes or politics. Entering the flat was like walking in on a still life. There was the postcard I had dropped on the floor in my haste to leave two days before; my cup and saucer still adorned the sink; the bed was still unmade, the bathroom cabinet still wide open.

'To hell with this bloody place,' I said aloud. My voice seemed to startle the still air. I decided to go out and have a meal in a restaurant. After which I would go to a film or perhaps even a play in the West End. Bad for one, to sit at home and mope. Get out and enjoy oneself, that was the ticket. Have a damn sight better time than one used to have when one was well and truly married . . .

I had a hearty Scotch to seal the bargain with myself, (I would give up alcohol later, when life had settled down again) then I changed into sports jacket and slacks. I was on my way to the front door when there was a brisk rap. I opened the door. Mrs Halliwell. As usual she looked as if she was dressed to visit the Palace. And as usual she regarded me as if I was a footman.

'Ah, Mr Beale, good day to you. Is your wife in? I would appreciate a word with her, if you please.'

I told her that Joyce no longer lived here. Her head snapped back in surprise as if I had leant forward and tapped her bony nose.

'I *see*,' she said. 'That is distressing news, Mr Beale. I copied out a particularly delicious recipe for cream of artichoke and hazelnut soup, something I had been intending to do for your wife for several months. Unhappily, I kept forgetting. My memory isn't what it was. And now that I have finally remembered, she is no longer here.'

'Sorry about that,' I said, wondering why I was apologizing. 'I'd take the recipe but I don't think I'll be making soup,' I said. 'On the other hand, I could give it to one of the stews—the flight attendants—some of them are super in the kitchen.' And elsewhere, I thought.

She peered at me in her incisive way. 'Are you quite well, Mr Beale? Are you getting sufficient to eat?'

'I'm in the pink, Mrs Halliwell. It's kind of you to ask.'

She nodded, agreeing. 'You're a pleasant young man, Mr Beale.' Her eyes hardened. 'And I cannot say as much for many representatives of the younger generation.'

I thanked Mrs Halliwell for including me in the younger generation.

She sniffed. 'I'm not at all sure that I'm doing you a favour, Mr Beale. In my day, young people were taught to look up to and emulate their elders and betters. Nowadays the young have managed to hoodwink their elders into emulating *them.* It's an extraordinary achievement but a self-destructive one, I fear. In the main, Mr Beale, I find them an arrogant and ignorant lot, lacking loveliness, graciousness, charm and manners. It is a great handicap in life to lack any of these qualities but to lack all of them is tragic indeed. How is your friend?' she asked abruptly.

'My friend?' I had to give my mind a mental boot to get it to think at Mrs Halliwell's pace. 'Oh, *him.*'

'Has he had any more experiences of a supernatural nature?'

I nodded and asked her if she would care to come in.

'Only for a little while, Mr Beale. I can't spare you more than a few minutes.'

I sat her down in front of the telly; she accepted a glass of sherry; I poured myself a modest Scotch.

'Your friend encountered a young woman, if I recall.'

'He's not absolutely sure that he encountered *her* . . . it was her aircraft he saw.'

'Ah yes,' she nodded as if nothing could be more commonplace. 'And what has taken place since our last conversation on the subject?'

I had the uncomfortable feeling that I was blushing. I had every reason to blush. 'I believe he has had . . . one or two more encounters with the aircraft. And he's heard odd signals—Morse signals. But apparently he's become almost accustomed to it all . . . it's odd what you can become accustomed to, isn't it?'

'Nothing the least bit odd about it,' declared Mrs Halliwell. 'What else?'

'Well, an occurrence that I can only describe as peculiar. I . . . well, *he* was in a pub and all of a sudden everything became turned *back* . . . back to the 'twenties, you see. The people in the pub, the bottles, the advertisements, it was all more than half a century ago.'

'And what happened?'

'Actually, nothing. A moment later, it was back to today again. Then later on, in a cinema, he suddenly found himself watching a funny old silent with Clara Bow instead of *E.T.*'

'Mischievous,' said Mrs Halliwell.

'I beg your pardon.'

'It sounds as if the lady has a sense of humour.'

I stared. 'How can she have a sense of humour? She's *dead*. She's been dead more than half a century.'

'A sense of humour is by no means unheard of in the other world,' Mrs Halliwell informed me. 'No doubt she was a high spirited young woman in this life. Why, then, should we assume that she lost that characteristic when she went to the other life? It's a pity that you find the notion so difficult to accept, Mr Beale. You should be more flexible in your thinking. Try, Mr Beale, try hard. You may rest assured that the spirits often delight in playing their little tricks. Sometimes I think it's nothing more than a device to gain attention. The princpal characteristic of this particular spirit seems to be persistence, would you not agree? It seems clear to me that such persistence must have a purpose. I imagine she wants to convey something, a message, of some importance I suspect.' She sipped her sherry. 'People have the queer notion that the spirits move in a totally aimless way, just wandering about, frightening the faint of heart. Nothing of the sort. There is purpose there, I am convinced. Case history after case history supports the theory. The purpose is communication.'

'But what is she trying to communicate?'

'My dear boy, how can I possibly say? Your friend will probably be able to comprehend, eventually. You say there is no family connection between the young lady and your . . . friend?'

Did the sly old girl suspect that there was no friend, that in fact I was talking about something that had happened to me? I told her that I knew of no family connection.

'Then I recommend most earnestly that you persuade your friend to consult an expert in the field, someone who will be infinitely better equipped than I am to explain the phenomenon and to unravel its meaning.'

'Yes, but he's a pilot, you see, and the company might find out . . .'

'There's nothing the least bit reprehensible about this!' she snapped, her wisps of eyebrows angling in outrage at the very idea.

'I know. But airlines don't like the notion of their pilots seeing . . . spirits.'

'Why? It's not something they can be *blamed* for!'

'I do agree, Mrs Halliwell. Wholeheartedly.'

* * *

As I drove home from Sunday dinner with my parents, I reflected on the fact that we had not mentioned Joyce's name once during the entire evening. True British phlegm at work. No doubt my parents had scores of questions but they didn't ask them. At the conclusion of the evening's jollities they were as ill-informed about the sordid details of our split-up as they had been at the beginning. We were like three condemned criminals locked together, talking continuously, but studiously ignoring the subject of our impending executions.

Blast Joyce for causing us all this upset! Blast her for making my parents spend a perfectly horrible evening in their own house with their own son. And blast her because I was driving along Baker Street alone, heading for an empty flat—a hideously expensive flat, at that, and one that I had no intention of maintaining on my own. I had to move. God knows when. I shuddered at the thought of all the arrangements to be made, the furniture to be loaded, the myriad *things* to be packed. Weren't we supposed to divide our possessions? What did she want? What did I want, for that matter?

It was all very depressing. Much better not to think about it right away. Much better to file it away for a while. Would there be a day when Joyce would come to the flat and go from room to room, putting chalk marks on this table and that lamp? Did I give a damn what she took? Should I contest everything? I didn't *know*, that was the point. The furniture belonged to both of us, therefore it belonged to neither of us. I rather wished a fire would come along and demolish everything, with the possible exception of my Oscar Peterson and George Shearing tapes; then we could simply divide the insurance proceeds.

* * *

I watched the news, then slotted a Shearing cassette into the deck. It was on George's second chorus of 'Lazy River' that I noticed the absence of the Azoulay. Funny, I had been gazing at the spot on the wall for some minutes before it dawned: the bloody picture simply wasn't there any more! I sprang to my feet and hurried to the spot, examining the brass picture hanger that was still embedded in the wall, looked on the floor behind the bookcase to see if the picture had fallen down. No sign of it. *She* had it. What the hell else had she helped herself to while I was away? What a bloody cheek! I stormed through the flat on a rapid tour of inspection. A couple of figurines and three old framed maps of Cumberland seemed to be missing. No doubt there were more, but it would take a closer look to find out. How dare she come strolling in to the place as if she still owned it, helping herself to whatever took her fancy! Bloody unforgivable behaviour! It was then that I noticed the note. Propped up against the flower pot on the mantel. *Dear Adam, I rang you but there was no reply. I hope you don't mind, I popped in and picked up a few more clothes, also a couple of things that I wanted and was pretty sure you didn't. Trust you're keeping fit. Joyce.*

I should have changed the locks the moment she walked out. She seemed to regard my home as sort of storage shed for her stuff. Was the insufferable one with her? Advising? Was she already sick of him? Did she look about the old place and feel a tugging at the heart? Regretting everything?

Damn and bloody hell!

I felt my flesh crawl at the thought of that smarmy bastard Jeremy walking around *my* flat, sticking his long nose around, sniffing here and there, feeling things with those long, mobile fingers of his. How dare he *presume!* God, if only it were possible to wring his scrawny neck!

I could kill, yes, by God, I could, I knew I could! How dare that swine steal Joyce. That's what he did, damn him to hell, he *stole* my wife! I felt the surging anger, that atavistic rage that has swept through man since time immemorial. At that moment it was incomprehensible to me that I had taken it all so placidly when Joyce broke the news. What was the matter with me? Was it shock? Was I too stunned to react? Too dense? Perhaps it was because I had been drinking earlier in the day. I was in no condition to cope with her pronouncement. By God, I should storm into that bloody office, go into that swine Forsythe's office and wring his scrawny neck right there and then! That would teach the bastard to go around stealing other fellows' wives! Kill the devil. Yes, I could do it. And, Lord, wouldn't it make those idiotic advertising people sit up and take notice! And Joyce! Yes, Joyce most of all. How prim and professional would she be if she saw darling Jeremy getting himself well and truly throttled! And serve him bloody well right! That would give all the advertising bods something *real* to think about for a change! People had the right idea back in the old days; they damn well did what came naturally—and there was no question that putting paid to a sod who stole your wife had to be categorized as doing what came naturally . . .

Then what? Mental glimpses of police and court rooms, prisons and warders. Thoughts to sober one.

But, by God, there really wasn't any need to kill him! No, a hard fist in the nose would do very nicely indeed! Flatten the sod all over his layouts. Then stalk out, past the rows of wide-eyed employees, out past the reception desk, a wry smile from Sally from Trinidad, then off to God only knows what conquests in the big world outside . . .

I slept soundly that night. At ten the next morning I rang Joyce's office.

Sally answered. When I asked if Jeremy Forsythe was in, she hesitated.

'I'm not . . . I don't think so, Mr Beale, I'm sorry. I can put you through to his secretary, Miss Nolan.'

'Who?'

'Mr Forsythe's secretary.'

'Yes, but what did you say her name was?'

'Miss Nolan.'

'How do you spell it?'

'N.O.L.A.N.'

The chill started in my shoulders and ran down my spine. Down. Not up. I recall distinctly. I asked what Miss Nolan's Christian name was.

'Doreen,' said Sally.

'Not Mae?'

'No, I'm sure of that. It's Doreen. Shall I put you through to her?'

'No, don't bother. Thanks anyway.'

'Nice to talk with you, Mr Beale.'

Evidently she knew she was not likely to be talking to me much in the future. Stupid of me to react like that to the name Nolan. It was common enough, for goodness' sake.

Was I glad that Forsythe was out of his office? Come now, be honest, I demanded of myself. Wasn't that a glimmer of relief that floated around inside when Sally said he was out? Relief or frustration? I had to tell myself the truth. It depressed me. A dismal thing, my anger: it couldn't sustain itself for the length of a telephone conversation: a thoroughly pathetic imitation of what my ancestors must once have felt. Those old fellows wouldn't have let it flicker and dim like a camp fire in a windstorm. Was this what civilization did? Shoving reason in the way? Intruding, sticking its idiotic nose in where it didn't belong? You couldn't help but admire the chaps who refused to permit reason to interfere, the sort who plunged ahead and did what they knew was right and to hell with the consequences. But, try as I might, I knew that wasn't me. I *cared* about what might happen afterwards. That was the whole trouble. Worrying about consequences. Or was it, I wondered, that the cause wasn't worth the awful consequences?

I pottered about all morning. Then, after a lunch of baked beans on toast, I went out and bought three pairs of socks, a Ray Bryant cassette, some bread, milk and butter and two large bars of chocolate. Then I discovered that my binoculars were missing. That bastard Forsythe! Helped himself to them while Joyce was picking up her clothes! Sod him! I felt an urgent physical *need* to punch Jeremy Forsythe firmly and expertly in the mouth. See him go down, eyes popping with astonishment, mingled with a healthy portion of sheer terror, to go sprawling, all legs and arms entangled and flopping about like limbs on a rag doll. Yes, by

God, that would indeed be marvellous. The old instinct doesn't lie, I decided. I would meet Jeremy in the street. Simply walk up to him and bash him. Then walk away. *Walk*. Not run. I nodded, liking the notion. Had another couple of chunks of chocolate. Liked the notion even more. I *would* do it. My plan was to visit the café opposite the agency office building. Take the table beside the window. Have a pot or two of tea while keeping an eye on the front door of the agency building. The moment the ineffable Jeremy emerged, I would stand up, walk out, across the street. Bop Jeremy a good one, stroll back and settle my bill at the restaurant, then go on my way.

As a species we had become a damned sight too civilized. Once in a while a chap had to obey the call of the primitives who had gone before!

* * *

They emerged together, arm in arm.

I sprang to my feet. Bastard!

I hurried to the door, passing through it just as Jeremy and Joyce reached the bottom of the steps and turned left towards Bond Street tube station.

I stepped into the street.

Then stopped, my right arm slightly raised.

They were grinning at each other, huddling close against the chilly wind. They were as happy as hell, damn it. I could never recall seeing Joyce looking so damnably happy. Happy? She was positively *radiant*; there was a joyful spring to her step, a light in her eyes.

I turned around in the middle of the street, spinning like some flat-footed dancer. A van had to pull up to avoid hitting me. Gratefully I slipped behind it, putting it between myself and the contented couple.

'Tired of living, are you, mate?'

'Sorry,' I said to the van driver.

'Been a bleedin' sight sorrier if I'd done you.'

I went back into the café and paid my bill, mumbling

something about forgetting it. The waitress shrugged, disinterested.

When I emerged from the place, Joyce and Jeremy were out of sight. I stood on the pavement and felt foolish. And hurt. What the hell had I done to deserve this? Did all those years count for nothing? It began to rain. In an odd way I was glad. The rain was a sort of flagellation, a punishment for being a stupid sod who seemed to be constitutionally incapable of doing anything right.

I went home and found the binoculars in a cupboard in the lavatory.

25

Another airmail envelope with the generous handwriting, the U.S. stamp and B. Sutton's return address in the top left-hand corner.

My news had taken her aback, she wrote. She hoped I was OK. She knew it must be a tough time for me; she had been through the mill herself, she said, and it was no fun for the participants, guilty or innocent. If there was anything she could do, etcetera, etcetera . . . She hoped I would find time to give her a call when I was next on that side of the water; she was, she said, still doing a little digging for bits of 'gen' re M.N. Was that OK with me? She hoped so. And she remained my sincere friend, Beverly.

I telephoned her from Terminal One in Toronto.

She seemed delighted to hear from me.

'Adam! This is fantastic! I was just thinking about you!' Her voice dropped to a more sober tone. 'How are you doing?'

'I'm in good form,' I assured her.

'It's great to hear your voice.'

'Yours too,' I told her. And meant it.

'I found one of her sisters,' Beverly told me. 'Mae's, that is.'

'Splendid,' I said. I supposed it was splendid; I wasn't quite certain any more.

'Her name's Sibeal,' Beverly said. 'She was born in 1911; she's seven years younger than Mae. She was married to a man called Frobisher in 1933. He was in steel or aluminum or something like that. Big wheel, I guess. She had two sons, Patrick and Egan. Patrick's a newspaper editor in Ohio; Egan an attorney in New York. Frobisher died in 1977. Now Sibeal Nolan—or Frobisher—lives in Scarsdale, just outside New York. Her address is 24 McGivern Lane. And she has two Cadillacs and four cats.'

'You've been busy.'

'You're glad, aren't you?'

'Of course,' I said, 'why do you ask?'

'Just wondered. I thought maybe with all your problems at . . . well, at home, you'd rather not be bothered with the Mae Nolan stuff.'

'I'm still most interested in Mae Nolan stuff.'

A soft chuckle. 'You're not just saying that?'

'Cross my heart. Tell me, how did you manage to dig up all the gen on the sister?'

'She has a library card.'

''Nuff said.'

'And I've located a lady in Maryland: Jack Thornton's niece.'

'Marvellous.'

'Are you sure you're OK?'

'Quite OK. Honestly.'

'Are you eating enough?'

Why were the women of the world so concerned about my dietetic intake? 'I'm eating heartily.'

'I hope so.'

I said, 'Do you think the sister might be willing to talk about Mae?'

'No idea. They tell me she uses the local library maybe a couple of times a month. Arrives in a chauffeur-driven Caddy, mink coat, the whole bit. Then bitches if the latest best-sellers aren't on the shelves. I know her sort.'

'Do you have her telephone number?'

'Sure,' said Beverly. She read it to me and I copied it down. Then she said, 'I was thinking about maybe going down to New York for a few days. A girl friend of mine wanted me to go with her. I could follow up on the Scarsdale lead when I was there.'

'I'd rather you came alone,' I said. 'As long as I can arrange to be there at the same time. I'd very much like to see you again.'

'I'd like that too,' she said. I loved the straightforward, obviously sincere way she said it.

'Do you have to go with the girl friend?'

'No. I just hope I don't run into her in Saks Fifth Avenue.'

'We'll stay out of Saks Fifth Avenue. How's Russell?'

'Growing like a weed.'

We said our goodbyes—reluctant goodbyes. The warmth in her voice was touching and enormously appealing. I kept comparing her casual American accent with Joyce's cool, precise tones: soft and cosy tweeds against stainless steel.

But did I really want to interview Mae Nolan's sister, Sibeal? Even if we succeeded in getting the old girl to talk about Mae, what would we accomplish? What questions could we ask? Was Mae a nice little girl? Did she play games as a child? Was everyone sorry when she fell into the Atlantic? I wondered if I was really achieving anything by stirring up a lot of old memories. Perhaps I would succeed only in upsetting an elderly lady who had never done me any harm. Wouldn't it be far more sensible to forget about 1927 and Mae Nolan and concentrate on today and Beverly?

Wouldn't it be infinitely more rewarding?

In retrospect, I suppose it is amusing that I believed the decision to be mine to take.

* * *

We took off a few minutes after seven with Captain Stevens at the controls, streaking down the avenue of runway lights, lifting off easily—we were two-thirds empty—and soaring into a pitch-black sky. The sparkling lights of Toronto disappeared rapidly as we sliced through the low cloud. A few miles south lay Lake Ontario: a hundred miles of fresh water beyond which lay New York State. Beverly was there, still thinking, I hoped, of our recent conversation. Was she already making plans for New York? No doubt she was nervous too. It would be our first formal rendezvous as male and female acknowledging a mutual interest in one another. Frightening thoughts probably lurked somewhere at the back of her mind: thoughts about Adam Beale turning out to be a psychotic killer, an airline pilot by day, outwardly as normal as the milkman or the bank manager, but in fact a horrible character who strikes up friendships with single women, luring them to New York, then bumps them off, mercilessly, strangling them in their baths perhaps, then cuts up their bodies, leaving them to be found by the maids . . . Women always take a chance with men until they get to know them. But Beverly, my dear, I informed her silently, I promise you have nothing to fear from me.

* * *

Near Gander I tuned in Oceanic Clearance, 134.6 on VHF.

'You're cleared via Track Whisky from St Anthony, Flight Level 370 at Mach .8.'

Next, twiddle to 15430 on the upper side band of

the HF range. The reward: the news from New York, loud and clear. And depressing.

'What we need,' declared Captain Stevens, 'is a Fourth World, for all the people who are pissed off with the other three.'

I heard the Morse signals when we were well out over the ocean. They were stronger this time, bolder.

I turned to the oiler sitting behind me; he was a fresh-faced fellow named Strang. Was he picking up any signals? He shook his head. He adjusted his volume, frowned as he listened. Another shake of the head.

'I can't hear them now,' I said. I was lying. Dot, dot, dot, dot, dot. Dot, dash, dash, dash, dash. Dot, dot, dot, dot, dash. Dash, dash, dash, dot, dot. Dash, dash, dash, dot, dot. Dot, dot, dash, dash dash. The same signals, coming from God only knows where . . .

I scribbled them down on a log sheet. Then I retrieved the piece of paper from my wallet. I compared the dots and dashes.

514882.

The same message—whatever it meant.

* * *

An odd in-between, a time of listening to endless records and tapes and hearing little, a time of taking up squash and abandoning it, a time of going to films and plays and remembering only fragments, a time of ebullience, of overconfidence and brittle high spirits followed by dark depressions and unexplained fears. I kept telling myself that my life had lost its bearings and that I had to get back on track—wherever and whatever the track was. In London, I was tempted to pursue my chances with one or two females of my acquaintance—stews, of course. I even got as far as telephoning one of them, a pleasant Scots girl named Louise. She said she would very much like to go with me on Saturday for a spot of dinner, but for one inconvenient detail: she was getting married on Saturday—to a pilot I knew well. I apologized, saying I had no idea; I wouldn't have dreamt of suggesting anything of the sort had I known; she said she quite understood and she wasn't the least bit offended and it was a very sudden thing; she and John had decided only a week ago. I wished her every happiness; she asked me if I would like to call in at the reception if I wasn't doing anything better; they were having a few friends, that was all. I thanked her for the invitation and said I would certainly drop in if I was in the neighbourhood. We wished one another heartfelt goodbyes—and she told me that she would have been delighted to go out with me if it hadn't been for you-know-what.

Joyce telephoned me that afternoon.

'Adam. It's Joyce.'

It was unnecessary for her to identify herself; we had been parted only a few weeks. I asked her how she was. Very fit, she told me. For some reason it put me in mind of a boxer training for an important fight.

'Would you mind if I popped around this evening?' she asked. 'I'd like to pick up one or two more things.'

I smiled to myself; I had had the locks changed. 'This evening's a bit awkward,' I said.

'Ah,' she said.

'I'm having an orgy tonight.'

'Pardon?'

'An orgy. Ten or a dozen highly compatible types. Various colours and sexual preferences. You can pick and choose. Would you and Jeremy like to come and join the fun?'

'Don't be disgusting,' she snapped.

The line went dead. Funny, that she should sound so damnably righteous after she'd been so busy sinning.

Joyce's father rang me half an hour later. For an instant I thought he was going to take me to task for being rude to his daughter; in fact, however, his mission was to tell me how badly he and Mrs Scrivener felt about 'all this'. I felt sorry for the poor fellow; he was so obviously performing a duty he found unsavoury.

I asked him how he was feeling.

'Coming along,' he said. 'A slow business, you know. And it makes you afraid to do anything the least bit . . . adventurous, you might say.'

'Very frustrating,' I said, 'for someone like yourself.'

'Yes,' he said. Then there was silence.

I said, 'You mustn't blame Joyce totally. I'm sure it was just as much my fault as hers.'

'That's generous of you to say so. How are you keeping?'

'Very fit,' I told him.

'Still nipping backwards and forwards to America?'

'Same old grind.'

'Look,' he said, 'if you're at a loose end any evening, you know you're always most welcome.'

'Most kind of you . . .'

I listened to myself trailing away to silence just as he had done. Neither of us wanted to complete our sentences—and probably for the same reasons.

'The trouble is,' he said, 'a thing like this upsets the balance; there isn't much in common any more, is there? Shame. We always got along so well—at least, I always thought so.'

'So did I,' I agreed. 'Awfully well.' Though, thinking back, it was hard to remember any particularly warm and enduring moments. The irony was that, now, when it was all over, we were finally talking like the dear old chums we were supposed to have been all along.

'Nan sends her very best.'

'Thank you. And please thank her. I do hope you're back on the golf course before too long.'

'Rather doubt that, old man. I have a feeling my golf days are over for good. How are your parents?'

'They're keeping well.'

'Delighted to hear it. Very fond of both of them. Tragedy, this sort of thing. It's not just the husband and wife who suffer, but the in-laws too. Doesn't seem fair, does it? Personally speaking, there's nothing I'd like more than to continue to see Rushford and Sheila but I suppose we won't. It wouldn't seem quite right, would it? And d'you know, to be perfectly honest, I'm not quite sure why.'

* * *

Then I had a birthday. I was thirty-seven. A sobering age. In three short years, I would hit Frightful Forty. My youth would be irretrievably lost; the rest of my earthly existence would be a steady decline. For the first time in my life the fact of death possessed reality; in the past it had always been something to acknowledge intellectually but never emotionally; it would, after all, barring unforeseen incidents, take place at some impossibly distant point in the future. But now, suddenly, that point in the future wasn't all that distant.

My parents took me out to a birthday dinner at a small restaurant a mile or two from their home—'not in the least pretentious but really quite a lot of fun'. We spent a moderately uncomfortable couple of hours talking about everything except Joyce. I kept wishing I had the intestinal fortitude to say, 'Look here, I know you want to know all the sordid details about Joyce and me, so ask away, I am now prepared to answer any question you may wish to put to me.' I didn't say anything of the sort. Instead I watched my father as he downed his steak and kidney pie with obvious relish. If death seemed ominously close to me, I wondered how he—at the advanced age of sixty six—could enjoy a moment's happiness. But I didn't ask him about it. We spent the evening in the British way: pretending that everything was exactly as it should be.

The next morning I left for Kennedy.

26

I felt a delicious thump-thump somewhere in my chest when I saw her coming through the La Guardia Arrivals gate with thirty or forty fellow passengers. There was a marvellous moment when she saw me, looked past me, unsure, then grinned as she recognized me and whipped off her glasses, waving a greeting, her small flight bag swinging perilously close to the shining bald pate of a man in front of her.

We kissed. For the first time ever. But we might have been practising for weeks, so smoothly did we perform.

'I wasn't sure it was you,' she said, cheeks flushed, beautiful eyes bright. 'I didn't expect you to be wearing your uniform.'

'We only arrived at Kennedy a couple of hours ago,' I told her. 'I just had time to get over here.'

'Gee, I don't *mind*,' she hastened to assure me. She stepped back to inspect me. 'It looks great. I love it. So *distinguished*.'

Just then a fat black woman with two round-eyed toddlers in tow asked me when the flight was coming in from Baltimore. I explained that I really hadn't the faintest idea; she frowned and shook her head as if to tell me that I should find out these things if I expected to make a living in the airline business.

Beverly laughed at my discomfiture. 'You should put up a sign saying I DON'T WORK FOR THIS AIRLINE SO DON'T ASK ME ANY DUMB QUESTIONS.'

While I had waited I had told an old lady where the washroom was, had pointed the way to the rent-a-car counters for a man with a red beard and confessed total ignorance about flights to and from Philadelphia, Washington and Toronto. I told Beverly that it was wonderful to see her. In fact, it was even more wonderful than I thought it was going to be.

'Me too,' she said, smiling softly, gently. 'Is everything at home . . . all right?'

'Everything is fine,' I told her. 'I booked you in at the Sheraton.'

'Terrific.'

'I booked two rooms.'

Another pinkening of the cheeks. 'I see.'

'Well, under the circumstances . . . you know.'

She reached up and kissed me again. 'You know you're one sweet guy. I could get to like you.'

* * *

While I was unpacking my bag I could have sworn I heard a little chuckle. I turned. No one there. Beverly was next door. I told myself that a sound had drifted in from the hall. I returned to my unpacking, finding that my toothpaste tube had been punctured by my razor which was now liberally caked with white goo.

I heard someone move behind me.

I whirled around. No one there. Cautiously I looked in every corner, even under the bed. No one, thank God.

Did I hear that giggle again?

Mae? Was it her? Popping in to keep an eye on me and see what I was up to? No, it was my own imagination, my idiotic, undisciplined imagination.

Half an hour later I met Beverly and we went down to dinner. She was looking remarkably fetching in dark blue. I ordered a vodka martini for her and Scotch for myself. The waiter departed and we smiled at one another across the small table. I said that this was delightful. She nodded, then we could find nothing to say to one another for a minute or two. It was ridiculous; damn it, we were both bursting with things to say and yet here we were, tongue-tied, like infants. Then, of course, we both started talking simultaneously.

'After you,' I said gallantly.

'I just wondered if you had any trouble arranging to get a few days in New York.'

'Piece of cake,' I said. 'How are things at the library?'

'Well, there was one little item a couple of days after you called me. A cop came in and asked questions. About you, I guess.'

An uneasy rumble down below. 'About me?'

'Not by name. But he knew *someone* had been asking questions about Mae Nolan some time back. He wanted to know what information we'd given out.'

'And?'

'I asked him why he was asking. He told me it was routine. They always say that in the movies, don't they?'

'Yes, I suppose they do.'

'I said that a man had been in some time in January. I said I thought he was a writer doing research and I also said I didn't think there was a law against it. The cop asked if you had come back. I said no. It was true, wasn't it? You haven't been back to the library.' She smiled.

I managed a smile too. But I thought of the company and Forbes's rapidly shrinking patience. 'What happened then?'

'Nothing. The cop took off. Funny, isn't it?'

'Hilarious.'

'But what I don't get is why anyone cares. What could be more innocent than making enquiries about a sort of celebrity who once lived in Abbottsport?'

'Has the policeman been in touch with you since?'

She shook her head. The drinks arrived. The waiter wanted to know if 'we folks' were ready to order yet. I shook my head; he said it was no problem and wandered away.

I made an effort to restore the gaiety of the moment.

'Cheers,' I said, raising my glass. 'Here's looking at you—which is a great pleasure.'

We chatted about England and New York, about the educational television network and about the BBC, about music, about pubs and vodka martinis. We had another drink and ordered shrimp cocktails and poached salmon.

'I've got a lead on a guy who's got movie film of a lot of famous airmen—Admiral Byrd, Lindbergh and all of them. Seems he's got some film that was shot of Mae and Jack Thornton at Roosevelt Field. I called him and he said he'd dig it out for us and put it on video tape, for a hundred dollars. I told him it was for a library research project and he knocked it down to fifty. Are we interested?'

I liked that 'we'. I told her yes and she said she would contact him next week; he was in California, so it would take a few days to get the video cassette. Did I want VHS or Beta?

'Since I haven't got any equipment of any sort to play it on, it's all a bit academic,' I told her.

'We've got a VHS machine at the library,' she said. 'I can borrow it.'

'OK,' I told her. 'We can view it in Abbottsport one day. Soon.'

She grinned in that superbly warm, intriguingly secret way of hers. 'I promise not to tell the cops you're coming.' She touched my hand. 'It seems nuts to me, but all I can figure is that someone doesn't want you to find out too much about Mae Nolan. But why? It beats me. The police wouldn't be interested in you—unless you're an international jewel thief or something. Are you?'

'Only in leap years.'

'Well, someone has told the cops to keep an eye out for you. But I can't figure out the reason. You're not breaking any law. You can tell them to get lost.'

'Yes, but bear in mind that I'm a foreigner. And a

pilot for a major airline. If the American authorities suddenly told Anglo-World that I wasn't welcome in the States it would make things extremely tricky. For one thing I'd be off the North Atlantic runs in no time at all.'

'That'd be *terrible*,' she said indignantly.

'Precisely.'

The shrimp cocktails arrived.

* * *

Why do certain combinations of line, of form, of angle, of shading, of texture combine to create a perfect representation of qualities—tenderness, humour, intelligence? Similarly, why are so many faces just that, *faces*, merely combinations of noses and eyes and mouths? I gazed at her and marvelled at the shape of her eyes, the unusual, very slightly Oriental slant of the lids. Why did that minute variation make all that beautiful difference. Why was the cheekbone so *right*, so ideally suited to the curve of the cheek and the delicate way it curved about her mouth? I touched her lips, running my finger lightly from one side of her mouth to the other, delighting in the shape and the silkiness of her skin. She smiled, the corners of her mouth angling gently, causing those tiny indentations to appear on either side; one very slightly higher than the other. I told her that her port side was up a bit.

'Is that bad?' she asked.

'Having a port side a bit up is considered very stylish in Chelsea,' I informed her. 'Women pay cosmetic surgeons enormous sums to have it done. And you, you lucky devil, you've got it naturally. I was wondering what difference it would make to your face if your nose was a sixteenth of an inch broader.'

'Do you think my nose is too narrow?'

'No. Actually I think it's perfect. That's what's so intriguing. Why is it perfect? Why would a little change ruin the whole effect?'

'I always heard airline pilots were smooth-talking sons of guns.'

'No, we're simple souls who say what pops into our minds.'

'I like what pops into your mind,' she said.

I wanted to tell her that she was totally, absolutely superb, that she felt incredibly *different* in my arms, that the warmth of her skin was miraculous, that the feel of her body against mine was extraordinarily exciting. But how can you say such things without mentioning all the others? Odious, indeed, are comparisons.

'You know what scared me?' she asked, that warm smile still on her lips. 'I knew I liked you. A lot. I knew I loved to talk to you, to laugh with you, to have dinner with you. But I didn't know if I'd like to sleep with you. But I do now. And, yes, I do like it. Very much. I like the rest of you just as much as the parts I'd seen before. I tried to imagine what you'd look like without any clothes on. I tried to imagine what *he* would look like.'

'He's fairly standard issue.'

'Yes, but . . . you know.'

'Yes, I know. I wondered the same things about you. And I enjoyed wondering. In fact I got quite randy wondering.'

'Just like now.'

'Exactly like now. Only now it's a somewhat more propitious moment, wouldn't you say?'

'I sure would, mister. You know something?'

'What?'

'It was a waste of money, booking two rooms.'

* * *

We had breakfast served in her room: orange juice and scrambled eggs, home fries, sweet rolls and jelly, an enormous pot of coffee and cream. We ate heartily; it had, after all, been an active night. Beverly put on a pale blue nightgown which was artfully cut to reveal large areas of delightfully formed breast; her nipples were intriguing shadows against the semi-transparent material.

'Captain Freeman was right,' I told her.

'Captain Freeman? Who's he?'

'He's one of ours. He says girls have better looking tits and bums than they did when he was a lad.'

I adored the way she coloured when she was embarrassed; the pinkening began in her cheeks and ended on either side of her brow, defining her temples in a charming glow.

While we were drinking our last cups of coffee, Beverly telephoned Mrs Frobisher in Scarsdale. I sat beside her, listening and breathing in the scent of her. A woman with a southern accent answered.

'Frobisher residence.'

'I have an overseas call for Mrs Donald Frobisher from London, England,' Beverly announced while I fondled her right breast.

'London? OK, hold on. I get her.'

Beverly covered the telephone with one hand. 'I'm trying to sound *serious*,' she hissed, colour adorably high again. 'What do you think you're doing?'

'Titillating, of course.'

She smothered a laugh then raised a cautioning finger. Something seemed to be happening at the other end of the line.

'Yes?' An imperious voice, obviously that of an elderly lady.

'Mrs Donald Frobisher?' Beverly enquired, imitating a telephone operator expertly.

'Yes, who is this?'

'One moment please. London? Mrs Frobisher is on the line now.'

She grinned hugely as I took the telephone. It was all a bit of a lark, playing games, half sexual, half serious.

'Mrs Frobisher? My name's Adam Beale and I'm calling from London. I was wondering if you'd mind if

I asked you a few questions about your sister, Mae Nolan.'

'How did you find out that Mae was my sister?'

'Just a few questions here and there.'

'My sister Mae died in 1927, Mr Beale.'

'I'm aware of that.'

'There's nothing I can tell you that you can't obtain from the newspapers and magazines of the period.'

'I was rather hoping to find out something about her as a person.'

'Why this sudden interest in my sister? Someone else was asking questions. Was that you?'

'I was merely making a few enquiries . . .'

'Well, there is nothing I can tell you. I'm sorry you've wasted a costly transatlantic telephone call. Good day to you.'

'Yes, but . . .' I was talking into a buzz.

'No dice?' Beverly enquired as I hung up.

'Why would she refuse to talk about her sister? Wouldn't the natural thing be to feel a little flattered that anyone still cared? Dash it all, it's been fifty years.'

'I like that,' Beverly said.

'What?'

' "Dash it all".'

'I thought you were complimenting me on my titillating.'

'I like that too,' Beverly assured me. 'Funny family, the Nolans. Tight-knit, like a secret society. Us Nolans against the rest of the world: that kind of stuff. I guess they like to keep to themselves and tell everyone else to mind their own business. It's a big family too: sisters and brothers and aunts and uncles, cousins, all over the country. Europe too, I think. I haven't tracked them all down yet but I'm working on it.'

'Was Mae the oldest of the children?'

'No, she had a brother, James Junior. He was born in 1903. Died in 1978. His widow lives in Palm Springs. I've got her address.'

'Do you think James Junior's widow would remember Mae?'

'Could be. They married the same year she died. June, I think.'

At which point my fondling of Beverly's right breast caused a reaction on the part of the lady and for the next hour or so we lost all interest in the Nolan tribe.

* * *

It was uncommonly mild for March. New Yorkers were hurrying about with raincoats over their arms, some in shirtsleeves, others with collars loosened, smiling up at the sun as they absorbed its warmth. Motorists drove by, windows rolled down, exhibiting uncharacteristic indifference to the torpid pace of the traffic.

Beverly and I walked along Seventh Avenue, then wended our way through to Fifth. It was one of those perfect times; for the moment everything seemed right with our world, the weather included. We walked arm in arm, our bodies in constant and quite delightful contact. We talked continuously, of capital punishment and abortion, of pornography and illiteracy, of the monarchy and masturbation, of kittens and seafood, of Hondas and Austins, of aviation and religion. Beverly told me that she had been educated in a convent; her father was Catholic, her mother a Protestant; we delighted in the fact; we had something of significance in common; it brought us even closer together. Beverly told me that her ex-husband, Chuck, had considered himself a devout member of the Episcopalian Church. 'But he never found the time to go to services. He was a hypocrite,' Beverly said. 'And I think that was the worst thing about him. Seems to me I could forgive just about anything except hypocrisy.' For my part I talked and talked; it seemed terribly important to make this dear, dear person aware of all the oddities and all the faults, all the hopes and secret fears. Was it her smile? Her warm voice? The firmness of her fingers on my arm? I heard myself tell her the most incredible things: about the frightful occasion, at the age of sixteen, when, excited beyond endurance by the large and rubbery breasts of my partner at dancing school, I ejaculated during a foxtrot; about the first sexual fumblings, about an abysmal failure with a prostitute, about examining my genitals at the age of fourteen and being convinced that my collection of components was incredibly ugly and would cause any nice girl to turn up her nose at them—and telling myself in all seriousness that I would have to be careful all my life never ever to leave the light on when I was with a woman in case she caught sight of them. She talked of menstruation and a memorable occasion during a school tennis match; she talked about a bald man who displayed his penis to her and a girl friend in a movie theatre . . . ('. . . but it was dark and we really couldn't see much') and about a lesbian who attempted to seduce her in a bus station in Toledo, Ohio.

We had lunch at Schrafft's.

'Do you see your ex-husband much?'

She shrugged. 'Once in a while.'

'Do you . . . feel anything for him? It's none of my business, I know, but I want to find out how I might feel about Joyce one day.'

'It's the strangest thing. I see Chuck and I don't feel anything. I wonder about it. "You lived with him for six years," I tell myself. "You've got to feel something." But I don't. He's just a familiar face.'

'I suppose I shall feel much the same about Joyce—or, rather, *not* feel. I rather hope I continue to feel nothing.'

'Was it a complete surprise?'

'Complete. Which only goes to demonstrate what a clot I sometimes am. A classic case of taking someone for granted. I suppose we'd been drifting apart for a long time and I hadn't realized it. It had become the normal order of things. I should have had the sense to spot that something was wrong and do something about it. But I don't know—perhaps subconsciously I didn't want to do anything about it. Hard to say. I've thought about it a great deal of course. To tell you the truth—and I seem to be doing a lot of that today—the only real emotion I've been able to identify so far is a very distinct dent in my pride. It hurts. Can't deny it. But one has to be careful. One's view of things can be somewhat distorted if one's pride is bent.'

'Do you hate her for what she did?'

'I wonder about that too. And do you know, I find I keep thinking about all the *time* I've invested in her. Odd, isn't it? And a bit cold-blooded too, in a way. When the break came, it was all very civilized. She even took her gamp.'

'Her what?'

'Her umbrella. It was raining.'

'How British of her.'

'Like a bit out of *Private Lives*, I suppose. I remember asking myself why we were so bloody polite about everything.'

'I wasn't polite when Chuck took off. I was scared. And being scared made me yell. Then I cried a whole lot. He lives in Cleveland now. Works for some machine tool manufacturer. He's a salesman. Calls me from time to time and comes up to Abbottsport to take Russell out to McDonald's and a movie—the usual thing. He comes on strong at the beginning, the all-American daddy, all fatherly and affectionate, but he can't keep it up. By the end of the day he's irritable like he used to be. He's got a problem. I hope his second wife can handle him better than I could.'

Back at the hotel, we telephoned the widow of James Nolan Junior in Palm Springs, California. The lady herself answered the telephone. She was a little deaf. Who was calling? From where? There was no Adam Beale at that number.

'I know that, Mrs Nolan. I'm Adam Beale.'

'Why didn't you say so? Do I know you? Are you

the fella who came by last week about the patio?'

'No, Mrs Nolan. I'm calling about your late husband's sister, Mae.'

'*Mae?* Mae's been dead I don't know how many years. Got killed in an airplane the same year Jim and I were married. 1927. That's . . . God, I've lost track how many years it was now.'

'Do you remember Mae, Mrs Nolan?'

'Remember her? Of course I remember her. She was my sister-in-law. Why wouldn't I remember her?' Then, abruptly, her tone changed. 'I don't want to talk about her.'

'May I ask why?'

'Why?' The old lady seemed nonplussed.

'I don't understand why you wouldn't want to talk about your late sister-in-law. She was a very brave girl. Someone to be proud of, don't you think?'

'No,' she said. 'I don't have anything to tell you. I've got to go now. Goodbye, Mr . . . er.'

'Beale.'

'Whatever. Can't talk to you. Sorry. Goodbye.'

She hung up.

'She sounded quite nice,' said Beverly. 'I think she wanted to talk about Mae but then she remembered she wasn't supposed to. Weird.'

'That's not the weirdest thing,' I told her. 'I think I've been seeing Mae Nolan's ghost or spirit or whatever it's called.'

Beverly took it well. The tip of her tongue emerged as if checking that the coast was clear before making the trip between her lips. 'Her ghost? Is this one of those cute English jokes?'

'I'm quite serious. It's what got me started on the whole business. I suppose if I hadn't had this . . . *experience*, I wouldn't have travelled to Abbottsport to find out about her, and met you. At first I thought I was going around the bend. Then I was convinced I was. Then I wasn't so sure.' I related the incidents of the monoplane near Kennedy, the signals, the sights. 'I'm more or less convinced that she's trying to tell me something. But I don't know what. Or why she should pick on me of all people.'

'You're both flyers.'

'Yes, but why not an American? I simply don't understand—and the trouble is, I daren't tell anyone about it. Not officially, that is. You can imagine how kindly Anglo-World would look on me if they found out I'd been hob-nobbing with a woman who's been dead more than fifty years!'

'And in the middle of all this, Joyce left,' said Beverly sympathically. 'Do you think this had anything to do with it?'

'I didn't tell her.'

'No?' She seemed surprised.

'I simply couldn't bring myself to tell Joyce. Yet I've told you.'

'I'm flattered,' she said. 'At least I think I am.' Her smile was brave. Did she look at me and wonder if I was all there? Who could blame her? 'You've had a bad time.'

'I've had better,' I admitted.

'And do you believe in spirits now?'

'God knows.'

'How can you still doubt? After this?'

'It might be an elaborate hoax. Not likely, I agree, but I still can't eliminate the possibility. God knows, perhaps there is something wrong with me; perhaps I'm imagining it all.' I glanced at her, anxious to see how she reacted. To my relief she was undismayed.

'That's a crock,' she said. 'There's nothing wrong with you, mister. I'll personally verify that fact.'

I smiled to myself. A stout one, Beverly, good for a fellow's morale. 'It's marvellous to tell you all this. I feel better than I have for ages. Do you believe in ghosts, the supernatural, all that sort of thing?'

Beverly scratched the tip of her nose. 'I'm not sure, but I think I maybe do. There's something out there that we can't explain. Things happen. I had an uncle who was captured by the Japs on Corregidor back in World War Two. My aunt didn't hear anything about him for two years, didn't know whether he was alive or dead—the Japs were pretty casual about prisoners of war in those days. Anyway she went to a spiritualist who said to bring him an item of my uncle's clothing and he would be able to tell my aunt whether my uncle was alive or dead. So she took a favourite sweater along and the spiritualist felt it, squeezed it gently, my aunt said. Then he told her not to worry; my uncle was just fine, he said, a little thin and hungry but as well as could be expected.'

'And was he?'

'Yes, he was okay. But the interesting thing was, the spiritualist also said to my aunt, "Your husband will be home by the fall of next year, so there's no need to worry about him any more. He'll be okay." Well, this part of the thing my aunt was pretty dubious about. At that time they were saying it would take another five years to beat Japan. But the spiritualist was right. They dropped the atomic bomb and it was all over, unexpectedly. And sure enough my uncle came home, a little on the skinny side, but okay, just as the man said.'

'Remarkable.'

'Sure. You wonder if it was just a lucky guess or whether he really did get some sort of signal from that old sweater. I don't know. Like I said, there are things you can't explain so I feel anything's possible. They say Nathaniel Hawthorne saw a ghost in a public reading room in Salem, Massachusetts. Seems there was this old man who had occupied the same chair for years and although Hawthorne didn't ever speak to him he got to know him by sight. Then someone told Hawthorne the old man had died. But when Hawthorne went to the library, there was the old man in his usual chair! Day after day! Nobody else in the library saw him, just Hawthorne. And although the old man seemed to want to say something to Hawthorne, the room was full of people, so Hawthorne didn't want to risk ridicule by speaking.'

'And what happened?'

'I think the ghost gave up and went away, to wherever ghosts go to.'

'Perhaps Mae Nolan will do the same.' I glanced at Beverly, afraid I suppose that she might be looking at me warily as one very naturally does look at a person who has clearly gone around the bend and has to be treated with circumspection because one is not at all sure what that person might do at any given moment. But she was smiling at me in that gentle way of hers. I said, 'I still can't quite believe this. If anyone had told me six months ago that I would be talking seriously about communicating with a girl who's been dead for more than fifty years I would have called for the chaps in the white coats.'

'Do you like her?'

'Mac?'

'Yes. Has she become a friend?'

'No, a bit of a pest, really. I respect her for her courage but I don't understand what she wants of me. She seems to delight in playing games, posing little riddles. She's one of the playful spirits. Some of them are you know. I've had it on very good authority.'

27

The narrow roads with their tall hedges put me in mind of English country lanes. It was flat around Chesapeake Bay, farming land on which they grew corn and soybeans, fruit and sweet potatoes. We had arrived at Baltimore shortly before eleven and had rented a Chevette. Then we had driven east, stopping for a snack of crab cakes on the way.

'Left here,' said Beverly who was navigating. She

had obtained the directions when she had telephoned the Porters from the Sheraton to tell them that we were on our way.

She pointed to a solitary frame house in an immense field bordering a river.

'That's got to be it.'

A burly man in a sweatshirt answered the door. He grinned, apparently pleased to see strangers.

'You're the folks looking for the stuff on Mae Nolan, uh? Sure, come in. My wife's upstairs. Fixing her face,' he added with a chuckle. He bellowed up the stairs. 'Hey, Nan, c'mon down! They're here!'

It was a cheerfully untidy place, full of books and fishing tackle, badly in need of paint and wallpaper. The man indicated the living room off the hall.

A minute later Nancy Porter appeared, a stoutish woman in late middle age, with pudgy, rosy cheeks and an amiable smile; she was dressed in corduroy trousers and an Army shirt with unfastened epaulets that flapped like diminutive wings when she moved.

We shook hands and introduced ourselves.

'We did a little digging,' said Beverly, 'and we found your uncle was Jack Thornton, the pilot Mae hired to help her fly the Atlantic.'

'You must have dug hard to find that,' said Mrs Porter with a smile.

'Real hard,' Beverly admitted.

Mrs Porter nodded her approval as we all sat down. 'You're right,' she said, 'Jack Thornton was my uncle, my mother's brother. I was maybe twelve or thirteen at the time. Just a kid. I hero-worshipped him. But he was gone before I ever really got to know him properly, as a person, you know.'

'But you do remember him?' Beverly asked.

'Remember him? Hell, yes, honey, you couldn't forget a guy like Jack Thornton. I thought he was the most handsome man in the world. And dashing. Young men aren't dashing any more. I always think, if things had worked out a little differently, Jack could have been as famous as Lindy, maybe more famous. He should have been. He'd have handled it so well. A modest man, my uncle. Charming as all get-out. But *naturally* charming, you know, none of this put-on crap you see on the talk shows. But he didn't get the breaks. Once in a while you need the breaks.'

'How did Mae Nolan come to know him?' I asked.

'Goodness knows,' she replied with a shake of her head. 'Back then aviation was kind of a family thing. There weren't many people in it, so everybody knew everybody else, sort of. I have an idea Mae wanted to fly alone at first but then she decided she needed another pilot. Seems to me she asked her instructor first. I forget his name.'

'Earl Diebner.'

'That's him!' She beamed at us. 'Wow, you kids really have done your homework, haven't you? Sure. Earl Diebner. They tell me he turned her down. Didn't like the odds, I guess. Can't blame him for that. Jack was flying out of Roosevelt Field at the time. I think he was test flying a new plane or something of the sort. He was a real good flyer. He could have beaten Lindy across the Atlantic if things had worked out for him. There was a $25,000 prize. Doesn't seem so much now, does it? But then it was a fortune. Some French guy was offering it for the first flight from New York to Paris. Jack went to everyone he knew, trying to raise the money to buy a plane for the trip. But they all turned him down. Lindy was smart. He got some businessmen to put up the dough. When Lindy took off I remember Jack saying how one side of him wished Lindy every kind of luck in the world and the other side of him wished he'd fail, so he could get his chance.'

'Was your uncle an experienced pilot?'

'Sure. He'd been flying since the war. The *first* war. Got to the front about a week before the Armistice. Didn't even get a chance to shoot any Huns down. Poor Jack, he just never got the breaks. If he'd gotten to France a year earlier, he might have done better than Rickenbacker and maybe he'd have come home the top American ace; he'd have been famous and a whole lot of things would have opened up for him. But that wasn't the way things worked out. When he came back from France he wanted to earn a living flying. But there weren't any flying jobs. Dad suggested the hardware business. Dad had a pretty nice little store in Chestertown at the time. Jack tried it for a few months. But it was too tame for him. Pretty soon he bought an old Jenny and went off barnstorming—flying about the country and selling rides for two dollars and five dollars and doing stunts in air shows. Flew for the Gates Flying Circus for a while—I guess you've never heard of them, but that was the big time back then. Jack used to fly for the wing-walkers and the guys who jumped from cars to planes and back again. Anything for a thrill, I guess. Did some movie stunt work too, out in California. Then he got a job flying the mail. He studied hard. He was serious about aviation. Said it had a big future.'

'Was he married?' Beverly enquired.

Mrs Porter shook her head. 'Lots of girl friends, of course. They were all crazy about him. But he didn't care for anyone until he met Val.'

'Who was Val?'

Mrs Porter chuckled. 'Finally found a name you didn't know! Val Llewellyn. Real sweet girl. He brought her home two or three months before he went off with Mae. He was living in New York at the time so we didn't see much of him down in this neck of the woods. But you could tell Val was something special, the way he looked at her. I was only a kid but I remember thinking: she's the one, she's the one who's won him over all the others. I think I had an idea there were thousands of others and they were all gnashing and wailing in every State of the Union.' A sad, remembering smile.

'Can you remember anything else about her?'

'She was from the midwest someplace, seems to me. Idaho maybe. Worked in a bank, somewhere on Wall Street, right downtown. Clever girl, had a pretty responsible job, they tell me. Quite a sense of humour too.'

'Were they engaged?'

'Not officially. I think they figured on getting married but Jack wanted her to wait till he'd done the flight. Mae Nolan was going to pay him a fat fee, for flying her. I don't know how much, but a lot. She supplied the plane, of course. All kinds of money in the Nolan family. But our family didn't get one red cent when Jack was killed. Maybe Val did but I couldn't say for sure. I never saw her afterwards. I hated the Nolans even then, before the flight. They had a couple of public relations guys on the job, handling all the press. The result was, all the news was about Mae, hardly anything about Jack. I think most people thought Mae was flying alone. Only a couple of reporters took the trouble to dig a bit and give Jack the credit he deserved. There was a lot of crap in the papers. Every day you'd pick up the paper and read more lies. The reporters just made the stuff up to fill the pages. We were suckers for it in those days. We believed everything we read. Now I don't believe anything I read.'

'Did you ever meet Mae?'

Mrs Porter nodded. 'A couple of times. She was OK, I guess. I didn't pay her much mind; I was only interested in Jack. We went to Roosevelt Field once, a few days before they took off. We looked over the plane and Jack told me how everything worked. He was very patient with me, with everyone. A beautiful person in so many ways. Oh I know, you're thinking I'm saying that just because he was my uncle, but it's true; he was a wonderful man.'

I asked her if she remembered anything about the aircraft.

She shrugged. 'I don't know one plane from another. It seemed pretty big at the time but I guess it wasn't.

There were two seats, far as I recall. And a big gas tank right behind. Jack told me they had to put in extra tanks because they were going to fly so far, all the way to Europe. He said it was real important to change the tanks in the right order, something to do with keeping the plane in balance, he said.'

I asked, 'Did he have diagrams pinned to the roof of the cabin showing the correct sequence of changing from one fuel tank to another?'

She looked quizzically up at the ceiling. 'Yeah, he did, come to think of it. I remember him explaining it to Dad. An hour on this tank, then the next. He said it would be something to concentrate on during the long trip. I can almost hear him saying that. I was standing right beside Uncle Jack. He was *God*,' she added with the wry smile. 'I used to think what a crummy break it was that he was my uncle, so we couldn't marry. Silly, the stuff you think as a kid, uh?' She stood up. 'I've got some pictures of him. You'd like to see them? You want some coffee or something? Beer? I don't think we have anything else . . .'

There were a couple of dozen snapshots in an old album: the same lean, good looking man with a pencil-line moustache I had seen in newspaper pictures. We saw him wearing a white open-necked shirt, shielding his eyes from the sun as he peered at the camera; sitting in a deck chair; arm in arm with a chubby woman ('Aunt Edith,' Mrs Porter explained); in flying garb, clambering aboard a single seat biplane; standing beside a slim, pretty girl . . .

'Val,' Nancy Porter said.

Beverly said, 'What happened to Val Llewellyn . . . afterwards?'

'Beats me. She left town, I think. Went back to Idaho or wherever. Half crazy with grief, they say. I never heard of her again. But to be honest, I didn't give her much thought. All I cared about was Jack. I couldn't believe he was dead. It was all some dumb mistake. He'd come through so many crack-ups—even flew a plane into a shack for a movie. We kept telling ourselves he was floating on wreckage or he'd been picked up by some ship without a radio and that was why we hadn't heard. I even tried to believe they'd find him on some little island that no one had even known was there. They'd call it Thornton Island, after him.' A sad shrug. 'But if that had happened it would have been Nolan Island, most likely. She was paying for every goddam thing, after all. I hated her for years; every time I heard the name Nolan I wanted to scream or burst into tears or something. Stupid, of course. It didn't do any good. And it wasn't her fault, not really. Jack knew what he was doing. It was his decision. He wanted to go. Hell, he'd been trying to do it on his own for months, years even. He figured this was his big break. I guess it was; but it didn't work out; he didn't get the breaks. I remember it all like it happened yesterday. For a few days the story about Mae and Uncle Jack was everywhere. The whole world was talking about them. You couldn't look at a paper without seeing their names—and *her* picture. Then nothing. It was over. Suddenly people couldn't even remember their names. Zilch. It was as if it had never really happened, as if it was just another story made up to fill the pages of those lousy papers. I hated everybody because they were going about their lives as if everything was still all right with the world. I thought I'd die; I wanted to. It hit me real hard because, honest, I don't think it ever occurred to me that Jack wouldn't make it.'

We looked at more pictures of Jack Thornton: in the uniform of a lieutenant in the Army Air Service, wearing breeches and a striped shirt as he lounged self-consciously before a barnstorming Jenny ('his first airplane—army surplus'), in a suit, holding a hat at his side, as a guest at a nephew's wedding ('the son of my Uncle Ferdinand, of Battle Creek, Michigan,' Mrs Porter explained). A handsome man indeed, with well-defined features, a humorous mouth, a ready smile, dark hair neatly parted and brushed flat on his well-shaped head. You could sense the charm in the smile and the bold eyes. There were newspaper clippings too, brown with age but carefully kept in a photograph album, each clipping protected by a transparent plastic film.

We had final bottles of Budweiser with the Porters. Mr Porter was retired, we discovered, a former steel-worker from Pittsburgh who now spent his time fishing and thinking about painting his house. We thanked the Porters for their time and their hospitality. At the door, Nan Porter said, 'Just thought. You got to see Dan McLeod.'

The name meant nothing to either of us. She chuckled.

'Got you again, uh? He was a buddy of Jack's. They were real close for a long time. Nice guy. Old now but still bright. He lives with his daughter. Hold on a minute. I've got the address someplace. We've been exchanging Christmas cards for five hundred years.' She hurried into the kitchen to return a moment later with a tattered address book. 'Here it is, Allentown. It's almost on your way back to New York.' She said how nice it was to talk about her Uncle Jack. Then she looked at me as she might have examined a picture. 'Matter of fact you look a little bit like Jack. Same sort of features—but he had a real neat moustache, just like Ronald Colman.'

* * *

We stayed that night in a motel called The Turn Inn. We watched 'Hill Street Blues' on television during dinner, a collection of cartons containing Chinese food. Then we made love while some earnest fellow provided us with an endless list of football and hockey scores and another discussed the weather and yet another beamed at a series of smiling, singing, joking guests all interspersed with barrages of commercials. I was superbly content.

'I liked the Porters,' Beverly said.

'It was clever of you to find them,' I said.

'But it hasn't helped much, has it?'

'It brought us here,' I pointed out.

I hadn't planned to say what I then said. It just seemed so perfectly natural that I did.

'By the way.'

'Uh huh?' she was snuggling comfortably into her pillow.

'Why don't you come and live in England? With me, I mean . . . not by yourself . . . that wasn't my thought.' Oh Christ, I was buggering this up. 'Properly, of course. I'll get a divorce and we can get married. If you'd like to, that is. Hell. I didn't do that at all well, did I?'

She said softly, 'I think it's very sweet that you goofed up your speech. You're usually so cool and correct, so British. But there is a minor detail. You haven't asked me.'

'Haven't I? No, no, I suppose I haven't. Well, will you? Marry me, I mean? It'll take a little time I expect, my divorce and everything . . .'

'What about Russell?'

'I rather thought we'd take him along too.'

She grinned. 'You're a sweet man and I'd love to live with you. Even marry you.'

We spent a few minutes kissing one another and saying all the breathless things that people invariably say to one another at such times.

I asked Beverly how she felt about living in England.

'As long as it's with you, it's OK. Do I have to apply for a visa?'

'I haven't the faintest idea. But I'll find out. I have a flat in Kensington at the moment. That's an apartment, of course. Come to think of it, you don't even know where I live, do you? Dreadful oversight. I apologise.

I'll write it down first thing in the morning. Don't let me forget.'

'He's giving me orders already,' Beverly murmured to the world in general.

'It's a nice enough place but I think we should buy a house in the outskirts. Golders Green, Hendon, Hampstead; I grew up in that area; it's rather pleasant and not too far out of town. Of course, the further you get out of town the better the house prices. We could go to some little place in the country, if you'd prefer it. There are some rather jolly little villages in Surrey and Buckinghamshire, actually some of them look a bit like Abbottsport, only older and, well, cosier in a way, I think . . .' I glanced at her. 'I'm rambling a bit, aren't I?'

'I like it when you ramble,' she told me.

* * *

Dan McLeod's daughter was an untidy woman, thin, with greying hair flapping across her forehead. Cigarette jutting from her lips, she regarded us with open suspicion. I identified myself as the individual who had telephoned the previous day. After a moment's thought she nodded and reluctantly admitted us to her dismal residence. While the Porters' home had been chaotic, it was a cheerful, positive chaos; this was the chaos of neglect, you could smell it. There was a sourness in the air, a gaseous pastiche of sweat and stale tobacco smoke, grease and grime.

'He's in the back room. What d'you want?'

I said, 'We're doing research on a woman flyer named Mae Nolan; your father was a friend of Jack Thornton who was associated with her.'

A slow nod. 'Yeah, seems to me he did talk about her. They got themselves killed, didn't they, the guy and this Nolan dame? What you doing, writing a book or somethin'?'

'We're not really sure,' Beverly told the woman in

brisk, librarian's tones. 'It depends what sort of information we're able to gather.'

We were shown into the shabby back room where Dan McLeod was occupying his last days sitting in a lopsided easy chair before an ancient black and white television set. He was a burly old man in his eighties; his sparse white hair was cut inexpertly so that it formed a sort of fuzz over his skull; his face was leathery and lugubrious, the colourless skin gathering in melancholy folds around his chin and neck. His sight was bad; he peered at us through narrowed eyes that were rheumy and bloodshot.

'What did ya say your name was?'

He sounded irritable; I wondered if he, like Earl Diebner, wanted to watch 'Barney Miller' rather than talk to us.

I introduced Beverly and myself.

'Yeah, yeah. What d'you want?'

'We were talking to Nancy Porter and she suggested that we contact you.'

'Who? Porter? Yeah.' He nodded; a ghost of a smile flickered at one corner of his mouth then vanished. Now he remembered. Sure, we were wantin' to find out about Mae Nolan, right? That was OK; for a minute there he thought we were more of those shit-bags of social workers. Anything we wanted to know, just ask. I gave him a bottle of J & B and he nodded, gravely, approving. He asked me to put the bottle on a nearby shelf, so he could see it. Now, about Jack. What did we want to know? It was all one hell of a long time ago. He met Jack when they were both flying the mail, operating out of Hadley Field in New Jersey. Jack Thornton was a real nice guy, a gentleman.

'Did you know him when he was contracted to fly Mae Nolan?'

'Sure I did. Matter of fact, we were both kind of interested in doing the Atlantic hop about that time. There was a twenty-five-grand prize going begging. Trouble was, it took dough. And we didn't have any.

Lots of guys were trying to be the first to make it from New York to Paris, and the other way, too, I guess, east to west, but it was tougher that way because of the prevailing winds. There were some Frenchmen, I forget their names. And Byrd, and some others. 'Course, Lindy beat them all. I kinda lost interest then. But not Jack. He had his eye on the Pacific. He figured he could be rich and famous by flying a hell of a long way. He was right. The trick was financing. Real expensive, breaking aviation records. My eyes started to go just after that. Had to give up flying. Sold insurance, until I ran out of relatives and guys I knew.'

'How did Mae Nolan come to know Jack Thornton?'

'Uh? Jack? Well, he was doing some test flying over at Roosevelt Field on Long Island. Mae saw him. Asked him if he wanted to fly her over the Atlantic. But I guess there were other things on her mind too,' he added with a hoarse chuckle.

'Other things?' Beverly queried. 'Do you mean there was a romantic relationship, Mr McLeod?'

'Romantic relationship?' The old man seemed to enjoy the phrase. He repeated it. 'Yeah, I guess you could put it that way.'

I said, 'What way would you put it, Mr McLeod?'

'Lust.'

'Lust?'

'That's what I said.'

'But you told us Jack Thornton was a real gentleman . . .'

'Not him. *Her*.' He shook his head and the corner of his mouth twitched momentarily. 'Just so happened I was with Jack the first time he and Mae bumped into each other. It was at Roosevelt. She'd just taken delivery of this new Bellanca. Real pretty airplane. Red with black trim. Well, sir, there it is in a hangar. Far as I remember we were on our way to Martin's diner for a sandwich and that airplane catches our eye. So we go in to take a peek. And a guy's whole life is changed.

Bang! Just like that. Funny about life. Sort of fragile, isn't it? There was Mae, kneeling on the floor beside the landing gear with some guy in overalls. They were talking about taking the pants off the wheels. Real prominent pants on the Bellanca. But they'd get plugged up with mud and all sorts of crap on the fields we had then. No runways—no, I'm lyin'; Roosevelt did have a sort of runway. But it was clay and clinkers, far as I recall. If it rained it got kinda soggy. What was I talkin' about? Yeah, Mae. Well, sir, I can tell you she looked real pretty down there on the hangar floor. She had a great figure; she used to dress in breeches and leather jackets. Very classy stuff. Custom-made. None of that off-the-hook crap for Mae. All her clothes had that sort of *casual* look, the look you don't ever get with cheap junk. Know what I mean? When Jack and me went over and spoke, she had a real irritated look on her face. You could see she was getting mad. What the hell were these guys doin', wastin' her time? A lotta rich folks have that look. Ever notice? I guess it comes with dough. Anyway, you should have seen the change when she set her eyes on Jack. I wanna tell you, it was something to see. Kind of *basic*, you know what I mean? The way some guy'll look at a real well-stacked dame. Undressing her with their eyes. Well, Mae did just the same when she got focused on Jack. Couldn't blame her, I guess, the guy was good lookin' enough to be a movie actor. Ever since then I kinda hoped I might see some dame lookin' at me that way! But no such luck. And I got a feelin' it sure as hell isn't goin' to happen now. Where was I? Yeah, Mae. She took a real strong fancy to Jack from that very first instant of layin' her eyes on him! My guess is, she wanted to run off to the nearest motel with him, right there and then—except it seems to me there weren't any motels. Things weren't so convenient for hanky-panky then. There've been a lot of bad things happenin' in all the years I've been around, but I tell you, one real good thing is that it's a whole lot easier for hanky-panky than when I was a kid. But what the hell, it's a goddam sight too late to worry about that now. Mind you, I often think it'd be nice to know what happened to 'em all. I guess they're grandmothers and great-grandmothers and all they got to talk about is their arthritis and how lousy their sons and daughters and goddam grandkids are to them.' He glanced meaningfully in the direction of the front of the house. 'I know how they feel. Mind you, Cathy's all right in her way. It's that son of a bitch of a husband of hers. Strictly from want, I tell you. Drives a truck. Drinks a coupla six-packs every night then wants to pick a fight with her or me. Always was a prick. Said so the first time I seen him. Haven't had no reason to change my opinion so far. She could've done one hell of a lot better for herself.'

Beverly said, 'Mr McLeod, to go back to Mae Nolan's feeling for Mr Thornton, was there, in fact, an *affair*?'

'Sure as hell was,' muttered the old man, nodding.

'Was it . . . well, *serious*?'

'Depends what you mean by serious. Did they go off to bed together? Yeah, they most likely did. Least, I'd be surprised as hell if they didn't, the way Mae was looking at Jack. Almost indecent, it was,' he remembered with a sniff. 'And, hell, Jack wasn't the sort to say no. But *serious*? Well, not as far as Jack was concerned, I'd say. He could forget women faster than anyone I ever known. And, of course, all the time this was happening Jack was kind of entangled with a real nice girl in New York. I forget her name now . . .'

'Val Llewellyn,' I said.

The old man smiled as the name came back to him. 'Yeah, that's it. You know about her, uh? Nice kid, Val. I liked her a lot. So did Jack. Fact is, she was the only one he *really* cared for. Oh, he did a hell of a lot of cuddlin' with others but Val was the only girl who mattered to him. Pretty good little pilot, she was too.

He taught her. Mostly out at Roosevelt Field, in a Travel Air. Real nice handlin' airplane, the Travel Air . . .'

'When did Mae Nolan hire Jack Thornton as her pilot?'

'Uh? Oh, not more than a week after they met in that hangar. I think she'd already been talking to some pilots. Wilmer Stultz and Clarence Chamberlin and maybe some others. Then I guess Mae decided it was going to be Jack, come hell or high water. She was like that. She'd make up her mind about something and that was it. I don't think Jack was all that crazy about the idea of being a sort of aerial chauffeur, but it was a pretty good opportunity and I guess he figured it would make his name if he pulled it off.'

'You knew Mae Nolan well?'

'Sure. For a little while. Mostly at Roosevelt Field. She stayed at a hotel in Garden City and she was at the field night and day, test flying and gettin' all sorts of instruments put in her plane—rippin' some out, putting others in. She was having a whole lot of trouble with her family too. They wanted her to quit before she killed herself. But she had her cap set on it and there was no changing her mind, just like she had her cap set on Jack. I remember her having one hell of a fight with her father. I could hear them goin' at it. She was bawling him out, said he was always screwin' up everything she ever tried to do. Of course the poor guy was just doing his best to stop his daughter from gettin' killed, which didn't seem to me to be too terrible a thing to want to do. But she didn't see it that way. Mae had quite a temper. She was something to see when she got mad. Had her own way all her life, that was her trouble.'

'Was she a good pilot?'

'Not bad. But she didn't have enough experience. She would've been nuts to try it on her own. She'd have killed herself for sure trying to get that Bellanca off the field all loaded up with gas. You needed to be one good flyer to get a ship to fly with that kind of load on board. There were telegraph wires and trees at the end of the field. A golf course next door. When she hired Jack Thornton it meant giving up maybe a hundred and sixty pounds of fuel. But he was a real good pilot and he knew navigation. I remember they talked about radios but the equipment you could get in those days was heavy as hell. Maybe two hundred pounds for a set that could transmit more than fifty miles. And they set off a lotta sparks; dangerous, with all that gas on board. I'll say this for Mae, she may have been hot-headed and she may not have been the most discreet gal I ever met, but she had guts. And she worked her ass off to make herself ready for the flight. She said she was going to do a lot of the flyin'; there was no way she was going all the way to Europe as a passenger. She made Jack promise he'd let her fly at least an hour or two, so she could spell him, so he could get some sleep. Jack said, "Christ, Mae, you really think I could sleep while you're flying?" He was just joking, you know, but she got mad as hell with him. Called him an s.o.b. and a few other things too. He promised he'd let her fly some of the time—but I don't think he had any idea of sleeping!'

'Was he very worried about the dangers?'

'Don't ever remember him talking about it. He figured he had a real good chance of making it. The big trick was getting the ship up over those telegraph wires at the end of the field. He told me, once he'd done that most of his troubles would be over. He liked the ship, the Bellanca. It was what Lindy first wanted for his flight, but things didn't work out, so he went to Ryan—which was a pretty wild thing to do, because, I tell you, I couldn't ever remember hearing of Ryan before Lindy did his thing. Poor Jack, could have been as famous as Lindy. He'd have had money and everything. He had the looks, just like Lindy did; he'd have played the part real well, a hero for the whole world.'

'What happened to Val all this time?' Beverly enquired.

'She was around, I think. She worked in New York someplace. She used to come out at weekends mostly.'

'While Jack Thornton was having his affair with Mae Nolan?'

'Oh sure; mind you, he was kind of careful to keep them apart.' He emitted a croaky cackle as the memories bubbled back. 'Always having woman trouble, was Jack! They fluttered around him. The thing was, he was a real kind-hearted guy. He loved women! I mean, he really *loved* 'em! So he might have cared for Val most of all but he could always find a little time for some others! Maybe it was just as well he went the way he did, he'd have been all worn out in another few years! I remember there was a rumour goin' around Roosevelt that Mae and Jack were makin' out in the Bellanca when they were supposed to be test flying! Beats me how they could manage it. There was no auto-pilot in that crate. But what the hell, where there's a will there's a way, I guess! They sure as hell looked rumpled sometimes when they got down!' The old head shook with wry pleasure at the memories.

'Did he intend to marry Val?'

'Val? Yeah, I think so. He was serious about her, in his own way. The others were, well, kind of a thing to pass the time. If the gal he loved wasn't around, he loved the gal who was around, you might say. Never any shortage of tail with Jack! I'll be honest. I envied the guy! But look what happened to him. Here I am still breathin'—just—and Jack's been gone all these years. Can't believe how long it is since all that happened.'

'How did Val react to the rumours about Mae and Jack?'

'Don't know as she ever heard any of 'em. It was just the guys around the field who talked. Like I say, Val worked in New York, at a bank, I think. She only got out to the field once in a while and you can bet no one mentioned any carryings-on with Mae when Val was around.'

'Do you know what happened to her after the plane went down?'

The old man shook his head. 'Went home maybe. I never saw her again. Got a letter from her. Real nice letter, just the sort of thing you'd expect from someone like her. She said she knew Jack had died doing what he wanted to do and she also knew that she loved him and that he loved her and the memories of him would keep her goin'. Real tough letter to read, believe me. I got Christmas cards from her for a few years, then they stopped. Maybe she got married, I don't know. Real shame she and Jack didn't get married. They'd have been happy. I always figured that would have been one of those marriages made in heaven, y'know. There aren't too many of 'em, but that would've been one. They were so right for each other. But things don't ever seem to work out the way you want 'em, do they?'

I asked him if he remembered anything special about the way the aircraft had been prepared for the flight.

Dan McLeod shrugged his big shoulders. 'Seems to me they had the usual instruments. Airspeed, altimeter, a sort of turn-and-bank thing with a spirit-level bubble—an inclinometer, we called it back then, a tachometer, oil pressure and temperature gauges; yeah, and an earth inductor compass; they were a real big deal in the 'twenties. Then they added that big gas tank right behind the two seats. Jack told me he tried not to think about what would happen if they flipped over on the take-off run and had a fire. "With that big tank up my ass they sure as hell won't have to bother crematin' me," he said. He laughed about it. Laughed too much, that's a fact. I guess he was kinda scared but he didn't want to admit it.'

28

Frederick Walton, Anglo-World's Director of Operations, had a peculiar way of sitting in his high-backed leather chair. His shoulders jutted forward as if he was about to propel himself into an upright position. He held his head at an aggressive angle, jaw set, challenging anyone to disagree with him.

I had no intention of doing anything of the sort.

'What the bloody hell have you been doing in America?'

'Nothing,' I replied. I found it necessary to clear my throat, wondering as I did so whether Walton categorized it as the aural equivalent of a giant blip on a lie detector.

He indicated a missive on his desk, tapping it with his right forefinger, repeatedly, like someone transmitting Morse.

'It doesn't say that here.'

'Nevertheless . . .' I began.

'It's a hell of a thing,' he snapped, 'when we have to concern ourselves over the behaviour of senior pilots in a foreign country.'

'I can assure you . . .' I began again.

'Christ, man, you represent us every time you're there.'

'I know that, of course, and, well . . .'

'It's a *hell* of a note.'

I should have said, coldly, 'If you will be so good as to permit me a moment's silence so that I can explain, I think you will see that the complaint is quite without foundation.'

But I didn't.

Walton said, 'The old man *insists*—absolutely bloody *insists*—that every complaint, no matter how trivial, be referred to him. It's bad enough when some idiot bitches about his bloody steak being overcooked. But he's going to bloody well *explode* when he finds that a senior pilot is creating problems on the bloody *ground*—and in bloody *America*, to boot!' His cheekbones took on a ruddy hue.

Captain Forbes was at my side. He said, 'If I might make a suggestion, perhaps the fair thing would be to apprise Beale of the precise nature of the complaint.'

Walton regarded the two of us without enthusiasm. 'I rather suspect Beale knows who is making the complaint. Don't you, Beale?'

'Not really,' I said. Again, damn it, I had to clear my throat.

Walton picked up a letter that had been typed on light blue airmail notepaper. 'Mrs Frobisher of Scarsdale, New York. She states that you *harassed* her.'

'I did no such thing!'

'She says that you were "unreasonably persistent" —her phrase I might add. In other words, you made a bloody nuisance of yourself, Beale.'

'That's quite untrue.'

'This bloody Frobisher woman has *connections*!' snapped Walton, his colour rising again. 'Bloody good connections, right up to the bloody White House, according to the New York office. Christ, man, you don't *harass* people like this!'

I gulped and tried to get my thoughts in order. 'Mrs Frobisher's sister lost her life trying to fly the Atlantic in 1927. I was merely asking her for some information about her sister.'

'*What?*'

I repeated my story.

Walton glared; his dark eyes had an unnervingly piercing quality. He demanded to know what the bloody hell I needed this sort of information for.

I had to admit that I wasn't quite sure. Which

prompted Walton to rumble anew about the special responsibilities of representatives of the line in foreign countries.

Again I told him that I had done absolutely nothing untoward; I had merely asked a few questions. I added that the truth of the matter was that I had chanced upon something fishy. Unfortunately I wasn't able to say just what that something was.

Walton sat back in his chair, breathing heavily as if he had just done a dozen circuits of his spacious office. 'Christ, Beale, you've been with the company long enough to know that we can't afford to bloody well *offend*!'

Yes, I said, yes, I quite understood and, yes, I would certainly see that I did nothing in the future that might create a situation of an invidious nature for the company and, yes, I most certainly did comprehend that if such a thing happened again the company would have no choice but to take me off the North Atlantic routes, yes, yes, yes . . .

* * *

I explained it all in a letter to Beverly:

'The company have made it pretty clear that they won't stand for me upsetting influential people like the Nolans. To hear them talk you'd think I was endangering Anglo-American relations for all time. Nonsense, of course, but airlines are supersensitive *when it comes to this sort of thing, as I'm sure you know by now. It's infuriating and frustrating, but I really can't see what I can do but obey. This is one of the countless times I've wished I was independently wealthy. How delightful it would be to tell A-W where to put their job. Unfortunately, I need them rather more than they need me. They provide me with a reasonably good income, and, infinitely more important, they also provide me with the means of getting to see you. Often. (How I wish there was an Abbottsport Interna-*

tional Airport and that it was served by A-W!) On the other hand, I suppose we can congratulate ourselves for hitting a Nolan nerve. The Nolans must *be as worried as hell. They've gone to so much trouble to put me off. I've thought about it a great deal but I still can't sort out* why. *Come to think of it, how did Mrs Frobisher (née Nolan) know that I work for A-W? I certainly didn't tell her. As far as I recall the only person I've told was that unpleasant cop in Abbottsport. Which leads one to all sorts of interesting speculations. Are the police being instructed by the family,* ordered, *to keep an eye on us? Do the Nolans still have that kind of influence in Abbottsport? It looks like it. But again, why bother about us? What have we done that makes us worth watching? I haven't a clue. Is it just that the family has a complex about privacy? Or are we on the point of uncovering something of importance? God knows. I wish I did. By the way, I have to report that Mae and her plane and her Morse signals (if they are indeed hers) have been conspicuous by their absence in recent days. It's as if she is content now that we've stirred things up thoroughly and got ourselves in trouble. The* only *absolutely marvellous, totally delightful thing about this whole bewildering business is that it has brought us together. My next critically important mission in life is to get you thoroughly hooked on fish and chips and brown ale, then I shall feel that I have done my stuff for Britannia and that we shall eventually win the Colonies back, citizen by citizen . . .'*

A mildly amusing closing. But I hated to send the letter. It was a document of capitulation, written evidence that they had won, that I cared far more about the security of a regular salary than about unearthing the truth.

The days passed slowly, tediously. I played some tennis, started half a dozen books—and finished only one. I wrote to Dan McLeod, Earl Diebner and Nancy Porter, thanking them for their patience and kindness and hoping they were keeping well. I stayed two days with my parents at Golders Green; I wasn't particularly keen on the idea but my mother seemed to think it utterly desirable, considering the 'circumstances'; she said she couldn't bear the thought of me living alone, her tone managing to infer God only knows what dissipations and unhealthy practices were going on nightly in Kensington. My father said it was all a frightfully bad show. He still seemed to blame me for the whole thing and clearly missed Joyce keenly. Why couldn't I have the sense to manage my life better, he was no doubt wondering. My mother asked, in her shy way, if there was anyone else 'on the horizon'. I told them that I had met a very nice girl in America.

'*American*?' My father snorted, apparently conjuring up images of a Red Indian squaw in full livery.

'Where did you meet her?' my mother asked. 'Does she work for the airline?'

'No, she's a librarian. In a little town in upstate New York.'

'*Librarian*,' muttered my father meaningfully.

'Is she going to visit England?' my mother enquired.

'I hope so. I'll bring her to meet you, of course.'

'That will be nice,' said my mother dutifully.

I slept in my old room. It had changed remarkably little; it was a sort of shrine to more innocent days. The bookcase still carried the W. E. Johns epics, the Billy Bunter annuals, the copies of *Flight* and *The Aeroplane*. One shelf was devoted to my models; a Hurricane, a Meteor, a Heinkel, a Dakota and a biplane which, to my dismay, I found I could no longer identify. All of them were heavy with dust. (My mother said she dared not touch them for fear of inflicting damage. It was rather touching that she still believed them to be worth preserving.) But in spite of her care, deterioration had set in as the plastic parts became brittle with age; the glue was drying; a propeller had fallen off here, a wheel there. The tiny pilots were still hunched devotedly over their controls, condemned to gaze through dusty windows until the plastic cabins became opaque or until the glue holding their painted bottoms to the seats finally gave out. The last time I had slept in that bed was with Joyce. Half a dozen years ago, it was, when a winter freeze-up had burst our pipes in Earls Court. We had scurried out to Golders Green with overnight bags while the plumbers repaired the mess. The bed had been too small for two adults. But in those days it hadn't mattered. Indeed, it had proved to be remarkably stimulating, sleeping together only a few feet from my parents. Each squeak of the bed produced new fits of giggles, hands pressed against mouths and free hands groping and caressing. Odd how everything seemed to be so bloody funny in those days. When did the chuckling start to dry up? Why didn't I notice it was happening?

* * *

It was raining hard when we landed at Kennedy. I was flying; I brought off a greaser, the wheels making contact with the asphalt so gently that it was hard to determine the precise moment when the 1011 ceased to be a thing of the sky and became wedded to Mother Earth once more. A thoroughly slick bit of work, with a dusting of luck mixed in for good measure. The elements had co-operated, graciously avoiding hitting us with eddies and vertical air currents just before touchdown. Smooth landings were good for business.

I telephoned the Abbottsport library as soon as I was inside the terminal.

A no-nonsense voice answered. I asked to speak to Mrs Sutton.

'Not in today. She's sick.'

The news rocked me back on my heels. 'Is it anything serious?'

'Not sure. Who's calling?'

'A friend. I'll call her at home.'

'OK.'

I dialled Beverly's home number. She answered.

There was an uncertain tone to her voice; she sounded nervous but she brightened the instant she recognized my voice.

'Oh, Adam, it's wonderful to hear your voice. Where are you calling from?'

'Kennedy. What's wrong? I rang the library. They said you were ill.'

'It's nothing,' she told me. 'Don't worry. I'm fine.'

'Are you sure?'

She started to say something, then she began to cry. She tried to disguise the sobs, but in vain.

Alarm flared deep within me.

'For God's sake, what is it?'

'I had a little trouble,' she said at last.

'What sort of trouble?'

'I got hurt . . . I fell down,' she said, sounding as if the thought had just occurred to her. 'Only bruises and a cut or two. Nothing really.' She seemed to take a deep breath to calm herself. 'I'm sorry. I didn't mean to cry. I don't know why I did. Dumb. There's nothing to cry about.'

She was hiding something, I could tell. I said, 'I'm coming up to see you.'

'When?'

'Now.'

'But when do you have to go back to London?'

'Don't worry about that. I can organize something. I'll be up there as soon as I can. Is there anything you want me to bring?'

'No, just yourself, Adam, just yourself. But are you sure you're not going to get into trouble?'

* * *

'You can't,' said Wheeler, the Operations Manager. His beefy countenance was dark with dismay. He shook his head. No, it was out of the bloody question.

'I'm afraid I've got to,' I told him. 'It's an emergency. A close friend . . . badly injured. A sudden thing. I've simply got to go there. To upstate New York. Rochester's the nearest airport. I'm flying there in an hour and ten minutes. I'm booked on US Air out of La Guardia.'

'And just how do you think Despatch is going to get a replacement First Officer at this short notice?'

'I'm terribly sorry but I wouldn't be doing this if it wasn't absolutely necessary. I know it's a hell of an inconvenience and I'll do anything I can to make up for it later on.'

'The way you're going on,' said Wheeler, wagging a righteous finger, 'there may not be a later on.'

* * *

I leased a Dodge at Rochester airport. The girl at the desk explained the route and drew red marker directions on a map of the area. In spite of her efforts, I was soon lost in the expressways encircling the city. It was an hour before I was on the right highway, heading south towards Abbottsport. Anxiety was a dull nagging ache. Beverly was *ill.* It was no cold or minor scrape. My mind seethed with ghastly possibilities. Had she been told that she was suffering from some unspeakable malady and had only weeks to live? It was possible, wasn't it? Such things happened. Every day. I kept remembering her voice. It had chilled me with its tone of desperation; it was the voice of a deeply troubled, cruelly frightened woman. She had tried hard to speak naturally, but she had failed. Something was seriously, hideously wrong.

It was dark when I reached Abbottsport. I hardly glanced at sleepy Main Street; I was anxious to find my way to her apartment building. The second or was it the third street past the post office? I tried the second and had to explore a couple of unfamiliar blocks. Then I saw her diminutive Honda beside a Chrysler.

She answered the visitors' buzzer promptly.

'Hullo? Adam?'

'Beverly?'

'Oh, Adam, come on up!'

I heard the click as she pressed the button to release the door catch. I hurried inside, through the hall and up the stairs to the second floor. Her door was ajar. She was waiting, wearing slacks and a shirt.

'Hullo,' she said, smiling a brave but not entirely successful smile.

I stared, appalled. Her face was badly swollen on one side, marred by huge ugly bruises and contusions. Suddenly, shockingly, I realized the truth.

'You didn't fall down. Someone beat you.'

I pulled her to me and held her close, stroking her head and feeling the tears on her cheeks.

'It's all right,' she said, as if I was the one to be comforted. 'I'm OK. You don't have to worry. It's nothing serious . . . nothing's broken.'

'How did it happen? *Who* . . .'

'I don't know who it was,' she said. She sounded apologetic; she seemed to blame herself for not knowing. 'There were two of them.'

I demanded to know if she had been to the doctor, to the hospital, if she had been X-rayed and had received proper medical attention.

She assured me that she had been thoroughly examined, that she was quite well. 'I look worse than I am,' she said with a trembly smile.

'Did they . . . try to rob you?'

'No.'

'You mean, it was . . .' I had difficulty saying it, 'a *sexual* assault?'

She shook her head. 'No, Adam, nothing like that. They were just telling me to get my nose out of the Nolan family's affairs.'

'*What*?' It was incredible, unbelievable. 'The *Nolans* did this?'

She nodded, looking past me, the tears still fresh on her cheeks. She said that two men had burst into the library early Thursday morning, just as she was opening up. They pushed her inside and locked the door.

She thought the men wanted money; she told them there was no cash in the library and that all she had on her was ten dollars and change, no more than sixty cents. But they didn't want money. 'They said I should quit poking into matters that were none of my business. I didn't know what they meant; I didn't, honestly. I never gave the Nolans a thought. Then the first one hit me in the face. Here, on the left side. Suddenly. Without any warning. I remember I was so . . . surprised. I fell down and looked up at him. And he said I should take that as a warning to mind my own business. And then the other kicked me. Three or four times . . . I don't remember exactly. I know I couldn't get up. He knocked the breath out of me. I was on the floor all curled up, trying to protect myself and crying out . . .'

'Bastards.' Anger pounded behind my temples. 'What happened then?'

'They left, I guess. I found I was alone. But I couldn't remember hearing the door. I think I lay there a while, sort of, well, trying to come to grips with what had happened. It was so unexpected. I couldn't believe it had really happened. I wondered if it was a dream and I was going to wake up in bed. And the phone started ringing. I answered it. Mrs Driscoll wanted to reserve *Space* by James Michener. I said I'd been attacked. And Mrs Driscoll said sorry, she'd gotten the wrong number and hung up. So I called the police.'

'Did you recognize the men?'

'No. I'd never seen them before.' She shook her head. 'Stocky men, both of them. One was in his twenties, one mid-thirties, I'd say. One had on a shiny plastic jacket. Black. The other one wore cowboy boots. I saw the boots when I was on the floor. Brown and yellow. But, honestly, I don't know if I could recognize the men again. I hardly saw their faces for more than a few seconds.

'Jesus Christ,' I seethed with impotent fury. I

wanted to hit out at someone, anyone. 'What did the police say?'

'They took a lot of notes and said they'd look into it.'

'That was all?'

She nodded. 'I haven't heard from them since. I've been here all the time. My neighbour, Gladys, has been buying groceries for me. She's been real nice. She drove me to the hospital . . .'

'And?'

'It was okay, Adam. Just bruises and contusions, like I said. Nothing serious. I know it looks real bad but it isn't.'

I kept muttering about what swine they were and how they wouldn't get away with this—already knowing that in all probability they would. 'What about Russell?'

'He's fine, just fine. He's asleep. I told him I fell down and'—she managed a wan smile—'he said I'm always telling him to take care, now he's going to start telling me the same thing.'

She nestled her head in my shoulder while I told her how badly I felt about getting her mixed up in all this.

'I'm glad I'm mixed up in it. Honestly. Real glad.' She touched my face, ran her fingers lightly over my cheek and mouth and eyes, as if she was a blind person trying to fix my features in her mind. 'It's all right . . . now that you're here. Was it difficult, getting someone else to take your place?'

'Piece of cake.'

'No, it wasn't,' she said. 'I can see right through you, Adam Beale, and you can't fool me. You're worried about what will happen.'

'I'm a damn sight more worried about you.'

'It won't happen again, I'm sure of it. They've done what they came to do. Now the Nolans have attacked both of us. Me, with a couple of goons. You, by complaining to your company.'

'The bastards have over-reacted,' I declared. 'Bullies always do. It wasn't enough to try and scare me off. They had to punch you up. Damn their rotten souls!'

Beverly said, 'The irony is, we'd just about run out of steam. We'd admitted it, hadn't we? We didn't know where to look next. So beating me up was kind of pointless. But I guess they don't know it.'

'Bastards.' How much did the Nolans pay those thugs? Was there a schedule of fees? So much for a bruising? So much for broken limbs?

I told her I intended to stay a few days, until she was completely fit and until we were sure she was safe.

'I'd love you to stay, Adam.' She gripped my arm. 'But I don't want to get you into trouble.'

'Why not? I've got you into trouble.' Easy to say, of course but I knew all too well that there would be a day of reckoning with A-W. Soon.

She seemed more relaxed now. She poured drinks and we toasted one another and I kissed her, carefully avoiding the bumps and bruises.

Then Russell emerged from his bedroom. Beverly instructed him to say hullo to me and he nodded sleepily and said 'hi'. This was Mr Beale, she told him. 'Sure,' he nodded, and went off to the bathroom.

'He likes you,' she said. 'I can tell.'

I wondered how Russell would take to Hampstead or Golders Green.

'Say goodnight to Mr Beale,' prompted Beverly when Russell came out of the bathroom.

'G'ni'.'

'Goodnight, old chap,' I said, feeling very protective. It was a not-unpleasant feeling. I watched Beverly as she followed Russell into his room; I heard her tucking him in and saying goodnight and to sleep tight. When I thought of those bastards punching her, I could feel the anger stinging like an ulcer. No wonder people went berserk at such times. Was any action more despicable than the beating up of a woman or child? And who was to say it wouldn't happen again, in this oddly violent little town with its peculiar prejudices? I wanted to stay here and protect her. Permanently. Which was all very nice except for the inconvenient fact of the Immigration people and my need to make a living. Very well, then, the answer was to take the two of them back to England with me. Immediately. Was *that* possible? I told myself that *anything* was bloody well possible. If it had to be done, it had to be done.

When Beverly returned to the living room, she smiled at me and said I was a sight for sore eyes. 'You know,' she added, 'we've found out a whole lot of interesting things about Mae Nolan. Like, she drank orange phosphates at the soda fountain; owned a Nash; she had an affair with a man who was sort of engaged to someone else and she was kind of headstrong and wouldn't listen to advice from her father. But so what? Who could possibly care about such things now, after all this time?'

I said I hadn't the foggiest.

She said, 'Has Mae been in touch with you recently?'

I shook my head. And laughed. 'We must be going around the bend.'

Beverly said, 'There's no one, absolutely no one in the whole world I'd rather go around the bend with.'

29

It was the same cop: pinkish, puffy features, hefty frame swelling mightily against starched and pressed blue uniform shirt.

He gazed at me, his arms folded on the counter before him. A bullet-proof glass shield separated us; it distorted his mouth, working ceaselessly, chewing.

I told him that I was making enquiries on behalf of

Mrs Sutton; she was interested in knowing what progress was being made in her case.

The cop's brows darkened. 'I remember you.'

I regarded him with what I hoped was an expression of haughty indifference. 'I remember you too,' I said. 'Vaguely.'

'What's your interest in the Sutton thing?'

'Mrs Sutton is a friend of mine.'

'Yeah?' The cop unwrapped a fresh stick of chewing gum and popped it into his cavernous mouth. He carefully folded the wrapping paper, once, twice, three times, four times, before dropping it into the ash tray at his side. 'Well now,' he said, 'I think it's real nice of you to show such an interest in a citizen of our little community.' He smiled nastily, as if he was telling a dirty joke.

It required an effort to keep my temper under control. But I had enough problems without antagonizing the police of what was, after all, a foreign power. 'Perhaps I should be talking to someone else. Can you direct me to the appropriate authority?'

I think he thought I was trying to be funny at his expense. The heavy brows angled; the eyes darkened. A beefy finger wagged at me through the thick glass. 'You think you're real cute, don't you? But if you've got any smarts at all you won't push your luck. Get it?'

'I'm merely making an enquiry about one of your cases. What's wrong with that? Aren't people supposed to enquire about cases in this place? Mrs Sutton was brutally assaulted. She wants to know if you've found her assailants or have any idea who they might be.'

'We're workin' on it,' he finally admitted.

'Have you made any progress?'

'Some.'

'Do you think the attackers were from out of town?'

'Could be.'

'On the other hand, they might be from Abbottsport.

Is that what you're saying?'

'Maybe.'

'Do you treat all assault cases with such gravity and urgency?'

The beefy jaw continued to work, like some industrial machine. 'I'm bein' real patient with you, fella. But I'm tellin' you, you're pushin' your luck with this one.'

Ah! I had an idea what he was thinking. I said, 'What's different about this case? Is it because of the people involved? Important people? Is that the point?'

I thought I had him. But I was disappointed. He regarded me pityingly.

'It was a simple domestic squabble, fella.'

'Domestic squabble? How the hell can you call it a domestic squabble when a woman is attacked by two men she has never seen before . . .'

'She told you they were two strangers, uh?'

'Certainly.'

He shrugged indifferently. 'Yeah, I guess she might say that. I mean, why wouldn't she?'

'What are you driving at?'

'The truth, man. And we figure she could've been screwing around with both of them.'

I stared at him. 'Are we talking about the same case?'

'You bet we are, fella. Lady gets around a whole lot. Guys get sore at her. Take a poke at her. Happens all the time.'

I wanted to reach through that damned glass barrier and wring his fat neck. 'That's not what happened! You've got it all wrong!'

'Yeah? Believe what you like, buddy. No skin off my nose. You asked me a question. I gave you an answer. If you don't like it, that's your problem, not mine.'

'The Nolans put you up to this,' I shouted at him, almost incoherent with fury and frustration.

'Who? Nolans? Never heard of 'em.' A porky finger indicated the door. 'Take a walk, fella, before I get on the phone to the Immigration guys.'

I stood there, gaping, shaking with anger. No doubt John Wayne would have known what to do. I didn't. So I turned on my heels and went out into the street, all too conscious of the cop's amused eyes following me every step of the way.

Damn him, damn him, I kept saying to myself as I strode along Main Street. Complacent swine, pleased as punch with himself. No doubt he was at this moment reporting to the Nolan family that he had done his duty and everything was in order.

I stopped to look into a travel agent's window, not to study the special deals to Bermuda and Florida, but simply to get my wandering, wavering thoughts in order. I hated myself for even permitting the notion to enter my mind for more than an instant. But was it possible that there might be a germ of truth in what the cop said? Was I, Adam Beale, in fact being taken for a sucker? Had Beverly concocted the whole story as a smokescreen over her own indiscretions? For a nasty, sickened instant the thought seared through my mind: I might be jeopardizing my job, my whole future, for a woman who was *loose*—and a liar to boot.

I gazed at tanned and tantalizing cleavages on a Bermuda beach. Four-colour separations, I told myself: coloured dots on a bit of paper. Joyce had told me that once. In another life.

Was that fat cop smarter than I thought? Had he in fact planted a few seeds of mistrust and were they now germinating?

Damn it, there were times in life when you had absolutely no choice but to have faith in your instinct. I loved Beverly. Therefore I had to trust her. It was a pretty poor sort of love if it could be compromised by anyone as insignificant as that fat moron in the blue shirt. Wasn't it?

I nodded at my reflection in the travel agent's window.

Mind made up, I went across the street to the liquor

store for vodka and Scotch, which was, after all, the official reason I had ventured out in the first place.

* * *

Beverly was hard at work at a child's blackboard and easel, writing names, connecting them with dotted lines.

'I borrowed it from Russell,' she explained, indicating the blackboard and pushing at her glasses with a chalky finger. 'You got wet.'

I glanced down at my clothes. They were spattered. I hadn't noticed that it had begun to rain. She smiled in that beautifully warm way of hers and told me not to catch cold.

I asked her what she was doing.

'I figured it might help to put together a Nolan family tree. Have a look at all of them at once.'

'Good idea.'

'That's what I thought. Now I'm not so sure.'

I sat down and watched her at the blackboard. There was an immensely appealing determination in the way she tackled her work. I wondered if she numbered among her ancestors any of those indestructible characters who had trekked across America in covered wagons, fighting off Indians and disease and God knows what else, without even a Holiday Inn to look forward to at the other end.

At last it was done. She stepped back a pace or two, her head turning from side to side as she checked the rows of names.

'Okay,' she said at last. 'Here we go.' She indicated the top of the board. 'Our saga begins with twenty-five-year-old Faolan Nolan of Ballyragget in the county of Kilkenny. Young Faolan was poor but ambitious. He'd made up his mind that there was no future for him in Ireland as long as it was ruled by the nasty, overbearing English. So he decided to seek his fortune in the New World. It took him a while to save up the £3.15s to pay for his steerage passage, plus a few more pounds to tide him over until he got himself settled in America. It was a big, dangerous step. But Faolan was determined. And in 1873 he said goodbye to his family and off he went to Liverpool where he boarded the *Atlantic* of the White Star Line, commanded by Captain James Agnew Williams, bound for New York. He was a lucky young guy, this Faolan Nolan, for on her very next voyage the *Atlantic* went down off Nova Scotia with the loss of more than five hundred lives—the worst disaster on the North Atlantic up to that time. But by then Faolan was settled in New York. And he wasn't alone. He had met a pretty young fräulein on the voyage. Her name was Greta Huebner and she was nineteen. She came from Plauen in the Kingdom of Saxony. She had a train ticket to Chicago; she had set out to join her aunt and uncle there, to work in their drapery shop. But she cashed in the train ticket and stayed in New York with Faolan. He got himself a job in a drug store, delivering, packing, cleaning, anything. In October 1873, he and Greta were married—she having sworn to become a Catholic and bring up any and all offspring in the Catholic faith. The next year the young Nolans had their first-born, Malvin. Fourteen months later James Mallory Nolan was born. He's of particular interest to us because he was Mae's father. Then came Fiona in 1879, Etta a couple of years later, followed by Ignatius, Hagen and finally Alroy in 1887. By this time Faolan was doing pretty well in the pharmacy business but rumour has it a lot of his income came from a sort of lottery that was popular in New York at that time. Illegal but profitable. Faolan was a smart operator. He prospered. Pretty soon he was a pillar of society, contributor to all the right charities; but at the same time he was a rough, tough businessman. You didn't play games with Faolan Nolan. He got into the wholesale side of the drug business. Before long he had branches and plants in

New York, New Jersey, Pennsylvania and Delaware. He built a big house on 58th Street near Central Park. Greta got kind of plump with all the good living. They had the usual family problems. Fiona was sick with tuberculosis in 1889 but recovered. The same year everyone thought Hagen had been drowned in a boating accident but he was found alive and well. And the family kept on prospering; the kids got married and went their various ways. Fiona married Paul Crosbie of Wilmington, Delaware, in 1902; Malvin married Gwendoline Halliday of Binghampton, New York, in 1905, Hagen's turn came in 1908 and Alroy's in 1910. But the one we're interested in is James Mallory Nolan. It seems he met a girl named Patience O'Connor who was born in Montreal, Canada, but had lived most of her life in New York City. She was, it's said, a direct descendent of Cabrach O'Connor Don who was so prominent in the 1641 war.'

'Oh *that* O'Connor,' I said.

She peered at me over her glasses. 'It also says her family had connections with no less than seven coats of arms: O'Connor Don, O'Connor Faly, O'Connor Kerry, O'Connor Sligo, O'Connor of Corcomroe, O'Connor of Kildare and O'Connor of Offaly.'

'When you start digging, you're merciless.'

'So James and Patience were married in June 1901 and took up residence in Syracuse, where the main plant was located. James, who was already well established in the family business, was appointed general manager of the plant in 1910. James and Patience multiplied, as seemed to be the Nolan practice. James Junior was born in 1903. A year later Mac came on the scene. She was born in Abbottsport, where all the Nolans gathered every summer. Then Tully in 1906, Tullia in 1908, Sosanna in 1910, Sibeal in 1911, Moira in 1913 and, with one great sigh of relief, I'll bet, the last of the production run, Myrna, in 1915. It seems World War One was great for business. It made millionaires out of Faolan and his sons. And by this time the family was so big that old Faolan decided to build a place in Abbottsport to house the whole tribe. He bought a couple of dozen acres of lakefront property and built his house: it had about twenty bedrooms and a boat dock and even a bowling alley —the family was nuts about bowling. Faolan is seventy now. He's retired and he and Greta live in Abbottsport all year round; at any time of the year you'll find visitors, usually family. But in the summer, gangbusters. They all come, all the children, grandchildren, fiancés, cousins, you name it. They fill up the house, all twenty bedrooms; pretty soon the old man puts up a sort of boat house down by the lake, with four or five more bedrooms, to handle the overflow. Faolan likes to have his family around him; it's a private army, with representatives in the law, in medicine, the police, the whole bit. He has a lord-of-the-manor feeling about that big house in Abbottsport. No one messes with a Nolan in Abbottsport. The kids have to consult with him on everything. You might say he's an Irish godfather. But one day in June 1922, old Faolan goes for a swim in the lake. He catches cold. It turns to pneumonia. They take him to the hospital in Rochester. But it's too late. He slips away, quietly, peacefully.'

'Farewell, Faolan.'

Beverley nodded. 'I keep wondering what the old guy would have thought about Mae learning to fly. He had pretty fixed ideas on what women should be and do. And I'll bet flying an airplane wasn't on his list. But I guess she held the old man in high esteem: she named her plane after him. Now let's take a look at James' and Patience's offspring. First, James Junior; he married Ellen O'Flynn in 1931. They had four children, three boys and a girl: Benedict, Michael, Cleary and Teresa. James died in 1978. Mae was the second oldest child and we know what happened to her. Next, Tully. He married Rose Fletcher in 1933. Two children from that union. It broke up in 1940. Divorce. And no doubt

Faolan turned over in his grave; the old man had strong views on divorce—as he did about everything else. Tully married June Darwin in 1943 and had three more kids, a son and two girls. Tullia married Andrew Stratton in 1930 and had Frederick, 1933, Donald, 1935 and Pamela in 1936. Sos married Eric Batterley in 1934. Six children. Sibeal married Donald Frobisher and had Patrick and Egan. Moira was the only one who didn't marry—except Mae of course. Moira lives in Florida, at Boca Raton. Last on the list is Myrna. Born 1915. Married Ralston Hartt in Boston in 1939. Had four sons, Randolph, Raymond, Riley and Roarke. Old Greta lived to be ninety-something; she died in 1947. Her offspring are all over the place—New York, California, Florida, Georgia, Europe. They may have unlisted telephone numbers and post office box numbers, but by God, if they have library cards I'll track 'em down!'

I wondered if the Nolans had any idea of the calibre of the opposition.

Russell came in and announced that he had been playing with Chuck and Mark and that he wanted a peanut butter sandwich and a glass of milk.

'What's that?' he said, pointing at the blackboard.

'Names of people,' Beverly told him.

'Are you playing a game?'

'You might say that,' she said as she fixed the sandwich.

'Is it fun?'

'Sort of.'

'How do you play it?'

'Carefully,' said Beverly, with the hint of a smile in my direction. She gave Russell his sandwich and he made for the door.

'See you,' he said to me as he scurried by.

'Cheerio,' I said.

The unfamiliar expression stopped him. He regarded me gravely. 'Uh?'

'So long,' I translated.

He accepted that, nodded and went on his way.

Beverly came and sat beside me and, hand in hand, we gazed at the blackboard. Beverly said it looked like something out of the Bible: 'Faolan begat James and James begat James Junior and James Junior begat Benedict and you can bet Benedict begat somebody too. It'd make a cute song.'

* * *

The flickering images—mobile patterns of black and white dots—represented people who had once lived, breathed and laughed. Their jerky, awkward movements, like those of animated mannequins, had once been smooth and purposeful. The smiles, the silent movement of their lips, the oddly tentative gestures: all were parodies, quaint re-enactments of what had happened on a Long Island field more than half a century before. The screen went black. Words appeared in fussy, ornate letters: AVIATRIX MAE NOLAN PREPARES FOR FLIGHT ACROSS ATLANTIC. Shirtsleeved mechanics tend to a high-wing Bellanca. A girl struts by, dressed in breeches and a striped shirt. She turns to smile at the camera.

Mae.

My heart thumped. An extraordinarily exciting moment, seeing her much as she must have looked those scores of years ago. Grinning to show the world that she wasn't afraid. Jaunty step. Hand on hip. Big grin. Inevitable checkered scarf at her throat.

THE AVIATRIX DISCUSSES HER ROUTE.

Now she is talking to a man, a good-looking fellow with a pencil-line moustache. Jack Thornton, of course. They are studying a chart, pointing, grinning, no doubt obeying the urgings of the cameraman.

THE DAWN TAKE-OFF.

The hangar lights are still burning; it is difficult to make out the shape of the Bellanca as it is heaved into the open. A glimpse of two figures in flying gear, helmeted, waving as they bundle themselves aboard. The propeller spins. The Bellanca moves ponderously across the bumpy surface of Roösevelt. Cut to the aircraft turning at the end of the field. The sky is a little lighter now. The Bellanca begins its run along the runway, 5000 feet of clay and gravel. At first it hardly seems to move. Then it picks up speed. It's a nail-bitingly long run, with the monoplane thrusting along, tail up, but its wheels still taking the enormous weight. Now, abruptly, the aircraft disappears from view, hidden behind the silhouetted trees. It reappears a moment later, climbing—just—clearing the telegraph wires, turning cautiously, weighed down by its huge burden of fuel.

BON VOYAGE!

End of clip.

We played it again. And again.

Beverly shivered. It was eerie, she said, seeing Mae and Jack Thornton.

'They looked so happy,' she said.

'They'd been having it off in the Bellanca; no wonder they looked happy.'

She said, 'Nancy Porter was right. Jack Thornton was a good-looking guy.' She leant across and kissed me lightly. 'But you're much cuter.'

'I know,' I said.

I thought about that take-off run, what it must have been like, in the cabin, watching the runway unwind, not sure that the wings would lift the awesome weight, and knowing that if the Bellanca did struggle into the air, one cough from the nine-cylinder Whirlwind would mean disaster, seeing the wires hurtling out of the shadows of first light, then slipping a few feet beneath still-spinning wheels . . .

I stopped thinking about the take-off. Beverly had an odd expression on her face. Her eyes were half-closed and she was frowning as if deeply troubled. Her lower lip trembled. I asked her what was wrong.

'Seeing that old film made me realize how dumb I am.'

'Dumb?'

She indicated the blackboard. 'All those names . . . they're just a lot of scribbles, not real people!'

'Don't say that . . .'

'But it's true!' Abruptly she stood and tossed her carefully assembled file away, scattering the pages. 'We're no further ahead than when we started! We're wasting our time . . . and you might lose your job and I get beaten up . . . and what for? We're just a couple of little puppets to that family . . . and they play with us any way that takes their fancy . . .'

She startled me by suddenly bursting into tears. I went to her and held her tightly. She quivered in my arms.

She sobbed quietly for a few minutes then stopped and dabbed at her eyes.

'I'm sorry. I don't know why I did that.'

'You've been under a lot of strain.'

'I figured it would all sort itself out on the blackboard. But it didn't. Why should it?' She blinked at the names on the blackboard. 'We've only got the children and grandchildren of Faolan and Greta.'

'Do we need more?'

She nodded, her lips pursed as if to keep them from trembling. She took a deep breath then said. 'How do we know Faolan didn't have a brother or sister or cousin who came over from the Old Country? Maybe Greta had relatives from Germany. It's possible, isn't it?'

'I suppose so.'

'There are just too many of them.'

'But perhaps there weren't any more. Perhaps you've got the whole lot of them there on the blackboard.'

She shook her head. 'I can't even find Mrs Villate. She doesn't fit.'

'Perhaps you overlooked her somewhere.'

She shook her head. 'No, I didn't.'

Which, frankly, I thought a little stubborn and inflexible of her. Uncharacteristic really. But understandable, considering the incredible number of hours she had devoted to the task. Now she was on her knees, gathering up the contents of her file folder, glasses on the end of her nose, sorting and checking in her indefatigable way.

When I asked her if she would like a drink, she merely nodded, engrossed in her figurings. I made her a vodka martini and poured myself a Scotch; I arranged the drinks temptingly on a small enamel tray. As I was doing so, I happened to look out of the kitchen window. In timc to scc a policc car cruising slowly by. The fleshy face at the window was unmistakable. It was turned in our direction. Coincidence? Or was that fat bastard obeying orders from the Nolan HQ to keep an eye on Sutton and Beale? Would he shortly be reporting that the two subjects were under surveillance?

When I went back into the living room, Beverly was still on the floor, surrounded by her notes and documents.

'This family bugs me,' she said unnecessarily.

'Have a drink. It'll go warm.'

It distressed me the way she took the glass and tossed off the martini as absent-mindedly as she might have swallowed a glass of water with an aspirin. The drink downed, she returned to her task, flipping through her notes, her finger pointing out the names, checking off batches of children, accounting for this uncle and that daughter, shaking her head, furrowing her brow, stroking her chin thoughtfully. Her dedication was quite delightful to witness.

I told her I loved her. She coloured, her lips curving in a slow smile, her eyes sparkling through the mist of the recent tears. Her hand reached out to touch mine and she said to hell with the Nolans and I said my sentiments exactly and she said she was sure Russell wouldn't be home for another half-hour, at least.

* * *

We drove to the supermarket and bought some groceries: grapefruit and oranges, milk and peanut butter, steak and potatoes, coffee and sugar, coke for Russell, beer for me. While we were lined up waiting to pay, the black and white police car pulled up outside. The chubby one got out and stood legs astride, hands on the broad leather belt that held his holstered revolver. He wore sunglasses. I asked Beverly if that was the cop to whom she had reported her attack. She nodded. The cashier said that our purchases totalled twenty-three dollars and seventeen cents. We paid. Glancing at the cop, I gathered up the bags in both arms and we walked out to the parking lot at the side of the store. The cop's eyes never left us. His head turned, following us as we approached and passed him. I wished him a good afternoon. He nodded, his jaw working on the inevitable piece of gum. How were his investigations coming along? I enquired. He nodded again and said fine, just fine.

'Why,' I asked him, 'are you watching us?'

His eyes opened wide behind his sunglasses. 'Watchin' you? Why, I'm not watchin' you, mister. Whatever gave you that idea? I got better things to do than watch you.'

'You seem to spend a lot of time where we happen to be.'

'Just protectin' the community,' he replied, that damned smirk on his fat lips.

We drove back to the apartment. Half an hour later, while we were unpacking the groceries, I happened to glance out of the kitchen window. Sure enough, the black and white police car was cruising by once more, slowing as it passed our building, the same fat face at the window.

'He gives me the creeps,' said Beverly.

I wondered if it was against the law to lift a child out of school and spirit him away across the ocean and set him up in an English school. And would the English school take him? Could one simply present a child and ask the school to educate him? What documents would be demanded?

'Do you have a passport?' I asked Beverly.

She nodded. 'But I think it expired.'

'How long will it take to get it renewed?'

'I'm not sure. A week or two, I guess. Why?'

'I'm taking you away from this place. Both of you.'

'When?'

'Today. We can go to Toronto. You won't need your passport to cross the border into Canada. And when you do get your passport we're going to England.'

Her eyes popped open wide. 'But, Adam, I can't just go at a moment's notice. I want to, of course . . . but I've got a job . . . and there's Russell's school . . .'

'I don't care,' I said. 'I don't give a damn about your job or Russell's school. You're coming with me.'

Which was, of course, splendidly take-charge of me—out of character too, after God knows how many years of obeying rules and regulations, largely because it rarely occurred to me not to, and because you don't last long as an airline pilot if you fail to obey rules and regulations. Now, all of a sudden, the complications of transplanting a couple of United States citizens seemed to be of minor significance, trivialities that could all be worked out later.

Unfortunately the glory of the moment dissipated rapidly. I discovered that Beverly was no longer listening. She had that curious glazed look, proof positive that her mental wheels had begun to revolve at a furious rate.

'*Patricia*,' she blurted.

'I beg your pardon?'

She was burrowing through her notes, her glasses

wobbling precariously on the end of her nose.

'Why didn't I think of it before, for goodness' sake? Dumb, dumb!'

Then, triumphant, she produced a xerox copy of a document. She clasped her left hand to her mouth as she read it. Her eyes sparkled.

'Mae's birth certificate,' she announced, holding up the document as if it were a valuable item at an auction. 'She was named Mae *Patricia.* June twelve, nineteen-oh-four.'

I nodded. I recalled one of the newspaper stories calling her 'Mae P. Nolan'. But what was so significant about the middle name?

'Exhibit B,' declared Beverly, producing another document. 'I got this from the Hall of Records. The tax on Mrs Villate's property here in Abbottsport. You see where the owner of the property is named? Right there. "Patricia M. Villate". And get a load of the handwriting. All right? Now look at this school picture signed by Mae. Uh?'

I had to admit that there were definite similarities. 'But what does that prove?'

She folded her arms and pulled them tight as if she was hugging herself with glee. 'I think it's going to help prove that Mrs Villate is none other than our old friend Mae Nolan!'

30

'Mae's dead,' I declared, firmly, as if it was a tenet of faith.

'Is she?' Beverly took off her glasses and gestured with them in the general direction of New England and the Maritime Provinces of Canada. 'It *fits.* Her age is right. And she's been living in Europe for aeons.'

'Hardly a crime.'

'You're right. But just think . . . what if Mae *didn't* go on that flight?'

'But she did go.'

'How do we know? We saw a plane take off. But can you say for sure that it was Mae Nolan sitting beside Jack Thornton? What if it was Val Llewellyn?'

I stared. 'Oh, come *on*.'

'It *could* have been, Adam. Admit it. It's not totally, completely impossible, is it?'

I admitted that it wasn't quite beyond the outer reaches of possibility.

'OK,' said Beverly, grasping the little finger of her left hand as if to signify that the first hurdle had been overcome. 'So let's see if we can figure out what happened. Here's Mae Nolan. Twenty-three years old. Rich. Ambitious. Determined to be the first woman to fly the Atlantic Ocean. She learns to fly. Works hard, scared that Elinor Smith or Katherine Stinson and God knows how many others all over the country and in Europe might be actively preparing for similar attempts. Every morning it's an agony opening the newspaper; she might read that some woman has beaten her to it and is already aloft over the ocean. But now, the weeks pass and as far as Mae knows she's the only one in the race. Then she hires Jack Thornton as her co-pilot. She's known quite a few men, has Mae: handsome men, well-connected men, talented men, men with bright futures, men with intriguing pasts. But they were a pathetic lot compared with Jack Thornton. He's perfect. Good-looking, witty, sexy. And he can fly like an angel. Mae is happy. Together she and Jack will fly to world-wide fame. She's paying him twenty-five thousand dollars. She tells herself he'd probably do it for nothing. There's a beautiful spark between them. The next few weeks are the happiest in Mae's life; Jack seems to be as attracted to her as she is to him. The two of them are together all the time, working on the Bellanca, test-flying, preparing for the great adventure. Their affair gathers momentum. They meet in her hotel in Garden City, spend hours together in the hangar and in the plane, kissing, fooling about while they're flying. It's a breathtakingly exciting period. Jack is the love of her life. There can never be anyone else. Mae adores him. The days roll by. Soon it's time; they're only waiting for the weather.' Beverly put her glasses on, then took them off again. She wagged a finger at me. 'I figure it happened some time during that last day at Roosevelt. The weather reports were indicating that a take-off might be possible in the next twelve hours. Maybe Mae heard some remark in the hangar, some crack by a mechanic about Gentleman Jack and his aerial harem. Or maybe Mae had become suspicious about Jack's comings and goings and had followed him into New York. Or maybe, because he seemed to be that sort of guy, Jack simply told her the truth. Told her he admired her but that his heart belonged to someone else. Val. That *hurt*! Really hurt!' Beverly sounded as if she was relating something that had happened to her. 'Mae was shattered. And what made it far, far worse was that Jack was prepared —in fact, *wanted*—to give her up, *Mae Nolan*, no less, for some nobody of a secretary! She *had* to do something. But what? Fire Jack? No, she thought of a better way. A way to take care of both Jack and Val at the same time. They were due to take off at dawn. What happened was, Mae persuaded Val to take her place. Maybe she said she couldn't go through with it now that the moment of truth had arrived; she was scared, sick to her stomach with fear. Or maybe she said her family had talked her out of it. Maybe she said if Val didn't go, she would abandon the whole thing. Val was as good a pilot as Mae, so why shouldn't she take Mae's place? Here was a once-in-a-lifetime opportunity. Val could jump in the plane and go off to become the first woman in the world to fly the Atlantic—alongside the love of her life. How could she say no? No way. So she didn't. She put on Mae's flying gear. It was still dark.

No one could see that it wasn't Mae in the plane. Dawn broke just as they began to taxi. It all worked out so beautifully. That's what *happened*, Adam. I'm sure of it! When the plane took off, everyone thought Mae Nolan was up there sitting beside Jack Thornton. But she wasn't. She had slipped out of the hangar while everyone else was busy watching the take-off. She hid out in a hotel or some log cabin in the hills. No doubt she had a few chuckles about the newspaper stories —she and Jack Thornton being tragically lost over the ocean. Big news for a few days, then everyone forgot all about it. It was ancient history. After a while Mae went to Europe—the discreet way, via Rio, maybe, so the chances of her running into anyone she knew were just about zero. She settled in Paris. Married Pierre Villate. Had a pleasant life. When Pierre died, she got a yen to come back to dear old Abbottsport. She bought the big house on the hill. And that's where the bitch is right now! And that's why the Nolans won't talk about her. They know what she did. And they'll go to any lengths to make sure nobody else finds out. They got scared about us. We were nearer to the truth than we knew. So they complained to your company and sent a couple of hoods to work me over. This is the skeleton in the Nolan closet—and it's for sure they want to keep it in there.'

I felt as if something odd had happened to gravity. I seemed to find myself suspended a foot or two above the apartment floor, revolving at an ever-increasing rate. Ideas whirled about in my head like a lot of bats gone mad. I tried to grapple with them one at a time. Mae *alive*? It was almost physically painful to absorb the notion, so firmly embedded was the belief that she had been dead more than half a century. I kept saying, no, it was impossible, quite impossible. And Beverly kept saying, yes, it *had* to be this way; there was no other. As far as she was concerned we were past maybes; we were now dealing with certainties. Together, standing in her small kitchen, the counter still cluttered with bags of groceries, Beverly and I prodded at the facts, manoeuvred them, cajoled them, until even I had to admit that what she was saying possessed a chilling plausibility.

Beverly's glasses were revolving between her fingers. 'You *did* see that plane, Adam; it was the same one that took off from Roosevelt back in 1927. Mae's plane. But Mae wasn't in it. It was Val. She wants to set the record straight. That's why she keeps contacting you. Poor Val. After the plane went down, the Nolans told everyone she'd left town, gone out west. They even sent Christmas cards to the Porters and Dan McLeod in her name, and a letter. Nice touch, uh? You've got to hand it to them; they're real pros, those Nolans.'

We gazed at each other, nodding, agreeing; I congratulated her on her perspicacity. But, we had to ask, what use was the information? We couldn't prove any of it. Everything we had was circumstantial evidence of the flimsiest kind. If we took it to a lawyer he'd laugh us out of his office.

Beverly had that far-away look that I was beginning to know so well. 'Mae did something to the plane,' she said, her hands shaping the air before her. 'Must have. She surely didn't send Jack and Val off in her plane, just *hoping* something would go wrong. That isn't the Nolan way.'

The same thought had occurred to me.

Now Beverly was waving her glasses from side to side as if to cool them. 'How did Mae do it, Adam? Fix the airplane in some way? Put something in the gas?'

'Possible,' I admitted. 'She could have done any number of things, I suppose. She might have sawn through a wing strut and hoped it would fail during the trip. But that doesn't sound like Mae. Besides, it would take a lot of experience in aircraft servicing to do it properly.'

'She could have gotten one of the Nolan goons to do it. There seem to be plenty of those guys around.'

Which was true enough, of course. But by all accounts Jack Thornton was a solidly professional type, the sort who would look his aircraft over before every flight. And undoubtedly he gave the Bellanca an inch-by-inch examination before he set off to cross the Atlantic. He would have immediately spotted anything as obvious as a sawn-through strut.

'So how did she do it?'

Russell came clattering in through the door.

'Still playing that game?' he asked, glancing at the blackboard. 'Who's winning?'

'We are,' Beverly told him.

'You mean, you're *both* winning? That's a funny game.'

'You're not kiddin', pardner,' I said, earning a beam of approval from Russell who evidently felt that at last I was beginning to sound like a regular human being.

* * *

We drove the little Honda up the hill behind the town. The view was attractive from up here. You could see the long lake that cradled the town and ran off to join the Cohocton River further south. The Indians who had once lived there thought the lake resembled a tomahawk; a boomerang was nearer the mark, in my opinion, but no doubt the braves' knowledge of the artifacts of the Antipodes was limited. Had old Faolan harboured a secret desire to get it renamed Nolan Lake? No doubt the old boy thought of it as his own; perhaps he had stood on this very spot, watching his various speedboats and cruisers streaking about its waters for lesser mortals to gape at.

'That's it,' said Beverly, slowing down as she approached a house on the highest point of the hill.

The trouble was, you couldn't see much of the place; an imposing brick wall and a couple of dozen trees obscured the ground floor and much of the first. There were black wrought iron gates at the driveway through which you could catch glimpses of various items of statuary. A huge Lincoln limousine stood in the driveway in front of three garage doors. It shimmered in the spring sunshine.

'Charming little residence,' I commented.

'Worth at least a million,' Beverly said. 'Maybe more; it's a while since I've been pricing houses.'

I mused, 'Poor old Jack Thornton could have been living there now if he'd played his cards properly.' I gazed through the great iron gates. Was that really Mae in there? *Mae*? Or had we jumped upon a collection of odds and ends of information and put together a theory to suit our own needs? Wasn't it possible that Beverly could have missed an aunt or a second cousin somewhere among the Nolan legions? By chance her name could be Patricia. By chance she could be approximately the right age. Names and ages didn't constitute proof.

But no such doubts seemed to have occurred to Beverly.

'The nerve of the old bitch,' she said, 'living there in the lap of luxury. After what she did.'

'It's only our theory,' I cautioned. 'We aren't absolutely positive she did it.'

'Yes, we are,' Beverly told me. Firmly. 'I know it, Adam, I feel it, I really do. What d'you say we call on her neighbours?'

'What for?'

'Just to ask a couple of questions.'

The next house was situated a quarter of a mile down the hill out of sight of the Villate residence. It was unpretentious but neat and well-cared for. The mailbox bore the name Pollard.

No iron gates barred visitors from approaching. We pulled up the gravel driveway and stopped behind a five-year-old Buick. A man in shirt sleeves appeared behind the storm door and greeted us with a 'hi' that was friendly enough.

Beverly said, 'Sorry to trouble you but I'm looking

for an aunt of mine, a Mrs Villate. I understand she lives in this area.'

The man nodded. 'Mrs Villate? Sure. Just up the street. Next house. You can't miss it. That-a-way,' he added sounding like someone in a cowboy film.

Beverly said, 'We haven't seen her for a long time. They say she's in poor health. Do you happen to know how she is at the moment? We don't want to call on her if she's real poorly.'

The man shrugged. He didn't know. Had hardly set eyes on the lady since she moved in a couple of years ago, maybe more, makes you wonder where the time goes and that was a fact. Seems to him he'd heard that Mrs Villate was confined to bed. Bad heart, he believed it was. Wished he could be of more help. Looked as if we might get rain.

We had a last look at the Villate house. Then we set off back to town, a little dejected because we were really no wiser than before.

We passed the A & P. And saw the police car. Parked at the side of the road, as if waiting for us to return from our ride. Sure enough, as we turned the corner to Beverly's apartment building, I spied the black-and-white pulling out into the traffic.

Beverly parked beside the Chrysler. She hadn't turned off the motor before the patrol car came cruising into view. Fatty at the wheel. I rolled down my window and waved to him.

'How very good to see you this morning!' I called.

He scowled and went on his way.

We watched the patrol car until it turned at the next corner.

Then Beverly said, 'It's Sunday tomorrow. I'm going to Mass.'

'Would you like me to come?'

She shook her head without looking at me. 'No, I think I'd rather go alone. Do you mind?'

No, I didn't mind.

31

There were showers earlier in the morning but now the sun beamed down out of a bright blue sky. Everything looked washed and rinsed. The moisture on the roof of the church became a wispy veil hovering above the tiles as, below, the faithful filed out into the sunshine, pausing to shake hands and exchange a word with the priest at the door. It was an attractively peaceful scene. I watched for Beverly. I had dropped her off at the church more than an hour earlier, when the skies were still heavy and dull. Then I had taken the Honda for a little jaunt, around the town, down in the Beach area, past the erstwhile Nolan mansion, out to the silent, deserted lake shore. I threw flat stones into the perfectly still water and had watched them skip just as I had done on the shores of the Serpentine and the Thames at Cookham. Then I had driven back into Abbottsport, past the Villate house high on the hill, stopping at the Paradise Restaurant for a cup of coffee. Charlie Vogel had flattered me by remembering me, waving a friendly greeting as soon as I pushed open the chrome-laden door. It was, he said, real nice to see me back in town. Had I found out anything more about Mae? A few things, I told him but they had to be checked out. He nodded understandingly. Then it was time to return to the church.

Beverly was one of the last to emerge from the church. And when she did she spent some moments in conversation with the priest, a tall, rangily-handsome man with curly black hair. He kept running his fingers through his hair as he talked to her. Was it a nervous motion caused by Beverly's proximity? I hadn't noticed him bothering about his hair when he was talking to the others of the flock. Did she stimulate him? Damn him for being stimulated. An admirable thing, vows of celibacy. At last he and Beverly parted, with a handshake.

I loved the way Beverly walked, with long, determined strides, her head held at a slight angle as if she was listening for some distant sound. As she approached the car I commanded myself, sternly, never ever to take her for granted. When our eyes met she smiled. But the smile was quickly gone. I leant across and opened the pasenger door. I asked her how she had enjoyed the service.

'I didn't,' she said. 'I felt like a hypocrite. But I had to go.'

'Of course,' I said, although it was many years since I had felt any such compulsion.

'Father Thorne's a nice guy,' she said. 'He comes in the library once a week. He likes mysteries.' She turned to me. 'I wanted to find out if he went to visit Mrs Villate.'

'And?'

She nodded. 'Thursdays. I told him a friend was in town doing research on Mae Nolan.'

'And you asked him to put in a good word for me with Mrs Villate?'

'Right.'

'Do you think that'll do the trick?'

She shook her head as she fumbled in the glove compartment for her sunglasses. 'Not really.' She slipped the glasses on. 'I had something else in mind. Let's drive, shall we?'

I put the little car in gear and we scurried on our way, past the police station where a black and white patrol car was angle-parked. But there was no sign of Fatty. I turned into Beverly's street. The sun splashed through the new leaves on the maple trees, all laden with sparkling raindrops, dappling the roadway ahead with a myriad tiny spotlights.

As I pulled into her parking space, Beverly said,

'What I had in mind was, you could go and see Mrs Villate the day *before* Father Thorne goes.'

'Which would be Wednesday.'

'Right.'

'But isn't he putting in the good word on Thursday?'

'Yes.' She interlocked her fingers. 'It's probably a dumb idea . . .'

'What is?'

'Well, I was just thinking . . .' The catch on her handbag seemed suddenly to have become an object of intense interest. She studied it for moments, opening it and closing it. Then she took a breath and turned to me. 'I know you'll think I'm crazy. But it might work.'

'What might?'

She spoke rapidly as if anxious to get it all out before I could interrupt.

'You go to the house the day before Father Thorne is due. You say Father Thorne had to go out of town and you're substituting for him.'

'Substituting?'

'Sure,' she nodded as if it was an everyday occurrence. 'You're dressed up as a priest, you see, the collar and all . . .'

'*Me?*' I stared at her, so fixedly that there was a dull roar behind my eyes. How the blazes could she think of anything so utterly absurd. 'Don't be balmy. I won't do anything of the sort.'

'Why not?'

'Because . . . because it's *wrong* for one thing!'

'Isn't it a whole lot *less* wrong than what Mae did?'

'Anyway, it's potty. They'd see through me in a minute.'

'I don't think so, Adam. Really. I've thought about it. You know something about it already, being a priest, I mean. And you can do a real good Irish accent; I've heard you. The important thing is to *act* like a priest, be believable. I don't know if it'll do any good, Adam. But you might get something out of her, uh? It's worth a try, isn't it? You've got to admit, it's worth a try.'

'No, it bloody well isn't,' I declared. 'Under no circumstances will I do anything of the sort!'

* * *

The Honda's brakes squeaked as I stopped at the gates.

Enormous, forbidding things, those gates, at least twelve feet tall, great sculptures in metal evoking images of Alcatraz and Wormwood Scrubs.

RING BELL commanded the sign. I obeyed.

There was a buzzing sound then a metallic voice emanated from a minute loudspeaker concealed in the wrought iron.

'Yes, who is it?'

I cleared my suddenly-dry throat.

'Father Meehan,' I replied, my voice wobbling slightly under the burden of its Irish twang.

The voice softened perceptibly. 'Father Meehan? Are you expected, Father?'

'I believe so.'

'One moment, Father. I'll be right out.'

A burly figure emerged from the house. I took him to be the chauffeur, in his black trousers and his white collarless shirt, with sleeves rolled up to the elbows to reveal disquietingly muscular forearms. He nodded a cordial greeting as he hurried up to the gate.

'So sorry to keep you waiting, Father.'

'Quite all right,' I said. I wondered if I could bring myself to add 'my son'. I couldn't. 'I'm here in place of Father Thorne. He's been called out of town. He asked me to come to see Mrs Villate.'

'Ah, she was expecting the Father tomorrow, Father.'

'What's that? Tomorrow? Good gracious, what have I done?' I made a show of consulting my notebook. 'Faith, I declare I've got the dates wrong. Father Thorne read them all out and I must have mixed them up in some foolish way.'

The chauffeur beamed. 'But maybe Mrs Villate'll be able to see you, Father. Why don't you come in?'

He pressed a button somewhere behind the sign. The huge gates swung open, silently, inexorably. I put the Honda in gear and drove along a broad driveway of Lord only knows how many thousand bricks laid in a herring-bone pattern. I pulled up in front of a magnificent entrance, all white columns, glittering brasses and an ornate broken pediment. It reminded me of *Gone With the Wind.*

'This way, Father.' I followed the chauffeur into the house, still mumbling about my having made a mistake in taking down my notes.

I tried not to gasp when I entered the house. The place was gigantic: acres of deep carpeting, enormous expanses of oak panelling, with tapestries, paintings and sculptures by the dozen. The air was crisply cool, air-conditioned to just the right levels of temperature and humidity. I sat down on a leather easy chair. The sound of a radio or television set drifted discreetly from somewhere to my right. You're bloody balmy, I told myself. You're going to be out on your backside in five minutes. Or less. No doubt the chauffeur took care of such matters. A tough-looking cove.

A tall woman of about forty, with short hair and large, hornrimmed glasses introduced herself as Miss Hecht, Mrs Villate's companion. I recognized her voice; she had a clipped economical way of speaking. Her English was faultless but I suspected that her native tongue was German or Swedish. She was the one who had spoken to me on the phone and had told me not to bother Mrs Villate.

But she was pleasant enough now, deferential even. A clerical collar and a funereal grey suit seemed to work wonders around here.

'We weren't expecting a visit this afternoon, Father. Father Thorne is due to call tomorrow.'

More flipping of the notebook's pages. More apologetic excuses: unfortunate error in appointments, dear me, must have mixed up names and dates. No doubt Mr Flanagan was expecting me today and here I had him down for tomorrow. Perhaps I'd better go back and start all over again . . .

'No, Father.' She raised a placatory hand. 'Would you mind waiting for a minute or two? Mrs Villate wasn't expecting you, you understand. But I'll find out if she can see you.'

I assured her that I understood perfectly. I was sorry to put her to so much trouble. No trouble at all, Father, I was told. Three times, if I recall correctly. I sat back. The radio or television set now seemed to be coming from my left. A voice carolled joyously that Coke was *it*. Another voice, one deep within me, told me to run like hell while I still had the chance. I wanted to. But how could I face Beverly? Lie? Tell her that they saw through me the instant they laid eyes on me? Tell her that the chauffeur tossed me bodily out of the house? What, I wondered with a quaking somewhere around my intestines, would Frederick Walton, Anglo-World's Director of Operations, say if he could see me at this moment, dressed as a *priest*, of all things? The thought was appalling. Did I still have a job? Or had the big cheeses at A-W had their meetings and had they —'regretfully', the letter would say—decided not to put up with any more of my nonsense? Hard to blame them, poor sods. How much confidence could you put in a pilot who did things like *this*, for God's sake? I *was* nuts. And no doubt Miss Hecht and that muscle-bound chauffeur had already realized it. And no doubt they had telephoned for help. And no doubt Fatty was strapping on his Smith & Wesson, chortling with glee at the prospect of getting me once and for all.

'Father Meehan? Oh, I'm sorry. Did I startle you?'

'Startle me? Why, not at all.'

Christ.

'Mrs Villate will be pleased to see you, Father. Please follow me.'

Heaven help me. The words actually sprang to mind. Under the circumstances it seemed a bit much to expect any assistance from that quarter.

Was I really going to meet Mae Nolan? Or was I just going to make a bloody fool of myself? Again? Was it really conceivable that the whole world was wrong about Mae and only Beverly and I were right? I tried to make casual conversation as I followed Miss Hecht up the grand, curving stairway. I complimented her on the house and its furnishings. She declared with some pride that Mrs Villate had exquisite taste. She pointed to the silk Tabriz and antique Oriental rugs. To the 17th century Daubigny landscape and the 18th century Aubusson tapestry; to the sculpture by Peter Lobello and the 13th century Khumer bronze head as well as the 17th century Sukhothai bronze head; not to mention the George III carved giltwood mirror and the incredible 19th century French stained glass skylight . . .

Breathtaking, I had to admit.

'Mrs Villate loves her things,' said Miss Hecht as if discussing a little girl and her dolls.

The upstairs hall was a spacious, luxurious world of white. Every footstep was cushioned by immensely thick white carpeting. The walls were white; the woodwork was white; the lamps were white; the curtains were white.

Miss Hecht paused before white double-doors. She knocked discreetly, turned an ornate knob, glanced inside then beckoned to me.

I swallowed and had to clear my throat.

'This is Father Meehan.'

For a moment the immensity of the bedroom commanded my attention. I looked from left to right before I really saw the bed—which was funny in a way because in any normal room the bed would have been overwhelming. A four-poster, it boasted an enormous, intricately carved headboard; it was surrounded by a rich valance and draperies hung from the ceiling. It belonged in the Tower of London.

Then I saw her.

I was totally unprepared for the sight that greeted me. She was grotesque. A monster, she must have weighed close to three hundred pounds. Like a beached whale, she lay in that elegant bed, her chubby arms jutting out at an angle because of the sheer bulk of her flanks; her nightgown had layers of ridiculous ruffles around her shoulders. The odd thing was that above the cornice of sagging chins there was a face that still bore traces of beauty.

'Good afternoon, Father.'

The voice was incongruously high-pitched; it belonged to a teenager. I tried to relate the face to the one I had seen in the newspaper pictures. Without success.

I said, 'It's good of you to see me, Mrs Villate. I seem to have mixed up my appointments.'

She shrugged. 'One afternoon's much the same as another. I hope Father Thorne wasn't called away by bad news.'

'Not as far as I know.'

'Have you been in Abbottsport long, Father?'

'Not long,' I replied in perfect truth. 'You have a magnificent house.'

She nodded, a trifle sadly, I thought.

''tis a fine afternoon,' I observed—with an admonition to myself not to overdo the lilt.

She sighed. 'The state of the weather isn't of much interest to me any more, Father.'

'Is that a fact?'

She nodded. Then she gazed at me. In spite of her bulk and her little-girl voice, she had a penetrating way of looking you over. My insides chilled. Did she already know I was a fake? Was she about to send for help? No. Not yet. 'It's Father Meehan, isn't it? You're from Ireland. I can tell.' The pudgy lips pursed themselves to form a fleshy smile. 'There's a touch of the blarney in your voice, Father. What part are you from?'

My mind seized up. 'Near Dublin,' I told her at last. Beverly and I had laboriously studied an atlas and had found a town which I could claim as my very own. Now, when I needed it, I failed absolutely to bring it to mind.

But Mrs Villate didn't seem to notice.

'My grandfather was born in Kilkenny.'

'A charming town.'

'It's a county, Father.'

'It is indeed,' I replied. 'But there is a town of Kilkenny too.' I prayed that there was.

'You're quite correct, Father. Now that you mention it I do remember visiting the town of Kilkenny. And you're right, it was charming.'

'Is Abbottsport your home town, Mrs Villate?'

'Yes, Father, I was born here.'

'How interesting,' I said. 'And you have spent your entire life here?'

'Oh no, Father,' She seemed mildly amused by my naïvety. 'In fact I left America when I was very young. Long before you were born, Father,' she added with an oddly sad little attempt at a girlish smile. 'I lived for many years in Europe.'

My pulse quickened. Europe!

I tried to sound only mildly interested as I asked her where in Europe she had lived.

'In France mostly. Switzerland and Italy too, but not so much as France. My husband was French, you see.'

I had to clear my throat. She *could* be Mae; it was possible. Just. And only just. But how to find out?

'Pierre died several years ago and I returned here to Abbottsport.'

It was a curious experience: one part of me grappled with the facts, quivering with excitement, at the same time trying to tell myself not to get carried away: the fact that she lived in Europe was no proof that she was Mae Nolan.

'And how many years did you live in France?'

Idle, inconsequential tone: friendly chit-chat between a priest and one of his flock.

'How many?' She looked up at the ceiling as if seeking the answer there. 'Goodness, I have to think about that, Father. Such a long time. Fifty . . . yes, fifty years, give or take one or two.'

God, it *did* fit!

'And may I ask what made you decide to go to live in France?'

Was it my imagination or did the question startle her? Did she stiffen momentarily as if the question had struck a nerve? If so, she recovered rapidly. She raised one of those flagstaff arms and moved it as if indicating far-away places. 'I went on vacation,' she said. She looked past me, into some haven of memories perhaps. 'And I met Pierre. I was very happy. I loved France.'

We talked about Paris. She knew it well, chatting knowledgeably about the rood loft and rood screen of Saint-Etienne-du-Mont, about the Place des Vosges, about the music salon of the Hôtel de Lauzun, about Richelieu's tomb in the chapel of the Sorbonne and the stained glass windows in the apse of the Sainte-Chapelle. She revelled in her memories; I sensed that it had been a long time since she had had an interested audience. She could hardly wait to get one topic dealt with before she dashed off on another. For my part I was quite content to let her talk. It might lead somewhere. Unfortunately it led to Ireland. In no time at all she was chattering about Dublin's horse-drawn cabs on O'Connell Street, about the grandeur of Powerscourt in County Wicklow, the beauty of the cliffs of Moher and the Giant's Causeway on the coast of Antrim. I became uneasy. My knowledge of the Emerald Isle was confined to a viewing of *Ryan's Daughter* and a couple of visits to Shannon Airport. I was all too conscious how lucky I had been when we had talked about

Kilkenny; it would be foolhardy to push that luck.

'I could sit and chat all day,' I said, glancing at my watch. 'But there are others waiting, I fear.'

'Of course, Father,' she said, obedient as a small child.

I dreaded this moment. In ten seconds flat I would be exposed. Then they would boot me out. Or worse. I opened the small attaché case. Beverly had painstakingly printed my instructions on a piece of oblong paper cut to fit the bottom of the case. The sight of those neat characters strengthened my resolve. I had to push on, insane as it was.

Did she wish me to hear her confession?

She nodded and, as if reciting a poem, asked me to bless her for she had sinned; it was, she said, a month since her last confession. But it was dull stuff: being short-tempered with a servant, a silly little fib, a bad case of gluttony. I doled out the Our Fathers and the Hail Marys. Was there anything else? I don't know what I expected her to say. In the event, she said nothing. I had no choice but to give her Absolution.

Then came the Communion. The incredible thing was how easy it was. I intoned the words with due solemnity. The old lady's responses were brisk and businesslike. Clearly, in spite of my fumblings, it hadn't occurred to her that I might be an imposter.

But was she Mae? I still don't know. I was no wiser than when I had driven up to those gates. And my time had almost run out.

I closed my case. 'I'm sorry to say I must get along. It's been a great pleasure meeting you, Mrs Villate.'

'It was good of you to spend so much time with a dull old woman.'

'You're not dull,' I assured her. 'Dear me, not dull at all.'

But, I thought, I wish I knew who the bloody hell you are.

'I hope we'll be seeing lots more of you, Father. Will

you be staying in Abbottsport for long?'

'I'm not at all sure. We must serve where we are needed.'

'How true, Father.'

I got up. I had achieved nothing—and it was better not to wonder about the consequences of all this when Father Thorne found out.

I was about to wish her a very good afternoon in my best Barry Fitzgerald tone when I noticed the prayer book on her bedside table. It was ancient, its tooled white leather worn and yellowed with age, the gold leaf of the cross now reduced to a few fragments clinging to the deep, finely worked indentations. It reminded me of the book I had once owned and cherished. A thought occurred to me.

I said how much I admired old books. Would she object if I looked at this one? It was a beautiful specimen, quite unusually tooled.

She turned towards the bedside table. Her prayer book? Did I wish to examine it? Of course she had no objection. She was delighted.

I picked it up and made a show of studying the cover.

'Marvellous quality leather,' I told her. 'You can't buy such stuff these days no matter how much you're prepared to pay. Something to do with the curing, I understand. This must be very old indeed.'

'Old?' She smiled. 'It's very nearly as old as I am, Father. I was seven when my grandfather gave it to me. It was my first Communion.'

'Fancy that now,' I murmured. Excitement bubbled within me. Her *grandfather* had given her the book. Old Faolan, was it?

I attempted to open the book. And failed. My fingers seemed to have acquired all the dexterity of a bunch of bananas.

'There's a catch, Father.'

'What?'

'A clasp on the side, to keep it shut.'

So there was. 'Of course, of course, how foolish of me.'

I managed to negotiate the thing. The covers parted. I made much of examining the paper, holding the book up to the light and running a finger across it, nodding at its fine texture.

Then I turned to the flyleaf.

And prayed.

Yes, there, in rusty, almost illegible script, was the inscription

To Mae,
With love on her first communion,
Grandpa.

Mae!

Bloody elusive *Mae*!

At last!

I had to take in air. Without realizing it, I had been holding my breath. *Mae*! Beverly had been right and the rest of the world had been totally, inexcusably wrong. I would never doubt her again. I kept turning the pages as I collected both my breath and my thoughts.

'This is your book, Mrs Villate?'

She nodded, smiling. 'Sure is. I've had it almost all of my life.'

I turned back to the first page and studied it for a moment.

'It seems to be inscribed to someone called Mae. I understood your first name was Patricia.'

The smile froze on her lips.

'I used to be called Mae . . . as a child, you understand.'

Somewhere in the house a telephone rang. Was it Father Thorne calling about his appointment tomorrow?

I said, 'Actually, Mrs Villate, I know all about your being called Mae.'

A creasing of the swollen brow. 'You know?'

I nodded. It was a delicious moment and I had a childish urge to prolong it as long as possible. 'As a matter of fact,' I said, 'I also know that you fooled a very large number of people in September of 1927.'

Her mouth dropped open. She didn't speak but her eyes were fixed on mine, unblinking, unwavering.

I went on, quietly, almost conversationally: 'I also happen to know that you caused the deaths of a pilot named Jack Thornton and a young woman by the name of Val Llewellyn . . .'

'You're not a priest,' she croaked.

Curiously, I got the impression that she was as dismayed about that as about my knowing the truth.

'Yes, I'm an imposter, Mrs Villate. Just like you. The world thinks Mae Nolan was a brave young flyer who died trying to fly the Atlantic. But we know better, don't we? You sent Jack Thornton and Val Llewellyn off on their flight knowing perfectly well that they would never reach the other side. You killed them. I'm interested in knowing how.'

She stared, her lips slightly parted, the tip of her tongue protruding, a pink blob.

'The whole world thought you were in the right-hand seat of that Bellanca when it took off from Roosevelt Field. But it wasn't you, was it?'

She didn't reply. No doubt I sounded like some prosecutor-general, rapping out the words that she must have dreaded hearing for more than half a century. I think I expected her to deny everything. To call the police. To scream for help. *Something*. But she just stared. And suddenly the tingle of triumph within me turned sour. And in its place I felt a weird kind of pity for the ugly great mound of flesh accompanied by an intense, almost painful weariness with the whole sordid business. It all added up to emptiness, to nothing. I was sick of the Nolans and their scheming. I wanted only to get myself out of it all as rapidly as possible.

I picked up my case and returned the prayer book to its place on Mae's bedside table, fastening the catch as if dedicated to leave everything just as I had found it.

Still she hadn't uttered a word.

I turned on my heel. Out through the bedroom doors without a look back at her. Along the upstairs hall. Down the curving stairway. With every step I expected to hear screams from the bedroom.

'Leaving, Father?'

Miss Hecht stood at the foot of the stairs. She accorded me a prim smile and opened the front door. I muttered something to her as I hurried out into the sunlight. The Honda was waiting where I had left it. It started, thank God, at the first twist of the key. I set off. The tyres purred over the brick driveway. The great iron gates swung open as I approached and I drove out to the road.

I turned towards the town.

* * *

'Mrs Patricia Villate died earlier today in Abbottsport,' declared the radio announcer in suitably sombre tones. 'Mrs Villate, 79, suffered a stroke late this afternoon. She was rushed to County Hospital but nothing could be done to save her. She was declared dead at 5.45 p.m. A member of the influential Nolan family, Mrs Villate had lived in Europe for many years. She had returned to Abbottsport following the death of her husband in Paris.'

Beverly listened to the broadcast as she sipped a vodka martini, a gentle, satisfied smile on her lips. I kissed her. She grinned at me and told me that I was brave and clever; I said I thought she was probably correct. Then I told her that in the end I felt nothing but pity for Mae, a fat, helpless old bag surrounded by her treasures that she could no longer enjoy.

'She had it coming,' said Beverly. She sighed and

sipped her drink. 'I'd give my eye-teeth to know how she did it. Would you still love me without my eye-teeth?'

'I can't promise. Your eye-teeth exert a powerful sexual attraction.'

'Your ear lobes do the same for me,' she said. 'But how did she kill them, Adam? Gee, I'd love to know.'

Me too. But there was something else I was equally anxious to know: whether or not I still had a job.

* * *

I had. But only just. And only after a wearisome series of interviews. With the Chief Pilot, the Association representative, the Operations Manager, the Superintendent of Personnel. I told my story again and again. I stuck reasonably closely to the truth—the research, the discoveries, the Nolan family, the assault on Beverly—omitting only the finale in Mae's house. I reported that Mrs Sutton and her six-year-old son were now safely ensconced in Kensington. I was, I said, very sorry that it had happened and the corporation could rest assured that such a thing would never happen again.

You could almost hear the corporate scales being loaded. On the one hand, the awesome weight of Failure to Present Himself for An Assigned Flight. On the other, the factors that might be considered in the accused's favour: Long and Reasonably Reliable Service, a Generally Good Record, Moderately Bright Promise (until the Incident in Question). Then there was the factor that may just have swung it all in my favour: Recent Marital Break-up. Incredible what corporations will forgive if there has been an RMBU.

A final interview with ruddy-cheekboned Frederick Walton. The corporation in its infinite wisdom had decided to give me One More Chance. It was made clear, however, that the corporate eye was well and truly on me. From now on, I had better conduct myself in a totally exemplary fashion, be a model of punctuality, decorum and efficiency. Did I understand? I did indeed. I exuded humility. And so I returned to line duty, to the right-hand seat on the 1011, back to the superbly logical world of vectors and VOR/DMEs, of transponders and terminal control areas, of instrument comparators and AFCS Modes. I was light-headed with relief.

Crew scheduling telephoned me a few days later. Tyler had been rushed off to hospital with a ruptured appendix. I was needed to take his place on Flight 881 to JFK on Wednesday morning, returning to Heathrow on Flight 882 the following day.

It wasn't until I arrived at the airport that I learned that the captain on Flight 881 would be none other than Porson, the gentleman who was in the left-hand seat on a pair of memorable flights. I also discovered that this was to be Porson's last trip before retirement. He managed a half-hearted smile when he saw me in Operations. No doubt he wondered why fate had chosen to put Odd Bod Beale in the right-hand seat on this, the final run of his airline career. What did Porson know of my recent escapades in upstate New York? Might he refuse to have me aboard? No, he evinced neither dismay nor delight on seeing me; he was his usual somewhat taciturn self. We scanned the flight plan and discussed the weather reports. Then we went out to the aircraft and flew it to New York. A perfectly ordinary, totally routine trip. We landed on 13 Right precisely three minutes ahead of schedule. It was all very slick and professional. Porson himself admitted that it wasn't too bad a trip, all things considered. I thought it best not to enquire as to what 'things' he might have been considering.

I stayed at the Sheraton that night; it seemed strange to be in New York while Beverly was in London. I thought of her, grappling with unfamiliar groceries and the buses, left-hand-driving and Mrs Halliwell—who had happened to call the very first evening Beverly and Russell arrived. I must say the old girl took them in her stride, welcoming them to the United Kingdom in the grand manner, like a plenipotentiary of the Royal Family, and recounting her memories of the Savoy-Plaza and Whispering Jack Smith. She then proceeded to tell Beverly what an agreeable young man I was, with which opinion Beverly seemed to concur. I had to ask the two of them not to talk about me as if I wasn't present; whereupon they giggled at one another like a couple of grammar-school girls. Before I left for Kennedy I telephoned Joyce and told her please not to telephone the flat. I had company, I explained. *Permanent* company? she wanted to know. Definitely, I told her. She seemed slightly put out—which pleased me, I must report. God, I was so lucky to have Beverly there. My secret fear was that I would return to London and find that she and Russell had gone. I imagined a note on the hall table, telling me that she was sorry but she simply couldn't take it any longer . . . The mere idea was enough to make me wake up at night, heart pounding, terror clutching me about the throat. The curious thing was that in all the years we lived together, it had never crossed my mind that Joyce might leave; where Beverly was concerned I could think of little else.

* * *

There was a jolly little ceremony in the New York manager's office. Captain Porson was the guest of honour. Toasts were drunk (in club soda, by crew members) followed by tedious and rambling speeches, recounting incidents which had involved Captain Porson and which, everyone kept saying, had been excruciatingly funny at the time. There were handshakes; then the presentation of an onyx desk set suitably inscribed. Captain Porson said he would miss flying in and out of Kennedy, but not much, and the chatter of his chickens would compensate him for the absence of airline gossip. More handshakes and promises to keep in touch. Then we strode out to the aircraft and made it ready to transport us back to Heathrow.

'A significant moment,' I remarked as we began to roll.

'Significant?'

'Your last trip with Anglo.'

'Nothing the least bit significant about it,' he sniffed. 'I've known this day was coming for years. Just another trip as far as I'm concerned.'

'The end of an era . . .'

'Codswallop,' said Porson but he accorded me a frigid little smile to acknowledge the thought.

I wondered what was really going on in that bullet head of his. Was he aching with regret that this was the end of his career? Or was he relieved that the days of responsibility were over? Nurturing a bunch of chickens seemed to me a poor substitute for flying 1011s all over the world.

We lined up behind a Pan Am 747 and an Air Canada DC-9. I informed the passengers that we would be taking off in a couple of minutes.

'That's if Pan Am doesn't leave his Before Take-off check until he's on the runway,' said Porson. 'Half those buggers still think they're in flying boats. Leave everything until you're lined up in the water ready to go, that's them.'

The sun was low on the horizon now. It was one of those tranquil spring evenings when the light is subtle and gentle and the grass looks like green velvet and you realize once again what an extraordinarily beautiful place the world can be. Mind you, I think it would have looked beautiful to me if we had been taking off in torrents of freezing rain, for I was going home to

Beverly and at that moment I was probably as content with my lot as it's possible for a fellow to be.

We followed Air Canada on to 22 Right. Behind me, Rowley, the oiler swivelled his seat to face forward for the take-off. The cabin staff were buckled into their seats. In the distance you could see Air Canada lifting off, trailing wispy jet fumes.

'Anglo eight eight two, clear for take-off.'

'Anglo eight eight two,' I acknowledged. 'Rolling.'

Porson eased the throttle levers forward, smoothly, expertly obtaining the EPR bug setting before the airspeed indicator registered 80 knots. Then up to take-off setting. By the book. Effortlessly, the big aircraft ate up the runway, vibrating ever so discreetly as the speed increased; the air streamed over her superbly formed wings, the speed providing strength, creating lift, making her throb with desire to take to the air.

My job was to watch the speed. At precisely five knots below the V1 (the critical engine-failure speed) I called, 'Minus five.' Porson acknowledged; the take-off was proceeding according to plan.

Then the shapely nose lifted. The rumbling of the main gear ceased. The 1011 lifted off, angled skyward at the ten degrees specified by the manual.

'Positive rate,' I called.

'Gear up,' Porson said.

We climbed away from Kennedy at V-Two (take-off speed) plus 10 knots at 15° of pitch, up into the tranquil evening. As the speed mounted, I retracted the flaps at Porson's instructions: to ten degrees at V-Two plus 10 knots; to four degrees at V-Two plus 20 knots, retracting them completely into the wings at V-Two plus 60 knots.

That was when I heard the Morse signals.

Dot, dot, dot, dot, dot. Dot, dash, dash, dash, dash. Dot, dot, dot, dot, dash. Dash, dash, dash, dot, dot. Dash, dash, dash, dot, dot. Dot, dot, dash, dash, dash.

The same sequence as before.

But the rhythm was more insistent, more urgent than ever. The pulses thudded in my ears, a tattoo that couldn't be denied.

I shuddered and felt the sweat on my flesh. Was it fear? Or frustration that the whole lunatic business seemed to be starting again? God knows. I remember the instinctive urge to rip off my headset in order to dispose of the bloody incessant dots and dashes once and for all. Damn the bloody dots and dashes. What the hell was I to do?

Porson was peering ahead at the evening sky like a sovereign surveying his domain. From the corner of my eye I could see Rowley, sitting back, arms folded.

Obviously neither of them heard the signals.

Christ, why couldn't the bloody signals go *away*? Some people had asthma to contend with. I had errant Morse signals. I knew them by heart now.

Dot, dot, dot, dot, dot: *five*. Dot, dash, dash, dash, dash: *one*. Dot, dot, dot, dot, dash: *four*. Dash, dash, dash, dot, dot: *eight*. Dash, dash, dash, dot, dot: *eight* again. Dot, dot, dash, dash, dash: *two*.

Five, one, four, eight, eight, two. The same numbers. Meaningless numbers.

But were they meaningless? Something occurred to me. The wheels began to turn.

No wonder I couldn't see it before!

When I had deciphered the Morse signals weeks earlier I had found myself with what seemed to be a random string of numbers: 514882. 514882.

At that time *this* flight was number 824. It had been changed because of some confusion with another airline. So Anglo-World Flight 824 became Flight 882.

882: the last three digits signified *this* flight.

514882.

What about five one four? Of course! Now it made sense. It was a *date*, for God's sake, with the numerals placed the American way: the five first, signifying the month, the one four signifying the day.

May the fourteenth.

Today.

The other numerals were eight eight two. *Flight* eight eight two.

This flight.

A warning; it had to be a warning; there was no other explanation, for the signals to be repeated over and over again for weeks on end . . .

I heard myself saying, 'I think there's something wrong.'

Porson didn't catch what I said. 'Mm?'

'Something's wrong.'

'Wrong?' His eyes scanned the instrument panel. 'What's wrong?'

I said I wasn't sure. His bushy brows glared at me across the centre console. You could imagine what he was thinking: Here goes Beale again. Why didn't they put him away in the funny farm after that first incident? I peered at the instruments before me, frantically seeking some clue. There *had* to be something. I had received a warning, the same warning over and over again for several months. Something *was* wrong. But what? The instruments revealed not the slightest indication of trouble. Rowley scrutinized his panel, checking the electrical system, engine health, oil temperature, quantities and pressures, fuel system, humidity control, APU control, cargo compartments . . .

'Well?' Porson's voice was a bark.

'No problems,' Rowley reported.

I said, 'I know there's *something.*'

'For God's sake.' Now he sounded impatient—and I could hardly blame him.

Every instinct screamed at me to turn back. We were in danger, frightful danger. I was convinced of it. But Porson wasn't. And he was in command. How could I persuade him to incur the awesome expense of turning back, dumping our fuel and then landing back at JFK?

I couldn't.

He asked me what made me think we had a problem. I had to mumble something about not being quite sure about that either.

'All right,' Porson said. 'Let's keep our eyes open, shall we?'

This was presumably for Rowley's benefit: a modicum of support for the First Officer, reluctant admission that if the First Officer said it, it had to have some basis in fact. I said I wished I could be more specific. He agreed that it would be helpful. It was, he said, bloody hard to take the appropriate measure when you don't know what the effing problem is.

No wonder he had that pitying look in his eye. Beale had finally gone off to do circuits with the bats in the belfry. Bleakly, I wondered what action the company would take over this. My only hope was that Porson might, in the euphoria of his final flight, neglect to report my outburst. That is, if we ever got to Heathrow. Something *was* wrong. But what, for God's sake, *what*?

The stew came up front. It was a relief to see her; her presence de-fused the tension. She was a tall redhead. Her name was Jocelyn; she possessed a pleasant smile and a superbly lithe figure.

'And what would you gentlemen care for?'

'Depends what you're offering,' said Rowley.

'That isn't on the menu,' Jocelyn informed him coolly.

'I'd like a salad,' said Porson. 'Haven't had anything since lunch. And I don't want anything cooked. Can't stay awake with a heavy meal. Just a salad. And a cup of coffee if you'd be so kind, my dear.'

'Certainly, Captain.'

Rowley ordered the roast beef. I asked for coffee only; my appetite had evaporated; my viscera felt as if someone was busy making a reef knot of the pipes.

32

In 27A, Marcus White swallowed the last fragments of the boiled sweet provided by the stewardess before take-off. They burned their way down his gullet. And then lay, glowing, stinging. Why, for crissake did he take the candy? Didn't he know that food was *poison* at times like this? Got to stop thinking about it. *Got* to. He took a pocket book from his flight bag, read for two minutes, then closed the book and leafed through a magazine. But the Tightenings wouldn't let him concentrate. Jesus, they were extra-specially bad this time. Was it something to do with altitude? The bits of candy were *growing*! *Filling* him! Only one thing would help. But he had to wait. A few minutes. A lifetime. He closed his eyes. Waves of light washed over him, splashing behind his eyes, reaching, spreading throughout his skull. It was hurting light. Stabbing light. The altitude, that was it. Goddam flying. Squeezed into a lousy aerial toothpaste tube. Marcus White just wanted to feel *normal*. That wasn't too much to ask, was it? Just wanted to get rid of that guy inside, the one with the wires. Son of a bitch kept pulling, first this way, then the next. He had every nerve on a winch. And he kept turning his handle. You could *hear* him if you listened *real* carefully . . .

Pretty soon they'd be serving drinks. Then dinner. Then a movie. Big stupid faces. Mouthing. For crissake, why ever did he decide to vacation in *Europe*? Why not Florida? Or Aspen? Or Sea Island? *Europe*. God, would this pile of junk metal ever get there? The Tightenings were getting to his throat now, closing it up, squeezing the sides together, making a braid, wrapping around itself . . .

OK. No reason to wait any longer. It was time. Next to him, the chubby old dame looked at him, startled, amazed, as if wanting to move out of the seat in an airplane was the most goddam unusual thing in the whole stupid world. Her chins spread like a pink flat tyre, then hung, baglike, when at last she raised her ugly head. She had cows' eyes. And she *bulged.* God, Marcus White hated fat. He pushed past her. Only moments now. He could begin to *taste* the feeling good even before it began. The son of a bitch with the winch was already easing off a fraction.

Walking along the aisle, between the rows of seats, Marcus White decided that the plane wasn't like a toothpaste tube at all; it was a can of human sardines. Except that sardines look neater in a can. And prettier. God, how long could that goddam aisle *be*?'

He latched the lavatory door behind him. The light came on. Not long now. He reached into his shirt pocket for the packet of cigars. Bless you, Carlos baby, for this custom job. Your own special blend, you said. A little of this, a little of that, all woven in with the dried leaves of *cannabis sativa* by your own magic hands. No wonder they call you the Jesus of Junk. What wonders have your talented fingers wrought? A dash of Dilaudid? A pinch of Pantapon? A drop of Demerol? Something for the highs, something for the lows? All blended. Perfection. Something to see you through that long, long trip, Carlos had said.

Hands shaky; match wobbling, falling. Try another one. And another. Hold on tight now. Concentrate. Another match. OK, got it going now. Nice friendly glow there at the end. A funny experience, puffing, after years of mainlining. You miss that beautiful explosion of softness and warmth in the abdomen. But it was a pleasure delayed. There were contacts in London. In Paris. In Zurich. Good people. People who understood. But, man, as smokes go, this was *something* . . . something *else*. Carlos had surpassed himself. A unique creation. He should patent it. One surprise after another. Hold it lightly with the lips. Draw in the air around it. Lots of air along with the smoke. Let the mixture stay down. Let it work its beautiful way into every nook and cranny. Nerves unwinding now. Warmth edging along muscles. Every pore opening wide.

Marcus White sat on the toilet. He was superbly content. Suffused in softness, in peace, in a delicious purple glow that stroked him with infinitely delicate fingers.

A genius, that Carlos.

Funny, there was a sort of glow *beside* him as well as *around* him.

A lot of smoke too.

Why, Marcus White wondered, would smoke come out of the waste towel compartment?

* * *

I listened but there were no more Morse signals, nothing but the crackle of static and distant voices from the rapidly receding shore. I found myself wondering how I would be able to support Beverly and Russell after A-W gave me the order of the boot. Poor Beverly, she deserved better luck. The men in her life kept turning out to be dead losses. I had uprooted her from her own country, taken her away to England where she knew no one except useless Adam and ancient Mrs Halliwell. And for what? How long would she stay now? How long *could* she stay? I glanced across at Porson. I didn't blame him for declining to take action. If I had been sitting in the left-hand seat I would have done the same. But you won't be sitting in the left-hand seat of a 1011 now, mate, I informed myself. Or in the right-hand seat, for that matter. Enjoy yourself; this is probably your last ride in an aeroplane. Ever.

Jocelyn reappeared with Porson's salad and the drinks. She made a chuckled remark about preferential treatment for the Captain on his last trip. Was there anything else she could bring?

'You said it wasn't on the menu,' said Porson with a wink.

Behind me, Rowley burst into peals of laughter.

Jocelyn said, 'It may be available later on, Captain, if you ask really nicely.'

'Thank you, m'dear, but I wouldn't want to disappoint you. I know all you young ladies consider me as something of a sex symbol. I'd hate to shatter your illusions.'

More hearty laughter from Rowley. Jocelyn departed.

The exchange depressed me. Silly sods, they were all fiddling while our Rome was burning. Or was about to burn. We'd been warned.

'Smasher,' said Rowley as Jocelyn departed. 'Married to some twit in a bank, they say. Something wrong there.'

'Possibly he's the managing director,' observed Porson.

'True. Hadn't thought of that. Hadn't occurred to me.'

Could I simply tell Porson that I had been receiving Morse signals over a period of several months, warning me of impending trouble on this flight and that I had only just comprehended the significance of the messages? I could picture his reaction. No doubt he would radio ahead and request Heathrow to have an ambulance waiting at the ramp, complete with strait-jacket, First Officer, for the use of. Why, I asked no one, didn't the bloody signals tell us *more*? Why make us guess, for God's sake.

I looked about the sky, half expecting to see the Bellanca.

Faint, incredibly distant Morse signals? I winced with the effort of trying to capture the mere hints of sound. A waste of time. There were no signals. Which probably meant that whatever I had heard or thought I had heard came from within. Imagination. Errant electric charges popping off in my brain. In no time at all, I told myself, the whole bloody thing will short-circuit.

That was when we heard the interphone message from the rear cabin.

'What?' Porson glared at me, then at Rowley. He was still eating his salad. 'They've got a bloody lavatory fire. What? You say it's under control? Keep me informed.' He pointed to Rowley. 'Go back and have a look. Bloody hell,' he muttered as he replaced the interphone. 'Stupid bloody smokers. We should toss the lot of them overboard.'

Lavatory blazes were one of the hazards of the business, usually caused by some nitwit of a smoker tossing a cigarette end into the waste towel receptacle. As a rule they were easily put out by the cabin staff wielding extinguishers. But there had been tragic exceptions: the Air Canada DC-9 at Cincinnati, 23 dead; the Saudi Arabian L-1011 at Riyadh, 301 dead; the Varig 707 near Paris, 122 dead.

When Rowley returned, he was ruffled and ruddy-faced, his tie askew, his white shirt smudged. 'Daft bugger was stoned in there,' he announced. 'Wouldn't unlock the door. Thought it was as funny as bloody hell. Had to drag him out forcibly.'

'Sod him,' snapped Porson. 'What about the fire, man?'

'Sorry. It's out,' said Rowley.

'Sure?'

'Think so. Still lots of smoke, though.'

'Keep an eye on it,' Porson told him. 'Go back in a few minutes. Look things over. Keep on looking. Damn things can smoulder for bloody hours.' He turned to me. 'Everything else in order?'

I had been scanning the instrument panels. Nothing untoward to report: no flashing lights or needles pointing the wrong way.

Porson informed the passengers that there was no

cause for concern. A minor problem. Apologies for disturbing the tranquility of the flight.

Rowley went aft again. He returned a few minutes later. The fire seemed to be out, he reported. But he seemed uncertain. Yes, he admitted, there were still traces of smoke about. Porson sent him aft yet again.

Jocelyn came up front to tell us how they had finally subdued the passenger who had caused the crisis. Got himself badly singed but seemed totally unaware of it. Happy as hell. Kept talking about colours and how they were his good buddies. He was now fastened securely in a row of unoccupied seats at the rear of the cabin.

Five minutes later Rowley reported that there was still a spot of smoke but everything appeared to be under control. Porson said he was going back to have a look for himself. Then he uttered a peculiar sound. A sort of half-word, half-croak. He had turned towards me, twisted awkwardly in his seat. He held his knife and fork in mid-air as if unable to push them down to his plate. He was gazing at me yet his eyes didn't focus on me. His mouth was half open, revealing the semi-chewed remains of a helping of salad. For an instant I thought he was choking; his eyes protruded; the colour drained from his cheeks. He tried to speak, spitting fragments of food across the cabin, gasping for breath, his mouth opening and closing like a fish's as he blinked in simultaneous surprise and indignation.

'My stomach . . . ' he croaked at last '. . . something wrong with the bloody *food*!'

Food?

I tried to grasp him; he was slumping sideways, the tray slithering off his knees, its contents tumbling, a pathetic confusion of lettuce, tomato, slices of boiled egg and cucumber.

Tainted? *Poisoned*?

God. I suddenly realized how Mae Nolan had made sure that Jack Thornton and Val Llewellyn would never reach Europe.

The circuit-breaker blew.

'Lavatory flushing motor,' Rowley announced, eyes riveted to his panel. 'That sod did it.'

'Same lavatory?'

Rowley nodded. 'Rear left centre.'

'Get Jocelyn,' I told him.

A nasty little chill. Unpleasant visions of wires burning, sparking, shorting behind the walls and beneath the floor of the aircraft. Out of sight. Out of reach. I was checking the generator power meters and DC ammeter when Jocelyn came up front. Her eyes opened wide when she saw Porson. The poor old sod was still groaning and spluttering.

'Have the girls served any more of the meals?'

She shook her head, her eyes still on Porson. 'The meals aren't quite ready . . .'

'Thank God for that. Listen, don't serve any of the food. *Any* of it. I think Captain Porson may have been poisoned. See what you can do for him. Find out if there's a doctor on board. It's up to you. We can't help.'

'All right.' She nodded. 'I understand. I'll be back in a mo'.' She touched Porson's forehead. 'Oh Lor'.'

Rowley and I checked the bus bars, unpowering the AC and DC bars one by one, checking and hoping, closing crossfeed valves, opening relays, cutting power to all but the essential systems. I called Gander, the nearest field. Explained our problem. Electrical fire. Couldn't be described as critical. Yet. Yes, smoke was already finding its way into the cabin. The Gander operator acknowledged our message in the unemotional, business-as-usual tone invariably used at such times. I found his level Newfoundland accent—one-third Scots, one-third Irish, one-third Canadian—curiously calming although I knew that his pulse rate must be quickening almost as rapidly as mine.

Rowley went aft, returning a moment later.

'I think it's getting worse.'

'Oxygen masks and smoke goggles,' I said.

Rowley tugged the oxygen mask over his head,

flattening hair across his forehead; it looked like a ginger net.

'Flames?'

'No flames, Not yet. But more smoke than there was.'

'Bugger.'

'It's coming in through the vents and between the panel joints up by the roof.'

'Passengers?'

'Getting a bit edgy, I'd say.'

I'd say too. And who could blame the poor bastards?

Yes, I informed Gander, emergency equipment should indeed be in readiness.

Jocelyn came up front with a grey, slightly overweight man wearing a denim suit that belonged on a teenage ranch hand.

'Dr Schofield,' announced Jocelyn. 'From Hackensack.'

God knows why she had to tell me where he lived.

Dr Schofield's voice was husky; he apologized; he had a cold, he said, and he was a gynaecologist. He glanced at Porson. 'You think he was poisoned? Jesus. I'll do what I can. How long before we land?'

'Ten minutes or so.'

'Let's get him out of here,' said Dr Schofield. And sneezed.

You have a lot to think about when you fly a final approach in a smouldering aeroplane. Your imagination becomes over-active. Every creak becomes the crack of structural failure. You picture scores of diligent little flames gobbling away at the aircraft's vitals, one after another until, with a rending and a tearing, the whole thing transforms itself into an untidy collection of components fluttering along in the sky. And you are disquietingly aware that even if you get the 1011 back on terra firma your troubles may just be beginning. Fires are full of nasty surprises. When you are aloft there is a limited amount of oxygen inside the aircraft and a fire can be relatively docile. But the instant the doors are opened a smoulder can become a roaring, searing ball of flame that streaks the length of the cabin, incinerating everything in its path. It's called the 'flashover phenomenon' by the experts. They know what to call it but so far they haven't offered any notably intelligent suggestions on how to cope with it.

A thought jarred me.

My bloody *insurance*.

If I bought the farm, Joyce would get it *all*.

It never occurred to me to change the beneficiary forms. Never thought of it. Not once.

I must have muttered something. Rowley glanced at me.

My God, I thought, I can't let it happen. I damn well *can't*.

Beverly, sweet Beverly. She was waiting. I *had* to make it back.

We descended. A few minutes more. I kept glancing at the clock. Was the damned thing still working? Had only thirty seconds elapsed since I last looked?

The smoke was getting thicker in the main cabin, Jocelyn reported. It was acrid stuff that stung your lungs. I told her we daren't lower the passengers' individual oxygen masks for fear of feeding the fire the oxygen it craved. The passengers would have to keep on coughing and complaining. She said she understood. The smoke was finding its way into the flight deck now, sneaking up through the floor, evil wisps that writhed around us , creating ethereal strata that blurred our familiar world.

I instructed Jocelyn to prepare the passengers for landing.

'It could get nasty when we're down. I'm not saying it will. But it might. OK? There's a chance the fire will flare up when we open the doors and let all that oxygen in.'

The girl nodded. Chin grubby from the smoke. And looking as if it might start wobbling. She was as scared as hell. So was I.

I glanced back. Porson had been strapped into the jump seat. Dr Schofield was tending to him, sniffing.

I had to dismiss Porson from my mind. I had no time to think about him. I cleared my throat and in what I hoped was a reassuring tone informed the passengers that we would shortly be landing. Everything was under control. The cabin staff were trained for such emergencies. Follow their instructions and all would be well.

We hope, I wanted to add. One feels an almost irresistible urge to be honest at times like this.

After I had switched off the interphone I told Jocelyn that her girls should keep stressing to the passengers how important it was for them to fix in their minds the location of their nearest exits. When the time came to escape the cabin might be full of smoke, blinding, bitter-smelling smoke.

More nods. I noticed the way Jocelyn kept fingering her wedding ring as she talked. Was she thinking of her husband? For some reason I hoped so.

'It's going to be all right,' I said.

'Rather,' she replied.

Thus did we spend a few precious moments doing our level best to deceive each other. We both failed utterly and completely.

Jocelyn went aft.

I wanted to tell Beverly that I was thinking of her, even now, even here.

The smoke was thickening in the cockpit, swirling about in an unpleasantly purposeful way; it looked as if it had seeped out of some foul bog.

Our Gander friend advised us that all other traffic had been cleared. We had the approach to ourselves.

'In-Range check,' I ordered.

It was Rowley's job as the pilot-not-flying to call out

each item: ignition, lights, belts, radios, airspeed and altimeter bugs, EPR bugs, fuel.

'Before landing check.'

I made sure that the nosewheel steering handle had been centred. Undercarriage down. No-smoking signs. Altimeters, annunciators, three green lights confirming that the gear was down and locked.

'Flaps to thirty-three,' I ordered.

'DLC,' Rowley reported after checking that the speedbrake lever was correctly positioned.

The runway swayed toward us. Lights winked in the deepening shadows ahead. Beside me, Rowley rubbed his hands on his trouser legs, one after the other. The runway was dry, thank God. We had enough problems without having to worry about skidding.

'Here we go,' I said.

Viewed through a curtain of smoke, the runway had an oddly insubstantial look, like an image on a badly worn film. Coming in faster than usual. Controls still operating, thank God. No time for niceties, no worrying about a gentle touchdown. The object of the exercise was simply to reconnect the 1011 with Mother Earth as rapidly as possible.

The threshold of the runway swept toward us. Vehicles buzzing about. Figures running. Arms pointing. At us. Ease back on the control column. Cut power. Now! An instant of waiting. Then, wham! The wheels made contact, tyres shrieking, structure gasping with the awful shock. No matter. We were down.

We hurtled along the runway, reverse thrust fighting the awesome momentum.

For some reason I wondered if there were any television cameras out there, busy filming our landing. Sorry, lads, for not crashing in flames and giving you some really spectacular footage . . .

As we slowed, emergency vehicles came bounding along on either side of us like a lot of little creatures rushing to their mother's aid.

Rowley was on his feet, grasping at the seats for support. He flattened his hand against the door to the main cabin, testing it to determine if it was safe to open.

'We'll look after Porson,' he bellowed at me.

Beside him, Dr Schofield nodded, still sniffing.

As I brought the aircraft to a halt, I turned off the systems one after another. Behind me, Rowley and the doctor dragged Porson through the flight deck doorway into the main cabin.

I unbuckled myself, flinging the harness straps back over my shoulders and scrambling out of my seat. I turned to follow Rowley and Schofield. But at that moment the cabin crew opened the main doors. With a roar, the fire sprang at me like an angry beast.

More scrambling. Up through the emergency exit in the roof this time, clutching at the inertial reel, feeling the heat from the cabin as I slithered down to safety, bumping against the 1011's metal flanks, glimpsing a nightmare kaleidoscope through doors and windows. Figures groping in the stinking, smoky half-darkness. Shrinking back as the fire burgeoned with terrifying rapidity. The floor alive with humanity, crawling, bumping, clutching. Voices, harsh and urgent. Cries of pain. Screams of panic. Names. Shouted instructions from the emergency crewmen in their asbestos suits. Heat scalded the air around us as we helped with the passengers. One after the other we bundled them unceremoniously off the escape chutes. The bastards kept coming, like rag dolls of assorted sizes rolling off an assembly line. Heavy, lumpy ones; skinny, brittle-boned ones; infants, ancients: an avalanche of flailing limbs and frightened eyes.

The last one was a stew. She jumped from a doorway as the chute beneath her disintegrated in flame. An asbestos-suited crewman caught her; they went rolling on the ground clutching each other like playful children.

Above them the 1011 had become an inferno.

'Everyone out?'

'They'd better be.'

33

'We got Porson back in time,' I told Beverly. 'But only just. The doctors said he would probably have slipped away if it had been another ten minutes.'

She hugged me. She had been hugging me ever since I walked into the flat. 'How is he?'

'Coming along quite well. I dropped in to see him before we left. He looks a bit green and he says his stomach feels as if a 747 had taxied over it. But I think he'll be back on his feet in a few days.'

'Poor Captain Porson.'

'His words exactly.'

She shivered and clung to me. 'Thank God you're back.'

And thank God Porson decided to have a salad, I thought for the umpteenth time. By so doing he became the first person on board to eat, since none of the hot meals was ready. Had everyone eaten more or less simultaneously there would have been a plane-load of poisoned passengers and crew flying over the Atlantic, then across Europe, the automatic pilot handling the controls, ensuring a smooth ride, until the 1011's three engines consumed the last drops of fuel.

'Did you see the woman who did it?'

I shook my head, remembering the furore when we got back to JFK. Police, FBI, a couple of Air Force officers, someone from the British Embassy and most of the New York staff of A-W. An endless succession of sirens and winking lights. Telephones jangling. Rumours of a woman named Brady being responsible. Something to do with the catering system. An ardent IRA supporter, it was said. Doing her little bit for the betterment of mankind by injecting poison into all the meals going aboard the British airliner. Some official saying inadequately, 'You were real lucky.' I said we had had help from above. The official had nodded knowingly.

Beverley's eyes narrowed; she seemed to be looking back through the years. 'You know what I've been thinking?'

I nodded. 'I know exactly. That was how Mae did it. Right?'

'Right. It was a cinch for her,' Beverly declared as if she was recounting an event in which she had been involved. 'She knew all about poisons. She was a pharmacy grad. And she could get whatever she needed from the family business. No sweat. Do you figure she used a hypodermic too?'

'Why not?'

'Sure. No problem to load up a syringe and take it into the hangar. Who would notice? Everyone was busy getting the plane ready for the big trip. How much food would they have put on board?'

'Not much, I imagine. A few sandwiches. Perhaps some fruit and a thermos of coffee.'

'She probably saw the stuff on a seat. In a bag. It would have taken about thirty seconds. Mission accomplished. With one squirt she'd gotten rid of the lover who spurned her *and* the other woman. That's what happened, Adam, I'm sure of it.'

'Me too.'

'They wouldn't have needed anything to eat for several hours, until they were well out to sea. Then, zap! Would the plane have crashed right away?'

'Probably,' I told her. 'There was no auto-pilot, so as

soon as the pilot let go of the joystick, the plane would almost certainly have started to turn away to one side. Even if the controls had remained more or less central, the balance would have begun to shift as the fuel was used up. Then they would have simply spiralled into the sea.'

'Nice girl, Mae.'

'Hell hath no fury,' I burbled.

'And don't you forget it, mister,' she said. And hugged me again.

It was one of those moments when happiness is so intense that it is almost painful. I remember glancing up, sending silent thanks. My life and the lives of some two hundred passengers and crew had unquestionably been saved. The method may have been a trifle more complicated than was absolutely necessary. But it worked. Eventually.

My eyes met Beverly's.

'I was just wondering,' she said, 'what you're going to say if they ask how come you were so sure there'd be a problem on that flight.'

A good question.

I glanced up once more. But I had a feeling that neither Val nor Jack Thornton were going to help me with that one.